Defined by Damnation

Defined by Damnation

A. J. Anderson

Cover by Shimhaq
Design by A. J. Anderson
1st edition 2025

ISBN: 978-1-7644094-2-1

For Richard.

Chapter One
Overture

All members of the Duralaans nobility were aware of the Tale of the Ten Kings. Cecilia herself had been told and retold the tale countless times over the seventeen years of her life, yet she never grew tired of seeing a new spin on the story.

"We, the rightful lords of Duralaans stand united today against the Heretic King," the actor portraying King Artorius announced. "With our paths paved by the Gods and our allegiance unbreakable as the heavens, we shall find no opposition too great."

The eight lords who gathered around Artorius cheered as they held their banners high, the fabrics woven with shimmering threads to mimic the gemstones that glistened from the chain that sat atop Artorius' shoulders. Cecilia thought it was a nice touch in concept, but one that stripped much of the grim realism that the better adaptations offered.

They followed their leader offstage, and after the curtain's fall and subsequent rise, found themselves within the throne room of King Grettir II.

Artorius' head whipped back and forth, dramatically taking in the sight before him. "This cannot be! The King, already dead?" The actor paused so that any members of the crowd who had not already heard the tale might gasp. "But who could have done such a thing?"

"'twas I!" declared a voice from offstage, followed quickly by the actress playing the role of Artoria, outfitted in the most comfortable approximation of the black steel the real woman had worn centuries before. "The bastard was mad with fear, only I could bring his tyrannical rule to an end."

"Then I thank you, good knight," Artorius said, prematurely drawing his weapon so that nobody could mistake the threat behind his next words. "Now, please step aside so that I might take my crown and throne."

"Your crown?" Artoria likewise held her spear readied. "The people of this city have already decided that I shall speak for them. You are too late, *knight*."

"I am appointed by the Gods themselves. What right do you have to deny them?"

"I do not see any gods. Only greedy men who wish to take what they have not earned."

Thus began the first duel of the performance, and a tragically short one it was. Artoria had been mighty, but Artorius was trained by proper swordsmen throughout his childhood, and the knightess proved no match. He slaughtered her, driving his blade through her armour—leaving the precise number of times he did so to be debated endlessly by historians—and left her a bloody mess on the otherwise pristine floor.

The nobles who had followed Artorius were horrified, having thought their leader a just knight, and not one to end a duel in such an uncouth manner.

Artorius slaughtered them also, unwilling to stand even the slightest hint of disloyalty.

The stage was cleared, the actors took their leave, and the night's narrator made his first appearance. "So began the reign of Artorius the First, with the murder of what were his allies and the woman he would later learn was his sister." That reveal only incited further exclamation from the crowd. "But a man does not become a monster overnight, and Artorius had only begun to tread the path he would follow for the rest of his existence. You know the myth, you know the Ashen Lord, let us now know Artorius, the man who was defined by damnation."

The music grew to a crescendo as the curtains fell once more, and the cheering of the crowd grew so loud that Cecilia did not realise Cassidy had spoken until her lips were practically pressed against her ear. "What does that mean?"

Cecilia took a moment to think about it, as well as to let the cacophony die down so her response might actually be heard. "I think he let the worst parts of his life dictate the person he would become."

Cassidy's brow furrowed. "Why would he do that?"

"Have you never heard the story before?"

Cassidy only shrugged, and Cecilia realised that, while noble children would be curious to learn about their land's history, their attendants might not be so inclined.

"Then I will not spoil it for you, I should enjoy seeing your reactions."

Cassidy giggled, only to stop suddenly as her eyes caught something at the edge of the seating area. "You may not have the chance."

Cecilia followed Cassidy's line of sight to find Amor, her family's ever-present attendant, with a disturbingly cold expression and a beckoning hand. "You should stay, Cassidy. Tell me all you think of the show tomorrow."

"Are you sure, my lady?"

"I am certain." Cecilia passed through the audience, feeling a sickness churn in her stomach the further she came to its edge. She wanted to delay what was coming. Though she did not know what words would come from Amor's mouth, she knew they would not be good, and her mind only hastened its weaving of the worst possible tapestries it could.

"My lady, we must leave immediately," Amor said as soon as she was within earshot.

Cecilia straightened her back. "What has happened, Amor?"

"Your father will tell you once you have returned to the summit."

"That journey is hours long; you would have me wait the whole while?"

"It is not my decision, all we can do is hurry." Amor left no room for argument and began a hurried retreat from the theatre, offering Cecilia no choice than to follow.

A carriage awaited them outside, one that bore none of the ornamentations Cecilia was used to, instead offering the privacy that the situation demanded. Amor held the door open for her, murmured some command to their driver, then joined her inside.

The journey was slow, their transportation forced to halt often as it struggled to weave through the noon's citizenry. Amor did not speak another word, and Cecilia did not attempt to provoke him. While much of her wanted desperately to know what awaited her, another hoped to cling on to however few moments she had left to be unaware.

—

Deep into that same night, Cecilia thought sleep might never come for her, and she was not sure she wanted it. Horrible things could come in the darkness of slumber, perversions of what the mind could not endure consciously, presented within a realm in which she would have no control.

No, Cecilia did not want to sleep. That would only mean hastening the next day's arrival. And the next day. And the next. And every day that would follow. Cecilia did not want to face what would come, no matter how far away it seemed, she could never be ready for it.

But sleep must have taken her at some point, for it is only within a dream that impossibilities could be made real, and the voice Cecilia heard could not possibly be real.

"Turning in so early?" Léonora asked as they snuck through the doorway, carefully ushering it closed behind them. They appeared as though they had gone weeks without sleep and their head was a mess of ragged blonde hair that had grown longer than Cecilia had ever seen it. But they had not changed all that much. Léonora had clearly continued to trim down their devilish horns and still wore clothing atypical of their station.

Though this particular choice was new. "Why are you dressed like a maid?"

"'twas all Cassidy could let me get away with." Léonora performed a twirl as they approached Cecilia's bedside. "How've you been, Your Grace?"

Cecilia sat up, heart suddenly racing. It was not the first time Léonora had used that title to address her, so they did not know how close to the mark it hit, and she was not sure she wanted to tell them. "What are you doing here?"

Their expression hardened and Léonora leaned closer, as though about to embroil her in conspiracy. "They elected me heir to the seat of Dominus. I was supposed to be sworn in, was only a few steps from the cathedral's entrance when I realised . . . I don't need to be the person they want. I ran, snuck aboard a ship bound for a port in Avalass, and came right here." They took Cecilia's hands, cold despite the infernal warmth their people were typically aligned with. "That ship will remain docked until dawn, then they journey for the Silver Isle."

"Why are you telling me this?" Cecilia asked. She was sure she already knew the reason, but there was no harm in certainty—not anymore.

"I always thought that this was the only life for me, that I needed to follow in the footsteps of my lineage and be what they had sculpted. Then you came into my life and showed me that there was room for hope. I could—*can* be anything I try to be. So let's try, Cecilia. Let's follow a new path."

Cecilia did not think, was sure that if she did she would fall into a void from which there was no escape. She only said, "Okay."

And they fled into the night.

By chance, Léonora had encountered Cassidy on her way back from the theatre, and the two had conspired a means to ferry Cecilia away from her home atop Avalass' mountainous shadow. Neither guard nor servant crossed their path, and a white steed safely carried them down the sloping road and into the city below.

Cecilia wrapped a thick cloak around herself as they ventured through the dim streets. Very few saw it fit to roam so deep into the night, but she would not risk any chance that she might be recognised. Léonora made no such attempt. Though they held as prestigious a role as she, they were far from their home of Cendela, and few would know their face in Duralaans.

It would still be a number of hours before the sun rose, and Léonora posited their best chance of sneaking aboard their vessel would be during the harried final moments before the crew set off. Once they were aboard there would be little trouble, the crew more likely to contract the service of any strays they found in their midst than throw them overboard, and Cecilia had brought enough coin to cool any heightened tempers. All they had to do was wait.

Léonora paid for a room overlooking Avalass' port at an inn unlikely to question two runaway youths, no matter how valuable their attire seemed. It was small and the bed unlike the quality of any Cecilia had known before, but she was happy to share it all the same. Happy to be far from the new reality that had ensnared her.

Léonora seemed to finally attain the sleep they so clearly needed, but no such luck had been afforded to Cecilia. Instead, she spent the night holding her friend close as she listened to the distant sounds of that which stirred in the dark.

She tried to imagine the source of each one. What was it that made the neighbouring room's mattress squeak so loudly? What had led the night's denizens to stay out so long and grow so temperamental? What motivated a merchant to rise before even the sun deigned to do so?

Each of these people must have known lives no less arduous than her own, yet it would be her responsibility to govern them all, to soothe the turmoil and make it hers. Cecilia thought the idea should have scared her, such was the thing she had chosen to run from, yet as the sun finally rose she only felt her spirits lifted.

The pair made no delay in hurrying to the docks, careful not to draw too much attention as they passed through busy crowds eager to get started on the day's work. The bodies offered natural cover as the two boarded the small merchant vessel Léonora had spoken of.

It was only when they had safely hidden themselves among the ship's cargo that Cecilia's doubts began to surface. Had she acted too quickly? What would her father say? Would he track her down and see that she returned to her land in shame?

Who would rule in her stead?

"What's wrong?" Léonora whispered. "They will not find us down here, I'm sure of it."

"It's not that," she answered.

"You needn't fear, Cecilia. Your brother will be a good king, whether or not his little sister is around should not affect him much."

Cecilia's heart had only begun to mend itself, and it was shattered all over again. "My brother is dead, my sister with him."

Léonora went quieter than Cecilia had ever known them to be, their mouth opened and shut many times over before they found the words they sought. "I see."

"I am my father's sole heir now. I am supposed to rule when he is gone," Cecilia explained, slowly so that her voice would not waver. "So who will replace him if I am gone as well?"

To that Léonora had no response, only the solace of their embrace to ease Cecilia's quivering body. They remained as such over an unknown passage of minutes, neither speaking again until they heard the ship's captain announce that they would soon depart.

"I do not know what to do," Cecilia said.

Léonora pulled away enough to hold her at arm's length and study her expression. They brushed away a few stray tears, then asked, "What do you want to do?"

Cecilia had not the faintest idea, but a feeling had been forming within her heart, and the words needed to describe it were beginning to make themselves known. "I want to help. Though the thought of ruling makes me sick, I do wish to be the one to ease the burdens of my people. If I must wear a chain and sit upon a throne to do so—"

"Then so be it." Cecilia thought Léonora would be disappointed or confused, but they were smiling.

"I'm sorry."

"You have no reason to be." They held her close once more and softly pressed their lips to her cheek. "Go, while there is still time. Be a fair queen."

Cecilia allowed Léonora's arms to leave her and made way for the deck. She took one final glimpse of her friend; a picture she would one day immortalise in paint. "I expect to hear all of your tales one day. Do not make me wait so long."

Their smile only widened. "I would not dare."

It was no less difficult to leave the vessel than it had been to board it. Cecilia merely had to discard her disguise and call upon all of the command her station afforded. The crew had no choice but to let her leave, their confused expressions the only question they would be allowed.

She also made sure to inform them of Léonora's presence aboard and the fact that the Kingdom of Duralaans required they safely transport her friend to safe harbour in the Silver Isle— though that particular demand also necessitated some small payment.

The vessel set forth shortly thereafter and Cecilia watched it go from the edge of the wooden dock. It was not until it had assuredly vanished over the horizon that she disappeared into the swell of people and set out to confront what awaited her.

—

Cecilia knew perfectly well for what reason that particular memory had sprung unprompted into her mind. Ten years in the past it may have been, but the results of that one decision had never been more pressing.

That picture looked down on her as Cassidy saw that she were properly prepared for the coming event. It took great effort to force her eyes not to glance at the piece that hung beside it. Her father had always considered it a fell omen, and although Cecilia did not believe in such things, she would not risk it on such a momentous day.

Her father was dead, and she would cling to what memories of him that she had.

Cecilia had not known precisely what it would mean to remain as heir to the throne, but she had followed the path without wavering, and done what she could to adjust it to fit her preferences. Not once had she regretted her decision, and Cecilia was certain that would not change once the Platinum Chain was laid upon her. Cecilia would see it through.

Cecilia would be Queen.

Chapter Two

To Be Expected

Thishis was the part of the job Elias Sorren despised most of all. The monotonous waiting for something—anything—to happen. Whatever could possibly justify his being there in the first place.

It had been a long hour since their man had entered the tavern. A long *and painful* hour since Elias' expert opinion had been disregarded and he had not been allowed to grab the guy the second he'd been spotted. Such was the lot that had been given to him; forever he would know the best course of action and never would his words be heeded.

There existed no doubt within Elias' mind that he knew exactly what would proceed within those rotting wooden walls. The—so-called—Kid would be allowed a moment of peace before being confronted and given the chance to surrender peacefully. He would refuse this offer, and a fight would break out, a bloody and ultimately pointless fight that would conclude with Eric Blackhand being tossed out of the establishment and into the waiting arms of his captors.

Disregarding a few minor and chaotic outliers, that was how it always went. Blackhand's kind were all the same; none in Elias' four decades of operation had yet surprised him. Perhaps that was for the best, life was a lot simpler when one was always right, but it made things far from interesting. And after so long being given precisely what he expected, Elias had begun to fear his senses were being dulled. Years spent without proper challenge would make no man any wiser.

Elias was no young man. His dark skin was marred by age, long hair and short beard greyed by years long gone. Time had left its mark on him, though not in a way that was exclusively parasitic. Elias liked to think he had gained as much as had been taken from him. Those years amounted to experience, each grey strand of hair a silent reminder of all he had and continued to know. And that knowledge continued to serve him, made sure he would live to see a few more grey hairs, wherever they decided to show themselves.

"Why do they call him 'The Kid?'" one of the other hired swords muttered, a man whose name Elias hadn't bothered to learn.

Once, when Elias had first come across the whisperings of an assassin with a hand of black metal, his drinking partner had implied there was a humorous origin to the name. An origin Elias didn't care enough to follow up on. Now he wondered if indeed it would have served him better to have done so, knowledge could be a powerful tool when used correctly. And even if not, it would have at least granted him something to make conversation. Even that would be preferable to the waiting.

"You can ask him yourself soon enough," another man responded, the youth in his voice dropping Elias' heart deep into the pits of his stomach. What by the names of the Old Gods did Lyre expect could be done with muscle barely finished suckling their mother's teat?

Elias' brewing anger would not be given long to simmer, as the obvious sounds of confrontation resounded from within the aged drinking den. "Waste of blood," Elias muttered. "And time."

At long last the doors to the tavern swung open, revealing a lone figure as they stepped out from the darkened interior. He wore a long coat, an old thing that was coming undone in patches and stained with blood—both dried and otherwise. He raised a hand to his face, tucking a sweat-matted strand of hair behind his ear, his right hand gloved in black leather. *Not metal after all.*

It took no thought, simply instinct, and Elias' blade was drawn, held out before him in warning. His allies were moments too slow for Elias' taste, and he decided he would be sure to learn their names before the day was over, but only so he might guarantee he never made the mistake of working with them a second time.

"Yield your weapons," Elias called across the street. "That'll be all the warning you'll get." The pit in Elias' stomach only grew, despite the bravado he attached to his words. While his side far outnumbered the lone man, the fate he suspected had been met by those within the tavern brought into question whether it would be enough.

Elias brought another hand to his sword's hilt, gripping it tight, and inspiring a few of his fellows to follow suit. There would be a fight, Elias did not see a way around it. All he could do now was hope the sheer numbers might overwhelm their foe. Blackhand took a step forward and—to nobody's disgrace but their own— some of Elias' comrades shifted back.

"Stand your ground," Elias growled through gritted teeth, praying to any god that was watching that their foe hadn't noticed the obvious weakness. Yet to Elias' surprise, the man opposite him ceased his approach, coming to stand only a few measured strides away. "That's more than enough."

Blackhand simply raised his hands in response, before removing his coat from his shoulders and allowing it to fall to the dirt beneath him, accompanied by the telling clatter of whatever miscellaneous weapons were hidden within. Elias continued to watch as Blackhand kicked the coat toward him, eyeing his foe with curiosity while he attempted to determine what game the bounty hunter thought he could play.

Elias pierced the silence with a sharp whistle, and one of his companions gingerly bundled the coat into a small ball and carried it away. He could see now that Blackhand appeared entirely unarmed without his coat, but of course that was ridiculous, he would not disarm himself without good reason. Elias would not let his guard down so easily.

"Take me to Carlyle," Blackhand said, his voice frustratingly quiet. "That's who you work for, right?"

"You killed the men we sent in only so you could surrender anyway?" Elias would not believe it. "What ploy is this?"

"I didn't kill anyone."

"No?" Elias waved one of his men toward the tavern so they might investigate the validity of Blackhand's claim.

"No." The bounty hunter didn't so much as acknowledge the mercenary who passed him, his gaze remaining all too chillingly focused on Elias.

"Why not? I didn't know you were a pacifist."

"I find it hard to believe you know *anything* about me."

"I know enough."

Blackhand scraped at the dirt with his heel. "I wish you were the first to say that. Should we get going? I'd rather not waste time here."

Elias considered his options for a moment. The entire reason he had been hired was to take in the man and force him to stand before Carlyle Lyre, the somewhat unscrupulous businessman and entirely unscrupulous lord who had been so far wronged by Blackhand. Yet Elias couldn't shake the feeling that something was off.

Eric Blackhand was a snake, and had escaped numerous attempted apprehensions, no matter how great the odds had been stacked against him. He may not have encountered Elias before, but that did not mean he wouldn't use every trick he could to circumvent him.

But Elias had a job to do. His own personal apprehensions could not come before the completion of that job. Elias had not become so well regarded because he balked at the first sign that not everything would go his way. So he lifted the iron bindings from his travelling pack and closed the distance between himself and his new prisoner.

—

Another hour had passed before their caravan set off toward Lyre's fortress. Eric Blackhand had not lied, the men who failed to make him a prisoner were alive, albeit in varying states of injury. Now he sat opposite Elias in the back of an open cart. With his eyes closed and head casually leaned back, there'd be no telling he were a prisoner if not for the thick bindings ensnaring his wrists. Now that he had a good look at him, Elias thought he understood how Blackhand had earned his nickname. 'The Kid' appeared far younger than Elias' most forgiving estimates had led him to believe, that youth striking him as too much of a surprise for his liking. *It shouldn't be.*

Elias tried to turn his attention toward the road, the ashy grey plains that surrounded this part of Duralaans were a captivating sight, albeit somewhat misery-inducing given the history. It was the hope of many that the land surrounding Mount Promethus would one day heal properly, but for all the time that had so far been given, the only thing that had been produced were fields of grey grass. Blackhand did not seem so interested in his surroundings, perhaps indicating that he was local enough to be used to the sight.

As of yet the man had provided no further opposition. Despite his decision to combat those sent to originally take him prisoner, he'd seemingly given up on freedom and accepted his fate. Elias was almost tempted to believe the act, but gullibility was not the reason he had lived so long and so successfully. The fact that Blackhand was so willing to meet with his captor was more than simple acceptance. He wanted this. Therefore, he would have some form of alternative motivation behind his choice.

Assassination? The idea seemed extreme but was not out of the realm of possibility. From Elias' understanding, Carlyle had been hunting Blackhand for months, perhaps he saw this as the only means of stopping that pursuit. Take the serpent's head and the rest comes undone.

Elias grunted out a few short laughs. "You think you're so clever, huh?" He made sure to keep the words quiet enough that they would not be heard by the man driving the cart. "But I see right through you."

Blackhand opened a single eye, meeting Elias' hard gaze before closing it again. "You think so?"

"I know your kind. You're so young, arrogant, brash. You think the world is yours and that the consequences won't apply to you. But you can take my word for it; the consequences always find us."

"My kind is no different than your own. You are human, right?" Blackhand smirked. "Unless you're just the smallest orc I've ever seen."

"You know what I mean."

"What? Because you've met people vaguely similar to me, you think you know who I am? What I believe?" He scoffed, finally deigning to meet Elias' eyes properly. Blackhand's mouth hung open as if he wanted to say more but seemed to decide against it.

"Go on. Get it out, *Kid*. Might be your last chance."

Blackhand did nothing but watch his captor for a long moment, the bastard must've actually thought he was in a position to be so arrogant. But Elias couldn't help respecting it. The refusal to offer any rebuttal to his prodding showed an admirable level of self-control, unfortunately not a trait many of Elias' foes had shown in the past.

"Let me tell you what I've learned. The more you think you know, the less prepared you'll be when you're faced with something you don't," Blackhand said as Lord Lyre's fortress grew nearer.

"And what experience do you have?" Elias asked, genuinely curious to know something more about his opposition.

"I thought you already knew everything about me."

The cart began to slow to a halt as they reached the great fortress' portcullis. Elias took to his feet and dropped out of the back, moving toward the two armoured figures on the approach. He waited to be close enough to whisper before speaking. "He's bound tight, but he's planning something."

"We can handle him. Good work, Sorren." The shorter of the two guards said.

"Right," Elias replied, as doubt wormed its way into his heart. "Just do what you can to keep him secured."

"Could always use the lower dungeons," the taller one said.

The shorter man seemed to think very little of that suggestion. "He's just one man, what do you think he'll do?"

"Lyre hired me to get this job done right, that's what I'm doing," Elias said, casting a glance back toward where Blackhand was still seated. The man was looking at the fortress, something curious and disconcerting in his eyes. "Use those dungeons. Better to be safe."

The two guards passed Elias and spoke to their new prisoner. "Alright, Blackhand. Hope you enjoyed the trip."

The taller of the two placed his hand on the captive and led the prisoner toward the fortress' entrance, while his partner approached Elias, tossing him a weighty sack.

"If you're happy with that, maybe consider taking up more of Lord Lyre's work," the shorter guard said, before turning to join his fellow in leading their prisoner inside.

Elias watched them go, unable to shake the feeling that there was some piece of the puzzle that had been obscured to him. He had not been given the chance to understand Blackhand's purpose, which told him that either he had lost his knack for reading a person or he was missing something. The key piece that would unravel it all.

It came to him as he noticed the faintest glimmer in the light. The firm hand the taller guard had placed on The Kid's shoulder was metallic. Some kind of prosthetic black hand.

Elias tried to catch the guards and his incompetent band of youthful mercenaries, but the portcullis' teeth sunk into the dirt a few steps ahead of him, and there was nothing to do except wait to learn whether or not he would be proven right once more.

—

Eric Blackhand had begun to wonder if the whole ruse had really been necessary. He had infiltrated the fortress of Carlyle Lyre so easily that it seemed the grandeur of the plan in total was overkill. But then in all the weeks he had been there, Eric had failed to gain access to the lowest levels of Lyre's expansive dungeon. That is, until he finally received direct orders to escort somebody into those levels. Though the man did not know it, Elias Sorren had given Eric exactly what he needed.

It wasn't that Elias was especially predictable. Eric only knew that the man was quick to see the worst in people and enjoyed a reliance on having all the facts necessary to complete a particular task. When Damian, Eric's young accomplice and stand-in, handed himself over with a suspicious lack of conflict, Elias could do nothing but assume his intent was malign. Enraptured by that mystery, he would be too distracted to consider the real Eric Blackhand was already inside the fortress.

Eric only wished he had thought of it himself. Such a level of complexity was a few steps beyond him, but when the letter containing those steps had been left to him, Eric saw no other option than to follow along. There was too much at stake for him to question such luck.

With a fleshy smack, Eric knocked his fellow guard unconscious, took the man's keys, and unlocked Damian's bindings.

The Kid rubbed his wrists, nursing the bruises. "Thanks."

"Careful, we're not done yet," Eric said, hastily continuing down the dark corridor in search of where he might find the particular cell he sought.

"Sure, I'm just glad you were right about that bastard."

Eric shook his head, stopping for a moment to decide how to explain his thoughts. "I wasn't right about anything. He was just wrong about me—or you, actually."

Such was the unfortunate truth Eric had tangled with the whole of his so far short life. There would always be those who thought they had seen enough of the world that nothing could ever surprise them again. Then there would be people like Eric Blackhand, who would forever venture against all odds to surprise them.

His thoughts were disrupted by a sound just ahead. Stifled whimpers echoed faintly through the corridor, the pain in the noise making Eric's heart ache as he forced himself to hurry. There was something horribly familiar about the sound. He knew who this was and could spare no more time in rescuing her.

Eric had not been especially quick to believe the rumours that his old friend had been taken captive by Lord Carlyle Lyre, but the particulars of her name and description narrowed the likelihood that this person was the same one he had once journeyed with.

Arriving before the cell, Eric clutched the cold steel bars, peering into the darkness. His heart was racing, eyes searching for the first sign of the being contained within.

Eric's search was met with coughing and a shrill voice. "You're new."

"I'm not with these people." Eric spoke slowly, fighting back the rising anticipation that encouraged him to race to the conclusion. "We came to get you out of here."

His eyes landed on a shifting form in the darkness, inching cautiously forward as a sliver of flickering torchlight framed one side of her face. She was too thin, the strips that her clothes had been torn into hung loose from her figure, stained in part with patches of dark blood. Her skin was a paler green than it had been when last he'd seen her and her black hair was cut short. Worst of all, the left of her devilish horns had been cracked, the tip outright missing. Yet, despite it all, there remained a flicker in her eyes of the spirit Eric could recognise from almost a decade prior.

She forced herself to her feet, attempting to take a step toward the bars. As she tried to move, her legs shook, wavered, then buckled, sending her falling forward. Eric's hands shot out, an act of pure instinct as he realised that he could not stomach to see his old friend in any more pain. He held her through the bars, even as he knew Damian was becoming more fearful of potential discovery, this was infinitely more important to him.

"Why?" she asked, voice hoarse and strained.

"Because you did the same for me, Sera," Eric whispered, and her eyes finally met his, wide as she studied his face. He knew it wasn't the nickname she preferred. It wasn't even one anybody actually used—besides him.

"Nath?" Seraph's eyes widened with recognition and shock.

The man who had once been Nath Whitsin backed away from the cell's bars, drew his firearm, and blew open the cell door.

Chapter Three

The Black Rose is Dead

She appeared to be of about eight years in age, wore an elegant dress, had her hair decorated in a complicated weave of braids and loops that kept the overall appearance of tidy nobility while the quartet of small pink flowers set atop her right ear said something of her innocence. She held a fifth flower in her hand, raised high above her head in offering toward the night's guardian.

Domina decided she posed no threat to him, an obvious conclusion in hindsight, yet the elf took great pride in his diligence. He had been paid in full to discern the night's threats from the friends, and he would do so to his complete capability. Even if that meant spending some of his limited time ascertaining whether or not the noble daughter offering him a pink flower meant him harm.

Domina put on his most approachable smile and reached out to accept the gift. Yet the girl did not seem content, pouting and shaking her head.

"Kneel," she demanded.

Domina would have scoffed if there were not the possibility it would offend the child. Instead he relied on his prior thesis and trusted there would be no harm in playing along with her. Once he was down to her level, the noble girl carefully reached out and tucked the flower's stem behind his own ear. Domina could only imagine what a picture it painted amid his jet-black hair, but the girl seemed proud of her work, giggling and running off back to where her parents mingled with their fellows.

Domina continued his patrol of the dining hall, large enough to fit the three noble families that had been invited, but not much more.

The room was cast in moodily dim light. Domina suspected that allowed the guests the sensation of privacy during their discussions, making them more likely to voice whatever unscrupulous thoughts came to mind, and making Domina's task of weeding out his target a whole world easier—or so he had hoped. Instead it seemed the dinner guests were resolute in their willingness to focus on the most inane and useless topics imaginable. One trio debated the necessity of the recent rise in the taxation of goods depending on how distant the place of sale was from the place it came from, another two smoothed over disagreements between their families regarding an arranged marriage that threatened to fall apart at any moment, and finally the four eldest members of the gathered families discussed which era of Santora's leadership had been the most trying for its people.

Domina had spent a great deal of time in that continent. In fact he had been born in one of its lesser-known villages. And of the three eras of government he had lived through, he could say with absolute certainty that none were any better or worse than the others. Domina had half a mind to say as much but making conversation was not his strong suit—and more importantly, not what he was being paid for.

The only person Domina thought seemed at all suspicious was one young woman with short black hair who he had found striding through the room as though in a great hurry. She was not somebody Domina had been informed would be in attendance, yet when he broached his concern with his client, Domina had been informed she was to be left alone and that her presence was veri-fied. Thus he was left without any notion as to how he ought to proceed.

The master of the house watched Domina from the upper bal-cony. Caster Hyde knew what was at stake, and while he seemed to trust the capabilities of his hireling, he still appeared incredibly uneasy at the prospect that failure was very much on the table.

"I must thank you all for joining us tonight," Lord Hyde spoke, finally deciding he needed to acknowledge his guests in some way. "Though I may be the lord of this house, tonight is not about me. My son, Henryk, is to inherit my seat, and I hope by this night's end you will all understand why."

The young Henryk Hyde raised a glass toward his father. The boy shared more of his mother's features than Caster's, but his blazing red hair made the relation clear at a glance, if he were to grow out his facial hair some might not even be able to tell that there had been a transition of power.

With the end of his short speech, Hyde cast another glance to-ward Domina, clearly eager for him to conclude his investigation. This had not always been his life; answering to the call of who-ever's coin purse rang loudest. He had once had purpose, a true calling he could claim with pride. But that path had only brought him failure, or perhaps he had been the one to introduce failure to the path of the righteous. Either way, he had known little success for himself or those around him. A part of Domina still yearned for more than he had, for heroics and grandeur, but such things did nothing for his livelihood, especially when he was so ill equipped to pursue such a life. So here he was, putting the enemies of others to the sword and being rewarded for it. Domina was certain that this was not an unfulfilling way to live, yet unfulfilled he was.

This particular job had come to him through pure stupidity and luck. A blood broker had offered him a hefty sum of gold in return for taking the life of Lord Hyde, he had made the mistake of as-suming Domina would not have any moral apprehensions to killing a relatively innocent man in cold blood. Sure, murder was no stranger of his, but he at least liked to entertain the idea that he only struck down those who in some regard deserved it. He understood many had reason to kill Hyde, Domina would be willing to bet that there were no political figures in the whole world of Avandoras that did not—in some way—deserve to be put to the sword. Alas, that was precisely what Domina was there to prevent.

While Domina had turned down the contract on grounds of morality, he was aware another had no such qualms. Over the last week he had followed the path of an assassin, uncovering the faint trail of the one who had taken up the task. They never met their client in person, setting up drop points to exchange notes, marked by a thin plume of smoke in the sky. The last of these had appeared the morning of the dinner, beneath a small tree, and while Domina had been too late to discover whatever message had been left, it was clear the killer was prepared to strike.

The guests had taken their seats at table, prepared to feast alongside their host. Domina stood by the backwall, hand on his blade's hilt as his mind raced with possibility. He was certain the assassin would strike that night, though he supposed that did not have to be during the dinner itself, even if that would provide the best opportunity for a stranger to slip inside. He cast his eyes over the food, considering poison for a moment, before outright dismissing the possibility. He suspected the manor's servants first of all, but there had been no sign of malign in any of them and no chance an assassin could have infiltrated as a recent addition to the house's staff. Domina had been left with the conclusion that the killer had to be somebody who had been invited into the house, yet none had so far shown any inclination toward harming the lord.

An old sensation began to creep into Domina's heart; this was going to become just another example of his many failures. Once again, he regretted taking on the title of his old travelling party as his own pseudonym. *The Black Rose*. Only a fool wouldn't see the clear omen in that name.

Domina knew his wit was nothing to boast about. His specialty was as a combatant, not a strategist, such had always been his greatest failing. He was no sleuth, so there was no hope of discovering whoever had taken up the contract, at least not as long as he limited himself to a methodology which did not suit him. Domina would not be able to uncover his foe, but a means of forcing them to reveal themself was beginning to become clear to him. Domina shifted toward Hyde's seat at the head of the table and leant toward his ear, this would require his cooperation.

—

Domina stood by a rising plume of white smoke, snuck a glance toward the distant city he had come from and the point where the manor's height stretched beyond even the city's highest of walls. The visual sent quite the message to any who considered a visit, none of Anderan's splendour could compare to the home of Caster Hyde. *Of course somebody wants him dead.*

A shadow emerged from the city's secondary gate and began a harried approach toward Domina's tree. He smiled.

The plan had been relatively simplistic, though not one Hyde had been especially enthusiastic to partake in. Thankfully, with enough explanation, the lord had agreed, and after a drink of his wine, supposedly succumbed to poisoning. Domina proposed that this would panic the true assassin, and with him following up this first step with the lighting of the conspirator's signal fire, their options would be limited.

The shadow began to take shape as it neared, a tall masculine image, draped in black robes to disguise their identity. He spoke, barely contained anger in his voice. "You said the job was exclusive."

Domina did not respond, considering whether or not this man would recognise the voice of his client—or lack thereof.

"Don't think I'm walking away like this." He stopped on the other side of the tree. "You'll pay me for the risk alone."

Domina stepped out, wearing nothing to hide his features, and by the way the man stumbled back, it was clear he recognised him. "We'll see what I owe you." The metal of his sword sung as it came from its sheath, the tip pressed against the man's throat only a second later. The black blade was nearly invisible in the night, the only sign of its presence a starry glimmer within the glass core that made up most of its surface. Domina knew the bizarre nature of the thing, knew that it confounded his opponents long enough to put them down. The hooded man was stilled by his fear.

"You . . . didn't hire me." The man gave voice to the obvious. "It was you, then?"

Domina tilted his head, trying to make out the man's shrouded face.

"You killed him, took my mark?"

"No." Domina flicked his blade toward the sky, knocking the hood away to reveal the man's face. It was not one he recognised. "Who are you?"

"Just a man down on his luck, looking for some easy gold."

"Hardly a definition I'd recognise." Domina returned his blade to its place at the man's throat. "You weren't at the dinner."

"Of course not." The man was incredulous. "No, there was no way I could get inside. Too much risk, even for me."

"Then how did you plan on killing him?" Domina stepped forward, forcing the blade's sharper-than-razor edge closer to his throat. So close to the man now, Domina noted a strong odour emanating from him, one that seemed familiar, though he could not place it.

"You really didn't do it?" His eyes went distant, contemplative. "He's alive?"

"How?" Domina's blade drew blood, a shallow cut, but enough to leave a clear message.

"Wait and see."

This man had never managed to enter the manor, yet he remained resolute that his method could work. Domina could not see any weapons on him, no firearms to end somebody's life from a distance. Even more, he seemed to believe his plan would still see success. Whatever scheme he had concocted no longer required his presence. It was in motion. The fuse already lit. All that it needed was time for the inferno to rage.

Then Domina recalled that the fire had not been lit, the vain attempt to add to the night's atmosphere. But with Hyde's apparent demise, they would want all the light they could muster.

"Mind turning us around?" the man asked, his lips twisting into a knowing smile. "I like to watch."

Domina realised what the scent was—he had known it was once before. During his time with the Black Rose, he had spent much time in the Santoran city of Spirallos. That city had been destroyed, much of it being blown to kingdom come—the result of a hundred barrels filled with cinder powder hidden throughout Spirallos. As the ash and smoke cleared, a distinct scent remained in the air for weeks afterward. That same scent he now recognised on the man before him.

A little more or less than a hundred barrels of the stuff had destroyed a city. It would only take one to—

From the corner of his eyes, Domina saw Hyde's manor light up. In a single moment every window flashed white with blinding light, then that same light consumed the entire structure, no doubt visible to anyone within a day's ride. He could almost imagine the sight, like the sun had risen too early, and with it taken nineteen lives.

Domina forced himself to avert his gaze, such a blast had blinded many who underestimated its effect, but a part of him thought he deserved to suffer in such a way. He'd failed. Domina had once again failed to save those who had relied on him.

He hefted the blade above his head, and in a single slash, bisected the man from shoulder to hip. It was a poor choice. There was more yet to learn from him. But it was all Domina could do.

—

Domina stood before the ruins of the manor, now little more than an ashen pit at the city's edge. The fire had burned for hours, not waning entirely until noon of the following day. There was a haunting quiet about the place, in stark contrast to the cacophony of the blast. The surrounding area had been evacuated, and the site of destruction remained deathly silent.

A breeze swept through, kicking up a cloud of ash and sending it toward Domina. He felt something come loose in his hair and watched a pink flower drift past him. The breeze ceased and the tiny speck of colour drifted down into the gaping chasm of ruin.

The guest families had been ushered out after Hyde had taken Domina's suggestion to fake his death. He thanked whatever gods were still listening that they had been spared. But the man he was supposed to protect was no more, reduced to ash alongside his wife and son. His line ended with him, though Domina suspected he had other relatives who would be quick to take his place.

Domina remained there for a long while, considering what was next for him. The chance that he could take on another job so soon after this blunder was abysmal at best and the more likely scenario was far worse. Failing a contract with such grandeur might not have been something new to him, but that didn't mean the consequences weren't going to be difficult to deal with.

He set off toward the city's secondary gate, better to move in present than future was the idea, and preferably with as little eyes on him as possible. It wasn't like he could afford to live in the city any longer, not without being paid, and that was no longer an option. But a question of purpose remained. Domina could not simply wander for the rest of his days. He needed something to work toward, a direction he could focus on. It had been easy enough to stumble upon the Hyde opportunity; he was sure it would not take him long to find something new.

Or perhaps there was another way.

Caster Hyde was dead, his family with him, alongside Domina's best chance at learning more—but not his *only* chance. The blood broker who first informed him of the contract operated out of Anderan. Indeed, his home was only a short walk from the Hyde manor itself, close enough that he would have been forced to evacuate alongside everyone else.

Domina decided to postpone his flight from the city. There was no harm in having a simple look through the broker's abode, and if he turned up with nothing of use, Domina could leave having lost very little by way of time.

While it was true that failure was a constant companion of his, their relationship was not exclusive. It was his persistence that had kept him alive for so long. Domina would survive this as well, and he would see the job done. It was all he could do.

Chapter Four

Raph

It pained Raph to no end seeing her home like this. Truly, it was all she had ever been able to call her own. Father was an unknown element; Mother had abandoned her for her own safety. The store she had owned and operated was all Raph had possessed for the last five years of her life.

The sign lay broken in two on the scorched tile path out front. 'Reckless and Abandoned.'

Fitting, Raph thought, a smile tugging at the corner of her mouth. That was a first for her life post Spirallos' destruction. It made her heart rot with guilt.

She struggled to find footing as she stepped inside her ruined home of antique artefacts of questionable spiritual significance, many of which lay shattered and twisted on the ground. Raph's foot caught on something beneath her, forcing her to take a moment to regain her bearing, before looking down to see what had tripped her. The split handle of her glaive was embedded in the rubble, the bladed end nowhere to be seen. She wrapped her fingers around it, gave it a single hard pull, then decided the effort was wasted. Just another fragment of a past that would not be reclaimed.

Why she had thought searching the ruin was a good idea, Raph could not know. It was a whim really. A sudden inkling that she should return to her old home so that she might find *something*. But there was nothing left. That discovery should not have surprised her. She had given the destroyed structure a brief search shortly after the initial calamity and seen just how thoroughly wrecked it was. Why would anything be different upon a second inspection?

As if by some divine influence, her questions were answered by the sound of disruption ahead. Raph was not alone.

She clapped her hands together, then drew her right back, like stringing an invisible bow. Iridescent energy crackled in the air between her fingertips as she approached the source of the disturbance. Raph usually felt a horrible sense of dread when she called on her power, sourcing from the entity that dwelled beneath the city, but now she felt surging adrenaline course through her. Something about the city's destruction had changed that terrible maw, and Raph's bond with the thing had changed alongside it.

She rounded one of the few standing walls of the shop to find a small shape scrounging around in the rubble among what was once the storeroom. She let loose the crackling energy, letting it disperse upon hitting the ground beside them. A few of the bright sparks flicked toward them, sending them recoiling in pain.

"Ah!" they cried, turning to see where the shock had come from. They were a boy, maybe a few years younger than Raph was, and he was angry. "That hurt!"

"Oh that was nothing." Raph readied another blast. "Get out of my store before I show you real hurt."

"*Your* store?" he spat. "You're Sera? But you're just a—"

"I'm Raph," she cut him off. "Short for Seraph, but nobody calls me that."

"Oh." The boy was somewhat embarrassed for a moment, before his anger seemed to return. "Well I can't leave yet. I need something."

"You blind? There's nothing left."

"No, they told me this store used to have a ton of magical artefacts. There's got to be at least one left."

"I know what this store had. I ran it!" she repeated, but the boy only turned his focus back to his search. Raph released another blast, far enough from him this time that it would do no harm. "I said *leave*."

"And I told you that I can't. Not until I find something," he spat back. "What do you care if there's nothing left anyway?"

"I care because . . ." Raph considered for a moment just how much she wanted to divulge. "Because this was my home. Destroyed or not, I don't want some brat poking around where I lived."

To her surprise, the boy actually stopped his rummaging, sitting back on his knees as he seemingly struggled to decide his next course of action.

Raph couldn't help but feel the tiniest bit poor. He was right that there was nothing left for her to protect. She had no tangible reason to stop him from taking what he could from what remained, and yet even in such a sorry state it still held such an important place in her heart.

She kicked at a loose piece of stone. "What's your name?"

"Nath," he answered, eyes fixed to the floor beneath him.

"What are you looking for?"

He shook his head. "I don't know. Just something to make me strong."

"What do you need to be strong for?"

"To avenge my mother."

Raph recognised his anger now, a simmering veil disguising something deeper, something more difficult to reckon with. *Pain.* "You'll fail."

"What?" He looked at up her now, clear blue eyes lined with dark rings that betrayed just how tired he must have been.

"You can hurt who you want to hurt, but it won't bring your mother back, and it won't fix how you're feeling either."

Nath got to his feet, standing about a foot shorter than her. "I know all that. My father said the same thing. But neither of you understand, it's not about making things better for me. It's just not fair that she died, and they haven't."

"Justice, then?" Raph tilted her head, letting the greasy black strands of her hair cascade down the side of her face.

"Yes." Nath's gaze whipped from one side of the shop to another. "Surely there's something left that can help me?"

"If it's help you want, then the best thing for me to do would be to tie you down somewhere and keep you there until you develop some sense," Raph suggested under her breath, though the boy seemed too distracted to hear it. "But that's not really how this works."

She began searching through the various pouches hooked to her waist, eventually fishing out a small gold locket attached to a thin chain. She presented it to Nath, letting it swing from her fingertip like a pendulum.

"This is the Locket of Chronara, do you know who that is?"

"Of course," Nath responded, though there was an apprehension in his voice that made Raph doubtful.

"Goddess of Time. This locket was gifted to one of her most beloved followers eight centuries ago."

"It'll make me stronger?"

"It searches the branches of immortal time and locates the strongest version of the one who wears it, changing them into that form as long as it remains open."

Nath's hand stretched toward where the locket hung. He met her eyes, his question remaining.

"It'll make you as strong as you could possibly be," she said as Nath tried to take it in hand, only for Raph to snatch it back. "I could give it to you. Got any coin?"

"Coin?"

"Yeah. No matter the state, this is still a store. I don't hand out godly artefacts for free."

"I don't have any money."

Raph shrugged and shoved the locket back in its pouch. "Guess we won't be doing business then."

She hopped from one clear section of floor to another, playing up her apparent lack of interest.

"Wait!" Nath called after her, stepping through the mess of rubble with far less expertise.

"Hmm? Remembered your coin purse?" Raph asked, reaching what was once the store's entrance.

"No, but there has to be something else I can do."

"Oh?"

"Your home's destroyed. I could help you fix it."

Raph stopped at the entrance, looking out at the ruined street before her. "There are more important things to fix than one little shop."

"Well it's clearly important to you." Nath stumbled his way over to her, standing on the other side of a half-fallen beam of wood.

She turned her attention toward him, some of the hurt in his eyes had cleared. "When this place was more than rubble and ash, I had a system in place for those who could not afford my goods," Raph explained. "They would perform tasks for me. However many I felt made up for the cost of the particular item they sought."

Nath's face fell, bracing himself for the brunt of her request. "And what will I have to do for that locket?"

"An artefact of the Gods?" Raph whistled. "It'll take time to earn it, but stay in this city and work with me to get these people's lives back on track, and then I'll let you have it. Even more, I'll help you find the bastards you're looking for and see that they die before you do."

Nath took a moment to consider it, but there was only one conclusion he would come to. If he wished to avenge his mother, Raph offered the only means of doing so, and hopefully along her path of righteousness his anger would cool, and his pain would be soothed. Raph could see there was good in him, she only hoped it was not too late to save it.

"Okay. You have a deal, Sera." Nath held out his hand.

"Raph." She took it and the pact was made.

—

Raph did not know why that day—coming up on twelve years prior—had come to her. Perhaps it was because Raph thought she had seen Nath visit her deep in the dungeons beneath Carlyle Lyre's fortress, the place she had remained alone for weeks without end. She wondered why, of all people, it was Nath Whitsin she had seen. Perhaps Raph's mind was trying to comfort her with memories of the good deeds of her youth. Indeed Nath had done good in the end. They both had.

Raph was not aware of herself. Her surroundings were odd. In one moment the world was dark, completely empty of any substance. Then there would be flickers, visions she attributed to her dying mind, faces looking over her, screaming and doing what they could to sustain her failing form.

Her eyes opened for a moment, but she quickly decided it would be preferable not to engage with whatever awaited her outside her mind. None of that belonged to her anymore, she could feel the hand on hers, the one she had no doubt belonged to whatever angel of death would carry her toward the Immortal Plane.

Though she accepted this fate, it was far from preferable. Long had she endured the work of Carlyle's premiere extractor of truth—too nice a name for one who had inflicted upon her endless waves of agony, but one that did not bring those memories so vividly to the front of her mind. Despite it all, Raph was sure she had never given them what it was they sought from her, although she could no longer recall what that had been which she had suffered so much pain to protect. Ironically, in her bid to hide what she knew, she had also hidden it from herself.

Raph tried to recall it, the reason she had come to the land of Duralaans in the first place. It had been of incredible importance. Something that would threaten all who called the continent home. That purpose began to repair itself in Raph's mind.

Then she saw herself huddled in the dark corner of that cell, thin, bruised, and crying. So she pushed the memory away again, burying it deep within her subconscious, and her quest vanished alongside it.

She could still feel the pain in her legs, her arms, within and without the body she no longer seemed to possess. Though she understood it still existed somewhere, it would no longer be hers. Raph would soon be dead. It would be nice to know that which she had given her life for, but those details were ultimately meaningless. She had succeeded, that would be enough. *It has to be enough.*

Her mind drifted back toward the dark, further inundated by memories of her past. Raph recalled the moment Nath had given up on working to earn the locket, his need for vengeance having refused to alleviate. She had only pretended to be asleep as the boy snuck into her tent and pilfered the locket from her score of artefacts.

Raph crept through the night then, following him to the edge of the forest of tents set up as temporary housing for those displaced by their home's destruction. It was there that he finally slipped the locket around his neck and allowed its power to strengthen him. Nath had become an older version of himself. Lean and strong, he was a man who could take revenge for the pain the boy had suffered. However, before he could leave to claim his justice, something caught his attention. Three shadowy figures snuck into somebody's tent, their daggers illuminated by the moonlight. Raph had watched in silence as Nath flew instantly into action, putting a stop to their dark intent before they could complete the act.

Raph returned to her own tent afterwards, satisfied that the goodhearted boy she had recognised remained. And to her surprise, Raph awoke to find the locket returned to her inventory, and Nath ready to continue his work for the people of Spirallos. She did not know whether his intent was always to use the locket that night to protect the people from ne'er-do-wells or if he had simply changed his mind at the first sign of trouble, but she decided in that moment that he had finally earned the artefact.

Even then, he did not leave the city, claiming it needed protection in that moment more than he needed his vengeance. Raph did not know how much of that was true, but she was glad to have him by her side. Somebody willing to do good for others more than he wanted to feed his own desire would be an incomparable ally. While he tried to at first maintain secrecy, the identity of their nightly protector was eventually discovered by the people of Spirallos. They took to calling him The Kid.

Raph missed that kid, the one who would do everything to protect everyone.

Yet he couldn't protect her.

After the city was rebuilt, they had journeyed together for a time, before going their separate ways after a particularly strenuous ending to one adventure.

The pain of that memory pushed Raph further inward, and the sensation of the hand on hers grew numb. Distant.

"*No,*" a soft voice spoke.

Colour erupted from the darkness, a blinding radiance that pierced her mind. The colour twisted and grew, like iridescent vines snaking their way toward her, their leaves silver mirrors awakening lost memories. Painful memories.

Raph fell among a bleeding maw of jagged teeth and red flesh.

Raph was left alone on the doorstep of a popular inn. She saw a woman garbed in red hurrying away before her daughter could understand that she had just been abandoned.

Raph discovered a long-buried evil, destroying the last map to its prison so none might set it free.

"You're not finished, Seraph," the voice continued, the one that had guided her since Spirallos' destruction; The Floral Maw and Goddess of Growth, Anni. Her form appeared among the vines, emitting the same mix of colour and light, an ever-shifting figure of a woman beyond the confines of mortality.

The vines wrapped around Raph, gently holding her as she grew comfortable with the overbearing light.

"I don't remember," Raph tried to say. Though she possessed no mouth from which she could speak, the words seemed to simply exist between them. "I don't know why I came here."

"Yes, you do," Anni insisted, her words supported by patience. *"I did not choose you because you were one to shy away from a painful truth."*

"You know what they did to me. You must have seen it all. I will not relive it. I will not go back." Raph tried to scream but found her thoughts breaking apart.

"Of course not. Never go back, Seraph," Anni said. *"Never remain stagnant."*

Raph felt weightless, drifting in place between life and death. The choice between the two belonged to her; she could return to the pain, a moment she did not know, a world of uncertainty in which she would have to fight to survive. Or she could let the end claim her.

Was that what she wanted? To be painless. To be unburdened. To drift weightless upon the cosmic sea.

Raph recalled Nath once more. He had every reason to pursue those who had wronged him, he may even have been morally correct to do so. Yet he remained for the sake of others, all the while she watched as his heart longed to be elsewhere. He remained despite himself.

"Deal," Raph spoke, though she did not know to whom.

Chapter Five
Blood Business

He had considered a variety of means that might have allowed him to enter the broker's home without permission. Kicking down the door had seemed the simplest solution, but the risk of the noise alerting any who passed by turned Domina off the idea. The chances of anybody patrolling the evacuated zone of Anderan were slim, but Domina wondered if testing that estimate was wise. The windows would pose the same problem, and while an external door to the cellar seemed promising at first, it had been barricaded from within. Domina decided the door would just have to do.

A firm kick, and it was open.

Clearly the business of death was a profitable one, as the broker's home was by no means a small one. Domina might not have agreed with the man's lifestyle, but he could understand what would lead somebody to act the middleman in making real the darkest dreams of those with the means to pay. Though it may have been nothing in comparison to Hyde's manor, it was large enough that a complete search would take more time than Domina could stomach. Their meeting had not been a particularly long one, Domina had never even managed to discern the broker's name, but he had been able to understand just what kind of man he was. *Organised.* Domina supposed that if he were the type to bring his work home with him, this broker would keep it contained. Domina thought a study may have sufficed, but he struggled to find such a room. It seemed odd that one such as he would not possess one, yet as Domina searched the home's floors twice over, he began to suspect his judgement had been wrong.

But this blood broker operated a business. He brought together those who sought the pain of others and those who had no issue with delivering such pain. Such work would inevitably birth documents, papers that would have to be stored *somewhere*. It was possible he managed his work exclusively from inside the ale house where Domina had first met him, but he found it unlikely the broker would have a personal quarters within the establishment where he could store his belongings.

Domina was searching for a place he knew must exist yet had not the first idea where it could be. It was the sort of complicated puzzle he had always failed to solve but had always seemed to find its way to him—not unlike the way the contract to assassinate Lord Hyde had practically been forced upon him through no effort of his own.

He searched the house for a third time, finding nothing more than he had during the last. It was made up of a dining room, two quarters for sleep, a washroom, and the main room he had first entered into. It seemed as though the broker did not live alone; the idea of that kind of man sharing his life with another made Domina uncomfortable. He paced the hall connecting the rooms, there had to be something he'd missed. Whether that be a single drawer or cabinet or—*the cellar*.

In all of his time searching the building, Domina had not found an entrance to the cellar from inside the house.

He sprinted outside, locating the external cellar door, then tracked its position as he backed into the house once more. The cellar would have to be somewhere below the main room, but there was no clear way to access it. There remained the chance that the door Domina had found was the only one, yet for it to be truly locked from the inside as he presumed, there would need to be another way in and out.

Domina took his sword in hand and tapped the blade's tip to the boarded floor.

BANG BANG.

Domina moved along, repeated the act.

BANG BANG.

He took a larger step away.

BANG BANG.

He repeated the test a fourth time, centre of the room.

THUNK.

Hollow. Domina jammed the blade between the gaps in the floorboarding, embedding it deep enough that he had a level of leverage, then wrenched it up. The board came unstuck with a splitting *CRACK*, and beneath, Domina found only a pit of darkness, slightly illuminated by the new opening in its ceiling. He removed a few more boards, leaving enough space that he might fit through, then removed a thin stick from his travel satchel. It was an old relic of the elven homeland, the secrets of which had been passed along through his family. In effect it was not very impressive, but it had served incredibly useful more times than Domina dared to remember. He scraped off the stick's outer layer, revealing the luminous membrane and providing a small area of bright light. As he let it fall into the darkness below, the alflight bathed the cellar in golden light, revealing the floor to be only a short drop from where Domina stood.

Domina let himself drop to the cellar floor, taking the light back in hand and raising it above his head. Immediately he was assaulted by a horrible odour further ahead, the familiar scent of rot and blood, accompanied by the hint of something subtler, almost citric if Domina's senses were not misleading him.

He waved the stick around, taking in what he could of the room while he searched for the source of the odour. The walls were smooth black granite, though in a select few patches there seemed to be a splash of dark colour Domina could not identify. It glistened when faced with the light and seemed to grow as it reached the floor, where a larger trail continued toward the back of the cellar.

Domina could see a staircase behind him, leading back to the entrance he had seen outside, and supposed an alternate entry might be ahead.

He ventured further onward, his fingers gripped tight around the alflight. Domina found himself wishing he still possessed both of his appendages, a feeling that had become more frequent with time. Yet he had never sought out a prosthetic. Something within had always held him back from replacing that which he had lost, despite the enchanted devices the arcane craftsmen of the more well-to-do cities could provide, they had never struck his interest.

The smell had grown almost overwhelming, and Domina was forced to smother his senses with his arm, though holding the light so close to his face also made it far more difficult to see ahead. His foot caught on something and Domina fell to the ground, catching himself with his hand, but dropping his source of light. It rolled along the ground then stopped as it hit the same thing Domina had tripped over. He took the light in hand again and held it up, investigating just what had sent him falling—and finding only regret.

The face was almost unrecognisable, corroded and burnt in some places, rotten and degraded in others. One of his eyes was no longer in its socket, the other was milky white. The corpse had no clothes, and the rest of his body bore much of the same damage, as though it had been burnt by some acidic toxin, then left to rot for days in the damp dark of the man's own cellar. Despite all of the damage done, Domina knew this to be the same blood broker he had spoken to not more than a week before.

He stood over the corpse, trying to determine what exactly its presence meant. He had been dead for a while, of course, potentially since the night Domina had met him. Domina thought it possible the client had discovered the mistake his broker had made in attempting to hire somebody like Domina and had him killed for it. But the vial that remained in the broker's hand made him think otherwise. It could have been staged, but Domina wondered if he had killed himself out of fear of what his client would do, perhaps deciding to send his family away beforehand. If the client had been responsible, that would not explain the missing family. Surely, they would have noticed their patriarch's disappearance and done something about it before the evacuation.

Now that he had reached the farthest end of the cellar, Domina found that there was no secondary entrance, the only way in and out had indeed been the door he'd found outside. The one that remained barricaded from within.

The blood broker's corpse lay next to a long wooden desk, fitted with an assortment of drawers and littered with papers. Domina glanced over a few of them, all seeming to be either the death contracts themselves or meticulous notes weighing the benefits and detriments to pairing particular clients with particular customers. Many bore the name Laurence Callum, and finally Domina knew what to call the deceased merchant of death, though to his disappointment, it did not yield any immediate familiarity. His was not a name Domina had ever encountered before, and it brought him no further leads toward whose conspiracy he had found himself a part of.

He began a long and trying search through each sheet of paper and scrap note atop the desk, flipping through every drawer and seeking any apparent mention of Hyde or his home. He turned the drawers inside out, letting anything he found to be irrelevant scatter across the ground. That mess only grew as he found nothing that brought him satisfaction.

Domina reached for the lowest drawer available but found it unresponsive, locked with no key in sight. Callum likely kept it on his person but—in his currently unclothed state—it was hard to imagine that remained the case. Domina considered cutting the desk open but preferred not to risk damaging whatever could be inside, and so he was left with frustratingly few options.

Domina attempted to pry the desk open, stubbornly yanking on the silver knob until he thought he'd heard a faint *click*. Domina paused and listened as he thought he could hear mechanical workings within the walls, heavy *CLUNKS* that only seemed to grow with time. Then the room was bathed in light as part of the ceiling folded away, leaving a long slit of an opening into a room Domina could not identify from where he stood below. A series of granite slabs emerged from the back wall, each stopping shorter than the last, until a makeshift staircase had been formed. It seemed there had been a second entrance after all, and so murder was back on the table, alongside the possibility that whatever Domina was looking for had already been removed.

He sat himself down and ran a hand through his long black hair. *Of course it wouldn't be that simple.* But he had hoped there would be something to send him on his way, a clue that he could use to unravel this brewing mystery, yet he seemed to have reached a dead end.

All the while he could see the outline of this conspiracy; a noble house dead and the broker who'd arranged the contract along with them. All of the makings were present, but he could not see how they came together.

The more he thought on it, the more bizarre it seemed that this Laurence Callum had originally sought Domina as a potential weapon against Hyde. For him to have considered Domina as an option he'd need to have known something of his work, yet he somehow remained ignorant to the fact Domina only pursued the ignoble to put to the sword. The only reason he would have done so, besides being a greater fool than Domina had taken him for, would be if he had actually hoped that Domina would put a stop to it—or at the very least attempt to do so.

"Gods be good, what have you gotten yourself into?" he found himself asking aloud.

Domina decided not to concern himself with the larger scheme, if he were to only focus on one piece at a time, then even he could unravel such a tangled web. Justice would be served.

Callum must have been afraid of his client, or at least of what they aimed to accomplish, and so brought the contract to Domina's attention so he might put an end to it. Then the client discovered his betrayal and came to find the broker in his home, forcing him to poison himself, before absconding with whatever evidence remained to implicate them in the assassination. The only people Domina knew for certain could know the identity of this person would be the dead broker and the dead assassin—once again he regretted his hasty decision to end the demolitionist's life.

Although, he supposed there could be a third body who might know something of this mysterious figure. If Domina was right that the Callum family had been sent away for their own safety, Laurence may have told them something of his reasoning for fear.

And so, a new problem arose; Domina had no idea where this family might be and no clue how to find them. He wasn't even absolutely sure they existed at all. But Domina had gotten lucky before, he could only pray such blessings would befall him a second time.

He climbed the new staircase and found himself exiting into the home's hallway. Domina could only guess as to what secret lever could open it from outside, perhaps one of the paintings hanging between rooms or a candlestick that would activate when lit. He did not bother to conceal his presence, better somebody discover the corpse eventually than allow it to remain hidden only so Domina might secure his own mystique.

Offering the cellar's external door a final glance, Domina took off down the street, making his way for the secondary gate he'd used the night prior. There was a small farming town nearby, Domina dared to hope Callum's kin would not have been sent too far from home.

"Leaving the city?" a voice from beyond the gate called.

Domina rounded the stone arch to find an armoured figure blocking his path. "I am. That's no problem, is it?"

"Shouldn't be." The guard shrugged. "Got a name?"

"Domina."

"I see." The guard's eyes shifted to something behind Domina—or someone. "Then I'm afraid there is, in fact, a problem."

Domina turned to face the end of a sword's hilt as it connected with his forehead. He saw stars as he fell to the ground, a shot of pain piercing through his mind.

He wasn't particularly surprised. This was just what he got for hoping that luck might be on his side for once.

Next came a hard boot to his face, and the world went dark.

Chapter Six
The Leading Lady

Presenting," Amor announced, his voice echoing throughout the monumental hall, "Lord Redan of House Rosse."

On cue, Redan Rosse marched forward. The sharp clap of his heels on the pristine tile served as the only permitted sound above a whisper as he approached the royal throne of Duralaans. He came to a stop before the dais, dropping to a single knee, and turned his gaze toward the great stained-glass work embedded beyond the throne.

"As Lord of the House Rosse of Duralaans, I swear my unyielding fealty to the gracious Queen Cecilia, eldest of the royal House Asche," he spoke, voice surprisingly shrill for one who commanded such power among the nobles. "Through times of war and ages of peace, our banner shall be yours to command."

Cecilia would have been honoured by his words if Amor had not already forewarned her that each lord and lady would simply be reciting the scripts they had already been given. Pretty words, though she wondered just how strong they would hold in the face of true adversity. Bonds of sterner material had crumbled under far less pressure. The depictions of war sculpted into the ceiling and laid into the tile told the tale of how easily mankind gave itself to conflict, lured by the promise of vain accomplishment. The human species had reached its pinnacle centuries prior and would never know such glory again, no matter how often it bled to prove otherwise.

"Your banner is accepted with the same grace with which it is offered, Lord Rosse," Cecilia declared, reciting her own lines in turn. It was perfect, they were no more than actors performing the latest production in a long line of coronations. The hall was their stage. The attendees were their audience.

Such restriction almost comforted Cecilia. There would be no surprise, no straying from the defined path, no freedom. Cecilia had once believed that to be the case for all facets of the monarch's life and had long feared the prospect for its lack of choice. With so many pieces firmly in place, centuries of history to define the course a king or queen were expected to take, whatever could she possibly do to shift the tides so set upon their course? For that very reason, Cecilia had always been thankful for her place as thirdborn heir to the throne, nothing short of the greatest of tragedies would place her upon the royal seat. And yet on the throne she sat. It would forever serve as a reminder of all she had lost, and all she had to live up to.

Lord Rosse stepped back toward where he had come, meeting a young aide of his house who bore a velvet pillow in his hands, upon which Cecilia knew sat a small ruby. Rosse carefully plucked it from the pillow and approached the dais once more. Cecilia gave him a gesture of consent, and the man ascended the steps toward her. Delicately, he reached out and inserted the ruby into its slot within the large chain that sat upon Cecilia's shoulders and ensnared her collar—the Platinum Chain.

It was not the same that had once been worn by the first monarchs of her line. That had long been lost, leading to the decision that a new chain would be forged for each individual king or queen. It was made of metals sourced all over the continent and decorated with a gemstone gifted from each noble house. It was the symbol of unity, power, and responsibility. All sat upon a single mortal's shoulders.

Another noble stepped forward to take position beneath the throne, the Lady Daphne of House Raleigh. It was another ancient house of the kingdom, one of the original eight to ally with the Ashen King and be deceived in his efforts to maintain the throne. Another four houses had arisen in the near nine centuries since that monumental event, yet Cecilia only counted eleven families in attendance.

"As Lady of House Raleigh of Duralaans, I swear my undying fealty to the gracious Queen Cecilia," Lady Raleigh said. "Whether through times of war or peace, our house shall answer to your call."

"Your allegiance is accepted with the same grace in which it is offered, Lady Raleigh."

The lady rose, an expression of serene assurance on her face as she approached her queen and slotted the Raleigh emerald into its place.

Cecilia counted the attendees again as Lord Leonis Trethellyn cut through the gathering and made his way down the aisle toward the dais. Indeed, only eleven of the twelve noble houses were present.

"As Lord of House Trethellyn of Duralaans, I swear our unyielding allegiance to the crown of Queen Cecilia. Whether in peace or war, you shall know our aid."

"Your allegiance is accepted with the same respect with which it is offered, Lord Trethellyn," Cecilia repeated her lines even as her mind raced to recall all who were supposed to be in attendance.

For a moment she thought it was the Lyre household that was missing. While it was true that their lord had declared his inability to attend, the man had sent his daughter to act on his behalf.

As Trethellyn's sapphire was placed into position and the next lord marched forward, realisation finally fell upon her. House Hyde was missing.

Cecilia's heart sunk in her chest; Caster Hyde had privately declared his intent to forgo the typical pledge of alliance, instead wishing to wait and see what style she took as leader before he offered his fealty. But Cecilia had managed to soothe his apprehensions and confirmed his plans to attend so he may not spark greater discourse. Perhaps his promise had been false, such things were not unheard of, but a rebel house so early in her reign could prove disastrous for her future prospects.

Cecilia waited for Phemus Anderthread to finish pledging his banner and offer his family's opal, then gestured for Amor to approach the throne. "Were you aware that House Hyde would not be present?" Cecilia spoke quietly once he was close enough to lend her his ear.

"I'm afraid so, Your Grace," he answered, voice thin but respectably tempered.

"And what reason did he give?"

"A great tragedy, truly." Amor paused, only continuing at the nod of Cecilia's head. "Lord Hyde and his kin are, as of a few nights ago, dead."

"By the Gods' grace." Cecilia felt herself grow cold. Never would she have suspected their current absence to be the result of such a tragic circumstance. Rebellion almost would have been preferable; those relations could at least be repaired with time. The dead were lost forevermore. "You will enlighten me of the complete details surrounding this tragedy once this is done with."

"Very good, Your Grace."

"And do not think to keep such details from me ever again, I must know of such things immediately from here on out."

"Of course, it is only that such details are currently so sparse that I did not already broach it with you."

"I understand, Amor. But never again."

He acknowledged her with an elegant bow, before returning to his place at the right of the dais.

The next house's representative was announced and allowed to stand before her, declaring their fealty and being met with the

Queen's thanks. This theatre continued until all were given fair opportunity to present themselves and adorn the Platinum Chain with their colourful heirlooms.

Kiara Lyre gifted her a shimmering diamond, Lady Stellari offered her garnet, Ennard Harald presented his topaz, and an amethyst came from Strados. Lord Zephyr Mars added a piece of amber, containing a blade of grass he claimed had been gifted by the old goddess of nature. Helen Wintre placed into the chain a simple piece of quartz and blessed her queen in the name of their new goddess of nature.

When the affair was finished, Cecilia rose and marched through the space between her sea of subjects. The weight of the chain felt off, and Cecilia knew why. It remained incomplete. She did her utmost to put such distractions from her mind, but from a dark place deep within came a wandering thought of doubt. Just what would her newly loyal brothers and sisters in nobility think of such a thing? They might understand the tragic circumstance behind it. Or they would see it as a fraying thread, ready to be unwoven entirely if only they were to tug at it.

—

It was the quiet sea that Cecilia imagined as her handmaiden undressed her, carefully stripping and storing the royal coronation gown, before fetching its supper counterparts.

Cecilia had an odd relationship with the life of nobility. She could enjoy the elegance and glory of it much of the time but would just as often find herself suffocated by the immensity of it all.

She supposed she had at least come a long way from her youth, there had been a time where she had planned to run away from the life entirely, to journey the world and know no restriction besides the limits of the vessel of her adventure. It was a dream she had shared with the heir of Cendela, someone she had met during her family's tour of the neighbouring continent. They had spent much of their time since sending letters back and forth, sharing dreams of the fantastic world they would uncover together.

Then tragedy had reared its hideous head, and Cecilia's elder siblings were killed. There was no warning, no time to say good-bye, only a messenger to inform the King that his children had been killed on the road, a group of eager bandits having seen the royal caravan as worthy pickings. In one act of cruelty, both Cecilia's family and dreams were taken from her.

Cecilia drew in a sharp breath as her corset was tightened around her waist.

"Apologies, my lady," spoke Cassidy, Cecilia's longest and most faithful of maidens. In truth, she performed better as friend than servant, but Cecilia would never let her know it. The girl took great pride in her work and visibly cringed at her mistake, her skin reddening almost to the point of matching her hair. "*Your Grace*, is what I meant!"

Cecilia slowly let the breath back out. "It is quite alright, Cassidy. Nobody is listening."

Cassidy took that in stride, more than willing to take Cecilia's words over whatever lessons had been drilled into her in youth. "Thank you, Your Grace. It is only so difficult to get accustomed to." She allowed the corset to loosen ever so slightly, before stepping toward the selection of gowns, a suitable collection of practically every colour rendered in shimmering fabric. "But I shall grow accustomed to it. I am certain you will rule long enough that such a title will become inseparable from you. At least in my mind."

Cecilia thought she should take that with pride, but found herself frowning at a nearby mirror. Her rippling hair had always been incredibly light, a fiery gold that appeared distinctly royal, but it had never been white—or grey. The mirror was too far away for her to get a proper look, yet even from where she stood, Cecilia thought she could see a streak of ash grey amid the gold. She turned her gaze elsewhere, landing upon the dresses Cassidy had prepared for the night, finding herself caught by a shimmering turquoise gown, its colour reminding her of her old friend. "Has your brother returned your letters?"

"I am afraid not." Cassidy's expression turned grim. "I have done what I can to locate him, but I have uncovered nothing."

"I see." While Cecilia had been unable to pursue her own dreams, Léonora had known no such restriction.

She had followed their pursuits from a distance ever since, sending hired swords to shadow their travels and report back to her. If Cecilia could not live the unrestricted life for herself, she could enjoy it vicariously through her oldest of friends. Cassidy's own brother had been one such sword, making use of his illusory magic to join Léonora's crew just as they had begun to make a name for themself among the pirates of Avandoras' sea. But communication with him had gone quiet over the last year.

"Keep trying, Cassidy. I'm positive he is only having difficulty in returning them."

"Certainly, Your Grace." Cassidy forced a smile and wiped her hands along her dress. "Which colour would you prefer for to-night?"

Cecilia pulled her eyes from the turquoise and gave equal attention to each. She stepped forward and reached for the gown of red and gold. Those had been the colours of House Hyde. If they could not attend themselves, she wondered if it would serve to honour them and their years of loyalty by bearing their colours. Or perhaps the other houses would see it as a desperate bid to garner quick favour with whoever was to take Caster's place as lord. It irked Cecilia to no end that she had to consider such things. Gone were the days she could choose her wardrobe for nobody but herself; every facet of the fabric with which she covered her body would be taken and dissected, diluted by countless accounts among the populace until they reached consensus.

They can certainly try.

"The black will suffice."

—

The feast was—by every possible metric—spectacular. There was a culinary delicacy present from every point of Duralaans, a showcase of what the land had to offer itself when brought together in such a way.

It was the hope of all monarchs to make their people see the benefits of remaining as one. Many had come close, but none had maintained a truly united front since the days of Artorius I, the aptly named Ashen King. His actions still haunted the land, but it had been under his banner that the original eight houses had forged an alliance, and then it was against Artorius they had warred once his betrayal was unmasked.

"I dare say your father would have openly wept at the sight of you tonight," said Lord Trethellyn, setting aside his platter of meat for the moment. "From joy, of course."

"Thank you, Lord Trethellyn. But my father only wept twice in the time I knew him, and neither were in joy," Cecilia replied, inserting as much pleasantry into her tone as she could.

Lady Helen Wintre placed her hand over Cecilia's, an informal gesture that would have been offensive if the woman had not known the new queen since infancy. "That is quite untrue, dear. I know for a fact that Raine wept from joy upon laying eyes on each of his children for the first time."

"Do not be so sure it was joy that brought such things upon him," Lord Rosse spat, gulping down a goblet of wine to chase.

"Raine loved his children, that was plain to see," Wintre retorted.

"Even so, he must have known what they meant for him."

"That being?"

Rosse smiled, enjoying his time in focus. "The beginning of his end."

"My father was a complicated man, on that we can agree," Cecilia interjected, wishing that particular line of conversation to be brought to an end. "And he was a good king."

The lords and ladies each raised their cups in salutation.

"The greatest!" young Anthony Mars added to the toast, the son of Lord Zephyr, who responded to his son's outburst with a chiding glance.

The party returned to their meal, Cecilia silently thankful for the moment of reprieve. She was determined to enjoy it for the short time it would last. These meals would be a rare occurrence going forward. While the twelve provincial families of Duralaans tolerated each other enough not to war, they hardly enjoyed spending extended periods under the same roof. There was more than enough bitter history between them all to bring ruin to the land as a whole if allowed to surface during such gatherings, though they were all united by the fact that they had at some point each bred into the royal family. Cecilia shared blood with everyone in that hall. They were the only family that remained to her.

Cecilia recalled happier days, sharing supper with her father, mother, and siblings. Happy to drop the royal charade for only an hour or so. There was little she would not give to have those times returned to her, but she understood they were more distant to her than even her dreams.

As tears dared to wet her eyes, the dining hall's entrance creeped open. Cecilia was glad for the distraction as she saw Amor approach her spot at the long table.

"Your Grace, Lord Hyde requests your attention," he spoke quietly.

From the dead? was Cecilia's first thought, only slightly less logical than the alternative. "An heir has been selected so soon?"

"So it would seem." Amor seemed no more enthused at the prospect than she.

"Problem, Your Grace?" That was Lord Phemus Anderthread, his aged face inquisitive.

"Not at all, though my immediate attention is required." Cecilia rose from her seat, smoothing out the fabric of her marble-black dress. Not even the candlelight disturbed its shadow, granting her the image of one who stood beyond the nature of light itself. "Please, do not wait on me, this shall not take more than a moment."

—

The Queen and her aide marched in tandem through the dark halls of Avalass' royal palace. They began to slow as they neared the drawing room where the new Lord of House Hyde awaited.

"Who is he?" Cecilia asked.

"The son of Lord Hyde's cousin," Amor answered.

"I was not aware Caster had a cousin, why have we not been acquainted?"

"He has been abroad, Your Grace."

That would only complicate matters. "How abroad?"

"The cousin was wed to Deserum's Princess."

Cecilia came to a stop. "He's of the God's Land?"

"He is. The father remained in Deserum with his wife, but Aester Hyde arrived in Duralaans a week ago."

Cecilia glanced toward the door at the hall's end, dreading who it would be she would face inside. "Dare I put my fear to words?"

"How odd it is that the heir returns mere days before the current lord meets an undue end."

Cecilia spoke quietly and slowly. "Do not let such suspicions spread, but ensure a closer examination is given to Caster's death."

"I will see to it myself." Amor ventured his own sneaking glance toward the drawing room, before returning to his queen's gaze. "The believed perpetrator is no longer of this world, however there was another unknown force at play."

"Continue."

"A mercenary who warned the late lord of a blood contract on his head. He was present at Hyde's final dinner, before disappearing moments prior to the explosion that ended his life."

"Do we know this mercenary's name?"

"Unfortunately not, only visual descriptions from the surviving members of that fateful party."

"Have him found post-haste and brought to the capital." Cecilia returned to her approach of the drawing room, Amor joining her in step. "It is imperative that my reign is not remembered as having begun with the destruction of a beloved house."

"You needn't be concerned by such notions. In truth, the attack took place before your coronation."

"True as that may be, memory is so often corrupted by falsehoods. We must ensure it is the truth that remains prevalent, or at least the closest to the thing we can muster." Cecilia reached the large wooden door, carved with the depiction of a historic moment from her people's past—a lone vessel leaving Duralaans to reap the rewards of the Divine Promise. They had expected to find an infinite expanse waiting to be conquered, instead they landed upon a place just as harsh as the home they had left, finding the promise of the Gods to be false. If they wanted to have their rewards, they would have to do what they had always done. Take it.

Queen Cecilia pushed open the heavy doors and stood in the doorway for a moment, allowing the weight of her presence to have the emphasis it deserved.

A man lay on one of the room's long couches, he wore extended robes of red and gold, a type of garb Cecilia knew was typical of Deserum's upper echelon. He made a show of slowly turning his dark eyes toward her, before plastering a look of shock on his face, as though he had only just noticed her arrival.

Aester Hyde swung his legs back to the floor and rose, making even more of a display as he came to his full height, brushing his almond hair back with a hand gloved in white. "Your Majesty, such a pleasure it is to finally make your acquaintance."

"Likewise, Lord Hyde." Cecilia stepped beyond the doorway, gesturing for Amor to allow them privacy. He bowed a final time, then closed the door behind her. "Please, enjoy the furniture."

Aester smiled, clearly an expression well practiced, invoking equal levels of respect and charisma. "Only if you are to join me, Your Grace."

Cecilia returned the smile and rounded the lounge to sit opposite him. "I must say your presence is a surprise. With Caster's death still so recent, I suspected it would be a while before a new lord were named."

"Yes, well thankfully I had already planned to ingratiate myself with my family's roots here in Duralaans." He leaned as far back as he could, resting his arms along the head of the lounge. "Often fate is cruel, but sometimes we are blessed with such good fortune."

"Indeed." Cecilia found it difficult to read this man. He was young for a lord, although she was likewise young for a queen. Nothing on the surface pointed toward him being of poor character, yet she felt a stirring unease within. "Perhaps you could expand on what it is you seek here?"

"Naturally, Your Grace. There were few options for me in Deserum, Father served singularly as consort and I the heir, only to inherit the throne in the most tragic of circumstances. So I took my leave. I'd always known of our Duralaansi heritage and believed that I might make more use of myself here. It seems I was correct." Aester's eyes went distant as he recounted, as though he were reading from his own script. "The weight of lordship was far from what I had expected to greet me upon my arrival, but I cannot help feeling as though it were destined to be."

"What might have your intentions been otherwise?" Cecilia prodded. "If such unfortunate circumstances had not fell upon the former Lord Hyde."

Aester seemed to take an odd moment to consider his answer. "This land had me enamoured from afar. Its history, its politics, its power; all ripe with potential. Yet I'm afraid it has been too long since anything of note has happened. Life has grown stagnant. The kingdom is but a shadow of what once was."

"Mind, you are speaking to the Queen of that very kingdom."

"I would say such things to no other. Indeed, you are the only one who could hear me and do anything about it." He sat forward, his expression taking on something of deathly seriousness. "Damnation comes whether you like it or not, and I fear your home will not be strong enough to survive. If I have seen all of this from across the sea, surely you have noticed it yourself."

"You need not concern yourself in such a way, you have enough to consider as is."

"I must disagree, Your Grace. If I am to become a part of this kingdom, I wish only to see that it is as strong as it can be."

"Then you can rest assured that I am already doing everything to return this land to its former glory." Cecilia rose, deftly adjusting the chain around her neck. "Will you be joining your fellows? There is still plenty to eat, I assure you."

Lord Hyde rose to meet her. "No thank you, Your Grace. I wish to announce myself at a later time. Though you can be sure my aid will be yours to command in the meanwhile. I shall remain here in Avalass until the family home is rebuilt." He stepped forward and took her hand in his, planting his lips on the silver ring circling her finger. "I look forward to witnessing your reign."

Cecilia noted a glimmer in his eye, something of anticipation. *A careful step will be required in the company of this one.*

Aester made his leave, crossing toward the door and opening it. Cecilia watched as he stepped out of the room, only to turn back a moment later.

"Your Grace, I apologise, but your necklace seems to be missing a piece."

He was gone before she could supply a response.

—

When Cecilia had returned to the dining hall it was alive with discord, so loud she had considered retiring early rather than rejoin the fray. But she had pushed open those doors all the same, such was the life she had chosen when she turned down Léonora's invitation to enjoy the freedom of the seas. She would not shy away from her choice now.

She smiled when it suited, offered brief agreement or consideration when demanded, and did what she could to enjoy the rest of her meal. But she did not pay any real attention to the debates that captured the families, her mind was once again elsewhere. Though this time it was not across the seas that her attention turned, rather the soil beneath her feet, and what lay within. Such ponderings were accompanied by an old poem that came to her unbidden.

Ash and cinder. Fire and blood.

With the night's affairs having reached their conclusion, Cecilia saw her guests to their private quarters. She bid them farewell and thanked them for their presence.

A crown of smoke and plate of white.

Cecilia returned to her own quarters, removing the chain with utmost care and placing it in its proper place within a locked box. She ran her hand along the cold platinum; her touch lingered on the empty socket where the Hyde agate should have sat.

Lord descend from your mount of fire.

Cecilia stripped herself of her gown, confident it had made the intended impression, and took herself to her bathing chambers. A bath had already been made up as per her stipulations. Cecilia let out a slow hiss of air as she let the water scorch her skin.

Cleanse the blood from our fields of toil.

Heat had always done well to soothe Cecilia, yet she found her heart racing in that moment. The first day of her reign had been trying but she was confident it had been handled to the best of her ability—something that would only improve with time. She would make sure of that.

And see us through the ashen night.

Cecilia exited her bath and returned to her chamber, ignorant to the water dripping from her body as she came to stand before the canvas painting that covered the entirety of the wall opposite her bed. It depicted the beginning of the Ashen Night with the eruption of Mount Promethus, its fire making a silhouette of the armoured warrior who heralded that particular age. An army gathered at the volcano's base, the united forces of the whole of Duralaans, bound together by a common enemy.

Cecilia understood that night had returned once more. The problem was that those around her refused to accept it, refused to understand the threat they faced.

Cecilia may have once shied away from her duty, but it was now clear to her why fate had forced this role upon her. Somebody was required to see the people through damnation once more. Heavy as it may be, she would bear that burden herself.

Chapter Seven

To Be Deserved

In no way were the incidents of late any fault of Elias Sorren. He had done all that he could to apprehend Eric Blackhand. He had taken the facts left to him and used them in the most logical and beneficial manner to achieve his goal. Elias could in no way be blamed for having not received the necessary details surrounding the affair. If he had been told Lyre was holding a highly valued prisoner beneath his fortress, Elias would undoubtedly have discovered Blackhand's true intent and put a stop to it before it was too late. As such, the predicament he now found himself embroiled by, could in no way be seen as the result of any fault of his own. But these scenarios tended to demand a scapegoat, and Elias feared they had already identified the perfect caprine.

Elias would not grovel for forgiveness; he would make Lord Lyre see the truth, and if he refused, then Elias would know better than to waste his breath on such an illogical man.

There was a knock at his door, returning Elias' focus to what lay beyond his own mind. "The Lord wishes your presence," came a deep voice.

Elias rose from his desk. He had been confined to these quarters since Blackhand's escape, having not even made it back to the town he'd come from before Lyre's men had retrieved him and demanded his immediate return to the fortress so the lord might decide which fate befit him. Elias did not fear what awaited him. He knew what man Carlyle Lyre was: harsh, conniving, and selfish, but not a fool. He would see Elias still held use, if only he were granted the full scope of the truth.

He opened the door to find three armed guards waiting for him, two of which Elias could best without much issue, but the third would likely get the better of him, in time. Flight was not preferable, of course, but Elias had never regretted keeping his options open under such circumstances.

"Well?" he said, putting a casual hauteur into his speech. Playing for pity would benefit him none.

"This way, sir." The leader of the trio gestured, before marching forward. Elias continued behind him, aware the other two followed a short distance from his back.

They continued in such a manner for a while, Elias becoming accustomed to the sheer magnitude of the place. He had not visited any other noble household in his time, so he supposed the size was unlikely to be abnormal, but it was the overall aesthetic and sensation the place imposed upon him that seemed most strange.

Lyre's home was considered a fortress by most, and they were far from incorrect in the judgement. It was crudely designed, built of thick stone with no more warmth than the little that the few candles interspersed through the halls allowed. It was a tall structure as well, the walls coiled around themselves and towered high toward the sky, and Elias was well aware the thing ventured just as deep into the soil beneath.

The sheer enormity of the place had been a conscious point of design. Built into a valley, the colossi of the Mount Promethus range acted as a natural wall surrounding all but one side. It was a place of great defence, rendering it a clear target for any who wished to possess such ease of safety for themselves. Its walls had fallen and been rebuilt time and again over the centuries, the result of countless bloody sieges, both failed and successful. The last to hold it was the Ashen King himself, before the hero king Artorius III ousted the harbinger of doom and awarded Sir Falk Lyre lordship and the fortress for his own. The Lyre family had since been intent to maintain hold of their well-earned gift, a desperation that had bred their particularly hazardous demeanour.

The escort came to a halt, having reached the two doors which led into the lord's main hall. The man hit his fist to the slab twice, and waited for response.

After an extended moment, the doors were pulled open from the inside, and Elias entered without hesitation, striding over the long silver carpet that led to where he found Lyre seated upon a throne chiselled from dark rock. The head of his seat overhung far enough that the lord's face was bathed in shadow, rendering his demeanour completely inscrutable. Elias stopped a few paces back, close enough to get as good a look at Lyre as he could, but far enough not to impress any threat.

Carlyle Lyre was a human in the middle of his life. His features were sharp and angled, hair a long black that was tied behind his head by a strand of silver thread. His skin was a dark shade of mahogany, though lighter than Elias' own, it only served to draw further attention to the light blue eyes that seemed to pierce the veil of darkness.

"Apologies for the extended wait, Sorren. I'm sure you'll understand I have had much to handle," Lyre said, his voice measured and calm. "But now we can turn our attention back to the issues we've shared of late." He rose from his throne, taking in hand a heavy cane carved from some dark gemstone. "I paid you to complete a task for me, in that regard you have failed." Lyre came to a stop mere inches from Elias, whose eyes found themselves drawn to a jagged key hung from the lord's neck, truly ancient if its appearance did not deceive.

"My payment has already been returned, Lyre." Elias did not shy back, even as the lord's gaze pierced into his. "Though I would debate your suppositions of failure."

"How so, Sorren?" He tapped his cane against the floor, and the two were promptly left in privacy.

"I was hired to take captive a man who was to be found frequenting one of Prometh's many taverns, such was the task I accomplished."

"Be that as it may, you failed to realise the man was indeed not Eric Blackhand."

Elias was glad to find that the lord was not offended by his challenge, seemingly more intrigued by Elias' side of the story than anything. Almost as though he had known this would be the way things went. "Only as a result of your people's failure to properly describe my target. There is little I can do with such lacklustre information."

Lyre seemed to enjoy the jab, drawing back a smile as he circled Elias, as though he were a predator eyeing his prey up and down. "You are so sure of your—" he seemed to debate with himself the correct term, "—abilities. As an analyst I was told you were quite astute, yet I find myself wanting."

"For good reason, Lord. I am quite capable when equipped correctly, but when given incomplete information and little more than children as allies, I cannot act to the best of my capabilities."

Elias heard Lyre stop his predatory study, standing somewhere out of view. "Then perhaps you should prove just what you can do. Tell me, Sorren. Who am I?"

"You are Lord Carlyle Lyre—"

Lyre cut him off, "That I already knew."

Elias raised his eyebrows, waiting to be sure it was right to continue. "And you are planning something." Elias paused, giving himself a few extra seconds to think, before deciding it would do better out loud. "I could not help but notice that the overall décor of this place is restrained and minimalist, it speaks to your character; you're efficient. You would not have kept a prisoner longer than necessary, yet you did keep this one long enough for their presence here to leak. You needed something from them—assumedly some morsel of information—but you did not get it.

Otherwise you would not need me." Elias debated stating the addition that came to mind, decided he could not help himself. "You would not *still* need me."

Lyre rounded on him, coming face to face, he remained amused. "I need you?"

"You'd have tried to kill me otherwise. Loose ends and all that."

"How astute." Lyre wandered back toward his throne, letting his cane fall by the wayside and planting himself in his seat, his hand came to stroke his chin by way of displaying his consideration. "What makes you think I am planning anything? Yes, this prisoner did possess knowledge I desired, but who's to say that is part of anything greater than itself?"

"Nothing more than a hunch, if I'm being truthful," Elias said. "But for your prisoner to have spent so long in your dungeons— as I've assumed—and to not reveal what you wanted, then they must be quite the hardy individual. I can only imagine what sorts of knowledge one such as them might possess."

Lyre leaned forward, resting his arms on his knees and further examining Elias. He hoped to take the lord's continued interest as a good sign.

"The way I see it, Lord Lyre, I did not fail. Nor was I able to complete my original objective. So, if you would allow me, I should like to do so."

"And what makes you believe you will do any better than you have so far?"

"If I am allowed to properly prepare this time, to know exactly what he does and what he wants, then I see no reason I cannot best him."

Lyre let silence overcome them, allowing the weight of his eventual decision to build as he continued to stare into Elias' eyes.

Sorren had no interest in the wider schemes at play. Blackhand had made a fool of him and Elias needed to redeem himself. Both so that he may claim his payment and so he could prove to himself that he had not yet lost his touch. With age Elias was aware his skills would wane, but he had hoped he still possessed another decade or so before his mind failed and the years of injury finally paid him back for refusing to lend them the proper time to mend. He considered for a moment that this whole affair had been an elaborate message from the Gods to tell him to finally pack it up, but that wasn't a real option. If Lyre did not kill him—which Elias was certain he would not—then the lord would not allow him to simply decline his second chance. Elias was in it now, all he could do was see it through before somebody else did for him.

"I would prefer to keep this whole debacle between as few people as possible. So I will maintain our contract," Lord Lyre said at last, leaning back into the shadow of his throne.

"I knew you would see reason."

"But I will only allow you two weeks. If after even that you cannot complete this task, I must seek more reliable means."

"It will not come to that, I assure you."

Lyre leaned forward again and collected his cane, tapped it thrice on the floor, then waited. Elias was not sure Lyre had stopped smiling the entire time they had spoken, as though he knew something Elias did not.

The doors opened behind him, and Elias heard small footsteps quickly approach, before stopping at his side.

"Elias Sorren, may you meet Oedon, my ward and prophet."

"Prophet?" Elias glanced at the child beside him, a young boy who could have known much more than his first decade of life. He had an almost regal look about him, hair long and blonde, the shimmering strands allowed to cover much of his face. His clothes were little more than rags, tattered black strips serving as a quasi-capelet. They left Elias with the impression of raven feathers shrouding his upper body, hiding away something inhumane which lurked beneath.

"The boy was cursed. Mama cut his eyes out, made him blind to the day-to-day, but able to see *everything* else." Lyre looked almost prideful in the way he measured up the boy. "I believe his abilities will pair well with your own. One who can expertly read the present, another who can see the complete picture of the future."

Elias could barely make out the boy's eyes through his hair. Indeed, they were missing, replaced by crystalline orbs fitted into the sockets. From there his cheeks were stained with what looked like black ink, shaped not unlike tears. "He's a child."

"Trust, if that were a concern to me, then I would not have introduced you."

Elias wanted to argue his point further but knew well enough that Lyre would not take to it. He wondered if this was his means of keeping an eye on Elias, to make sure he got the job done this time and didn't take any opportunities to get away. "Very well. If that's what it takes, I'll accept it. Can't be much worse than the swordsmen you left me last time."

"Oh no, Oedon is far more than them." Lyre stood again and passed his gaze over them both. "Do your job, Sorren. Bring them both home. For my sake, and your own."

Oedon offered his patron a bow that befit his royal appearance, then began his way toward the door. He stopped, glancing back toward Elias as if waiting for him to follow. Elias gave Lord Lyre a sharp nod, then followed the boy out of the hall.

Oedon was quick of step for a child, and Elias almost struggled to keep up with him as he paced through the winding corridors of the fortress.

"You will require your tools," the boy said, clipped with a slight accent; it was not a question.

"Just the travel pack in my quarters."

"We are to pass it on the way, but we should act with haste."

"Right." Elias wondered just how this blind boy was so adept at navigating the halls. Possibly, it was no more than muscle memory, but Elias would not be so sure until he had properly tested the bounds of Oedon's so-called abilities.

They stopped by Elias' room, and he collected his pack. He preferred to travel light as a general rule, a man who needed excess to survive would do better to remain in the dense cities than risk the wilds. Out there he had to be able to survive with nothing but the skin on his back and the strength in his arms, though it never hurt to have a few supplies on hand to ease the difficulty, and Elias would not have gotten as far as he had without his blade.

Elias shifted his gaze toward the door, checking that it remained closed, then he slipped an item from the pack and clipped it to his belt. The thing appeared to be a compass, nothing worth more than a moment's glance. But if somebody were to examine it for any longer, they might notice it did not possess an arrow to point northward.

The pack slung over his arm, Elias found Oedon waiting for him, the boy taking off the moment the door was closed again.

They walked wordlessly for a few minutes, before coming to the fortress' stable. A cart had already been prepared for them, two large mares harnessed and ready for the journey.

"You lot really are efficient," Elias found himself murmuring.

"Time is of the essence. If we are to secure Blackhand and his devola friend, we must act now," Oedon explained, taking a moment to hoist himself up into the cart.

"Is that what you see?" Elias doublechecked that the cart and horses were properly secured, then climbed into the driver's seat. "With your . . . whatever you call it?"

The boy took his time to consider it, leaving Elias with the idea that Oedon even relied on his power to so much as choose his words. "Yes."

"Very well, what's the destination?"

"Do you know Harbinger's Rest?"

"Quite the ride, but I'm familiar."

He received no further conversation from Oedon and took it to mean he had said all he believed necessary. It was no bother to Elias; a quiet companion would be far more tolerable than a loud one. That only meant it would take longer for him to get a proper read on the boy.

Elias did not enjoy relying on another to define his course, it left the individual with too much power over him. Perhaps he deserved it for allowing Blackhand to slip through his fingers or perhaps he needed to be more ruthless when picking his clientele. But more and more figures of power had become like Lyre in recent years, they presumed to know better than he and thought to tell Elias how to do his job. Trust had become a thing of the past as more feared that which they did not have complete control over.

Am I any different? Elias wondered. Making snap judgements of character was a part of his job, and while he credited it as the reason he had survived so long, he also saw that it was a sign he too refused to trust those around him. But it had kept him alive, and would no doubt continue to do so. Now was not the time for regret or change. Now was the time to do what he did best.

"We'll make a stop by Prometh on the way," Elias said.

"Why? That is not where they will be," Oedon replied, a hint of agitation in his tone.

"Lyre's prisoner would have been far from well after her time down below. Blackhand couldn't have taken her far."

Elias smiled when he received no further response. *Good.* Oedon could rely on the future as much as he liked, but there was no comparing to the here and now.

He urged the mares forward and out of the stables, with some good luck they would arrive in town by midday, and Blackhand would be where he belonged by supper.

"Trust me, kid. I know what I'm doing."

<u>Chapter Eight</u>
Just Us

Eric thought that as long as his hand remained on Raph's that he could not lose her. As though he could keep her tethered to the mortal plane, even as the Gods hoped to claim her.

He and Damian's flight from the fortress had not been nearly as precise as their infiltration. Damian had put on the other guard's armour and helped Eric escort Raph to the stable. They knew that their hurried escape had drawn eyes, but Raph was too weak for them to wait any longer.

There had been a short pursuit, but Damian had managed to lead them away while Eric raced back to Prometh. It was not the safest place to lie low, but it was all he had for the moment.

"We can't stay here," whispered Raph, her voice threatening to break with every word. She had spoken only a few times after rousing from her state of unconsciousness, and had maintained her insistence that they move as soon as possible.

"I know. But you're still weak."

"I'm not weak." She tried to invoke strength in her statement, and Eric's heart broke to hear her fail.

"In this state? Yes, you are."

She attempted to sit up, and Eric rushed to brace her with his hand—a hand that was deftly brushed away. Raph came to a hunched position on the bed, breathing heavily from the exertion.

It was a small room, one of the lower levels of the town's foremost tavern, reserved for those with a need to sleep but no money to afford it and those who meant to hide. Eric felt like he fit well into both categories.

"Listen to me, Raph. I didn't save you just to watch you kill yourself like this," Eric said, putting as much plea into his tone as he could.

"I didn't ask for you to save me."

Eric couldn't help but laugh. "You'd rather that I didn't?"

"No!" Raph exclaimed, meeting his gaze with a steely glare. "But you've put yourself in more danger than you understand."

"What do you think I've been doing all these years?"

"I don't know. You left because you said you wanted a quieter life; said you were sick of the violence." Raph took her turn to laugh. "Now here you are, back in the life you said you hated. But you're different."

"Sera . . ." Eric tried to choose the right words, so much had happened since their last meeting. There were a hundred things he wanted to say, but none felt right. "A lot has happened."

"I can see that. And I'm not judging you for it. But if you're back on this path, for whatever reason, you need to do what has to be done."

He began to pace the room, trying to consider their options. "Where can we go? I don't have many friends here. I suppose we just get as far from Lyre's territory as possible?"

"That too, but I had something specific in mind."

"Okay." Eric stopped, it hurt him to see Raph's condition, the marks had begun to heal with time and the limited medicine he had available, but the remnants were a harsh reminder of the cruelty she had suffered, and Eric did not even know why. Raph seemed to notice his pity and wrapped a blanket around her shoulders. "Where?"

She took a moment to steady her breathing before speaking again. "My memory is patchy, but I remember now why I came to Duralaans. Do you know the Tale of the Ten Kings?"

"Vaguely. I think my father told it to me once." Eric knew the epic was somewhat entrenched in the history of his homeland but had never dug too deep into where the line between fact and fiction was drawn. "Guess I shouldn't be surprised you'd go from fighting a god of death to chasing legends."

She shrugged. "An early retirement doesn't appeal to everyone."

"Clearly." Though it was not by choice that Eric had abandoned his respite.

"But the legend, it centred around the first king of Duralaans After Celestial Abandonment, Artorius I."

"The Ashen King?"

"Anni feared he would return and sent me to stop it."

Eric had always been somewhat aware of Raph's goddess friend but had never been sure just how she worked. She seemed to be among the new gods that had begun to appear since the Reckoning, but exactly how far her power reached remained a mystery to him. Above all, it was comforting to know Raph had not been alone in the years since Vécar. It had been difficult to leave his allies after that fight, but with the threat eliminated he had felt that he needed time to rest. Really, he still did.

"I can't remember everything I discovered. I think I destroyed one of the maps to his tomb, but I don't know if there are more," Raph continued to explain, pausing between words as she played catchup with her own memories.

"Could that have been what Lyre wanted from you? Would *he* want to bring back Artorius?"

"It's my best guess so far. Part of me doesn't exactly want to remember what they tried to get from me in that dungeon."

"Then you don't have to. We can just retrace your steps, relearn what you knew."

Raph raised her hand to silence him. "No. I remember one thing: the map was only the simplest means of understanding where Artorius was sealed, but there was another way. She turned her body to face him, letting her legs hang off the side of the bed. "A cipher was made, one that hid the way to Artorius' tomb. But its secrets could only be revealed by at least five of the eight keys held by the era's noble houses." Raph winced and her mouth drew back in pain; this time she did not push Eric away when he came to her side. He did not try to touch her again, only wanting Raph to know he was there for her if needed. "I think I tried to steal Lyre's key, and that's how he caught me."

"So, if we could get hold of a majority of the keys—or even just half of them—then we shut down all hope of finding Artorius and bringing him back?"

"I think that was the idea, yes."

"What if we just destroyed the cipher, do you know where that is?"

"It was built into an ornamented cylinder and eventually placed inside the palace archives deep below Avalass." She offered him a pointed glance, but also a smile that Eric had not the strength to return. "Don't worry, that was my first plan too."

Eric was far from glad to consider rushing into such a deadly quest with his friend still so wounded, but not all houses were as cruel as Lyre was known to be. There was a way that they could get through this without risking further harm—to anybody. "So, who's first?"

"The home of House Wintre in Harbinger's Rest."

"Alright. That's not too far. What about Damian?" Eric felt poor for not thinking of his fate sooner.

Raph's eyes narrowed for a moment, clearly trying to decide whether that was a name she ought to know. "Who?"

"He helped me get you out, led off our pursuers."

Her eyes dropped, betraying the same emotions Eric felt. "I'm sorry, Nath. If he's not returned by now—"

"I know." Damian had been stronger than Eric had expected for his age, braver too. Eric could only hope he had come to the decision that joining them in Prometh would be unwise and had found elsewhere to wait for the trouble to die down. "Are you sure you don't want to wait any longer?"

Raph answered him by coming to her feet. Eric tried to brace her, but she shut him down with a cold glare. "Don't."

"I'm only here if you need me."

"I won't," she said, but the expression that crossed her face made it clear that she regretted her wording. "I mean that I won't heal properly unless I do it myself."

"That's not true. If you hadn't helped me for so long I'd never have made it this far. Do you think that makes me weak?"

"Don't be stupid, of course not."

"Then why are you different?"

Her stance grew steadier, and she risked a step forward, followed by another after the first's success. "Because I am. We come from very different lives, Nath. That just means we find our strength in different places. If you can't accept that, maybe we should go our separate ways again before it's too late." She continued to find her balance, eventually coming to a level of stability she could accept.

Eric traced his fingers over the metal of his prosthetic, keeping his mind distracted so he would not offer her any more aid than she wanted. "This place is my home, Sera. You tell me it's under threat? Then you'll have me until this is done. I will not turn away now."

Raph smiled again and offered Eric a hand. He did not take it, instead standing on his own and taking his firearm from where it sat on the bedside table. He holstered it, then pulled his leather poncho over his shoulders.

"I got you some new clothes. Might not be perfect, but they'll be nicer than what you have now."

She stepped toward where the folded garb lay, gaining more confidence with each footfall. "Thank you, Nath." A look crossed her face as though there were more she wished to say, then it was gone.

"I'll meet you outside." Eric stepped out, taking a moment to reflect after closing the door behind him. Raph had always been stubborn, but never so stoic as she had become since they'd last been together. He felt a new pang of regret for his choices in the past, if they had continued to travel together this may never have been, and their currently tumultuous standing might have been less ruinous.

Eric made his way to the lobby, offered the attendant his last few coins for payment, then stepped out into the street. It seemed to be about midday, the streets were quiet, most of the town's inhabitants likely performing their duties.

Mount Promethus towered in the distance. It had long been dormant, but the threat of its returned fury loomed even in Eric's mind. He could not fathom the fear it must invoke in the townspeople. Or perhaps it was familiar enough that it instilled no dread at all. The town must have had plans established in the case of another eruption, it stood to reason that the mountain's presence was simply a part of life. Not something to fear, simply nature.

Eric wondered if he could ever live that way. Accept that which he could not control and dwell plainly on what he could. But if that were the case, he would not be himself, he would be another who merely looked like him. It was true that he had changed a lot in only the last few years, but Eric had to believe that he was still the same person deep down, despite it all. And yet there he was, not even calling himself by his own name. Instead using a pseudonym derived from his father's and the description of the prosthetic that replaced his missing appendage.

It all seemed so ridiculous in hindsight. Eric had chosen a black hand because it reminded him of the state he had last seen his true one in. Charred and black. A constant memento of what he had lost. He could not help but outwardly bear the marking left upon him by his life, as though it meant anything to those who saw.

A shape in the corner of his eye tore Eric from his musings. A cart made its way into town, driven by a man Eric recognised in an instant.

He threw himself back into the inn, ignoring the attendant's confused outcry, and racing back toward their room.

Raph cried out in shock as Eric rounded a corner and ran right into her. "I thought you'd be outside."

"We need another way out. Sorren is here," Eric said, trying to recall where there might have been a second entrance.

Once again Raph appeared to try and dredge up any familiarity with the name, quickly deciding it was a waste of time. "Who?"

"The man I tricked so I could get to you."

She whirled on the spot, sending the long dress she now wore rippling around her. "Damn it all. Could we fight him?"

"I'd rather not."

"Nath, we killed the *Lord of Death* seven years ago. We can handle one man." She pushed past him, summoning flickers of energy that laced her fingers with vibrant light.

Eric grabbed her arm. "Seven years ago you weren't recovering from your deathbed, I had a talisman that made me the strongest version of myself possible, and we had two more allies backing us up." He released her arm, but she made no further move. "We aren't the people we were seven years ago. Not right now."

"I can handle it," she insisted, but Eric could tell her heart was not behind the words.

Murmuring echoed from down the hall, the hoarse tone of Elias Sorren. "They'll have come through recently. That's a human and a devola. They might have been injured. Might have valued their privacy."

"I'll follow your lead, Sera," Eric said softly. She turned to meet him, unadulterated anger flaring within tear-lined eyes. "I can't imagine what they did to you, and I know you could kill him if you had to. But I'd rather play this safe, with all you've told me, there is a lot more at stake than us."

"I need to do something, Nath. I need to make this right."

"You will. We survive the day, stop Artorius from ever returning, and then I promise you will have your justice."

She held his gaze for a long time, before reaching out, and placing a shaking hand on his shoulder. Raph's head dipped as she allowed a few shuddered breaths to escape her. "You remind me of someone I used to know."

"She was smarter than she had any right to be." Eric wiped the tears from her cheeks.

"She had to be." Raph's eyes found his, some of the anger having quelled. "Let's run."

And they did. Sprinting through the narrow halls, Raph quickly overtook Eric. An almost second sense seemed to overtake her as she navigated toward the backdoor. It was locked—a problem easily amended, and so they continued their flight around the building and toward where their horse had been hitched.

"I got to get my own," Raph said, pulling herself up into the saddle.

"If we weren't in such a rush, I'd love to take us shopping." Eric joined her as she grasped the reigns, bracing himself for what he expected to be a hasty exit.

But the horse did not move.

"What're we waiting for?" He peered around Raph's shoulder to find a strange figure standing in front of the beast: a child draped in black rags, with long golden hair.

"I told him he would not succeed if he came here," the boy spoke, placing a pale hand on the horse's snout. He smiled.

"Move, kid!" Raph spat. She was trying to manoeuvre the beast around him, but it was entirely unresponsive.

Eric felt a chill as he spotted the boy's eyes. Both sockets had been stuffed with shimmering crystal replacements. "You're with Sorren."

"Allegedly," the boy whispered. "Don't spend too long in Harbinger's Rest." He stepped aside and their horse immediately raced forward, leaving him in the dust as they flew through the streets and toward the main gate.

"You know him?" Raph asked, forcing as much speed out of the horse as it could muster.

Eric hazarded a glance behind them, they had gone far enough that the boy was out of sight, yet he couldn't shake the feeling that there remained eyes on them. "No."

"How'd he know where we're going?" Raph asked as they passed by the gate, leaving behind a pair of befuddled guards.

"A good guess?"

Raph took a moment to check for pursuit herself. "I don't like it."

"Change course, then? Start with a different house?"

"No. We see this through and get out of Harbinger's before Sorren can catch up." She allowed the horse to slow its speed enough to not exhaust her too soon. "Still with me?"

"Still with you." Despite the threat they now faced, Eric could not deny that he was glad to see Raph back in good spirits. Whether or not it would last for long, he was glad to see a glimmer of his old friend again—perhaps they were not lost after all.

Chapter Nine
Tethered

Domina had never been to prison, never been bound in steel within a dark room, with a single tiny source of light well above his head. Odd, given the Black Rose had been a group of thieves originally, but Domina supposed he was lucky enough that he had only joined them after that life were well behind them. Apparently that luck had run out, and he hadn't even committed a crime to warrant it this time—*karma, then.*

He sat in the corner of the cell that served as his accommodation, bound to the wall by a chain latched to a metal link around his remaining hand. Domina had no measure of just how many hours had passed since he'd been placed inside. The light outside his tiny window seemed to eternally offer nothing but a faint flicker of orange light. Presumably, it was candlelight from a higher floor—of course the only opening he had to the outside world would actually lead to nothing but more prison.

After his encounter with the city's guardsmen, Domina had come to within the dark box of stone, no clue as to what had transpired between his moments of lucidity. All he had left was his patience.

Domina had made the informed guess shortly after waking that his imprisonment was a result of being present the night of Hyde's death, and his attempt to leave the city so soon after had been cause for suspicion. He could not blame them for being so quick to reach such conclusions, but Domina would prefer them stop wasting time and start questioning him so he might clear up the confusion.

He would not soon forget his current purpose, and the longer he waited, the less likely he was to ever find anyone who would know the truth behind the deaths of late. But all Domina could do was wait and see what fate had in mind.

Domina must have lost himself to sleep, as the sound of stone grinding against itself startled him awake. What he had believed to simply be a window, was actually connected to the cell's entrance, being pulled back so that a small set of wooden steps could be lowered in. Domina rose to his feet and attempted to step forward, before being reminded by the immutable tension of chain that he was not allowed to go anywhere.

"Don't trouble yourself. I'll come to you," a cold voice spoke from outside.

Domina could see shadows wavering above, what appeared to be two figures making conversation he could not discern. One of them lowered in respect before disappearing, leaving the other to join Domina below.

The figure who entered was not tall, yet bore an impressive presence all the same, with a lean figure hidden behind a blue cloak. Domina had learned to read a person's strength based on the way they moved, and he was sure this person was not one to underestimate.

She stopped on the lowest of the steps, content with her position above Domina. "I am called Chora, what do they call you?"

"Domina," he responded. "Can we make this quick? I have no idea how much time I've already wasted being here."

"Very well." She took a seat on the steps, making herself comfortable as she placed one leg higher than the other in a way that did not seem especially dignified. Domina could make out some of her clothing beneath the cloak, layered fabrics that could offer decent enough protection despite their appearance. "What involvement did you have with House Hyde?"

"I was hired to protect their lord. Somebody wanted him dead, and thought I could save him," Domina explained, trying to get closer, but quickly realising the folly again.

"I have been made aware that you found the assassin too late?"

"Yes, a demolitionist."

"Traces of cinder powder were found within the ruins of the manor, as well as some remnants on the assassin's person."

Domina was surprised but also glad to find this Chora to be so quick to follow.

"I am sorry that you have been entangled by this affair, it is clear to me that the truth is as you've described it."

"So I'm free to go on my way?" Domina wanted to step forward again, thought better of it this time.

Now Chora did not respond. Domina could see hints of her face, but it was smooth and reflective, more likely to be a mask than her true visage. Whoever this person was, privacy was valuable to her, masked by more than the porcelain that covered her face.

"Why not?" Domina demanded.

"The Queen wishes you be escorted from here and given proper judgement in Avalass."

"The capital? No, I have work to do here."

"Your work is voided by the Queen's will."

Domina scoffed. "You might as well just let me rot here."

"If the choice were mine, I would consider doing just that. But I have my orders, and you should be thankful your queen has taken notice of your plight."

Domina had nothing left to say, only glancing down at his bound hand for a moment, before looking back to find Chora gone. For a second he thought his mind had made the entire conversation up, something to entertain itself after the hours of monotonous silence, but then an armed figure entered the cell with a large ring of keys in hand. He kept a distance from Domina as he made his way around toward where the chain was fastened to the wall. With a twist the lock came undone, and the chain dropped into his hand.

Like a dog on a leash, Domina was led by the guard up and out of his cell, finding Chora waiting for them in the hall. The corridor was just as miserable as the cell itself, a long hall of flat grey stone, broken occasionally by torches and the rectangle slits that played at being windows. A guard was stationed every few cells, and Domina could feel their eyes on him as he was handed over to his escort.

Chora took the chain in hand, gave him a single look up and down, then took off in the opposite direction down the hall. Domina stumbled at first to match her pace, finding it difficult to get reacquainted with movement after however long he'd spent restrained.

"Will I at least get my things back?" he asked.

"Your belongings have already been placed in my carriage," she responded, refusing to tear her sight from what was ahead.

"Should I expect company?"

"Duty demanded I travel alone."

"And what duty is that?"

"I am of the Artorian Guard, we are Her Grace's hands throughout her kingdom, able to do what duty forbids her." Domina would have expected to hear pride in the voice of such a statement, he was surprised to find only doubt. Not as though she were attempting to deceive him, though the thought did cross Domina's mind, it seemed more as though she did not quite believe herself.

Domina put the issue at hand back into the centre of his focus. "Like dealing with suspected lord killers that earn her attention?"

Domina was met by no response.

They stepped out of the gaol, finding a pitch-black carriage already waiting for them, two white horses hitched to the front. Chora opened the door for Domina, standing silently for a moment before Domina figured she wanted him to enter. As soon as he'd crossed the threshold, the mysterious woman latched the end of his chain to a railing on the carriage's exterior and closed the door behind him. He heard something lock and decided to sit down.

So it seemed he would be contained for another indeterminate series of hours. Thus, even more of his increasingly limited time would be wasted.

After only a few moments more the cart had begun to move, though Domina had no means of telling where they were or where this Chora would take them. He had her word that they were making for the kingdom's capital of Avalass, but he was undecided as to whether he was willing to trust or accept that possibility. A powerful house had been consumed by flame, and Domina had reason to believe he was the only one left with even the slightest clue as to who had orchestrated that murder. If he took too long, Domina feared that trail would go cold entirely, and then there would be no making back what he had lost.

He wondered exactly what it was that had garnered the Queen's interest. If Chora truly believed that Domina had not been behind Hyde's death, then what need would Duralaans' monarch have for him? It all seemed odd, and Domina couldn't tell if that was simply how the crown did business or if there was something else that he had not yet unearthed at play. The guards seemed to follow the orders of this supposed Artorian, but that only meant that she was somebody to be obeyed, not that she could be trusted absolutely.

"How long will we be riding for?" he called out, hoping to be heard over the noise of the carriage, yet with no response it seemed he was not so lucky.

Remaining was not an option, whoever this person was and no matter who they acted on behalf of, Domina had decided that to stay would be folly. He needed to follow this lead wherever it led, and he had no time for pointless distractions.

He looked over the inside of the carriage. It was small, enough space for two seats with leg room between, and storage beneath both. The windows were dark, practically black, just enough translucency to allow light through, but not enough to have any idea what awaited him on the other side. There was also the considerable issue of his hand being entirely bound to the cart itself. His first idea of simply leaping from the cart and running as far as he could was—decidedly unlike Domina—out the window. Patience would have to become his ally once again. The journey to Avalass would be a long one, the horses could not travel the whole way without rest, and surely neither could their driver. All he could do was wait.

—

Domina had not felt tired, and he did not remember the sensation of sleep coming for him, but he woke up to find the cart suddenly still. He could hear nothing from outside, as though pure silence had fallen upon them.

"We stopping?" he called out, again finding no answer. Domina thought to pound on the roof to catch Chora's attention but was instead caught by the fact that he now found his hand was no longer bound by anything. "Chora?"

Still no response.

This isn't right. Domina was no stranger to the supernatural, and the eerie silence, the cold stillness of the air, it all stunk of the immortal currents that upheld reality.

Domina kicked open the carriage's door and leapt out into what he found to be a wintry forest. Flakes of snow drifted from the black sky, landing on Domina's grey skin and turning to smoke rather than liquid.

The chill of the landscape seemed to infect him, seizing Domina's heart with panic, as though his body realised what had happened before even his own mind.

"Glad you could join me, sweetling," came a whisper that reverberated among the dark trees encircling him.

Domina whirled to find the carriage gone. In its place sat his blade, embedded in the snow.

"How useless you are without your toy," the voice came this time far closer, laced with a teasing edge. Domina could not help but yield to its will.

He spun again, the sword suddenly in his hand, yet it was only the woods that he found.

"That's better." Laughter surrounded him, somehow coming from near and far simultaneously.

"Who are you?" Domina called out, turning on the spot, wary as to which direction this entity would approach from. "What is this?"

"I have gone by many names in my time, but it is my occupation that has remained solely consistent." Domina knew the voice well, yet part of him did not want the identity confirmed.

"And what would that occupation be?" He brought his weapon around him, as though preparing for assault from all directions. Something was different about his sword, there was no glimmer of steel or glass, only a black void where the blade should have been, an appearance the sword had not possessed since—

"I fix broken things. Blind warriors, kings bereft of heirs, and dark elves in need of retribution."

Thus the veil was lifted, and Domina could not shy away from the truth any longer. "Morguein Frieda."

The darkness lifted, and a woman stepped out of it. Hauntingly beautiful she was, with a long pearl-white dress trailing behind, alongside her contrast of black hair.

Frieda spread her arms wide. "Look how you have ruined yourself."

"I'm still breathing, aren't I?" He kept his blade trained on her, though he understood how ridiculous the notion must have seemed to the witch. Domina was well sure that whatever plane he now stood in, it was not one he held much power within.

"Breathing, yes. But you've lost your touch," she said, slowly making her approach. "Your blade no longer sings to me."

"Sacrifices had to be made." That was all Domina wanted to say on the matter, he was unsure exactly how much she already knew and felt it better to keep whatever he could to himself for as long as possible.

She made no attempt to hide her contempt as she studied his face. "I can tell."

"What are you doing here? Did our contract not end when the sword lost its power?"

"Oh, of course not. My child may have been slain so that you could best your accursed foe, but our deal remains intact." She looked as though she were explaining herself to a child, Domina was in fact a few centuries old himself, but there was always the chance this woman-shaped entity was far older. "I promised to mend you, Domina. To hold all of those shattered pieces of your selfhood together."

"And what was it you got in return? I don't think we ever got clear on that."

"Nothing you did not already provide." She stood a hair's breadth from the blade's tip. "And nothing you could not provide once more."

"For what?"

"So that you may be strong again, do not think I have ignored the patterns that have followed you throughout life." She began to circle him, completely unbothered by the threat of the sword. Domina blinked for only a moment and suddenly it was no longer Frieda speaking to him.

A tall elven man strode through the snow—at least, it had been snow. Now the two were within the forest that had been Domina's birthplace, and the chief of his home village glared at him. "You were not fit for the simple life we had built. You dreamt of greater prospects, and where did that get you, child?" asked Zephyrus.

Domina backed away from the elder, he was not quite right, not truly there, with his overall appearance more like a poorly re-membered version of the man than how he truly existed. He found himself stopped as he backed into something immobile. Domina turned warily to find himself staring up and into the penetrating eyes of a towering devil.

Azazel had been incredibly imposing in life, but his hair had never been so blood red, his eyes not that intense fiery gold that now looked down on him. "You failed us, Domina. Led my troops to their demise, allowed Forkh to escape." They were on that very battlefield now, the one where Domina had led Azazel's force into the dark mage's trap. Instead of besting their foe, they were corrupted and given to undeath, becoming Forkh's own legion and disappearing far across the sea, where Domina could do nothing for them.

The battlefield grew quiet, the sounds of war coming to an end, and then the only two who remained despite the devastation were Domina and the Black Rose himself.

"I understand you always did all that you could," Esgar Rosse spoke softly. He at least appeared just how Domina recalled him—tall, thickly muscled, and wizened by his many years. He sat on a rock, appearing entirely relaxed despite the circumstance. "But for some, that is simply not enough."

Flares of light appeared in the sky; their time was running out. Domina stepped toward his old mentor, suddenly overcome with the need to fix things, even though he knew this particular failure was long a fixture of the past. "I'm sorry, Esgar. I can do better, more, I know I can."

"You've had time to do better, son. What've you got to show for it?" Esgar paid no mind to the raining rocks of fire that grew nearer.

"Nothing. But I can do this. I can make things right for Caster, for his family."

"A family of the dead?"

"Something has to be done for it."

"And who are you to be the one to do it?" He rose from the boulder, and the world almost seemed to shake with each of his steps forward. "You, without your greatest asset?"

"Is that all I am?" Domina took a discarded sword from the ground, taking in his own reflection on the bloody blade. "The dark elf who wields Anamrath?"

Esgar smiled, but Domina knew it was not his. "We shall see."

The rain of fire met the surface and Esgar Rosse died once again. But amid the fire Domina spied a second form, a woman in a billowing dress, now stained black.

When he next opened his eyes, Domina had returned to the carriage just as it seemed to be slowing. Something felt different within him, there was a new pit in his stomach, something hollow that longed to be filled.

The cart stopped, and he could hear Chora drop from her seat and slowly approach the carriage door. Now was the time to act, catch her off guard, break the chain, take one of the horses, and hope she wouldn't be willing to leave the cart behind just to pursue him.

The moment he heard the door unlock, Domina threw himself forward, kicking it open and knocking Chora back a few steps as he leapt to the ground. No sooner had he touched the grass than Chora charged him, tossing off her cloak and brandishing two scimitars. She struck at him with twirling motions. Domina could barely avoided each attack, forced by the chain to shimmy along the side of the carriage. He swung his bound hand toward her blades, hoping they might chip the chain enough that he could yank himself free, but the Artorian swordswoman seemed too capable to fall for such a trick.

"Whatever delusion led you to this, I recommend you stand down," she spat between strikes, not quite leaving any room for Domina to yield if he did decide to.

"I told you; I can't go to Avalass now." He shot out his leg and caught her in the stomach, forcing her to rebalance herself for a moment.

"That is not your decision to make." She threw her sword at him, too quick for Domina to avoid, but luckily it hadn't been aimed for him, instead it embedded in the cart right beside his neck. In the moment it had caught his attention, Chora was on him, blade pressed to his throat. "I thought it would be fair to let you sleep outside of the carriage, I believe I was mistaken."

"This isn't over, Chora. Whoever had Hyde killed is still out there. I can find them, but not if I waste time in the capital."

"I am sorry, Domina, but that is not an option."

"Just give me a short while, I will come to Avalass with what I find."

"These are the Queen's orders; I will not betray them."

"Then you leave me no choice."

The seams of reality parted before them, leaving room only for a sharp void in the shape of a blade. As the hilt formed in his hand, he drew it around him in a circle, severing the chain and knocking Chora's blade wide.

She leapt back, taking a moment to study the change in circumstance.

Domina did the same. Chora had displayed admirable skill and speed, and Domina was slow, even with the strength Anamrath gifted him. He would not succeed in a drawn-out trade of blows, Domina would need to end this quick. One swing might be all he had.

He aimed the sword's tip away from its target, lowered his body, and took a deep breath. *The blade hungers.*

The Artorian warrior charged forward, her own weapon angled not unlike his, but it was she who unleashed her strike first. Domina felt the urge to act immediately, instead forced himself to wait. Just one more second and then—

He swung his own blade diagonally toward the sky, catching her own steel the instant before it would have been ready to deliver unto him a lethal fate. Anamrath knocked Chora's scimitar off by an inch, then sliced clean through her mask.

Both warriors remained in place for a moment, breathing heavily. Domina coughed, he had avoided death, but her sword had delivered a shallow cut across his chest. Chora was similarly wounded; her mask had been bisected diagonally, leaving half of her face visible to him. She appeared young, comely—perhaps that was another tool of hers. At a glance he would never have expected her to be a trained killer. He was not sure how the

Artorian operated, but such anonymity likely made their work easier. She did seem oddly familiar to Domina—or perhaps that was a trick of theirs too. The trickle of blood that began to appear where the void had met flesh was new, however.

Domina had forgotten how light the blade felt in his hand, how easily it cleft apart that which would stand before him, how simple it would be to kill her now—how immensely the blade desired that outcome.

"Do not give my blade your death," Domina urged her.

Chora remained still. She did not appear afraid, more so disturbed by the nature of the power Domina now wielded.

"Which way to the nearest town?" he asked.

Now she shifted, pointing down the road the cart had been set down. "Haval is that way, about three hours by foot."

"Would that be the closest town from where we came?"

She considered it for a moment. "I believe so, yes."

"Then it shall do." Domina allowed his void blade to dissipate, leaving only the pearl hilt that could be easily tucked away. "I want you to take the carriage now and travel back the way we came for about an hour, doesn't have to be exact, just long enough to let me make some headway."

"You are not the one to give me orders."

"I know, and it's not an order. We are on the same side here; I will find whoever placed the mark on Lord Hyde's head and I will see them brought to Avalass."

"I do not believe that you understand just what task you have committed yourself to."

"Maybe not, but I must do this. Just as you have your duties to the Queen, I have duties to the dead."

Chora did not say another word, she simply collected her broken mask, blades, and cloak, then mounted her seat atop the carriage. She offered him a final glance, before bringing the carriage around and driving it back the way they had come.

When Domina was confident she had gone far enough that she would not see him any longer, he stepped off the path, only to be caught by something glimmering in the dirt. He knelt down to find a broken necklace, the chain links severed—likely an unintended result of his strike. Attached to the chain was what appeared to be an odd key, a small but intricately designed piece of metal, with jagged teeth on both sides, and a hollow stem. It was a shame Chora had lost it, though Domina was sure he would have a chance to return it to her when he eventually made his way to Avalass. But that would have to wait.

Instead of following the path to Haval, Domina made his way toward the expansive woodlands only a short distance from the road. Chora knew his heading and would no doubt attempt to re-capture him if they were to encounter one another in the town, so he would wait just a little bit longer and allow her to overtake him.

Domina thought he was getting quite good at practicing patience. Unravelling this web of intrigue remained a priority, but foolishly rushing into it would ultimately counteract his intent.

Thusly Domina found a thick tree he could rest beside as he continued to consider his current tact. It was still little more than hope that was leading him forward, but that would have to do for the time being. Domina was back. With the aid of his lost sword he could return to the man he had once been.

This was good, the start of a new day and a new Domina—or perhaps an old one returned from the grave.

It was shortly afterwards, when he heard Chora's carriage pass by, that he realised he had indeed met the woman before; Chora had attended the dinner at Hyde's manor, offering brief conversation with some of her fellow guests, before hurrying out and disappearing into the night.

Domina could not help but feel as though fate had done him a favour that he had only turned a blind eye toward. Or perhaps it was nothing at all.

Chapter Ten
Curtain Call

I refuse to allow our blood to be tied to theirs," squawked Lord Ennard Harald. "I bid you, Your Grace, see this farce annulled."

"Oh, ignore his ramblings, Your Majesty. Davick will make a fine husband and deliver some much-needed grace upon the Harald name," Lord Anderthread retorted.

Harald cackled. "Grace? Your son is a cad and a womaniser; he will do nothing but taint our name with his bastards and dirtied blood."

"You dare?" Anderthread placed his hand on his sword hilt to accentuate his offense, but Cecilia knew the show to be only bluster. If the crown were allowed to gamble, there was no small sum Cecilia would place on the bet that Phemus Anderthread had not the faintest idea how to wield the weapon without harming himself in the process.

"Calm yourselves. Need you be reminded of the titles you possess?" Amor interjected, stepping between the two. "You would do well to remember your decorum in the presence of your queen."

Anderthread backed down, though Harald did not miss the opportunity to goad his fellow lord with a smirk.

The two turned their eyes toward their queen in question, and once she was sure they were done with their arguing, Cecilia spoke. "The marriage is done. If you wished to do something about it, I am afraid you have missed your opportunity. Instead, the choice shall now go to your children. If either of them were to bid me annul their marriage, I should do so. But until that point, this discussion is over."

"Very well, Queen Cecilia," said Anderthread.

"Yes, very good," Harald agreed, with no lack of begrudge.

The two offered a bow, before exiting the throne hall.

Cecilia waited until they had completely disappeared behind the heavy doors. "What is next, Amor?"

"Aester Hyde has requested your presence at table, I believe he may intend to court you."

Cecilia fought to suppress a laugh. "No, I do not think so. Lord Hyde is simply eager to make himself known, how better than to dine with the monarch?"

"Very well, shall I have something prepared for you to wear?"

"No need, Amor. I can handle that myself."

He began to make his leave but took pause after a few steps. "Another note, Your Grace. Artorian Chora sent word; the man connected to the Hyde assassination had been taken into custody by local law. Unfortunately, he managed to escape her during their journey here."

"I was not aware that Chora remained in Anderan's vicinity."

"It seems her return to the capital was delayed."

Cecilia was discomforted by the fact she had not been kept aware of Chora's halted return, but figured Amor would have informed her if he knew more himself. "Thank you, Amor."

"Shall I send word in return? What is to be done of it?"

"I wish for Chora to return to Avalass, she need not concern herself with any further distractions."

Amor offered his own flourishing display of courtesy, then disappeared down one of the hall's many corridors connecting to the larger palace.

Cecilia allowed herself a moment to relax, letting her back rest upon the rocky throne. There was no seat quite like it, allowing her gaze to pass beyond the grand window opposite her and look upon much of the land that fell within her grasp.

The current throne of Duralaans and its encompassing palace had been built as high upon Mount Avalass as could be reached during the Ashen Night. It had served as a symbol; the new king of Duralaans would sit above the ash clouds of Mount Promethus and guide his people out of that dark age and back toward the light. Symbols held much power, such was the reason for the recreation of the Platinum Chain as the monarchy's chief relic of leadership, but Cecilia frequently wondered if it was too often that they allowed such things to define them. If not tempered, tradition and history could become a crutch.

The Queen gave up her seat and made way for her quarters, passing a few of the house's handservants along the way and offering them polite greetings. Yet it was all an act, her mood in truth had been sour since her coronation dinner had proven her worst fears true—which were only further cemented by the many noble squabbles she had dealt with in the days since.

The noble houses, the very people who she was duty-bound to keep in line, refused to do anything but bicker like children. It mattered little what they demanded, be it annulled marriages, expanded borders, permission to increase taxes, all appeared to the new queen as little more than pathetic bids to maintain or increase their own power. Few showed genuine concern for the people they allegedly stood to protect, and the ones that did seemed too distracted by their petty arguments to consider what might actually be for their betterment.

Was that the truth of Cecilia's duty? The chain bound her to these men and women, forced her to be the platinum link that maintained the bond of Duralaans' jewels. Yet they were resolved to repel each other and would sooner destroy their bonds than accept their necessity.

Cecilia arrived in her quarters, grateful to find that Cassidy was not present. The aid of her handmaiden was never unappreciated, but sometimes Cecilia found it grounding to perform her own menial tasks. A queen need not be so far above her people that she allowed it to become impossible to exist without them—though she supposed such a notion would be comforting to the commonfolk, if the queen relied so heavily upon her people, then she could never do away with them.

Cecilia changed out her decorative gown for something simpler, a plain black dress, tied at the waist by thin links of silver thread. Cecilia adjusted the chain around her neck, finding the weight of it had grown bothersome after wearing it for the entire day, but the thing should remain in place as long as she acted as queen, a dinner with the lord of a noble house was unfortunately considered such an occasion.

She ventured back the way she had come from, through the towering corridors of what was now her palace, and outside to a carriage in waiting.

The road that led to the palace was small but relatively safe, a mark toward just how difficult it had been to place the new royal abode so high in the world. A journey all the way to the main city below would take hours. When it was necessary for the crown to make such a journey, the Old Palace would serve as their temporary place of residence. Thankfully, Cecilia would not need to journey that far tonight. Aester Hyde had been placed in one of the guest houses that rested on a lower level of the mountain and would not require such lengthy travel.

Her fingers traced the empty socket that remained within the chain. Some had suggested she fill the hole with an agate of her own, but she had explained that it was the symbol that mattered more, the gesture of the stone being handed over willingly. A counterfeit would mean nothing.

It should not have come to this, the coronation was meant to be the simplest part of her reign, yet even that had shifted toward ruin. Cecilia had not ceased to wonder what symbol the incomplete chain appeared to be in the eyes of her fellows—a dangerous one, she posited. Something that could prove the defeat of all that she hoped to achieve.

The carriage arrived at its destination, and Cecilia was escorted into and through the manse. The place bore little by way of décor. It had served every noble house numerous times throughout the years, and none were permitted to leave anything that would align the interior with any one aesthetic in particular, so as not to leave the impression that any one family had a greater relationship with the crown than others.

Lord Aester Hyde sat at the head of a long oak table, his fingers steepled together as his eyes took in the dark slate. He rose to his feet upon witnessing the Queen's entry. "Your Majesty, such a pleasure."

"Trust that the pleasure is reciprocated. The House of Hyde has always been a steadfast ally of my family, I should like to maintain that strength of bond," Cecilia said, allowing her current aide to draw out the chair opposite Hyde, before seating herself. "It is truly welcome that you should ask for my presence at dinner rather than to beg for something more beneficial to yourself."

He chuckled quietly, then sat back down. "Can I assume my fellow nobles have been far from tame?"

"You can assume whatever it is that pleases you, though I should do nothing to confirm."

"Of course. Forgive my curiosity, I simply wish to better understand the way of this land." Aester snapped his fingers, and a hand was quick to fill his and Cecilia's cups with a yellow wine, something she could only assume he'd brought with him from Deserum.

"Understand it, yes. But do not give yourself over to it. Distinction has become a rarity I should like to see more often."

"Is that so?" He sipped at his drink, making a display as he savoured the flavour.

"Regrettably, the old guard want nothing more than to sustain themselves. They fear losing what they have." She tasted her own cup, finding it oddly sweet and not entirely dissimilar to the flavour of honey. "It is no fault of their own, of course. Merely a trait they have inherited from their predecessors. But even so soon into my reign I find it difficult to stomach."

"Then Duralaans is not so much different from Deserum."

Cecilia regretted then not studying the history and politics of the surrounding lands. She had a base awareness of the horrors inflicted upon Santora under Gallius Wilfre, and the impossibly quiet genocide of Cendela's draconic people, yet she remained blind to the affairs of Deserum, the former home of the Mortal Gods who had once helped forge civilisation. But she also knew her lack of knowledge was somewhat purposeful on their part. Deserum had maintained silence in conversation with the rest of Avandoras, as though they did not want anybody to see through the continent's spectral shield.

"Might you tell me something of your homeland?" she asked.

"Of course, Your Grace. What do you wish to know?"

"It is what you wish to say that I would like to hear. What do you think of the land that raised you?"

Aester turned his cup in place for a moment, a solemn expression falling upon him. "It was a shadow, through which you could see the outline of what once was. Only if you tried to reach out and hold it, you would see it for the illusion it was."

"I had feared as much. It is as though our lands can do no more than rot. I had thought that perhaps our new pantheon of gods might bring with them a new age of prosperity, but perhaps we are simply damned."

"Such dreadful words I did not expect to hear from my queen."

"I fear it is such dread that will be seen as the symbol of my reign in the centuries to come."

"At least your reign will be undisputed. In Deserum there were no less than five who proclaimed themself rightful monarch." Aester took a moment to drink more. "A disaster—about a century ago—shattered the land, made it nigh impossible to traverse safely. The crown could not keep its underlings in check, and so they forged their own crowns. But when new roads had been built and the King was able to have his words heard again, the fledgling found themselves unwilling to yield the power they now held. Thus Deserum remains a place of discord and little unity today."

Aester finished his cup and waved away the handservant's attempt to refill it. Cecilia could see that there was something else eating at his mind, an itch plain to see. "You have more to say."

"If I may, I fear that I see the beginnings of such issues here in Duralaans. If such a calamity were to befall your kingdom, would your nobles stand together, or might they take the opportunity to seize power for themselves?"

Cecilia did not respond. Of course he saw it too. She could not help but feel both embarrassed by her people and respectful of his insight. "It should not be about power."

Now Aester remained quiet, clearly intrigued by his queen's thoughts.

"It is not for such things that I wear this chain; I should surrender it to another if I knew it would maintain my people's own strength."

"But it will not?"

Cecilia finished her own cup, now finding the sweetness almost revolting, not something many would prefer to consume in Duralaans. "I have watched these people since I was a child. I have seen them bicker and insult one another to no end. I have no reason to believe they would do anything different if somebody were to deliver them this chain and the power it holds."

"Then what is there to do?" He was testing, trying to draw out a particular result.

Cecilia did not want to give it to him, though she found herself wishing to divulge just how manic this role had made her feel. But some things were for her, and her alone. "I have thought much of it, the riddle of how to make the unwilling compromise. Is it more morally appetising to force them toward peace or to allow themselves to wander confidently into damnation?"

Aester shrugged. "Sometimes a subtler hand is required."

"Control is control whether it lurks in shadow or daylight."

He pointed a finger toward her. "But it is easier to stomach, for the controlled and the controlling. Is that not the purpose of a monarch? To guide the people toward their best outcome?"

"Maybe once, long ago. But truly it is just a symbol now, a fragment of the old days that we cling to for posterity alone."

"I thought you better than that." Now Aester accepted the re-fill. "I thought you would not allow yourself to be so defined by your circumstance."

"We are all defined by something, *Lord* Hyde." She put extra emphasis on the title; he would not have been where he was if not for the death of his own kin. She hoped Aester respected that.

"Yes, but it is what we make of that which matters. You see the corruption in your ilk, what are you to do about it?"

Cecilia had no answer, it had been something she had considered much, the necessity to mend her kingdom. Yet she knew not how. Perhaps all the monarchs before her had faced the same predicament—all who sat upon the throne had the ability to see the issue at hand, just not what to do about it.

But who is Aester Hyde to know of such things?

"What are you doing here, truly?" Cecilia asked.

"I have not the faintest idea what you mean, Your Grace." He responded, acting more interested in the ornamentation of his cup than her question. "I told you there was little for me in Deserum."

"And you arrive here perfectly timed to inherit the lordship."

"A twist of fate, as I said. Are you accusing me of something?"

"Only of thinking beyond yourself. You have been leading me as long as we have spoken tonight."

"I meant no offense, I assure you that I only wish to better understand who you are."

"Then you can speak plainly."

A smile spread across Aester's face, and with a wave of his hand, the manse's attendants were dismissed. Cecilia similarly sent away her own company, eager for the shield of pleasantries to be removed.

"While our gods may be long gone, their arcane lore remains. Techniques passed down from generation to generation. There is one we knew, possessed by an ancient entity and able to see the threads of time and fate."

"And I presume he saw something of Duralaans' future?"

Aester's smile widened. "The return of an old foe, long buried, long awaiting his vengeance."

A chill coursed through Cecilia. Her heart raced. Breath came short. She need not guess which villain he spoke of. "Then we are doomed."

"If you should resign so soon, or perhaps this is opportunity?"

"To unite the people against a common threat." Cecilia did not think the words, but they came to her all the same, the dark path that had haunted her every thought. "Is there anything more? Who should release this foe? Who could even find him?"

"That much our prophet did not say."

Even now Cecilia could not understand this man's motives, so intwined Aester seemed by plots only he would know, yet she could not see the form they took. Again, a problem she knew existed, but could not properly face. "Why tell me any of this?"

"It is as I have already said, I look forward to witnessing your reign unfold, and just what peculiarities it should entail."

The doors to the dining room were thrown open, the manse attendants entered bearing platters of roasted bird, smeared with a fruity sauce, and the rest of the night continued with minimal conversation.

It seemed that Aester was well and truly satisfied by what he had put on offer and Cecilia was thankful for that to be the end of it. He had given her plenty enough to consider as it was.

Chapter Eleven

Until Sunrise

Nath!" screamed a voice that belonged to his sister. She had always been so strong, so smart, so quick to find the best solution to any situation.

"Nath!" His father. The man who had done everything to rebuild his son after his wife's death, even as he himself must have been suffering just as much.

"Nath!" Now Sera. She had been his closest friend in youth, taught him how to use his grief to help others, and stood by his side as they fought against impossible odds. He could never repay the debt he owed her, even if she claimed it had long since been paid in full. "Nath!" she repeated, shaking him awake. Her face would be the first thing he saw that day, but he was disheartened to find it wrought with worry.

"What is it?" he mumbled wearily.

She was so close to him, examining his eyes as if she expected something to burst forth from them at any moment. "Are you alright?"

"Yeah, of course." Eric sat up, placing a hand on Raph to force her to give him some distance.

"You were crying in your sleep." She let herself sit back, rubbing the sleep from her eyes.

"Oh." Pictures of flame were all he could recall from his time asleep. "The fire threw me off is all."

"What fire?" she asked, leaning forward a touch, and gesturing to the slight opening in their tent. "The one outside?"

He could not hear it anymore, no doubt having died down during the night, but the smell of wood gone to char remained. "Fire's made me feel off for a while now." Eric found himself reaching to where his hand should have been but found only the stump of twisted flesh that was left. "It must be pretty late still. You should get back to sleep."

"I don't think that'd give either of us much comfort."

Eric sat further upright and pulled his knees close to his chest. "You know, I used to think that there'd be a day when this was all over. I even thought that day had come; we took down one of the worst evils ever known, why shouldn't we get even just a little time to rest? That all went up in flames." He found where he had placed his prosthetic and began to manoeuvre its metallic joints. "Why can't we stop?"

Raph looked so tired to his eyes, and he felt more of a fool for thinking what he had endured could be compared to her own life. "This is all I've ever done, Nath. It's a part of me. To stop would be . . . like death." Her hand traced a small scar on her cheek, an injury Eric knew she had gotten after falling off a building in her youth—one of the less horrible sources of any of her wounds.

"Right, I'm sorry. Sometimes I just get exhausted by it all."

"I really shouldn't have woken you up."

"No, I get it. You wanted company," Eric tried to joke. "Besides, I must have woken you up first."

Raph shook her head with a weak smile. "Oh, who says I sleep in the first place?" The expression died shortly thereafter. Raph was studying him; Eric could feel her eyes on his even if he didn't meet her gaze himself. She placed a hand on his arm. "Why did you come back?"

"You were in danger."

"I'm not a fool, Nath. You didn't get all of this put together"—
she gestured toward the scattered items of his arsenal laid out on
Eric's side of the tent—"just to save me."

Eric sat quiet for a moment. One part of him wanted nothing
less than to put the last two years to words, but another wished
desperately to confide in his friend once again.

"You don't have to tell me. I'd rather not talk about my time
in the dungeon, so I understand if you don't want to tell me about
your own stuff."

"I want to, Sera. But I don't think I can." He looked at her now,
and it was not concern that marred her eyes, that emotion had been
replaced with one Eric had not witnessed in a long time.

Raph lowered her hand, finding Eric's own fingers and lacing
them together with hers. "Then let's not talk." She rested her head
against his. "Let's just stay like this for a bit."

They sat together as the hours of night passed them by, content
with the presence of one another, and no more.

At one point, Raph interrupted their long silence to give voice
to another question. "Do you want me to stop calling you 'Nath'?"

"No," he said, without a second thought. "I like that that's who
you remember me as; you might actually be the last one who
does."

Raph must have understood what that meant—that there existed nobody else who would know the name Nath Whitsin—
because she squeezed his hand tighter and would not choose to let
it go until the sun rose.

—

They set off early the next morning, racing to pack up their small
camp and get to their destination without further delay. With no
disruptions, they ought arrive at the city of Harbinger's Rest before that day reached its end, and hopefully well before Elias and
his companion caught up with them.

Raph held the reins once more, being the better rider between them, and allowing Eric the freedom to wield his firearm in defence if necessary.

"Have you been to Harbinger's Rest before?" Raph asked, half turning toward him as she drove their mount ever forward.

"Once or twice, but never especially long-term," Eric said, pushing down the voice within that debated the truth in that statement. He reasoned that relative to some species, even a decade could not be considered long-term. "What about you?"

"I passed through during my original search. The lady of House Wintre is a pretty ardent follower of Anni, so she was willing to point me in the right direction."

"You think she'll be just as hospitable this time?"

"I can only hope so." Raph hesitated. "Though Lyre might have sent word ahead, told her to be wary of us."

"Do you think she'd listen?"

"Maybe. I guess we'll just have to wait and see, huh?"

Eric hardly liked it, but sometimes that was the only option on the table. "Suppose so."

That day would be their sixth spent on the road. Day after day they had woken at the cusp of dawn and only taken rest upon reaching the darkest of the night's hours, a cycle that had kept them at a pace that ought to have kept them far from their pursuer's grasp but had begun to prove exhausting.

"Should I ask what kind of work you've been doing under your new name?" Raph asked. "It's not that I think you would have done anything overly problematic, but it would be nice to know what kind of infamy I've attached myself to here."

"Nothing outrageous," Eric answered, though he knew his work was also a far cry from the noble quests he had taken in youth. "Mostly bounty hunting, some protection jobs, escort stuff. Anything that would give me the coin to stay alive and keep myself sated."

"*Sated?* What does that mean?"

"As in . . ." Eric regretted saying that much, explaining those feelings would require him to delve into what had led to them, and that seemed too heavy a topic for the moment. "The need to do something good never left me either, it just changed form. From vengeance to justice, and back again."

Raph glanced back at him. "Then you do get it, you understand why I couldn't stop and come with you?"

Something about the way Raph worded the recollection irked him, or perhaps it was the recollection itself and the feelings attached that made him feel so raw. "I always have. But I also knew it would have killed me if I hadn't taken the chance."

"You don't give yourself enough credit, Nath. You might not have that locket anymore, but I'd hazard you're not far off from being that man."

That only pained Eric further. All it took was the memory of what it had felt like to become the most perfect iteration of oneself to inflict a numb sensation upon him, like he was still falling from that high, and perhaps would never fully return to the surface. "That man still had both of his hands. Whatever path would have led me to him, I've long passed it by."

"Well, I never said that you were him, just that you're getting pretty close." She shot him back a wink that managed to lift Eric's spirits enough to forget that numbness. "You're better like this, anyway. I couldn't stomach spending another second with that version of you"

Eric laughed. "Is that right?" He had always admired that vision of what he could have been. It was difficult to believe anybody could have thought poorly of that man.

"It was a lie, a fantasy that served its duty, but is better left as just that. I thought you might have finally realised that when you gave it up."

There had been many reasons he'd thrown away the Locket of Chronara, and while some form of self-realisation could be attributed, Eric knew there was much about his inner turmoil Raph did not know—even if others had so easily seen it. And Eric did not believe that this was the time to change that. "I wish it was that simple."

"Well it's good that we're back together, then. I have no idea how you've done it without me."

"Oh, I've done a lot. Just very little that was any good." He allowed himself to trail off, the need to share his pain with Raph was returning, and he would not allow himself to put that on her. *Not today.*

Today they would reach Harbinger's Rest. It was not a large city, a large amount of the space behind its walls being taken up by the manor of the residing noble family, alongside lodging and training grounds for their forces.

Raph slowed their horse to a steady trot as they neared the gate, coming to a stop before a burly woman standing guard.

"Halt!" Two more armoured figures appeared from behind the gate, flanking either side of their mount. "What purpose have you in Harbinger's Rest?"

Raph answered without delay, "Spiritual. We are followers of the Floral One." That elicited an amused chuckle from one of the guards. "I came through here not too long ago to visit the local mission; I wish for my friend to see just as much."

"How long will this visit take?" the guard asked, allowing the spear in her right hand some slack.

"We plan to be gone by tomorrow morning," Raph said sharply. "Forbidding any setbacks."

"Got a place to stay?"

Eric had an answer for that one. "Rickard's Respite. I've stayed there before, and the owner owes me a favour or two."

"Very well then." The guard waved her backup away, and they returned to their places hidden behind the city gates. "Enjoy your time at the Rest, stay out of trouble."

They were allowed to continue onward, entering the city proper and passing down the main street. A few of the city's people watched the pair with suspicious glances as they passed by.

Eric had no delusions about how he looked; it was his choice to present himself in such a way that most would not consider approaching him. Dark fabrics, messy red hair, and a leather poncho which allowed for the slightest glimpse of the fully equipped bandolier beneath, all fit together to craft the perfect image of Duralaans' most reprehensible sort. It could be a benefit in his chosen line of work to have those he interacted with made wary of his presence, it also bought him a level of solitude few could find naturally, yet there was always that very human part of him that was continuously pained by the reactions he inspired. Eric wondered what it said about himself that he continued to act thus despite that pain.

If one did not know where to look, they might never find the residence of House Wintre. Unlike so many other noble families, Lady Wintre's home did not tower over the rest of the city, large as it was. Instead, the space it occupied sat tucked away just shy of the city's centre, its surrounding wall made up of perfectly habitable housing which had been carefully placed to hide away the exact location of the lady's domicile.

Thankfully, Eric's occupation while he had stayed within Harbinger's Rest had demanded that he knew the city's ins and outs, including the location of what appeared to be a completely inconspicuous wall of stone, that just so happened to be guarded by Wintre's own soldiers.

They led their horse to the outside of Rickard's inn, hitched it to a timber post, then proceeded through the twisting alleys of the city and toward that stone wall.

"So, we just talk to them?" Eric asked, finding his anxiety growing the closer he got to their destination.

"It worked last time."

"They just let you in?"

"Pretty much."

"Gonna tell me how, Sera?"

"Just watch." She shot him a smirk then hurried onward, the stone wall coming into view as they rounded a corner, sitting at the end of a dauntingly long alley.

Posted a short distance from one another were a number of House Wintre's knights, armoured in white plate and decorated by plumes of blue feather. There were easily twenty of them, standing with their backs to the edges of the alley so they might each have vision of any who entered as well as the stone wall at its end.

Raph slowed her pace as she noticed the garrison. "They're new."

Eric matched her speed. "There were guards last time I was here."

"Not that many."

Eric's hand drifted toward his holster, though he didn't expect his weapon to prove much use against their armour. "So what now?"

"We'll need a rain check on the show, it won't work with this many eyes. We can try asking for an audience?"

"I can't say I have a better plan."

Together, they continued down the alley, coming to a sudden stop when the first two guards stepped out before them.

"Turn around, House Wintre is not accepting callers at this time," one of the knights spoke, though Eric could not tell which.

"I visited not so long ago. Lady Helen treated me as a guest, and we discussed our shared religious interests." Raph planted her hands on her hips. "Just tell her Seraph is here, no need for trouble."

"As I said, nobody is being accepted. Your name is irrelevant."

"Why? What's changed?" Eric asked, it couldn't have been so long since Raph's last visit that Wintre's tolerance for visitors had shifted so drastically.

Neither knight spoke for a painful few seconds, and Eric found it difficult not to stare at the gloved hand which seemed to clutch the knight's sword too tight for comfort. The tension was broken as a different voice said, "The recent tragedy in Anderan has necessitated greater care be taken in protecting the noble houses." Whichever one of them it was that spoke, they drew out there words as if they thought Eric and Raph were a pair of infants, careful to not necessitate a repeat of the explanation.

Eric was not sure what they meant. "Forgive us, we've spent a great deal of time travelling here. What tragedy?"

"The family of House Hyde were killed, their home destroyed by inferno."

Raph took a step back, mouth falling agape. "Destroyed? Completely?"

"Correct. Now step away," the knight said, revealing some of their blade's steel.

"Yeah, I believe it's about that time," Eric agreed, placing a hand on Raph and guiding her away. She seemed distracted by what they had learned. It truly was a tragedy. Though Eric had no particular care for the nobles of his homeland, he begrudged death of any sort—an undoubtedly hypocritical stance given his occupation.

The whole walk back through the alleys and streets, Raph seemed deep in concentration, as though she was forcing herself to be absolutely sure of their circumstance before she returned to normalcy.

"Do you know what this means, Nath?" Raph asked, startling Eric with her sudden change in demeanour.

"That this just got a lot harder for us?"

"The opposite, actually." Raph smiled.

They reached Rickard's Rest and entered the old inn, finding the proprietor and operator at his service desk. He seemed tired, despite the relatively early time of day, and unleashed a cacophony of sputtering coughs as he noticed their entry.

"Welcome to Rickard's Rest," he wheezed. "We have rooms aplenty, just take your pick. The price is inarguable, so don't bother."

"I beg to differ," Eric said, resting an arm on the rotting wooden desk. "You owe me, old timer."

Rickard's eyes seemed to finally focus properly on Blackhand, he shook his head back and forth. "Oh no. We are well even. You took care of those boys, and I took care of you after what happened to your pa."

"You forget? I did two jobs for you."

Rickard huffed. "I did not forget, I simply do not enjoy being cheated out of payment by a common sword."

"I don't use a sword," Eric shrugged, "and I'll pay for the room. It's something else I need for the favour."

Rickard sat back, cast his eyes toward Raph. "And you are?"

"Thinking . . ." was all she offered as reply.

Eric leaned forward, granting the old man some small taste of privacy, as though the two were conspirators in a dastardly plot, and not the men they really were. "I know you have friends inside the big house; I need to get word to them."

Rickard offered only a grunt by way of response.

"This is important. Raph here knows Lady Wintre. We just need to set up a meeting."

"Nothing's getting in or out, kid. All of my people have gone quiet. Everyone's scared they'll be the next Hyde."

That caught Raph's attention. "What happened there, really?"

"Don't know." Rickard scratched at his stubbled chin. "Some say accident, others reckon it was a paid killing."

"All the more reason we speak to Wintre now," Eric pressed on.

"I can't do the impossible, you'll just have to wait until all this blows over."

Eric lowered his voice ever more, as though what he were about to say was the most valuable secret he possessed. "Please, Rickard. We might never have known each other so well, but we're family. My mother always spoke highly of you."

"Don't do that," he said, projecting a cold exterior, but the softening of his eyes betrayed his true feelings. "Don't use her memory against me."

Eric backed away from the desk. "That's alright, then. We'll find a way."

"You'll stay here and pay full," Rickard grumbled. "And we'll just have to see what can be done for your other needs." He looked again at Raph. "And what was your name, girl?"

"Wintre knew me by Seraph, use that name and tell her I'm the same chosen of the Floral Maw she met a month ago."

"I won't be telling her much of anything myself, but I'll see if word can be passed along."

"Thank you, Uncle," Nath said—for in that moment that was who he truly wanted to be again.

They were led toward their rooms, separate quarters for the two of them, though Rickard had graciously decided they would only pay the price of one.

Raph did not go to her room, instead she followed Eric into his. It had been the same one Eric had lived in after the death of his family, weeks of his life he had lost locked within, too broken to do anything but dwell on what had been reduced to cinder. It was not until a group of street toughs had begun harassing Rickard that Nath had forced himself back together and into the Eric Black-hand he was today. Eric imagined he had lost enough pieces of himself that it was impossible to rebuild the person he was properly, but now returned to his home during the darkest nights of his life, he wondered if that had simply been the excuse he used to reckon with what he thought he needed to become.

Raph spoke as soon as the door was shut behind her. "We only need three of the keys."

"How's that?" Eric asked, removing his poncho so he might shake it out.

"The Hydes had one, just like the other houses who fought against Artorius, but their home is destroyed, and if their key went with it, then that's one less anyone else can possess."

Eric sat with the revelation for a moment. It was promising, but almost too perfect. "Unless they didn't keep the key in their home."

"Except I saw it myself. Caster Hyde showed it to me in person. He kept it on display alongside all the other trinkets his family had."

"Which lords haven't you met?" Eric asked, incredulous. She had certainly found herself living a more interesting life than he in the near decade since his last proper adventure.

"Only those two. Caster was paranoid, apparently somebody had told him there was a mark on his head, and he was looking for any explanation."

That would explain the lord's demise, but Eric had never heard of anyone having the mind to simply put out a bounty on a noble's head. No blood broker with any sense would take such a client—unless they thought there was no other choice. "Who organised the mark?"

"We didn't know, but I guessed it was Lyre coming for the key." Raph must have been able to tell Eric wasn't quite following her logic, as at odds with each other as the nobles could be, they would not dare risk the consequence of high treason. "Lyre made a bid to take Hyde's key once before, offered his daughter in trade, but Caster feared what he wanted it for and denied him."

"Could he really have killed another lord so easily?"

"Not easily, no. If it was Lyre, then it'll come out eventually. But I'm sure he won't wait that long before making his next move."

"Well I trust Rickard. He might downplay his connections, but I know he can get it done. It'll just take time."

Raph stepped toward the window, looking out at the city beyond her, then noticing something beside the sill. Eric could not see what she was looking at, but he knew that had been where he'd etched a tally mark for every day he continued to live longer than his father and sister. She traced her finger over the markings and said, "Sorren could get here any hour now, and Lyre won't wait around for us before he does whatever he's planning. We might not have time."

Eric had feared as much and begun laying out an alternative plan within his mind. It was far from preferable, would cause a not-insignificant amount of trouble, and bring Eric face to face with the living embodiment of his recent life choices. But Eric was rarely one to know the luxury of preference anyway.

He pulled the poncho back over his shoulders, checked his pistol was still in working order, and flexed his prosthetic hand. "Then we don't wait."

—

The sun had set and night fallen, no sooner would Greydeath take their meeting. It was only through reputation that Eric knew of the orc underlord, and that reputation was enough for him to never wish to find himself sharing a room with the monster. Alongside this was the fact that Eric Blackhand had taken up the bounty on Greydeath's brother not a year earlier and did not know whether or not he was aware of this detail. It was a risk, a monumental test of chance that Eric knew must be endured. There was far more at stake than himself, as long as Eric reminded himself of that, he would be willing to do anything—or so he liked to believe.

Raph stood by his side as they trekked through the darkened streets, having profusely insisted on joining him in the beast's lair. Eric was sure they appeared a perfectly odd pairing to any who witnessed them. While Raph's willowy teal dress and simple green vest may have made her look far more innocent than she truly was, Eric only hoped to obscure exactly what curious items his arsenal contained beneath his poncho—not that many could likely name them at a glance.

The firearm he carried was a rarity in Duralaans, a weapon he and Raph had designed during their days still in Spirallos. It was far less limited than the similar pistols which some artificer's had conceived of in recent years, sourcing its power from the combination of materials both natural and arcane. An infernal gemstone could be a dangerous thing when used carelessly, but tuned with the right runes, and contained within a casing of metal tempered by a dragon's flame, its destructive fire could be targeted.

The rest of his arsenal contained items of far less ingenious craftsmanship, being the things he had spent his days tinkering with during his so-called retirement. But they had proven their worth enough times that he would not consider running into the throes of danger without them.

They neared Greydeath's base of operations, and Raph leant toward Eric to ask, "This man can really get us inside?"

"More or less," Eric answered, knowing the true details would only serve as complication.

"What does that mean?"

"Just be ready to run."

They entered the towering structure which was Greydeath's headquarters, a place that most in Harbinger's Rest must have thought of as a place of healing. By day, Greydeath spent his time treating the sick and injured, a seemingly noble practice that just so happened to make him one of the most valued members of the city. It did not matter that he killed as many as he healed, so long as he healed the right people.

A few members of his cadre were stationed throughout the facility, watching the two as they passed through the halls. They did not speak, but each time Eric and Raph passed one by, that figure would peel away from the wall they stood at and begin to shadow them. This trail grew to five by the time they reached Greydeath's study, found at the summit of numerous sets of stairs and encompassing the majority of the tall building's highest floor.

Eric placed his hand on the brass doorknob and took a moment to reconsider his decision. This plan could very easily prove to be the cause of his death, if he was not careful, and Eric wondered if that was a possibility he truly felt ready to confront. He looked to Raph and—seeing that she appeared to reciprocate no such fears— opened the door.

They found Greydeath sat upon a tall leather-backed chair, bent over an expanse of papers. He cut an imposing figure.

Rippled with muscle, he had squeezed himself into the nicest clothing he could fit, and a pair of relatively small spectacles sat upon his nose.

The orcish people had been humanity's only true competitor outside of their own race within Duralaans' bounds, believed to have been placed among them so that the human people would be constantly challenged to grow stronger, and prepared for what would await them beyond the sea. In retrospect, those had been cruel times, the orcs being whittled down in number and forced to the northernmost reaches of their home. Their kind had shown just as much animosity as humanity had, only they had emerged from that battle the loser, and had stewed in anger ever since.

Eric could certainly understand why so many still feared them. Their blue skin, solid black eyes, and numerous bony protrusions were a frightful sight, yet Greydeath seemed perfectly native to such a dignified environment as his study.

"We are closed," he said, voice a deep but soft rumble.

"I'm not here for your day trade," said Eric, walking right up to Greydeath's desk and slamming his hands down. It was the prosthetic that made the most noise and caught Greydeath's attention.

"Oh. Hello, Blackhand."

"You know me?"

"Of course, you killed my brother," Greydeath said with no inkling of malice, confirming Eric's fears all the same.

"Just business, you understand."

"I would if that were true." Greydeath stood now, rising to tower over everybody else in his presence. "Does the name Eric Whitsin mean anything to you?"

Eric tried not to react, kept his tone neutral. "He was my father."

"Yes." Greydeath removed his jacket, he wore only a black vest beneath it, allowing the threat of his massive arms to make their point. "I recently discovered this man was quite indebted to my brother, a debt he failed to pay off for many years."

Eric could not stop himself from snarling. "That's not true."

"But it is." Greydeath rubbed his knuckles as he turned toward the great window behind him. His house of healing came to stand as the tallest point of Harbinger's Rest, a far from subtle statement about who really ruled the city. "My brother was forgiving, and thought to extend the time this man had to pay back what was owed. Time after time, he extended such kindness, but your father never learned."

"Because he increased the debt every time Father tried to pay him back." Eric glowered up at Greydeath, feeling heat rise within him, and growing less concerned by their difference in stature.

"My brother was a businessman, forgive him for needing the money to keep himself afloat."

Eric understood he needed to change the subject, Greydeath was only toying with him, and he needed to see things through without further issue. "This isn't why I came here."

"No, but I have been waiting to meet you for a long time, so you will hear what I have to say first."

Eric's hand shifted toward his weapon, but he forced himself to be patient, for at least a little while longer.

Greydeath turned back to smile at Eric. "My brother had your father killed to send a message; debts are always paid in time."

"You think that's news to me?"

"Stop interrupting." He opened one of the desk's draws, began searching for something inside. "Of course you'd know the truth. You had to. How else would you have gotten your revenge? In time you would find and kill my brother; he was always a smart man, but not smart enough to avoid death forever. So I waited and waited, yet his death never came. I wondered, 'Why does this man take so long?' Then it struck me."

Eric instinctively caught the scroll Greydeath had found and tossed toward him. He waited for further explanation, but the orc seemed content to allow Eric to learn at his own pace. Slowly, Eric unravelled the paper and began to read.

Greydeath continued, "This man was waiting for a *just* reason to kill his enemy. This man had a noble heart."

The scroll was a contract, one made between a blood broker and his hireling. The target was described and named as Orgoth—Greydeath's brother.

"So, I gave him a reason."

Two signatures were on the paper. One writ on the front from the client—signed by Greydeath himself—and another to be left by the assassin on the back, a signature Eric knew just as well. It was his own. "You put the bounty on your brother."

"Somebody had to, why not do it myself? Call it thinning the competition." He placed five more scrolls on the table.

Eric quickly skimmed through each. All were similar contracts, Greydeath putting a mark on one of his enemies, and hiring a particular killer to see his wish fulfilled. All were names Eric recognised because they were jobs he had completed himself.

Raph stepped forward. "Why are you showing him this?"

"Because I want him to understand just how far back our relationship goes, and how much further it could go yet." He held his hands behind his back, appearing as formal as he could. "Let's dispense with the cloak and dagger. We are allies. You have done me well and I have paid you well for it. Let us strengthen this allegiance."

Eric's mind went quiet, processing Greydeath's words as little more than a dull ringing. All this time Eric had thought he was taking up random jobs to eliminate individuals of malintent. Was it different now that he knew it had not been so random? But who was Greydeath if not one more creature of darkness who profited from misery? He was no different from the men and women Eric had already killed, yet it had been he who had benefited from every drop of blood spilled.

Eric had never fooled himself into thinking his work was good, but he had hoped the choice to live such a life would mean an ultimate tipping of the scales toward justice. Now the ends behind his means were revealed to him, and they appeared as black pits of cruelty mimicking the shape of eyes.

"Well?" Greydeath pressed. "Name what it is you came for, let me show you how valuable this partnership can be."

Eric couldn't help but laugh, he had been afraid whatever Greydeath had up his sleeve would prove ruinous to the plan—if anything it only cemented his commitment.

Perhaps in the grand scale of things, Greydeath's healing work amounted to more than the harm he inflicted. Perhaps the people Eric had killed for the orc's pleasure deserved the fate they got. He did not care.

Eric Blackhand drew his firearm, raised it toward Greydeath's confident visage, and unleashed that destructive fire.

Chapter Twelve
The Light in the Dark

Raph did not like this Greydeath character any more than she liked any person who was so confident in themselves that they did not consider the role others played in their lives. Whether it was Florian of Spirallos or Carlyle Lyre himself, they always found a way to make themselves the centre of every story. Greydeath had thought himself beyond retribution and had found himself paying greatly for such a mistake. Raph had no qualms with what fate had bought him, but she feared what would come of it once his mass grew cold.

A streak of crackling flame burst from Nath's weapon and tore through the left side of Greydeath's temple, leaving only a gaping chasm of charred flesh in its wake, before next shattering the glass window behind the orc. Greydeath's remaining eye went wide for a stunning second, before he stumbled back, and fell through the broken window, disappearing as gravity took him beyond their sight.

The guards had moved as soon as Nath's firearm had been drawn, too late to stop him, but fast enough to have their justice.

Raph acted with just as much haste, redistributing the arcane currents that remained following Nath's use of his weapon to rapidly heat the steel of their enemy's swords. As they attempted to draw the weapons, each man became instantly dismayed to find their weapon scattering to the floor in molten droplets of metal. Nath took the opportunity provided to turn from one guard to another, firing on each of them in turn, and letting them drop to the floor.

Raph took a moment to consider what had taken place. She had expected Nath to make some form of deal with the underlord, using his criminal prowess to possibly sneak them into the manor grounds or even to steal Wintre's key itself. Now she found herself at a loss, unsure whether Nath's actions had been a premeditated part of a larger plan or motivated purely by what Greydeath had revealed.

Nath gripped his firearm tight in hand, staring blankly at a nondescript point within the study. "Shouldn't be too long now, let's just wait a moment."

A fire rose within Raph, an anger directed toward just how blasé Nath was acting despite the way things seemed to have rapidly spiralled out of control. "For what, Nath? What was all that?"

He turned toward her, though without meeting her eyes. "It doesn't matter. The plan stays the same."

Raph paced in a small circle, trying to understand what had overtaken his wit. She knew Nath had done work as a bounty hunter since their time in Haevahn, and that life brought burden on a person, Raph had only hoped those burdens would not find their way to her so quickly. "Are you okay?"

He tucked his weapon away beneath his poncho, acting as though he had not heard.

"Did you know you were working for him?"

Nath rounded the desk and peered out through the window, taking in his handiwork. "It doesn't change anything." He waved for her to join him. "Come here."

Raph crossed the room, careful to step over the array of corpses. Her focus remained on Nath, rather than turning toward where Greydeath's corpse must have landed far below. There was a solemn rigidity to his expression, recalling memories of how he had been following their confrontation with Vécar—and even then he had still been willing to talk to her. Though Raph had always been one to keep her pain internal, it comforted her to know she was not alone in it, and she enjoyed seeing another who could move beyond that darkness. But it had been a long time since she had been able to offer an ear to her friend, and she wondered just how much of that darkness had consumed him since. Was she much the same?

"There they are." He pointed out a line of armoured knights headed toward where Greydeath had embedded in the dirt. "Get ready. As soon as they enter this place, you make a sprint for the mansion."

Raph's jaw dropped. "That's the plan?" She'd have smacked him across the face if she were not afraid the force would send him to join Greydeath in the dirt. Instead, she forced him to actually face her.

He tried and failed to pull away. "What?"

"They'll kill you, Nath!"

"You're meeting with the lady of House Wintre, I'm sure she can pull a few strings if you get her on side."

"Don't you think getting her to give us the key was a big enough demand?" Raph asked, her voice rising with frustration. "You should have told me this was the plan; how much time it saves us won't matter if you die."

"This is important, isn't it? If we don't do this, Duralaans and everyone who live here are at risk."

Raph gripped his arms so tight, she wondered if her nails would soon draw blood. She didn't mind so long as it woke him up from his mania. "So you throw rational thought out the window? There were ways to do this."

"This is one way. A good way. You have your chance now; I just needed to do this."

Raph was beginning to see the depth of his troubles, how tightly he had clung to the path she had once shown him. "I'm sorry I let you get dragged into this; I should have come here alone."

"Alone, and still Lyre's prisoner. I thought we went over this, Sera, how many people would that help?"

She let him go, feeling a sickly knot twisting within her stomach. "Don't call me that."

"Then you might as well stop calling me 'Nath,'" he spat, though seemed quickly made ill by the vitriol in his own words. "We're not those people anymore. I've changed. You've—"

"Changed? What would you know of who I am now?" As much as she felt it, Raph was not mad at Nath. Something else had earned her ire, an indistinguishable concept that lacked a face for her to challenge, making Nath the next best stand-in.

"Nothing," he laughed, "because nothing is all you'll tell me."

"If you were so curious about my wellbeing, maybe you shouldn't have left."

"It was never about you. I was just . . ." He hesitated, placing his prosthetic hand in the other and caressing the metallic fingers. "I'm not like you. I can't keep moving from one thing to another, as much as I've tried. I never moved past that anger that first drove me, never learned to be guided by a true sense of justice, not like you." A calmness came over him, a sad shift in his expression as he seemed to discover his thesis. "Larina was right, it's all just a distraction. Just a lie. I'm not a hero."

Raph could only stare at him, feeling as empty as Nath appeared. There was something akin to a scream within her, a growing sense of urgency that drowned out the quieter part of her which demanded she do what she could to help her friend.

Nath must have noticed her turmoil and decided to make her decision before she could. "Don't pity me, Raph. It's too late for that. But if everything you've said is true, we need to do this. We have to stop Lyre and whatever else might be coming to destroy this world."

"I know." Raph could hear the knights making their way through from below, their heavy footsteps growing louder with every moment. "Why didn't you ever tell me you felt like this?"

He shrugged, a weak gesture. "You had more important things to do. Better you focus on them than waste yourself on my problems."

"You helped people as well, don't act like that means nothing."

"Like Greydeath?" He shook his head. "Because it looks like that's the only person I've actually been helping."

The clatter of armour and boots grew louder.

Eric continued, "Just get the key. I'll keep these fellas distracted as long as I can."

Raph forced herself to nod, the time to debate was over. "Don't you dare die." Then she did slap him, forced by an urge to leave a proper impression on him, before Raph stepped out of the window and fell toward the ground. Gravity had hold over her for no more than a heart-pounding second, before Raph called upon her own innate arcane properties—a blessing stemming from the inherited link all devolas had to the infernal plane of Diavollos—to soften her landing.

A crowd had gathered around the corpse of Greydeath. Most seemed rather glad to see the orc dead, and none stopped Raph as she made her hurried journey toward the mansion's entrance.

She forced herself to put emotion aside, they would do nothing for her in the presence of Lady Wintre. All that mattered was securing the key.

Despite how folly Raph believed Nath's plan to be, it had worked. Only two of the knights remained guarding the entrance to the Wintre manor, though they seemed far more alert than they were earlier. If it came to it, Raph could easily best them in combat, though it had not been violence that had secured her entrance originally.

They spotted her, immediately recognising Raph as the same devola who had attempted to gain access hours prior. "You will come no further!"

Raph ignored their command and channelled as much of Anni's power as she could. The pale green of her skin began to glow, eyes became nothing but pits of bright light, hair billowed around her face like a halo, and her horns appeared less devilish and more like a holy crown.

The two guards staggered back, struck with equal amounts awe and terror.

"I shall see the Lady Wintre this moment." She used her power to further project her voice, knowing it would sound deafening in their own ears, but no louder than a whisper to any who passed by.

"What are you?" one of them whispered.

"I am the sole vessel of the Goddess of Growth, the light that pushes back the rotting end, the one who will not remain stagnant. I am harbinger of tomorrow's sun. I am Seraph." She did enjoy playing up the drama of it all from time to time.

The guards took a moment to collect themselves, before speaking again, "We will alert the Lady immediately."

"I shall follow."

They did not deny her.

The two armoured men escorted Raph through the deceptive stone wall and into Wintre's grand courtyard. It was just as magnificent as it had been during Raph's last visit, the path lined by tall trees with bright pink flowers. Given Anni's connection to nature, it was a common theme among her followers that they would tend carefully to their gardens, and it appeared Helen Wintre was no different.

Raph wondered how much of the work Wintre had actually done by her own hand and how much was the work of her servants.

Curious glances were cast in Raph's direction as she was ushered into the entrance hall of the manor, a wide chamber facing a tall spiralling staircase.

"If you would wait here, I shall alert the Lady to your presence."

"Of course," Raph said, and once he had ascended the stairs, she let her display drop. It felt like finally taking in air again after holding her breath for too long. What was an incredible display, also proved to be incredibly taxing, and she could only hope it would not be needed again for a while more.

During her last visit, Raph had come across Lady Wintre by chance, having met her in the local temple of Anni's worship. It felt like divine providence to have met precisely the person she needed to further her quest. The woman was kind, nurturing, but also exhibited a hint of cold calculation. Raph wondered if Wintre was aware of Lyre's schemes and thought to help her just to cut him down a notch, but she also saw the Lady's faith was strong. Perhaps she simply saw the threat that Artorius' return presented and hoped to do no more than stop it.

Helen Wintre appeared at the top of the spiral, seeming to have just been roused from sleep, with her short hair tussled, and dressed in an elegant silk blue nightgown, but she did not seem at all vexed. Wintre smiled as she took her time to descend the staircase and meet Raph at its floor.

"Seraph." She spread her arms wide in greeting. "Such a pleasure to be in your company once more."

"I hope I did not wake you, my lady." Raph pinched a corner of her dress and offered her best approximation of a curtsy.

"I am not so far aged that I cannot be woken without invoking wrath," she jested. "But what does bring you here so late? Would you not prefer tea as with our last meeting?"

"I fear time is of the essence."

Wintre's kind expression turned serious, eager to know what help she could be. "Then speak, whatever the Growth asks of me, I shall do all that I can."

Sometimes Raph had difficulty keeping all of Anni's titles in line, she had to remind herself often that most did not have such a personal connection with the goddess as to use her given name. "My quest to cut off all access to Artorius continues."

"Did you find the map? I hope my information was not so outdated that it proved no use."

"No, it was fine. The map is gone, and I have now turned my attention toward the cipher."

Wintre listened with an impassable expression, she at least seemed curious, but also somewhat wary.

"It is an artefact, made to store the details of Artorius' imprisonment, not unlike the map. Eight keys were made to it, but only a majority of five are needed. I fear that somebody seeks to attain these keys."

"But they could do no harm, even with all of the keys. The cipher itself is well and truly sealed beneath Avalass."

"I would prefer Artorius' return be an absolute impossibility. Why leave it to hope that nobody could gain possession of the cipher?"

"I do not disagree." Wintre tightened her gown, as if getting suddenly cold. "Such was the reason I had my key hidden where nobody could find it."

"As long as it exists, I assure you that's not true." Raph stepped forward and called on some of her power so she might emphasise her next words. "*Tell me where it is.*"

Wintre took only a moment to consider, then said, "The lake of Vyx, deep within the old wood."

Raph had heard something of the place. It was a mystical forest, rumoured to have ties to an ancient entity of great power, one that took to acting as guardian of the items left in its lake. "You have my utmost gratitude, Lady Wintre. I would not ask so much if it were not important."

Wintre straightened somewhat, appearing with as much dignity as Raph would expect from the Queen herself. "There is no need for you to explain yourself to me, Seraph. If it benefits the Growth, I am quite happy to oblige."

Raph turned to leave, before remembering the issue of Nath. "There is actually something else you could do for me."

"Speak it."

"I have a friend who has offered myself and our goddess much aid recently, but a misunderstanding has left him at the mercy of this city's law bearers."

"I see . . ." Though Wintre's twisted mouth and furrowed brow told Raph that she did not.

"If he could be allowed to go free, I would be in your debt."

"What is the mouth of the Floral Maw doing associating with common criminals?" Wintre's eyes narrowed, but the hint of a smile on her face told Raph it was from a place of curiosity rather than suspicion.

"He's not a criminal, just too quick to make judgements."

"I will see what can be done for him, but perhaps for such a thing I may ask a favour in return?"

Raph's head tilted in question.

"Just today, Her Majesty the Queen requested my presence in the capital so I may destroy my key alongside the other noble houses." She shrugged dramatically. "Now I told her that would not be necessary—after all our key has long been lost. But if you, my dear Seraph, were to prove me wrong, then I would ask that you complete the Queen's request on my behalf."

Raph was taken aback. "I'm not quite sure that would be best. I'm not one to treat with royals."

"But it will aid your quest, will it not? You will see with your own eyes that the remaining keys are destroyed. What better way to ensure your enemy is banished eternally?"

She considered it. At first the idea seemed to Raph as a distraction from her main task, but she quickly found herself agreeing with Lady Wintre. If the keys were to be taken to the capital, that was where Raph needed to be.

She offered another curtsy. "Thank you, my lady. I will see it done."

"The thanks is mine, Seraph." She mimicked the gesture. "Do not be such a stranger this time."

"I apologise; it has been a busy few months." Raph made her way back to the entrance—stopped. "Perhaps I could ask of you one last favour?"

—

Stellarhoof was a proud beast. With a coat of black-speckled white and a mane of red, she was the fastest horse Raph had ever ridden—it seemed there were some benefits to having access to the resources of a noble house.

She rode through the streets, passing by where Greydeath's corpse had been, and offering a prayer to Anni that Nath had made it out safely. She wanted to free him herself, but for whatever reason, her heart would not allow it. He would surely insist on joining her for the rest of her journey, and Raph did not know whether she could stomach that.

Whatever place he was in now, she could not give Nath what he needed. Any words she might attempt to pass off as wisdom would surely turn to bile in her mouth, and even more of her own pain would be passed on to him. She would not burden him any longer—not now that she was beginning to understand why he had walked away.

They blew past the main gate and followed along the moonlit road back out of the city. It would be a short, but not insubstantial ride before she reached the forest. Raph could only hope she would arrive before dawn. The Lake of Vyx was said to only be visible under moonlight, with the forest under the protection of a legendary beast by day. It would be vastly preferable that she did not have to wait until the very next night before she could claim this first key—that was as long as the lake's guardian judged her worthy, and this entire leg of her journey was not rendered pointless.

Raph led Stellarhoof away from the main path. She could see the faint outline of her destination in the distance, appearing to her like a purple cloud hanging impossibly low over the ground. As it grew closer, Raph could make out the thin white trunks attached to the swirling tufts of purple. They were trees, their leaves made of wispy threads of what looked like mist from a distance but seemed to actually be something like silk. The moonlight gave the impression that the silk was luminescent, like it absorbed the light and then projected it back down, lighting up the forest floor entirely.

She drew to a stop as they reached the cusp of Vyx Forest, taking a breath as she absorbed its beauty. Whatever grass might have covered the forest floor could not be seen through the purple threads that had fallen from the trees above, creating an environment that was the same above as below.

Stellarhoof grew restless as they passed the forest's boundaries. Raph found it difficult to coax her into continuing, like the place itself was trying to deter them.

"Easy, girl." Raph patted her mount's strong neck. "Just a forest, nothing to fear here."

As if on cue, a shrill whistle pierced the silence ahead of them. Stellarhoof whinnied in response, throwing her head back and forth. Raph gripped the reigns tight, struggling to maintain control over the beast, but she only grew more anxious.

"Calm, girl!" Raph demanded, but the steed only stamped her hooves in response.

Raph had ridden horses before, but she had never received any proper training in the skill. Taking a horse across a continent was easy enough but calming one frightened by some supernatural entity was another thing entirely.

She pulled harder on the reigns, the rough rope digging painfully into her palms. "Just be steady!"

But it was no use. Stellarhoof reared back and Raph was thrown from her saddle, landing with a pained grunt on the ground. It may not have looked like a typical surface, but it sure felt like one.

Raph could only watch as the horse sprinted back the way they had come and disappeared beyond the tree line.

At least she'd taken Raph as far as she needed to go—for the time being at least. Better not to think about how she was going to journey all the way to Avalass afterward.

The whistle returned, clearer this time, and Raph decided to head toward it. There was no map that would lead her to the mysterious lake she sought, so an equally mysterious whistle seemed the best alternative. It came again, lasting a moment longer. Another few seconds after that it returned, longer still. Over and over, the whistle came, with shorter intervals between the trills each time. It even seemed to become more distinctive, almost musical as it beckoned her forward.

Then it was right before her eyes, appearing so suddenly that Raph almost strode right into it; a brilliant glistening pool of water that seemed to stretch impossibly far. Her eyes couldn't even make out where the water came to an end. Raph looked to the sky and found this to be the only spot the trees came to a stop, allowing the moon to shine down on the lake.

Raph gasped as she returned her gaze to the water and found that a large stone had appeared within its centre, serving as the cold throne of the fey beauty which sat atop.

The woman-shaped being combed her fingers through her hair—the same purple as the trees, it trailed over her figure and into the water. She wore no clothing, putting her odd skin tone on total display—an off-white, almost green colour, that Raph had only ever seen as a trait of elves. The whistling emanated from her, and this time it did not stop.

Raph could not help but step toward her, mesmerised by the figure. Her music struck something nostalgic in Raph, drawing out memories of the past. For a moment, it was her mother sat on that rock, carrying the tune of a lullaby Raph once might have known by heart.

Raph did not even realise she had stepped out and onto the lake itself, somehow standing atop the liquid surface as though it were solid.

"Are you . . ." Raph hesitated; it was cold, unbelievably cold. "Vyx?"

The woman's hand stopped, and she turned her eyes on Raph—they were hollow and dark, except for a single pinprick of light in both.

Raph fell, hitting the water and then sinking far below.

<u>Chapter Thirteen</u>
To Be Decided

Elias had made a mistake, he was apt enough to admit that. He had taken the easy way instead of thinking about the bigger picture, let his suspicions get the better of him. It was a concerning position to be in. To have been so confidently wrong. To have outright ignored information that would have seen him successful. But he just had to remind himself that it wasn't so simple.

Blackhand and his friend had been in Prometh, it was not Elias' fault that he had the bad luck to arrive a few moments too late to catch them. Those were circumstances beyond what he had the power to control, letting himself be concerned over their impact on his own task would only open him up to the mess of possibilities that entangled all of life. He was simply better off not thinking about it.

Oedon remained insistent that Harbinger's Rest was the way to go, even if their detour had cost them valuable time. Now Blackhand had a head start and was not travelling with a whole cart towed behind him—Elias knew that he could not afford another mistake.

The all-seeing boy had continued to speak minimally, sitting himself in the cart behind Elias and keeping largely to himself. Whether that was by preference or because he held a grudge against Elias for not following his direction, he did not know—and frankly didn't much care. But they were supposed to be on the same side, and Elias had told himself he'd get a better understanding of his partner before it was too late.

"Tell me how it works," he said, cutting through the silence.

"My sight?" Oedon responded, his tone flat and disinterested.

"Sure."

"Will it change anything?"

"You tell me," Elias snickered. "Look, if I understood this stuff better, I'll know that I can trust you're not leading me astray."

Oedon went silent for a while, then ambled his way into the seat beside Elias. "What do you need to know?"

"How do you know where they'll be?"

"It is simply what makes the most sense to me," the boy explained slowly, still choosing his words with caution.

"Well, Prometh made sense to me. How would you know better?"

"It is a difficult thing to describe. Most akin to an instinct that only I possess. If I focus I can see it clearer, but usually it comes as little more than a sensation."

"I'm sorry, kid, but none of that's doing it for me." Elias was hearing what he expected: vaguely spiritual nonsense that ultimately just boiled down to guesswork and luck.

Oedon went quiet again for a time, before taking a concentrated breath and pointing toward something ahead of them. "See that tree?"

Elias saw many. "Which one?"

"Any tree is fine."

Elias cast his sight over the plain before him. A few trees were scattered about, though none stood out to him as more important than the rest. "Sure, I'm looking at a tree."

"Okay, now close your eyes."

"Not doing that unless you want us to ride off the road."

Oedon paused again, and Elias wondered if he should start timing the gaps between his sullen silences. "Very well. Just don't look at it again."

Elias had no interest in doing so. "Easy."

"Now take a guess at how it currently appears."

Elias couldn't help but laugh, though he understood he had nobody to blame but himself for encouraging such nonsense. This was just what he got for being curious. "It probably looks the same."

"Right, that is the same principal my prescience works on."

"It's guesswork?"

"Based on what I already know. Now tell me, what would that same tree look like a day from now?"

Elias' patience was truly being tested, perhaps their pairing was Lyre's punishment, though he supposed Oedon was not enjoying his presence any more than he was. Better to be a good sport about it. "Probably not all that much different."

"Right, but you are less certain. Now imagine it ten years from now."

"Kid, I have no idea if I'll still be living after so long, let alone what some tree will look like."

Oedon seemed to grow frustrated for a moment, before returning to his calm demeanour. "Just try."

"Fine, I reckon it'll be quite a bit bigger. Unless someone cuts it down."

"Thank you. You made that prediction based on what you know currently, correct?"

"Sure, that's how I do my job. It's what I'm good at." Or at least he had been.

"And that is essentially how my sight is able to work. I use what *has* happened to make an informed decision on what *will* happen."

Elias went silent himself for a moment, churning the mystique into logic. It made some sort of sense to him but wasn't quite fulfilling his curiosity. "Except that's not prophecy. That's not even all that different from what I do."

"*Except* I can see a lot more than you. The future might not be perfectly defined, but the past is, and I can see *all* that is past."

"Really?" Elias was attempting to process such a thing. "The entire past? All of history?"

"It is not as though I am constantly flooded with other's memories. But it is always there. Deep down." Oedon started picking at his fingernails, a telling sign that it was more of a burden than he was letting on. "Everything we do today is defined by something that has already happened, that is the single immutable truth of reality, and it is how I am able to see the future."

"Then what is it that defines me?"

Oedon's fingers froze. "Are you sure I can say?"

It was not a happy memory of his, but there was also no way this kid could know about it through any natural means. "I've already lived it; your words won't hurt me any more than that."

"Okay." Oedon glanced up at Elias, and he was taken aback by the genuine concern the boy displayed despite the unsettling appearance his crystal eyes and black tearstains offered. "Your brother fell in love. A wealthy man from a nearby town visited and swept him off his feet. He was happy, but you felt that something was wrong. Something about this stranger concerned you. But you did not have the words to describe it, and your brother disregarded your fear as—"

"He didn't think that." Elias cut him off. "No, he just never cared to listen."

Oedon looked as though he wanted to argue the point, so Elias was grateful that he did not. "Should I continue?"

"No, that's enough."

"Do you understand now?"

Elias wasn't sure that 'understand' was the right word. He could recognise the boy's ability to infer bits and pieces about the future based on what he knew, but the larger scope of his apparently boundless knowledge was less easily reckoned with. "How'd that happen anyway?"

Oedon did not respond.

"Hey, you know my sob story. Let's have yours."

The boy turned his head outward to view the passing trees. "I come from a place called Deserum, do you know it?"

"Loosely, haven't heard anything nice."

"It was once . . ." Oedon went quiet again, what Elias was quickly finding to be an annoyingly frequent act of his—perhaps he was reliving that once upon a time when Deserum was not the shattered land Elias knew it to be today. "But by my birth it had become a place of war. If you were to survive, you needed power, and I had none. So my mother took my eyes and replaced them with these gemstones, in the hopes that a deity would take purchase within me."

Elias forced himself not to react too harshly. Different kinds of folk had different kinds of rituals. He was not the right man to decide which were right and which were wrong, even if he did believe maiming a child was very much wrong, no matter what holy powers you hoped to gift him. "That worked?"

"Yes." His voice was a trembling whisper of air. "It did."

Elias didn't know what to say to that. Comforting the distressed had never been his strength, let alone one with so much baggage. "That's rough, not much other way to put it. You're young too, at least I was a man by the time my brother died. How old are you anyway?"

"I was born 870 years After Celestial Abandonment."

Elias shot the kid a look, he'd guessed as much, but to have it confirmed was still shocking. "Twelve?"

Oedon shrugged. "Many of Deserum's people still possess the blood of the Auratum."

Those had been men and women chosen by the Gods after Duralaans' conquest of the world, gifted incredible power in return for their surrender. Elias supposed their minds also developed at a greater rate than a human's, though it could also be that Oedon had simply been forced to grow up before his time. "Either way, you shouldn't be doing any of this."

"I can see the future, Sorren. You are not one to tell me what I should and should not be doing."

"Working for Lyre, that's what you've chosen?"

"There is no such thing as choice. Have you not been listening? Every decision we make is defined by infinite hands we will never see."

"Then how come you can't see the whole future, huh? Like the tree. Get to a certain point and it really is just guesswork."

"Don't take it so literally."

Maybe it comforted the kid to think it was all predetermined. But Elias had seen enough bizarre occurrences to know there had to be a level of random chaos to existence—how else could Elias' recent string of failures be explained?

"We may be provided moments of decision in life, but the path we ultimately take is already set. *That* is how I knew they would be in Harbinger's Rest before even they had decided upon that course. And *that* is how I know you will continue to Lady Wintre's city, even after I tell you the devola will instead be in the Vyx Forest."

"Oh." Elias thought he was starting to like this kid. "Am I so predictable?"

"No more than everyone else."

"Well, I can't say you're wrong. Blackhand is the job, no reason that's changed. But just because we grab him first, doesn't mean we won't get his partner later."

"Do not explain yourself to me. I know who you are, and I know I cannot change that."

Elias patted Oedon's shoulder, the closest he could be to comforting. "For what it's worth, I'm sorry Lyre stuck you with me." Lyre may not have known Elias well, but he thought he'd made his preferences in allies clear. "We're too much alike in how we think, that's why it's difficult for us to work together."

"Listen to what I have been saying, Elias. You cannot change who you are. You are not the one I hold that against."

Elias thought to dig deeper, but the sight of Harbinger's Rest coming into view seemed more pressing. He considered straying from the course and instead making for the forest Oedon had mentioned, but if this truly was another opportunity to make good on his deal and finally catch Blackhand, then he had to see it through. Technically, Oedon hadn't claimed that he would catch Blackhand in Harbinger's Rest, only that the hope of such a thing would continue to drive him. Elias was not so sure whether he should clarify, lest he risk becoming so reliant on prophecy as the child clearly was.

One question won't hurt. "What will we find here?"

"There is no reason for me to tell you, you shall see for yourself soon enough."

Elias thought he should be aggravated by the refusal, instead he felt that he only now properly understood something of Oedon's mentality—though it still did him no favours. He wondered just what he would do if he held the same power as this child. Blackhand could never have gotten the better of him for starters, but Elias also supposed that he would not be so inclined to share his knowledge with others. Not out of any sense that they did not deserve to know what he did, rather for the simple fact that at a certain point it would become irritating to constantly explain the workings of one's own mind.

They arrived by the city's main gate, finding a large assortment of armed figures standing guard. *What has he done this time?*

"Stop there!" An armoured woman brandished her spear, cutting off their progression. "What's your purpose in Harbinger's Rest?"

"We come on behalf of Lord Carlyle Lyre of Prometh," Elias answered, bringing his cart to a stop. He noticed Oedon leap into the back and start rifling through one of his packs. "We're hunting a target, a man stole something valuable from the lord, and he needs it back."

"Lyre, huh?" The guard embedded her staff in the ground and used it to lean on. "This target have a name?"

"Eric Blackhand."

She seemed taken aback for a second, then smiled. "You don't say?" She waved off her companions. "Leave the cart and come with me, I don't know what god favours you, but you've been blessed today."

They left their vehicle and followed the guard through the city's streets. Oedon held a bound sheet of parchment in his hand, trailing behind Elias and their escort at a wary distance.

The guard explained the situation along the way. "Fella came through just yesterday, killed one of our best healers, then let himself be taken in." She shook her head as she cast her gaze toward a particular spot in the dirt. "Just awful. It was late at night, but a poor lot of people had to see it."

That struck Elias as odd, and he wondered if there wasn't a chance they had followed the wrong man once again. Blackhand was a killer, that much was a known fact, but as far as Elias knew he had never gone so far as to hurt anyone that didn't have a few marks against their name. That much he admired about his enemy. "The deceased, they have a name?"

"Haras Goorak."

That explained it. Haras Goorak was one name. Greydeath was another. The orc was a monger of murder and theft who'd long haunted the underworld of Duralaans' east. Blackhand had spent a great deal of time hunting the orc's enemies, a fact that had led Elias to believe there may have been some connection between the two. Clearly a connection that had withered.

She came to a stop outside of a small brick building with barred windows, a distinct appearance Elias knew to house a selection of cramped and miserable holding cells, what could be used to hold a man in the short while they had before relocation or execution. "Here you are," she said. "Just head on in and they'll see what can be done. You'll need proof of your work before they let you claim him, but that's on you."

Elias thanked her and waited for Oedon to catch up. "I'm having trouble believing it. Seems too simple, right?"

"It is not," Oedon stated, tone flat—factual. "Eric Blackhand is inside that building. He is yours now."

This series of events had not encompassed Elias' most tumultuous job, but he was no less glad to know it was at an end. "Well, shouldn't keep him waiting."

They entered the building, finding it just as cramped and lightless as it appeared from outside. Just short of the entrance was a small wooden desk with a single man hunched over it, seemingly asleep. A corridor behind him appeared to lead toward the holding cells, though the darkness made it difficult to see especially far.

Oedon slammed the parchment on the desk, waking the man with a start. He glanced around the room, then squinted at the two of them, struggling to return to lucidity.

He groaned as he rubbed his neck. "Who's this?"

"My name is Elias Sorren, this is Oedon, we come on behalf of Lord Carlyle Lyre to take Eric Blackhand into custody," Elias said, hoping he would not need to repeat his purpose a third time that day.

Oedon slid the paper further toward the man. "That is a contract from our master stating that you are legally obligated to obey us, lest you suffer the consequences of disobeying a lord of Duralaans."

The man, clearly longing to be asleep once more, raised his hands in surrender. "You don't have to tell me twice." He pointed his thumb down the dark corridor behind him. "He's just down the hall. Good luck getting him to go anywhere."

Oedon made way for the holding cells immediately, but Elias found himself struck curious by the man's words. "How's that?"

"Technically, he's a free man. Lady Wintre absolved him of his crimes just this morning, but the guy refuses to leave. Cell's unlocked and everything. I guess the guy likes it in there."

Or Blackhand has a new scheme in mind.

Elias followed Oedon into the darkness, finding it incredibly difficult to see as they progressed past the cells, he only hoped Oedon's purported prescience was not made ineffective by a lack of light.

Elias found the boy standing still before the last cell door, ushering it open with a light push. "It is unlocked."

"Let's hope he didn't slip out, who knows how long our friend back there's been asleep." Elias could see through the crack of the door; it was even darker inside. "You don't have a light, do you?"

Oedon snapped his fingers, and a small crystal appeared floating above his hand. It emitted a faint light, nothing blinding, but enough to offer an idea of what awaited them.

"What is that?" Elias asked.

"A light."

Elias decided that he did like this kid. Raising a son of his own had never been something he'd considered, but a few times he had come close to apprenticing promising youths making a start in the mercenary world. For one reason or another they had all fallen through. Perhaps, if Elias could get Oedon away from Lyre, he could show him how to properly use his abilities. There was a real chance he could be better than Elias one day—given the proper tutoring.

Through the creaking door, Elias found more darkness, slowly being explored by Oedon's crystal. His heart pounded. Elias was rarely one to find himself ridden with anxiety, but something about finally coming so close to success had ignited that cold sensation in him, and the creeping pace that Oedon was revealing the room did not help.

Eventually, the light unveiled a face Elias did not recognise.

The man pulled back as the light grew closer to him. "Oh, give me a break," he groaned, raising his right hand to defend himself from the light—a metallic, black hand.

Elias crossed his arms over his chest, smiled. "Eric Blackhand, nice to meet you good and proper."

There was defiance in the prisoner, despite how tired and weak he appeared, huddled in the corner of that cell. "Elias Sorren, I know your name too."

"Good, saves us from introductions. You're coming with us."

Blackhand leaned forward, far enough that the most of his face was again taken by shadow. "Make me."

Elias drew his sword and pressed it to Blackhand's throat. "I need you alive. Don't make me risk losing my payout."

"Tempting, but I need me alive too." He pushed himself from the ground, dusting off his clothes, before straightening out his back with a grunt. "Shall we?"

There was the infuriating arrogance that Elias knew this man for. Everyone he had spoken to during his early work gathering intel had explained that Eric Blackhand acted with an all-around disinterested confidence that made it hard to read him. Their issue was thinking that there was anything to read beyond that cocky exterior, whereas Elias knew well enough that was the complete extent of depth Blackhand possessed.

"Are we walking or do you have a cart?" he asked, raising an eyebrow appraisingly.

Elias returned his blade to its sheath and cast a glance back toward Oedon. "We have to get some shackles on him."

"There should be some in the pack."

Blackhand seemed to only just take notice of Oedon, his eyes flickering with something like recognition.

"Alright, let's get moving. We still got your friend to grab," Elias muttered, holding open the cell door and gesturing for the others to exit before him.

Oedon took the lead, and Blackhand followed closely behind. "Guess we stayed too long." Blackhand whispered to Oedon.

"Don't be so sure, Whitsin."

It struck Elias as bizarre that they spoke in an almost familiar way, and Whitsin was not an alias he knew Blackhand to have adopted at any point. He could not see the bounty hunter's own reaction, but the way he began to trail further behind the child told Elias he was similarly taken aback.

Elias thought to thank the lawman at the desk but found he had returned to slumber. No wonder Blackhand had remained, he'd practically been left with the building all to himself. A man like that no doubt had no place to call home, so of course a gaol would be the best he could hope for. They collected a satchel of what Sorren presumed was Blackhand's belongings and left the place behind them.

As they trekked back through the streets without any further talk, Elias noticed a few dirty glances cast from the citizenry they passed by. Blackhand had made quite the statement killing Grey-death, but that just meant Elias Sorren being the one to take him into custody was all the more impactful. He offered a few of the onlookers a wave as they slunk past. *Let them know the man who would take this troubadour far away from them.*

Their cart awaited precisely where they'd left it. Oedon hopped into the back and dug out the binders he'd mentioned, tossing them down to Elias so he could wrap them around Blackhand's wrists.

He realised there may be an issue. "Does that hand come off?"

"It does," Blackhand responded with a knowing grin.

So the cuffs would be utterly useless, with Blackhand able to remove his prosthetic and slip right out at any time. "Do we have rope?" he called up to Oedon.

"Not very much."

"Enough to tie him up?"

"You do not believe he knows how to escape such a thing?"

Elias realised he was acting a fool; there was a very simple way to solve the issue at present. "Oedon, just tell me what I have to do to stop him from escaping."

Oedon cast his crystalline stare toward Blackhand, smiled "Nothing. He will not leave us."

"Truly?" Elias looked over their captive, he was still smiling, but there was something off about him. The smile did not meet his eyes, it was hollow—empty.

As usual, Oedon offered no further dialogue—what Elias took to be the boy's difficult form of confirmation.

Elias shoved Blackhand toward the cart. "Climb up, you're with the kid." Elias himself returned to the reins. "Where was it the devola would be?"

"Vyx Forest. But I said that you would have to choose between the two, you chose Whitsin."

"That's not his name," Elias murmured, finding himself irritated by the fact that Oedon knew more about the man he had spent so long studying than he did. "So where do we go, then?"

"We will find Seraph in . . ." Oedon's voice broke. "How odd. I cannot see her."

"What does that mean?" Blackhand spoke up, a hint of panic in his voice.

"Something is obscuring her, I cannot see through."

"Fat load of good that sight of yours is turning out to be." Elias sighed. "Well, we can't go back to Lyre yet, not without the both of them."

"We've already used half of our time, Sorren," Oedon said.

Elias had practically let himself forget the time limit Lyre had placed on them. It had taken them too long to get to Harbinger's Rest in the first place, and now they didn't even know where this Seraph girl would be, let alone how long it could take to find her. "Is there some way for you to get a message to him? Just to keep him informed, maybe get some more time?"

"I have a whisp shell, but it is meant for us to inform him when the job is complete. Only one message."

Elias laughed. *Of course.* He turned to address Blackhand. "You wouldn't be willing to give her up, would you?"

"If I knew where she was?" Blackhand played at actually considering the idea. "No."

So Elias' overarching gripe with this entire job had returned; lack of information. If Caryle Lyre, in his supposed wisdom, had given Elias even a sliver of what it was this woman had that Lyre needed, he might have been able to deduce where she was headed, even with Oedon's power proving itself ineffective. But once again he had been set up for nothing greater than failure.

Was that the plan all along? Perhaps Lyre had intended for him to fail over and over again. This could very well have been some sick game he enjoyed: making a smart man play dumb.Lyre was planning something, Sorren knew that without doubt, so why not give his allies everything they needed to help him succeed? What was so terrible that he had to hide it, even toward his own potential detriment?

Elias Sorren held himself toward a particular standard of professionalism. He had no personal qualms with Eric Blackhand or his friend, but he had been hired to do a job, and that job he would do. His mind was in spiral, running rampant with logic, and coming to conclusions he did not enjoy. "Give me the shell, kid."

"Why?"

"Just do it."

Oedon's brow furrowed with consideration, but the whisp shell was already in his hand, as though he had known what decision Elias would make before he knew himself. "I see."

Elias took the shell in hand. He had used such things once or twice before, a simple piece of arcane trickery. You thought of whom you wanted the message to reach, spoke, and whatever sorcery had been imbued into the item would do the rest.

"Carlyle Lyre. The target is in our possession." He was purposefully vague in the words he used, let Lyre come to the wrong conclusions. "We're currently outside of Harbinger's Rest. I'll take us halfway to you, and you'll do the same if you really want them. Three days. Don't keep me waiting."

He crushed the shell in his hand and let the fragments scatter to the wind.

Chapter Fourteen
Starving

Five days Domina had spent in Haval, secure in the knowledge that Chora had likely passed through before him and decided to leave holding the belief that he had in fact lied about his destination. Bolstered by the belief his ploy had worked in his favour, Domina took his time in searching the place.

If Callum's family had chosen Haval as their place of escape, Domina did not want to alert them to the fact somebody was seeking them out. They had reason enough to flee Anderan, discovering another pursuer on their tail would only force them to run even further.

So Domina paid for accommodation in the town's better inn and took to slowly making his rounds of the people who called Haval home. Whether that entailed listening to their conversations without notice, asking the tavernkeeper seemingly innocuous questions about how many of her patron's faces were new, or keeping a lookout for anyone who walked the streets with a particularly strong display of anxiety, he was sure that he would find Callum's kin—if in fact they were in Haval at all.

Domina had developed a pattern; in the morning he would explore the town's marketplace, then he would seek out those in need of labour for the most part of the day in the hopes that he might develop a level of trust with those he helped, before taking to one of Haval's taverns at night. It allowed him to see many faces and hear many stories each day. Interesting as they were, none had so far told him of what he needed to know.

"That'll be the last of it," Aaric called as Domina hurled the last sack onto the cart. Apparently, Aaric Oltz typically had one of his workers load the cart for him, but business had called them away early, and so today Domina took their place. "Wouldn't hurt to have a man like you full-time."

Domina put on his best smile, not something that came natural to him, but a gesture he believed he had become quite skilled at performing. "Afraid I have enough to concern myself with as is."

"For the best, that is. My boys would kill me if I put them out of work." He reached out a hand and Domina took it. "Hope to see you around, Domina."

He watched as Aaric went on his way. Helping the man with his work may not have put him much closer to finding his veiled foe, but it was still good work done, and he relished these minute opportunities to aid the people. It had been a long time ago that his life had not been so filled with grand exploits and adventure, Domina's exploits of youth had been those of a hunter, seeking the beasts of Mina'lla to quell his people's hunger—in many ways Domina was still a hunter, only his prey had changed drastically.

"Excuse me?" a soft voice came from behind him.

Domina turned to find a young woman, her hands clasped anxiously before her as she looked up at him.

She was small, her subtle stature only further diminished by the way she held herself with a slight slouch. "You're the elf, right?" She blinked at him, awaiting an answer, before seemingly realising she wasn't being clear enough. "The one helping people, I mean."

Domina put on that smile again. "Yes. I'm new here, so I thought I'd do what I could to get to know the locals."

"That's quite kind." Her eyes flicked to the ground. "Would you be able to help me as well?"

"I don't see why not. What did you have in mind?"

Her eyes met his again. "Could I fetch you some tea before I get into the details? There's quite a bit that I need to explain."

Domina gestured for her to lead the way. There was obvious fear in her, whatever task she had for him was no simple affair—not quite like loading a farmer's cart or helping an aspiring arcanist piece together her latest creation. The latter task had been an interesting, albeit confusing thing. Domina was none too interested in the practices of the world's specialists in all things magic, but if the same threads they used for themselves could be made more accessible to the layman, he saw no reason that would not be for the best. As long as they did not fall into the wrong hands.

Domina wondered if this woman could be the one he sought, if her nervous demeanour was the telling sign he had hoped to find in one who knew her husband had brought ruin upon her family. "My name is Domina," he said as they walked. "What is yours?"

"Amity," she answered.

That was not the name Domina had hoped for, and pressing further for her inherited name would only gift him her suspicion. Instead, he continued the pleasantries with a related topic. "That is an elven name, no?"

"It is. My grandfather migrated here from Haevahn a few centuries ago, we've lived here since."

"I visited the homeland a few years back, it's not quite like the stories. Not anymore."

Amity nodded sombrely as she turned toward what Domina presumed was her own place of living. With a turn of a key, she found her way inside, allowing Domina to enter before her.

It was modest abode, a wide living room greeted them on entry, though the shuttered windows rendered the interior difficult to discern clearly. "Apologies for the state. I've been out all day, haven't had time to open up," Amity explained, though Domina noted she did nothing to amend the lack of light. "How do you like your tea?" She hurried for the kitchen.

"I've always been partial to lemon."

"Lovely choice."

He listened as she began to prepare their drink, taking the meanwhile time to further examine the interior. It struck him as though nobody had lived in the place for quite some years. Dust coated the furnishings, cobwebs had been built in the darker corners of the room, and Domina found that the whole of it gave him the impression of a place stuck in a single moment. "How long have you lived here?" he called out.

There was silence for a moment, then finally came a response, "All my life. Like I said, my family are from here."

"Of course, but I meant to ask how long you've lived in this house yourself."

"Ah." Silence again.

"You might tell me if I'm prying too much," he added, worried he was getting close to scaring her off.

"That's more than okay. In fact, I only moved into this house recently."

"That so? Where'd you call home before this?" Domina knew he was treading awfully close to the edge, but trusted he'd know to stop before he went too far.

"My husband and I lived in Anderan for a long while—" She cut herself off abruptly, as though she also realised that edge was coming uncomfortably close.

"Well, I just came from Anderan, in fact."

"You did?" That fear in her tone dissipated slightly, replaced with a hint of curiosity. "Terrible, what happened."

"It was." Domina approached the kitchen. "A good thing you left when you did."

"I suppose so," she whispered, but Domina discovered her voice was no longer coming from the kitchen, in fact the room was empty—the tea left only as its base ingredients.

Domina's hand went for the hilt tucked into his belt, but he quickly decided better of it. Afraid as this woman might be, she would not be a threat to him or anyone else. "Your husband was Laurence Callum?"

"*Was*?" came the quivering voice behind him.

"I'm so sorry." Domina found Amity a few steps into the kitchen, a crossbow, of all things, held in her shaking grasp.

"What did you do?" She took the tiniest step forward.

"Nothing, it's what I want to do that matters." Domina raised his hands, palms spread flat facing her. "I am looking for the people who took his life, as well as those of Lord Hyde and his family."

"He warned me somebody would come looking, told me I had to be ready."

"I understand. But I am not here to hurt you, I am here to find—"

Her fingers found the lever, a dangerous thing given how unstable her hand was. "You were asking for me, hunting me down."

"Because I am trying to understand who killed your husband."

There was a loud snap as the bolt was let loose, and Domina's body with it, allowed to act purely on instinct. His hands were already raised; it was simple enough for him to catch the bolt out of the air. Then the rest of him flew into motion. The world went dark as Domina's hand grasped the hilt of Anamrath and the blade came to life. After that it was like all colour had been sapped from the world. Darkness smothered everything except the terrified woman before him—the woman who now had Domina's starving blade at her throat.

"Please," she whimpered. He could see her legs were trembling, knees threatening to let her collapse to the floor. "I don't know anything."

"I'm not going to hurt you," he said, understanding just how difficult that was to believe given their current position. He shoved her back and she tumbled from her feet, it was meant less as a form of intimidation, and more as the quickest way to get her away from the weapon in his hand. He left her there, refusing to let himself get any closer. "I only want to know what made your husband send you away. Who hired him?"

"I told you already. I don't know."

"That's okay. Amity, that is completely fine. But if there is anything you remember, any mention that caught you as odd—even the smallest thing—I must know." He tried to put his weapon away but found his arm unresponsive—he had forgotten just how trying the Anamrath could be.

"He was scared," she whispered, clearly fighting off total terror. "He dealt with a lot of bad people, but he'd never been like that."

"Did he describe his latest client at all?"

She could only shake her head.

"There were papers missing in his cellar. Do you have any idea where those could have gone?"

She could only shake her head.

Domina felt his arm struggle against his mind, wishing to be used, hungering for something he could not allow it to feast upon.

Then her eyes went wider—a small feat given how wide they already were. "There was one thing, only one thing that he told me when he sent me away." She looked up at him, and Domina realised she was waiting for his permission to continue. He gave it. "Laurence told me I could not go to Meergard, even though I have people there I can trust, even more than here."

"And that was odd? You cannot think of a reason why he would want you to stay away?"

She shook her head again. "I wanted to be with them. I was scared. But he told me to come here instead. Said this was his safehouse, I didn't know this place existed."

That was something Domina could work with. "Thank you, Amity."

"Please don't hurt me," she begged again.

Domina took a deep breath, forcing all of his mental energy into his arm. He imagined every muscle, every single tendon and nerve, then forced them to act according to his will. The blade disappeared and its hilt returned to his belt, the effort may have left his arm feeling terribly numb, but at least the threat was gone.

Amity breathed easier. "What is that thing?"

"Just a sword," he replied. "And like any sword, it's too dangerous for its own good." *Or mine.*

She found her feet once more, coming to a shaky stance outside of Domina's reach. "You should get rid of it, Domina. Before you hurt someone."

"Yeah." He pulled his black cloak around him, hiding the hilt from view. "Thank you for everything, Amity. I am sorry about your husband. I will see those who did this brought to justice."

She offered him a small smile, though the terror remained behind her eyes. "Do what you can."

Domina left without another word, certain his further presence would only lead to more issue. The sun was on its way out of the sky, but he found himself without interest in visiting a tavern that night. Domina's whole body was starting to ache from the fight with the weapon that was supposed to be his. He also knew the trying patronage a night out could summon, and he did not know if he had the strength to leash Anamrath a second time in one day.

Upon reaching the inn, Domina tossed the keeper a few coins, then hurried to his room. Once inside, he immediately tore the hilt from its place and whipped it at the opposite wall, colliding with an almost satisfying clatter. Domina stared at it for a few seconds, feeling a sense of calm wash over him—then the hilt twitched, and in an instant flew back toward him. He managed to catch it before it smacked him in the face, but his heart leapt with panic as he saw the blade come alive.

Thankfully, it had not pierced his skull, instead Domina held the sword far enough to his left that the blade sat just past his ear. "What is this?" he asked the blade.

There came no response and Domina felt as a fool for his attempt. Despite the semi-sentient nature of the weapon, it had never been conscious enough to make conversation, instead communicating its thoughts with sensations that passed through Domina's own flesh. But it had been a long time since he last possessed the weapon, and Domina knew that whatever rules Morguein had bound the blade to the last time did not necessarily remain. For instance, Anamrath had never before perverted Domina's perception quite like it had in Amity's home. Sure, he had felt his senses heightened in combat or been granted a greater level of focus with it in hand, but he did not recall such clear tunnel vision coming over him.

He did not want to consider the fact that it very well could be that such a thing had happened once before, only he had not been allowed to remember. It was a frightening prospect, but he knew the blade could control his body, could push him toward committing acts he did not wish for, but twisting his memory would be new. And Domina could not say why he might suddenly be allowed to remember.

Domina lowered Anamrath and looked down into its empty black blade. He contemplated leaving it behind. For a long time Domina had survived without it and had found decent enough success in its absence. But Domina also knew just how much he was capable of accomplishing with the weapon in his hand. That was too much to pass up, not with so much at stake. Domina promised himself he would reconsider once this quest was over, with justice served he could return to his old way—of course he could.

Placing the hilt down on his bedside table, Domina tried to settle in for the night. He had the next day's destination and would need to be rested well enough to do whatever had to be done in Meergard. The mystery client had organised one death so far through Laurence Callum, it would serve to reason that it may not have been the only one. It was possible his reason for wanting Hyde dead was not personal, but rather an issue he took with the noble houses in general; a man willing to see the most powerful people of Duralaans dead would certainly be one to fear. Of course, Callum would have been at risk for his part in the scheme, he would have been stuck between the fear of his client and fear that the crown's justice might discover him. Domina could only hope he would reach Meergard in time to put an end to the client's schemes.

It would be a week's ride at minimum, and his foe had a natural head start, given how long Domina had already spent travelling from Anderan, and then during his lengthy exploration of Haval. He realised that his prospects of reaching the coastal city before another noble house met an undue end were slim. He would be left trying to piece together an answer from another ruined grave and likely find as little to show for his work as he had so far.

But perhaps Domina did not need to visit the place *in person*.

He threw himself to the floor and raced out of the room. The hilt of Anamrath remained beside his bed; it would be with Domina if he needed it, somehow it always was.

A few drunken wanderers glanced Domina's way as he passed by, undoubtedly perplexed by his bizarre demeanour. He wondered whether waiting until morning would have been a better idea, but given how much time had lapsed already, sooner was better than all else.

He ducked through a narrow alley. The arcanist he'd aided a few days prior had boldly declared that the mess of metal and crystal she had pieced together could communicate with another being across untold distances. Domina was sure that could include the Lord of House Trethellyn who ruled over Meergard, though he had no idea what he could actually say to the man to get him to leave. Simply threatening him with mortal danger might be the prod he needed to get to safety, but it could also encourage a level of arrogance that might only hasten Lord Trethellyn's demise—not what Domina wanted. Simply explaining the situation in whole could work but also might do no more than aggravate the man he was probably about to awaken from slumber.

Enna Hollow's home was hard to miss, appearing like a disaster waiting to happen. At its base was a relatively plain structure, but clear alterations had been made at some point to its foundations, and various pillars protruded from the ground to hold up the wider levels above. It seemed to stand as a symbol of constant evolution and growth. The pinnacle of the tower was what sat at the peak, a great glass dome visible even from where Domina stood below, shimmering with an array of colourful lights. No doubt an eyesore to her neighbours, but it told Domina that Enna had not yet taken herself to bed.

He pounded on the glass door that served as entrance, oddly opaque despite what had been used to make it. Even odder was that no sound came as he hit the door, giving the impression that Domina had somehow missed it, despite the fact that he could feel its warmth against his knuckles—the warmth was bizarre too, now that he considered it.

"It's late, Domina." A voice came from the door itself, accompanied by a slight echo. "I trust this is important?"

"Incredibly. I know that I promised my help came without strings attached—"

"But strings we all have," she cut him off. "Care for a drink?"

There was no time for an answer, as the door quietly slid open. Enna Hollow stood directly in front of Domina, her sharp eyes trained on him, depicting a level of focus her messy golden hair and the dark rings beneath those eyes did not quite uphold.

Her eyes fell to his hand. "Put the sword away, please."

Domina had not even realised it had come to him, but sure enough his left hand held it tight, the blade alive and dark. "Of course." He put Anamrath back where it belonged, with far less issue than earlier in the day, it seemed finally willing to obey him. "What've you got?"

Satisfied, she turned away and crossed the room to find a glass cabinet on the other side. "You got a preference?"

"Anything fruity."

"Oh, really?" She crouched low, running a finger over each bottle's label, before making her choice. "Not what I'd pick for you, but I guess we don't know each other so well, huh?"

Domina had come to stand toward the chamber's centre, unnerved as the door slid back in place behind him. Whatever walls the house once possessed had been knocked away, leaving the impression of a single massive room. A spiralling staircase rose high, passing a few levels above and coming to a stop at the glass observatory at the peak.

Enna handed him the bottle. "It's plum cider."

Domina took it and cautiously raised it to his lips, he did not suspect poison from this woman, but the past few days had set him on edge. Forget simply giving up his accursed black blade, Domina desperately needed a good and proper retreat. He let the bubbling liquid into his mouth and found himself delightfully surprised by how much he enjoyed the taste.

"So . . ." Enna watched him. "What do you need?"

He handed the bottle back to her. "I have to warn some people very far from here of an impending danger."

She shrugged. "Send a bird."

"Time is of great importance, and I cannot risk this message being intercepted."

Enna remained focused on him for a moment more, then her eyes shot wide with realisation. "Oh."

"Does it work?"

"I haven't tested it."

"What do you need to test it, then?"

She raised a lone eyebrow and Domina got the message. She took a long swig of the bottle herself, then forced it back into his hands. "Drink up, bud. If this fries your soul, you'd be better off not feeling it."

"Is that a true risk?"

She shrugged. "Any possible success or failure is purely hypothetical. But . . . sure."

Domina weighed that against his need to see this through. In the back of his mind there was something trying to run far away, black tendrils seizing his mind and begging him not to risk it. But Domina had never been afraid of death, indeed he had lived far longer than any human would ever naturally dream of. It was a purposeless end that chilled his heart. "If I die, will the message still get through?"

Enna took time to seriously consider the possibilities. "It should. My fear is not that your soul will be unable to deliver the message, rather that it won't be able to return to your body afterwards."

The mention of the soul brought an idea into Domina's mind, and he took a long drink of the cider as he allowed the terrible solution to develop.

—

The instrument Enna called the Telanimus was no more than a quartz slab surrounded by large crystals of varying colours and shapes. They seemed to pulse with light every few seconds, sending a bolt of colour through the thick silver ropes ensnaring them and into the slab itself, igniting the veins of crystal within the quartz.

"What do I do?" he asked, finding a hint of anxiety had crept into his heart, and deciding that coming to understand the contraption would kill the parasite.

"You lay on the slab, wear the crown, and then . . ." She had been hurrying around the observatory, running through what Domina presumed to be her final checks, before stopping in place. "Well, I don't know after that, but you should be alright to figure it out yourself."

Domina did not share her optimism, but pessimism would do him no better. He could only trust that the arcanist knew well enough what she was doing.

Enna fetched a metallic ring, about the size of a person's head, and brought it over to him. "Put this on, it should temporarily sever your soul from your body, then hopefully call it back."

"And if it doesn't," Domina removed Anamrath from its holster, "I have this."

Enna looked at the black blade with awe. "What is that thing, really?"

"A blade."

"You think it'll help keep your soul tethered?"

Domina approached the slab. "That . . . or destroy it entirely."

The exact way the blade worked had never been properly explained to Domina, but over the years he had come to understand that it feasted on souls, tearing them from the deceased and seemingly destroying them. It was a cruel fate, keeping the dead from joining the Immortal Plane—if it still existed at all, Domina had never been offered a proper answer. But such demands were the cost of keeping the sword powerful, though Domina had long suspected there was an ulterior reason Morguein wanted a steady source of souls.

In theory, Anamrath could feed on Domina's own soul, acting as a counterweight to the Telanimus' ability to send the soul a great distance. When the instrument was deactivated, he hoped that the sword would be enough to return his soul to Haval and then back to his body—though there was always the possibility he would only be added to the collection of souls the blade consumed.

"We're ready," Enna said. "Get on."

Domina ran his hand along the quartz slab, it was cold except for a small pulse of heat every time the crystals came alit. He sat atop and placed the ring around his head, the inside was decorated with more crystals that rested uncomfortably against Domina's skin.

Enna put her hand on his shoulder and pressed his back against the slab, then began fastening him down, leaving only his arm free to keep hold of Anamrath.

Domina had the sword as only the hilt, raising it to sit just above his waist. "Count me down, I need to activate this at the same time as the instrument."

"Will do." She cranked a heavy lever, and the slab turned downward, bringing his head almost perpendicular to the floor.

Domina could feel the blood rushing through his body. "Is this necessary?"

"Probably," she offered. Domina could no longer see her but could practically hear her shrug. "Three . . ."

It was happening. He kept the hilt in position.

"Two . . ." Her pitch rose with anticipation.

If this were to kill him, Domina thought it would not be without purpose. He had done enough. He had helped people, despite those he had let down—he had helped just as many.

"One . . ."

But such thoughts eroded in his mind. He simply couldn't force himself to believe them. If he died right then and there, Domina knew that it would be as an abject failure.

"Now."

His body was shot with pain at two distinct points. The blade came to life, penetrating his abdomen and pinning him to the slab beneath. In his mind was the other pain, a burning sensation that seemed to creep through his entire essence, igniting every part of what made him who he was. Both sensations felt at odds, the sword desperate to take him, and the artifice struggling to send him far away.

Domina could only scream.

Even as he thought he saw a familiar figure stand before him— a woman in a black-stained white dress, her face youthful and inhumanly smooth, her long black hair billowing behind her like a cloak of rippling dark.

Domina tried to call out to Enna, tried to warn her of the presence, but his voice was overcome and could only continue as an anguished cry. Morguein lowered herself to meet his eyes, then placed her hand on his cheek.

The moment her skin touched his—Domina was gone.

A dark room, illuminated only by the moonlight creeping through the window. Domina stood before a large bed, encompassing two elderly individuals.

"Lord Trethellyn?" Domina spoke, his voice echoing unnaturally around them.

The man's eyes shot open, glancing wearily around the room, before landing on Domina's apparition. Trethellyn did not speak, only stared up at him with mounting terror.

Domina had no idea just how he appeared to the old lord, but he knew he did not have time to assuage his rising fear. "I bring warning to you, Lord Trethellyn."

"What are you?"

"I am the Black Rose. Now, heed my message, Lord of Meergard." Domina raised his hand, bringing a finger to point down at the man. "Death came for Caster Hyde; it now comes for you."

The man sat further up in his bed, casting a momentary glance toward his wife. "How?"

"I do not know the shape it will take. Be wary, cloak yourself in mystique, and await my arrival. I will be there as soon as I can, I must ask that you survive until then."

"Who . . . or what is trying to kill me?"

"I know not who. But they are dangerous, cunning; take every caution if you hope to live." Domina could feel himself waning, he was being pulled elsewhere.

"I don't understand, how is it that you know all this?"

"I was there at the end of Hyde's life, and I will not allow his killer to go unpunished." That did not seem to comfort Trethellyn in the slightest. Domina wanted to explain more, but suddenly the room was gone, replaced entirely by darkness.

"Enna?" he called out, received no response. Domina had not returned to her observatory, though that was obvious enough. It was what place he now inhabited that was a more difficult question to answer, but the colour of the darkness struck him as familiar. "Morguein, are you out there?"

Silence.

Domina supposed it was a fitting fate, to die by the weapon he had used to take the life from so many others. Yet he was not dead, he remained conscious enough of his surroundings that he had to believe there could be a way back. The sword was his, bound to him by contract, that had to remain true even with him a part of its blade.

Domina stretched out his open hand and summoned Anamrath.
Nothing.

Worth a shot, he thought.

Anamrath was a thing of consumption, constantly desiring more and more. It existed as an absence of all, absorbing even the colour of the world alongside the souls it came into contact with. How was one such soul supposed to escape such a thing? Of all the people he had killed, none had so far managed it. There was little chance he could succeed where they had not. But none of them were attached to Enna's strange contraption.

Domina felt a pulse of heat run through him and briefly light up the dark. Enna must have realised he had failed to return to his body and reactivated the machine. He felt his soul ignite, ready to be sent wherever he willed it, yet Domina found himself unable to return to his body.

It did not matter. He was precisely where he needed to be.

With each pulse, Domina could make out distinctly human outlines within the darkness—the souls of those he had killed. With the next electrifying sensation, he attempted to shift his own soul, keeping it within the void, but moulding it through the Tel-animus' power.

With his soul as the matter and Enna's creation the forge, Domina turned his soul into a pointed edge. The darkness peeled away from him, unable to exist in the space his new weapon in-habited. He saw the souls surrounding him grow nearer, drawn toward the blade he had forged and adding themselves to its form. Within the pitch-black void of endless consumption, Domina birthed a blade from the very matter Anamrath hungered for, that which repelled the soul and that which fed upon it—*Anamchara*.

Domina raised the white blade above his head, brought it down upon the void, and sliced it in two.

An ear-piercing sound went riot inside his head, Anamrath might not have been capable of speech, but it could certainly scream. As the dark gave way to light, Domina could faintly make out the world outside. He reached out, and with the next pulse of the machine, sent his soul back to his body.

Domina did not realise just how numbing the void was until he felt himself returned to his flesh. Immediately, he tore Anamrath from where it punctured his body and threw it to the ground.

Enna squealed. "It worked!" She threw the lever in the opposite direction and the slab of quartz mercifully flattened out.

Domina let himself rest for a moment, taking measured breaths to remind himself what it was like to feel oxygen in his body. Everything was cold, as though he had been sapped of all the life his body possessed and was only now slowly coming back to normalcy. He had not spent long within the blade, but it had taken an exhausting toll on Domina. He could only imagine the misery of those still caged within. None of his victims were good people, but he did not think that such a fate was deserved by any.

"Maybe a few tweaks are needed . . ." Enna began mumbling to herself. "But this could be incredible. Domina, if I could only study your sword—"

"No," he stopped her. "Not that I take issue with you examining it, I just don't believe it would let you."

She crossed her arms over her chest. "I suppose I'll need to find my own, or at least something to serve as a suitable substitute." Her eyes widened as she noticed Domina was still strapped down. "Let me get those. Did it work, by the way?"

Domina found it difficult to recall exactly what had happened. "I believe so. Trethellyn seemed scared enough to take the threat seriously."

"Grand, just grand." She removed the final binding. "I think we make quite fine partners."

"I haven't done partners in a long time."

"Oh, you should. I miss my last one . . ." She trailed off, and Domina decided he did not want to know what had come of them.

He held out his hand. "Thank you, Enna."

"No need, we both got something out of this." She gave him a hard smack on the arm. "Now I'd like to get some sleep."

Domina couldn't help but laugh. He could see the sun rising in the distance, its rays penetrating the multicoloured glass dome and bathing them in light. "Enjoy it. I don't know when I'll get to rest again."

"Then I'll make sure to sleep long enough for the both of us."

Domina returned to his feet, taking a moment to make sure he was indeed stable, before glancing down at Anamrath. It might have been better to leave the thing there after all; having almost trapped his soul eternally, he thought perhaps it would not offer the aid he had hoped. But then he recalled Hyde, and the past seven years—though they were not an exact string of failures—Domina knew he could do so much more.

He collected the discarded hilt, making up his mind with the fact that leaving it in Enna's care would only be passing the burden to another.

Domina snuck a final swig of Enna's plum cider as he passed through the lower level, then stepped out into what would surely be a new day.

Chapter Fifteen
The Lake of Vyx

Raph recalled the journey to Vécar. It had been a difficult task to track down the Death Lord, then an even more horrible effort to actually confront the entity. There had been four of them by the time they had located Lost Haevahn and stood upon its necrotised soil, but they had not been ready for the true cost of the fight that would follow.

At the base of the Gildroot, a once beautiful golden tree cultivated by the elves in mimicry of the Gods, Vécar had made the old elven capital his domain. And the four heroes stood ready to face their foe, aware of his intent to spread undeath across the world. In that moment they offered him a final ultimatum. His answer came as no surprise. Violence ensued.

The girl charged forward, defending Nath as he fired on Vécar from a distance. She turned the environment against the Death Lord, reinvigorating the dead roots that had overtaken the ruined structure and ensnaring the villain. Despite his seemingly frail appearance, he had proven quite the foe, calling upon the power he sapped from his legions and their souls to threaten Raph and her allies with a terrible miasma of rot and decay. When Vécar had finally seemed to weaken, a great dragon was added to the fray, likely a once pristine beast of white scale, long gone to a dead grey. Horrible gashes where it had once been sliced still hung open, and chunks of flesh had been torn from its large body, yet it fought with such ferocity that it was difficult to believe the creature no longer possessed any whisper of mortal vigour.

But that girl was not Raph, had not been for the seven years that had passed since she had originally witnessed that day. Now Raph could only watch as her own past played out before her, the only audience to her own life. She was struck by just how young she had been, not even a woman and Seraph was at war with the embodiment of death itself. This girl had protected so many people, saved so many lives, and yet who had been there to protect her?

Before she knew it, Raph was marching toward her younger self, drawing on her own power to do what nobody else had. But Raph was too slow. The dragon fixed its gaze upon the girl and unhinged its decomposing jaw. A white light awakened inside its throat, the deathly flame desperate to envelope her, but the young Raph was distracted, eyes closed as she still focused on turning the resurrected plant life against Vécar.

This was not a moment Raph recalled. She knew she had managed to ultimately emerge from Haevahn with her life, yet she could not see a way the girl before her would escape the fate coming for her.

Then Nath was there, placing himself between Raph and the beast. His firearm began to glow. The crystal that provided its power seemed broken, unruly as he kept a finger pressed down on the trigger and refused to release it. With every second that passed by, that energy built toward climax. The crystal crackled with ferocity begging to be set free, fiery light almost consuming Nath entirely. Then the moment before it seemed as though it could be held back no longer, Nath threw the weapon into the dragon's waiting mouth and wrapped his arms around Raph as the fury of the eight infernal circlets was unleashed behind him.

Raph felt that she should have known who had saved her life, but then recalled just how little time there had been to speak with

Nath after the battle's end. She wondered just how much could have been changed if she had pushed herself to do more.

Naturally, the beast had in fact not been killed and rose again to continue proving a thorn to the four's efforts to defeat their true enemy, and Nath wasted little time throwing himself back into the fray.

"I suppose this is one of your memories?" came a voice from behind her.

Raph turned to find a young man before her, garbed in a simple grey tunic that was emblazoned with a symbol that reminded her of those used by the noble houses, though not one she could instantly recall. His hand rested casually atop the pommel of a greatsword that seemed just as familiar.

He smiled, his features deceptively soft, invoking notions of kindness and warmth, yet Raph felt perturbed by him. There was something cold behind his eyes. "I should be gladdened to no longer be alone here."

Reason found Raph, the initial shock of revisiting the past fading away and allowing the truth to find purchase. "We're inside the lake."

"I should think so." The man let his eyes turn to the battle that ensued beyond them. "Quite the contest you faced. Where is this?"

Raph noted how truly enraptured he seemed by the display, what was to her a painful reminder she might prefer to leave in its place, appeared to this man as all too spectacular. "Haevahn. Or the ruins of it, at least."

"Ruins?" He looked back to her, seemingly perplexed. "What calamity fell upon this place?"

"I don't know the specifics. Divine retribution, I think?" Raph found pause as she realised why she had found it difficult to place the emblem, though it seemed much like what appeared on the banner of House Raleigh, it was bizarrely altered in some aspects of its design. It was simpler, less embellished on the whole, like it had been created in this form initially and then altered and refined over the years that followed. "We're from different times."

His eyes narrowed and a smile tugged at the corner of his lips, this fact came as no revelation to him. "So we are."

Raph considered her situation and the limited options before her. Encountering somebody from the past could be problematic, though she supposed the structure fate provided would counteract any potential cosmic disaster their meeting might cause. "Do you have any way out of here?"

"Not quite, I doubt I've been inside any longer than yourself." He hoisted his sword up to rest on his shoulder, the act drawing attention to the shining platinum accessory that sat on his shoulders and circled his neck. It seemed lacking, eight slots remained empty where Raph supposed one might decorate it with diamonds or some other valuable gemstone. "However, I did not come to this place for no reason. I seek an item of great value to me, and I must not leave this place without it."

"Then our goals are aligned." She cast her eyes around them in a complete circle; it seemed an exact recreation of her memory. "But where would we go?"

"With this being your past, I presumed you might have a suggestion?"

"Afraid not. You got a name?"

"Artorius, and yourself?"

Raph felt her heart skip a beat and forced herself to look away, as if continuing to take more interest in her surroundings than his identity. "Raph," she eventually replied, once she was sure she could force her voice to be steady.

"A pleasure." He took her hand in his, stunning Raph as she watched him bring his lips to her skin. "I am most certain that with you as my ally there can be no obstacle too great."

Raph pulled her hand back, consciously not so fast as to invoke any suspicion, even as she inwardly longed to wash away his touch. "We should get moving then. I don't expect anything we need to be in the past."

"Well put." His friendly demeanour shifted to something more serious, an expression Raph thought came more naturally to him.

"Does anything around us seem odd, unlike how it should appear?"

Raph examined her surroundings, with greater focus this time. The fight had reached its conclusion, one of their people having lost consciousness during the confrontation, leaving only three standing before their slain foe. Raph rounded the corpse of Vécar's dragon, slowly nearing the conversation that ensued before her.

Once, over a century prior, Larina Yukkie had been Vécar Forkh's lover, had known the elf he had been before his waking thoughts were entirely consumed by notions of death and power over the soul. When that madness had taken him, Vécar disappeared, and Larina sought him out, chasing the creature to the farthest reaches of Avandoras and discovering what had become of her lost love. It had been during that journey she had crossed Raph's path and joined her company, seemingly having made her peace with the necessity of their quest. Yet when the deed had been finally realised, Larina was no less distraught. "What did we think we could do here?" she had said, and even repeated now her hollow tone chilled Raph to the core. "Death to the Death Lord? Is that justice?"

Nath approached, still bearing the visage of his locket's empowerment. "I'm sorry, Larina. I know that he meant much to you, but that was the past. This was not your husband; this was an evil that needed to be destroyed."

"Nath, sweet fool," Larina crooned. "Don't try and dull my senses with your own." She placed a finger to her chin, a mocking display of thought. "Or are those Raph's delusions that you spout? Sometimes I cannot tell where her words end and yours begin."

The young Raph roared at the elf woman. "What are you saying? We did this together; you can't change your mind now!"

"Quiet, child. We all know you would have done this alone if it were possible."

"We helped so many people today. Think of them, Larina. Come back to yourself," Nath implored.

Raph could see something of consideration flicker to life in Larina's expression, but it died as quickly as it appeared. "But it wasn't about them, was it? All that anger, all that pain, you just wanted a place to put it."

"Please, Larina. Let's just think things through and we can talk about this when we're calm," Nath said.

"You couldn't save your mother, couldn't avenge her either."

"That's in the past, please just listen to us now," Raph added.

"So what do you do? You hurt everyone else, pay back your own pain tenfold. When really you'd do this world a lot more good if the only person you hurt was yourself."

Spiralling streaks of golden energy shot from Raph's hand— not the younger version from her past, but the Raph of the present. The bright lights twisted in the air, drawing nearer to each other as they shot toward their destination. To Raph's surprise, the light actually managed to strike the memory of Larina, sending her flying back into Vécar's throne with an explosion of gilded light.

The memory seemed to stop there, as if unable to reckon with her act. She had thought about that moment many times over the years. Given the chance to actually see a different outcome, Raph acted on pure instinct.

She could sense Artorius' approach. "I presume that did not happen originally?"

Raph offered no response, instead approaching where Larina had fallen. The elven woman appeared uninjured, though she lay upon the throne without movement. "Are you in there, Larina? Vyx?"

"What is this?" Artorius appeared perplexed as a shallow trickle of water reached his feet. He stepped up toward the throne to avoid it. "Was this place always flooded?"

The ruins had been built far inland, there was no way any water could reach it, yet as she kept her eyes trained on the liquid, Raph could see the water was rising. "No, this is very much new."

It reached the first step, and Artorius was forced up to Raph's level. But the water only seemed to quicken in response. In no great passage of seconds it had reached her feet, appearing from no source she could identify, and rising to engulf her body up to the waist in moments. She managed to stay above the rising water level, but Artorius seemed weighed down, despite not visibly wearing anything of significant weight.

Raph reckoned with whether or not she should lend him aid, and whether it would leave any impact on the course history would take. She was aware of the legends surrounding the man; he had once visited the Lake of Vyx during his original quest for the throne—a visit he had survived. If Raph hoped to do the same, tying her fate to a man she knew would not die seemed her best chance.

She ducked below the water and swam down toward Artorius. It was impossibly dark below the surface and only grew darker still as the water's surface ascended in the opposite heading. Artorius only seemed to fall further as she attempted to reach him, the floor of the old structure refusing to obey natural order and meet him. She called on Anni's power, wrapping Artorius in golden vines and keeping him momentarily in place, it was just enough to give Raph the chance to grasp his hand as it desperately stretched toward her.

Immediately Raph was drawn down by his weight. It occurred to her that Artorius still clung to the hilt of his sword, yet fully submerged by the dark liquid as she was, there was no way to demand that he let the thing go. Instead they could only struggle to swim back to the ever-distant surface.

Raph could feel her chest and throat tighten, her body's means of begging her to take what she knew would be a futile breath. With nothing but watery darkness to be seen, she could not gauge whether they were making any progress—even as the pain shooting through Raph's body told her that time was coming short.

Artorius' grip on her hand loosened and slipped from her grasp, forcing Raph to watch as he drifted down and was consumed by the abyss. It was not long after that she lost her own battle with her body, instinctually driven to take a deep breath—only to find herself choking.

Raph found her body overtaken by a fit of violently coughing. Water shot forth from her mouth as she collapsed to what was now solid ground beneath her. It took some time for her to feel a semblance of normalcy return, even as Raph thought she had successfully expelled the water from her lungs, her body continued to ache in memory of the experience.

When such pain had subsided, she allowed herself to sit back on her knees and take in her surroundings. Raph had been returned to the Vyx Forest, and she now sat in the centre of the clearing where the inhuman woman had sung. Yet the lake did not remain, the waters replaced by a layer of white grass. Artorius was not far, standing on his own two feet as he similarly examined their situation.

"You shouldn't be here," Raph said, finding her voice hoarse and painful.

Artorius did not turn as he addressed her in return, "I find myself disagreeing."

Raph thought to speak, then came to understand his meaning. They were still within Vyx's lake, the drowning they had experienced no more than the creature's means of transporting them to the next aspect of her domain. "Well this isn't a memory of mine."

"Nor mine." Artorius made a display of folding his arms across his chest and furrowing his brow in thought, as though preparing to reveal something especially profound. "Perhaps she is trying something else."

"For what?" Raph knew the lake's entity was not a simple thing, very few ever wished to encounter her, and even the few who did had no pleasant memories of the meeting—those being the ones who lived to tell such tales. "Is she testing us?"

"Distracting."

"How do you mean?"

Artorius collected his blade from where it had been embedded into the dirt, holding it at the ready for any provocation. "I fear we have been led astray. Perhaps there is no reward awaiting us at the end of this insanity, only death." He strode to where Raph still knelt, offered a hand. "Do you know any who have successfully acquired a thing from this creature?"

Raph forced herself to stand without such aid, not for her ego, but so that this man would not see the advantage to strike. He was her enemy, no matter which iteration it was she encountered. "I've heard stories."

"Or lies."

"So we've both wasted our time?" She stretched her limbs, realising the sensation of suffocation had not entirely disappeared, as she forced herself to take deeper breaths to sate her aching lungs.

"I would not be so quick to make that assumption." He started toward the tree line. "No matter the depth of our situation, we should not stay here."

Raph found herself agreeing. She would be a fool to have not considered the possibility that Vyx was no more than a predator, using the treasures lost to her lake as lure to draw the foolish toward a breathless demise. But she could similarly not discount the truth that Vyx's lake was no mere legend, it was an aspect of lore that had been shared for centuries, and Raph thought there was little reason that any would wish to hide her true nature.

No matter the creature's actual morality, no good would come from remaining within that grassy clearing, and Raph joined Artorius as he re-entered the forest proper. "Going anywhere specific?"

"I thought to retrace the path I took in entrance, but this place has changed shape." He stopped. "What of you?"

Raph shook her head, and with it the memory of that haunting whistle that had guided her returned. "Wish I could tell you I was paying so much attention."

A cacophony resounded in the distance, seeming to echo as the ground shook beneath their feet. "What is that?" Artorius was taken by the noise, staring toward the direction from whence it seemed to have come.

Smoke began to creep across the sky, blanketing the night with grey, alongside bizarre bursts of red streaking through the veil. Artorius took off toward it, leaving Raph confused and not entirely sure she wished to follow him toward the calamity, before deciding once again that they would do better together.

She'd lost sight of him quickly, Artorius being far quicker on his feet than Raph would have assumed, and disappearing among the strange trees. Raph had no hope of matching him, not with her breathing difficulties growing by the second, making it so such great exertions left her panting hungrily. With her body remaining within the lake, it was only a matter of time before she truly did drown—it was no small miracle that she had not already.

Finally, Raph found the forest's edge. She must have exited somewhere to the north because the monumental mountain of the kingdom's capital was within her sight. Raph had expected to find it was Promethus that had erupted, just as it had in the Ashen Night's beginning, instead it was the sky above Avalass that was consumed by fire and smoke. She could only imagine the horrific state of the city itself.

Artorius stood atop a small hill before her, seeming entirely transfixed by the vision before him, Raph would not have been surprised to find him weeping at the sight. "What power is this?" he spoke, apparently to nobody in particular as he did nothing else to acknowledge Raph's approach.

Raph found herself similarly consumed by the display—not in awe as Artorius was, rather she felt as though it were her own heart which had erupted, its molten hearth melding with her veins and igniting an infernal terror like none Raph had ever known. This was not something of any past she knew. This was to come.

"We should keep moving," Raph said, though she was not sure where they might go.

Artorius had not noticed her arrival, being startled by her voice, and requiring a moment to familiarise himself with his company once more. "Where?"

Raph had no answer for him. They needed to leave, that much was clear, even if the precise means were not. But left without means, what could they possibly do to save themselves? Raph realised it had been a mistake to not provide response; Artorius simply allowed the mountain to consume his focus once more.

"It wishes that I see this moment. For what reason?"

"Maybe you're right that it is only feeding on us, that display might be nothing more than . . ." Raph paused as she recalled his own words, "distraction."

Her appeal to his own reasoning broke through his thoughtless state, and he turned toward her with his natural seriousness returned. "Fair point, my lady. But there is no other destination I can fathom being worthwhile."

Now it was his reasoning that landed a mark on her. Considering her own conceit that what they faced was some form of test, Vyx's means of deciphering whether the pair deserved that which they sought, it could serve to reason that Avalass would be the site of their next test. Raph had ended the vision of Haevahn by fighting back against Larina's accusations, perhaps it was in Avalass that Artorius would face his own challenge. She felt that there was only one way to know for certain. "What did you come here for?"

Artorius' visage shifted slightly, growing somehow colder than he already appeared. "Is it necessary that you know?"

"I have no idea. But I'm trying to understand what it is this lake wants from us—if not only our death. I'm wondering if what it is showing us is in some way connected to what we seek."

His lips twisted toward a smile, even as his eyes did not reflect the display. "Why come to this place alone?"

Raph was taken aback by the query, how it was related to her own question, she could not guess. "Excuse me?"

"You and I both came into this lake without company, for what reason?"

"Does that matter?"

"No less than your own query."

Raph huffed in annoyance but decided to entertain him—if only so that they could move on and waste as little additional time as possible "I came her alone because this duty is my own, and I will not allow others to suffer on my part."

Artorius seemed pleased by her answer. "And you are stronger for it. Allies, friends, companions would serve you poorly. Stronger we are when left with nothing but our own hands to shape the path before us."

Raph shifted on the spot, not at all comfortable with her enemy's suppositions. She had no want for his thesis on such matters, even less so given his history. "We're wasting time."

"Do you disagree? I saw your confrontation with that undead creature—"

"A fight we only won because we were many," Raph argued, cutting him off. She would not allow her victory to be turned into his weapon.

"But could you have not been stronger had you not been forced to rely on your fellows?" He clucked his tongue in disappointment. "A king does not let himself be supported by those lesser than him, he stands above, and apart."

Raph fought back the urge to combat the man properly. She could see clearly the man he was to become, the vain despot who would cloud the land in ashen darkness. Yet duelling him would do no good. The constraints of fate would refuse her the glory of stopping his march of vengeance before it was allowed to begin. The effort would only be a waste of time and breath.

"I tell you this so that you understand why I will not divulge my purpose to you. Know only that I seek an item of great value and be satisfied that I continue to walk beside you." He stepped forward, beginning his trek toward Avalass. "We both know it is not for my sake, trust who you wish and pay the price."

Raph followed him, intent to keep to her decision to tie her own fate to his but none too pleased to do so. She had studied some of the Ashen King's history during her travels, but not enough of those tales told of what led him to tyranny, though Raph supposed she was finally beginning to understand. Artorius had trust in none but himself, a characteristic Raph could not help but pity him for—all while wondering if she was as dissimilar to him as she might like to be. Raph could no longer be sure whether her decision to leave Nath in Harbinger's Rest had been for his sake—or hers. She had wanted to push him away since he had returned to her life, had told herself it was because she needed to heal on her own accord. Because that was what she had always done.

Because it's who you have to be, were the words she had told herself time and again.

Whilst Raph had allowed her thoughts to distract her, she had seemingly crossed an impossibly great distance. The gates of Avalass were before her, and the forest from which she had come had disappeared beyond the horizon. It was no surprise that natural distance would not prove an issue within such a place, such bending of space could even prove that Vyx did, by some measure, wish that they reached the capital before succumbing. Even so, Raph had to allow herself a few moments more to shake off the bizarre sensation the experience had placed upon her.

She noticed that, despite the eruption of the mountain before her, no magma appeared to consume the city's streets. Ash was all that drowned the capital, the same which had earned Artorius his moniker.

The king-to-be did not slow as he entered the city, fixated upon whatever destination he held in mind, and refusing to be addled by the devastation that would surely come. Raph watched as ash fell upon his shoulders and clung to his form, seeming to solidify as more of the lifeless substance found him. Artorius was transformed into the Ashen Night's lord within moments, armoured by the pale plate he wore in every artist's depiction of him hence, with his winged helm much like a crown and the ash that fell from him a cloak. Raph tried to brush away the few stray specks of grey which landed upon her own flesh, yet they were so stubborn as to not be removed.

No sign remained of the capital's populace, the streets rendered empty for the sake of whatever Vyx hoped for them to see.

Yet even in their absence, Raph could guess at the great number who called the place home, the sheer immensity of the city itself offered enough to reason that tens of thousands surely inhabited Avalass, perhaps with countless more who took the shadowed alleys and forgotten nooks as their dwellings. Such thoughts only further steeled Raph's resolve, these would be the first to suffer if this vision were made real. But Vyx was no omniscient creature, in all likelihood she had only called up such a sight for it was what she saw within Artorius' heart. This could still be avoided.

Artorius quickened his pace as he reached a series of steps that stretched high above and led to what appeared to be the capital's royal palace.

Artorius reached a series of steps which led up to the capital's original palace, the same structure the man would one day inhabit as monarch. Raph could not help but feel unease grow within her, born from more than the heightening tension in her lungs, and becoming only more pressing as Artorius ascended.

"Wait!" Raph cried, stalling for time she did not possess. "We don't know what's up there."

Artorius glanced back at her, helm covering his face entirely. Strangely, the wing-like plate which curled back from the front of his face and spread out at the sides of his head, bore no slit through which he might see. The lower half of his face had similarly been covered, with the porcelain that masked it shaped to mimic his natural appearance. That glance was all the response he offered, before continuing toward the palace.

Raph raced after him, concern mounting despite her awareness that everything before her was still no more than an illusion. Artorius acted as though he knew more than he would say, had told her that he would not willingly divulge any more than he pleased about his quest. Raph could not trust somebody who so openly kept secrets, could not stand by the side of one who did not trust that she could be of aid. There was no time to further consider whether she had done the same to Nath, the mistake that trusting Artorius for even a moment had been was all that she could think on.

"We have to stop, Artorius. It's not too late. There'll be another way out of this." Raph didn't know what she was saying, but she was certain she needed to stop him, just as she had done so with Larina.

"I am aware of what awaits me. I know the way out." His voice was made metallic and immortal by his mask. "You will not ward me off this path."

"Is a path that leads to all of this so worth it? Look around, Artorius. Vyx is testing us with our mistakes, do not repeat yours." With each word, Raph felt more strongly that her own theory had been correct. If only Artorius word turn back from the damnation that awaited him, he might prove himself worthy of what he sought. "Is this what you want?"

Artorius stopped only once he had reached the landing at the stairway's peak, but did not turn back toward Raph as he said, "It is not what I want that is of issue, for this crown was laid upon me before I had even the chance to take my first breath." He took a deep breath then, as though it were a luxury he had rarely been afforded in the past—Raph certainly wished she could do the same. He gestured toward the miserable scenario that unfolded before them. "Gaze upon a place without my hand to steady it; forever clinging to destruction." He raised a hand toward his face, seeming to only then realise his visage had been masked by the grey slate.

"I have seen the future of this place. It is not as you say."

"Then for what did the Gods choose me?" he said, voice level but for a quiver of rage, and Raph realised it came to him as naturally as air did to the lungs. Beyond the veil of pleasantry and stoicism, Artorius was a man of fire, blood, and fury. "Damned am I by what they forced upon my head. The only mortal who might succeed those who could never fathom the true weight of a crown, nor the choking grip of a chain." He clutched the platinum accessory in his hand; the thing shook in his grip as he seemed to reckon with the idea of tearing it free. "I walk the road of kings in shackles. My feet bleed. The gold leaves me blind. My every thought is of misery as I lead the way to paradise. And there is no greater privilege."

"For one who claims not to entrust himself to others, you do spend so much of your time following the will of another. Gods or not, why let them decide who you are to be?"

Artorius turned toward her at last. "Because I am King. Only the fool would turn down so ostentatious an opportunity. Yes, this path is one I am damned to follow; thus it is *my path to walk*, and you are all so very privileged to have me to lead the way."

He turned away once again and continued toward the palace. Raph attempted to follow him but found herself slowing as her breath left her. Droplets of water splattered across the ground as she fell into another fit of coughing, struggling once more to grasp at whatever little air remained to her. She could see Artorius open the palace's grand doors, struggling in no way like Raph did—as though he were not drowning at all.

As though he had never entered the lake to begin with.

Raph tried to stand but found her body too weakened to oblige. So she placed her palm flat against the warm stone beneath her and used whatever of her connection to Anni's power she had been allowed to ensnare Artorius' feet.

Raph forced herself to laugh between desperate gasps for air, the only thing she could think to do so she might be distracted from the doom that approached. "You're not him at all."

Artorius half-turned back to her.

Raph smiled. "Hello Vyx. Care to explain the point in all of this?"

A feminine laugh echoed in the space between them, followed by a distinct whistle. Artorius sliced his blade through the vines, freeing himself and leaving Raph weaker still.

Artorius crept forward, and with each step his ashen coating flaked off, revealing a new form beneath. The shape grew, towering over Raph's crippled self. Light purple hair trailed alongside the shape. Her flesh shimmered with silver scales, broken only by what appeared to be gills and fins. She appeared as a monstrous cross between the humanity of land and something from the darkest of depths. She crawled toward Raph on bone-thin limbs, her jaw unhinged to reveal a mouth wider than her lips should have allowed. Rows upon rows of tiny dagger-like teeth lined the inside of her gaping maw.

Raph scrambled back, kicking to get as far away from the creature as possible. Her breaths were coming shorter, and Raph could feel water choking her lungs and throat. It was not long before her body gave out and she could only watch as Vyx loomed closer, bringing her twisted visage inches from Raph's own face.

She forced her eyes shut, what was to come did not need to be witnessed. Instead Raph thought of her past: the help she had tried to give Nath, their reckless journey to Haevahn, and their eventual victory. She hoped his words had simply been a moment of dark passion; he had to know the things he did mattered, even if they were ultimately choices he made for himself. Perhaps Raph finally understood him, after all she too had endeavoured to help others her entire life, yet with death so near, she did not feel satisfied as she should have. Her work was not finished. It never really could be. There was always more to help. They needed her. They needed what she had been denied.

"And what do you need?" asked a voice without body.

Raph needed to live, so she might grow stronger and face the threat on the horizon. Such was the path that had been chosen for her, the path her mother had unknowingly set her upon the night she'd left an infant on the doorstep of Spirallos' kind innkeeper. She had survived on that kindness, but she was a child then, and surely much stronger now. Strong enough to survive on her own.

Raph's eyes fell upon the specks of ash on her body. Had Artorius believed the same? Was that what Vyx had hoped to show her?

I need help. She tried to say the words, but all that came from her mouth were watery sputters.

As her vision began to fade and the world grew closer to darkness, Raph wondered if her admission had gone unheard—had come far too late.

It had not.

The next moments of Raph's life came in brief flickers, surrounded on all sides by darkness.

The weight of the world returned as she was carried out of the water.

Her fingers wrapped around cold metal.

A purple-haired woman returned to her lake, sparing one last glance to make sure Raph would be fine, before disappearing under the shimmering water.

House Wintre's key rested within Raph's grasp. It had been months since she first set out to acquire one such key. She had finally done it, and it had almost cost her everything. Yet there was still a final step she had to take.

In one way, she and Artorius were not entirely dissimilar. Raph would not trust that the nobles set to gather in the capital would happily destroy their own keys, she had to see it done herself, had to be absolutely certain the threat of his return would be put to rest. But she was not Artorius, and she was completely capable of accepting aid when absolutely necessary—how else could she define Anni's gifts? Raph was certain she could do so again when the time came.

Though she had done some reading on it and had only just witnessed its shape in Vyx's visions, Raph had never herself visited the Capital of Duralaans. It was time for that to change.

<h1 style="text-align:center">Chapter Sixteen
Chokehold</h1>

I have never seen you in such a state as this," Cassidy mused as she helped Cecilia dress.

The Queen looked over her own body. She did not look to her own eyes so far from her typical appearance. Perhaps she had thinned somewhat—Cecilia had so much that needed to be done that her opportunities to eat had been few, and even when she could sit for a meal, her mind was so far away that she rarely finished what had been prepared, instead offering it to be enjoyed by the house's attendants.

Cassidy must have noticed her concern, for she was quick to say, "Oh no, I did not mean you have withered, Your Grace." Her deft hands worked quickly as they tied the shimmering blue sash around Cecilia's waist. "It is only your eyes that seem different."

"I suppose I have not slept as soundly of late," Cecilia reasoned, more so with herself than her handmaiden.

"It is no surprise; you have had many particulars to address since coronation."

"Yes." Cecilia's voice was a whisper, her mind threatening to stray—as now seemed to be a frequent occurrence. She did not think Aester's words would have had such an effect on her. Cecilia knew well enough the threats posed to her land; there was no reason that the lord's warning should be anything new. "Have you heard anything of your brother?" She decided to direct the topic away from herself.

Cassidy's hands began to slow in their movements. "I fear not, Your Grace." She rounded Cecilia, took in her work with disciplined pride. "Perhaps it is time we let that go."

With each day that passed, the time since either had heard of Léonora and their crew grew more distant, and the chances of such changing neared impossibility.

Cecilia felt Cassidy take her hands. "You have quite enough to concern you, Cecilia." She uttered her queen's name as though it were an entirely normal thing to her, forgoing the usual dismay she would display following such a mistake. This was purposeful. "If I may be so bold?"

"Of course." Cecilia traced Cassidy's fingers with her own, taken with surprise by how similar they were to hers. Yet they did not carry the weight of a whole kingdom in their grip.

"I find it distasteful that you were forced into this position, you had such dreams, yourself and Léonora." She smiled, as though recalling an old memory. "You once told me that the two of you would one day not be rulers of land but of the entire sea."

Cecilia did not smile, the memory felt to her more like salt on a wound than nostalgic. "If that is all, I have duties I must fulfill today."

"That is my point, Your Grace." Cassidy squeezed her hands. "Is this truly what you want? I understand that you see this as your duty, your role as last daughter of the King—may his soul find rest—but is it what *you* wish for?"

Cecilia parted her lips to answer but could not force the words to come. No, this was not what she wanted. Her heart still longed to be free from the chains of monarchy, but she remained steadfast in the vow she had made to herself after learning the fate of her siblings. "If it was not me. If I did not wear this chain and guide my home away from ruination, then who would?"

The Queen invited no answer, turned and marched out of her bedroom. Amor stood at attention, his salt and pepper hair neatly combed back, white garb pristine and unblemished—Cecilia hoped she appeared anywhere near as put together as he did. She certainly did not feel so.

"Grand Magus Corwyn is preparing the ritual as we speak, Your Grace. I would offer it shall be ready well within the hour," Amor began, settling into the same pace as she.

"It is to be Lyre today?"

"That is right."

In the days since Aester's warning, Cecilia had quickly pieced together a plan and set upon its execution. It was clear the evil that he spoke of referred to the Ashen Lord Artorius, and there were only two ways he could be found and freed. Eight keys had been gifted to the houses who stood together during the Ashen Night, and five together could unlock a cipher left in the possession of the monarchy. Cecilia had that cipher, locked deep within the mountain her palace stood upon. If unlocked it would present the location and means of freeing Artorius—a purpose Cecilia had long questioned.

Why allow the return of Duralaans' greatest threat to remain a possibility?

Knowledge of the cipher's exact history was scarce also; nobody could confirm for her who had commissioned its creation nor when exactly it had fallen into her ancestor's hands—the same was true of the keys themselves. It was as though they simply appeared one day, existing only to tempt the weak of will.

A second route to the lord remained in the form of a map, one that had been created at a similarly unknown point and then lost at another. Even with the map in hand, one could not unlock Artorius' tomb—wherever it had been buried—so it remained a factor of little concern in Cecilia's mind. The keys were the threat, and they had to be removed from the table.

Cecilia had taken to speaking with the lords and ladies of the noble houses, particularly the ones who held the keys. It was a trying prospect, given they had long since returned to their homes throughout the continent, but with a ritual performed by Duralaans' foremost practitioner of the arcane, the distance could be temporarily closed. It was not something that should be practiced frequently, at most Cecilia could commune with one noble per day, and even then it could not be for so long. The method had evidently taken a toll on her, but it was working.

Lord Rosse exhibited no true interest in the matter, taking a great deal of time to even recall that he held such a relic in his possession. He came to agree to Cecilia's terms as long as the other houses did the same.

Daphne Raleigh required greater haggling, but Cecilia was aware of difficulties she had faced of late, difficulties that could be alleviated while also benefiting the Queen's own agenda. The Orc, a savage humanoid people who lived in the northmost reaches of Duralaans, had long been an enemy of the kingdom. As such, they frequently raided the farms and towns within House Raleigh's domain. In return for the destruction of Lady Raleigh's key, Cecilia swore she would send the Artorian Guard to lend Daphne their aid—an offer that was quickly accepted.

Lord Zephyr Mars also wanted a return for his sacrifice: a relic of equal value from the crown's own vault, an item that he would select himself during his next visit. A trade Cecilia was more than happy to agree to, she did not know exactly what was kept in the vault besides the cipher and could not bring herself to believe that any of them could hold much importance—lest she actually know of their existence.

Leonis Trethellyn was trickier. When Cecilia managed to contact him, the lord seemed entirely stricken with fear, insistent that something was coming to take his life from him. He did not articulate what had allowed this fear to take root, but it was clear it had completely consumed his attention. Cecilia offered a visit to the capital as a reprieve from that which daunted him, and he accepted without much thought, the necessity to destroy his key a non-factor as far as he seemed concerned.

With Hyde's key most likely destroyed, and Lady Wintre insisting her own key had long been lost, there were only two that remained. One was the key of House Asche, a key Cecilia already possessed. King Raine had been Lord Asche until the title of monarch passed to him with the untimely death of his elder brother. Cecilia had never felt more akin to her father than she did now. He had kept the truth of his burdens from her, but she believed they could not have been so different from her own.

So it was time for her to speak with Carlyle Lyre, a feat Cecilia did not believe she had ever accomplished. The man had not attended her coronation and there had been little opportunity for them to cross paths prior, given how far he lived from the capital. At most, Cecilia thought she may have met him on a visit to Prometh with her father, though that had been before Carlyle had inherited his title.

She knew he had become a ruthless lord, though not one who deserved no respect. He may have been considered cold to those outside of his dominion, but those under his jurisdiction thrived. Prometh was the only city that stood to rival Avalass, its people considered incredible craftsmen whose innovations could be found throughout the land, a fact that the House of Lyre had turned toward prosperity for their people.

Amor stopped a few paces behind Cecilia. "Something you may wish to address in the meanwhile, Your Grace."

Cecilia shook herself out of her recollection. "Yes, Amor?"

"Artorian Chora returned just this morning. Given all that took place surrounding her travels, I presumed you'd wish to speak with her?"

"You presumed correct. She is in her quarters?"

"Yes, Your Grace."

"Then I shall meet with her alone." Cecilia changed course, making way for the lower levels of the palace. While much of it had been built atop the mountain, the royal house burrowed twice as far into the rock itself; providing quarters for attendants and easily defended bunkers in times of mortal danger.

The death of House Hyde had remained a constant point of mystery for her. Such senseless violence, for what? The perpetrator was dead alongside his victims.

The assassination had unfolded the same night one of her own guard had been within the city—for what purpose, Cecilia did not know. Chora had been sent to smooth over Caster Hyde's doubts, but Cecilia had been informed she had done so days before Hyde was alleged to have been killed. The Artorian should have returned to her post in the capital immediately, yet she had remained, only to then have this mysterious dark elf slip her fingers and fail to bring him to Avalass. Cecilia could not guess what role this man might have played in the events, but she would learn no more without the chance to speak with him personally.

All of this unfolding so close to her coronation, how Cassidy could be so surprised to see her in such disarray was only another mystery to add to the pile.

Cecilia felt the cold platinum of the chain around her neck, once again traced the edge of the empty slot. That particular part of the chain sat where she could not see it, allowing her mind to imagine it were a yawning void, one that could never again be filled. It had been opened, and no matter what she stuffed in its place, there would be no sating it.

The door to Chora's quarters was not only closed but locked. Cecilia rapped her knuckles against the wood. "Artorian Chora, it is Cecilia." She heard no response but could make out the faintest sound of shuffling feet. "I would like to speak with you."

The sounds ceased, and Cecilia felt her concern mount to a point. Then the door opened, and Chora stood before her. The first thing that caught Cecilia's notice was the thin scar that crossed the woman's face, though she appeared otherwise entirely fine. She was dressed in a plain tan tunic, standing tall, but still a head shorter than Cecilia—as most were.

Chora bowed. "I offer my utmost apologies, Your Majesty. I have no excuse for my failures."

"That is quite alright, Chora. May we sit?"

Chora's delayed answer betrayed her, but she could not turn down a request directly from her queen. She bowed her head and allowed Cecilia to enter.

The quarters of the Artorian were sparse, simply decorated by only her bed and desk. Cecilia sat herself on the mattress, even as Chora stood uncomfortably over her.

"Tell me about your journey," Cecilia said.

"You already know the whole of it, Your Grace."

Cecilia smiled as she shook her head. "I do not believe so."

"I was sent to deliver your message to Hyde." Chora shifted on her feet as she spoke. "He changed his mind and agreed to pledge his banner at your coronation."

"A coronation he did not attend."

"Your Grace?" Chora was taken aback by Cecilia's callousness, though she had no time to be anything besides blunt.

"Of course, he was killed a few nights before. But you similarly failed to attend my coronation. What was it that delayed your own return?"

"I . . ." Chora's eyes went distant, she was struggling to find an answer, something that would not be difficult had she been offering the truth. "You wished that I bring the dark elf here."

"Yes, but I did not send those orders until after I had discovered Hyde's death. That was on the day of my coronation." Cecilia maintained an impassive expression, but beneath the veneer of carelessness, she was examining every twitch of emotion in the woman before her.

Chora's face told the tale of conflict, part of her had something it needed to divulge, but then there was the other part keeping it at bay.

Cecilia gently patted the space beside her, choosing warmth as the tool that would extract what she needed. "Sit, Chora. Don't force me to make it an order."

The Artorian held herself back for a moment, but soon yielded to Cecilia's power as monarch and stepped forward to take her place on the bed.

"I cannot say," Chora said, her voice little more than the subtlest suggestion of speech.

"I am your Queen. You will do as I command."

"I don't understand why you are doing this."

"What do you mean?"

"You gave me my orders, wrote that I mustn't speak of the matter." Chora seemed to question her own choice of words for a moment, then added, "Even to you."

"What?" Cecilia's knew her emotionless visage had begun to crack but was more concerned with getting as much out of Chora as she could.

"Is this a test, Your Grace?"

"I wrote no such thing."

Chora could only stare back, eyes wide with confusion and some deep terror. Cecilia recalled just how young the Artorian was, wondered if this encounter would leave a scar worse than the one on her face.

The Queen tried her best at being comforting, and placed her hand on the woman's shoulder, forced herself not to take offense when Chora shuddered in response. "You are speaking to me personally now, that supersedes whatever you believe I gave you in writing."

They sat together in silence, until Chora offered the slightest nod.

"Do you still have this missive?"

"No, you—" She stopped, corrected herself. "*Whoever* sent it, they ordered it be destroyed."

It was poor but expected news. Cecilia forced an encouraging smile onto her face. "That's alright. Now, can you tell me exactly what they wanted you to do?"

"It was already organised. I was only the proxy."

"For what?"

"Paying the blood broker and communicating with the assassin."

Cecilia's body chilled as she understood where this was going, but she had to hear it all. "To kill who?"

Chora could no longer meet Cecilia's eyes. "Not just to kill. They wanted Hyde and his home completely destroyed."

Cecilia pulled Chora closer. "Why?"

"I had to take something from Hyde's home. Their deaths, the explosion, it was all a distraction." She took in a deep breath, let it out as some semblance of her Artorian strength returned. "They wanted me to take a key."

Abruptly, Cecilia stood, her eyes immediately turning to the open door. She crossed the room and had it closed and locked before allowing herself to speak again. "Where is this key now?"

Chora's expression turned to disappointment. "I lost it in my fight with the elf."

"It was supposed to be destroyed," Cecilia said, to herself more than the woman before her. Everything had gotten so much worse with only a few words, or in truth, with those few words Cecilia was awakened to how bad her situation already was. The keys resting in the hands of the nobles was poor enough, having any of them possessed by a complete unknown introduced a new slew of horrible outliers.

No. Cecilia took a moment to calm her mind. A person needed five to unlock the cipher, as well as the artefact itself. This changed nothing. If Lyre could still be convinced, they would have the keys destroyed, and the threat would be gone. But what kind of wrinkle would the knowledge of the Hyde key's continued existence be to her plans?

The nobles could not know, Aester Hyde especially. Perhaps after the threat had passed she could hunt down the remainder. But not yet.

"You will accompany me from here on out." Cecilia spoke with authority. "We must uncover who it is behind this insanity. You will help me and I will ensure you remain safe." She opened the door, glancing pointedly toward where Chora still sat on the bed. "Come now, there is work to be done."

The sound of her footsteps were enough to tell Cecilia that her Artorian followed close behind. On top of the missing key was also somebody willing to impersonate their queen, and the fact that they were skilled enough to succeed told Cecilia that this person was either within the palace or easily able to access it. The Artorian were trained to recognise their monarch's handwriting, so to fool one of them, this person must have had access to letters of Cecilia's to study. That fact did nothing to narrow the possibilities; she frequently sent missives across the whole of Duralaans for a variety of necessities. Anyone with access to even one of those could have used it as a base for their forgery. She would have to confront that issue at a later time, however. For the moment it was Lyre she had to face.

Chora followed her closely as they worked their way up to the higher levels of the palace. There were three major spires that towered above the mountain. One housed the throne room, another Cecilia's bedroom, but the third served as her current destination. The Grand Magus had long served the royal family, the current one in particular had actually served three monarchs in his years, drawing on the essence of the Immortal Plane to lengthen his lifespan beyond the confines of mortality.

They found Grand Magus Corwyn awaiting Cecilia in the third spire's highest chamber. The windows were sealed, a single candle serving as the only source of light. Corwyn stood still at the back of the room, an ornate multilayered robe hiding away his frail and weathered skin, his hood pulled so far down that the only hint of his facial features was the long white beard that had grown all the way to the floor.

His fingers twitched and the door slammed shut behind them. "It is time," came his voice, booming within the small room, strengthened by power his frail form did not imply.

Cecilia knew the procedure well enough after running through it six times so far. She stepped into the centre of an intricately designed web of arcane symbols and held aloft the flickering wax candle, as long as it burned she and Lyre would be able to speak.

"You must not enter the circle," Corwyn spat.

Cecilia turned to see Cassidy had stepped forward, quickly ushered her back with a raised palm. The Artorian seemed discomforted by the overall air of the ritual but accepted her place by the wall.

"Proceed," the Grand Magus whispered, evidently trusting Cecilia enough at this point to not run her through every step himself.

She focused on the flickering flame. It was small, weak, and she found it hard to believe the power channelled by it. Then Cecilia closed her eyes. It took only a moment to begin, she simply thought of her target, and when her eyes opened again Carlyle Lyre stood before her.

Lord Lyre cut an imposing figure. No taller than Cecilia was he, yet the man seemed to tower over her, shrouded by a black cloak lined with fur. His chest remained bare, goading Cecilia with the key he openly wore around his neck. "My Queen." He displayed no pleasure in using her title.

"Lord Lyre." Cecilia matched his disinterest. "I trust you are well?"

"Well enough. Business has called me away from home, and I fear the affairs that await me shall try my patience."

Cecilia did not allow herself to be offended. "Then allow me to offer a distraction."

Lyre's eyes narrowed, the first sign of proper emotion from the man. He appeared to Cecilia as though he were standing in the room with her, yet there was something unnatural about the vision despite how real he seemed. Like her mind could sense that something about what her eyes were seeing was entirely wrong.

"For centuries our houses have held a relic. It offers little by way of use to any of us but could prove an incredible symbol if we seize the opportunity before us." Cecilia paused, testing her grounds with Lyre. When he did not interrupt, she took it as encouragement to continue. "I move to have the eight original houses meet here in Avalass so the Artorian Keys may be destroyed together."

Lyre hid his reaction well, a faint twitch of his left eye the only tell that he had not enjoyed her request.

"I understand you all pledged your service to me, but such an affair was necessitated by tradition. We need to find something else to serve as common ground. I believe this will unite us."

"Us?" Lyre spoke up. "Only eight of the houses possess keys, what of the other four?"

Cecilia had considered that point. The other four were newer, and as such could not be bound by destroying items they did not possess. "I will deal with them in due time, but I can only handle each issue as it presents itself."

"What issue might that be?" Lyre laughed, a harsh and clearly forced sound. "We have possessed these relics for centuries, why destroy them now?"

"Our alliance has never been so fragile, long has it been allowed to be withered by time. We require a crucible to reforge our bonds."

"We each gave you our pledge, what makes you believe that is not enough?"

Cecilia considered revealing the root of her fear, decided it was better kept to herself for the time. "A pledge is no more than words. Statements, beliefs, concepts do not define a person. Actions do."

"So early in your reign, and you already ask so much of us."

"I apologise, Lord. I did not realise that key was so important to you."

Lyre's lips twitched upwards as he fought back what seemed to be a genuine smile. "It is of sentimental value, no more."

"Then allow me to have a replacement forged, a gift in return for your sacrifice."

He pursed his lips. Lyre must have thought he was losing the contest of wit. "Forgive me, Your Majesty. I do not trust your reasoning. Why has this thought only occurred to you recently? We were practically all present for your coronation, that would have served as better opportunity for such a demand."

"But you were not present." Cecilia found a lever. "What was it that kept you from attending? I'm sorry, I haven't had to a chance to ask."

"That is quite alright." His voice grew low. "There was an attempt on my life, I feared travelling so soon after."

"That is terrible." Cecilia put no true sympathy into the words. "Odd, is it not? Hyde dead, an attempt on your life, now even Trethellyn fears death comes for him. All the more reason we must stand united. Surely you do not believe we are better separated?"

Lyre did not offer his stance, instead he turned the conversation back toward his own point. "Tell me truth, Cecilia. What sparked this line of thinking? Why do you fear Artorius now?"

And so there was no way around it. No other lord or lady had been so intent on discovering Cecila's reasoning, and she could not risk losing Lyre now, not when he was the last one needed. She took a deep breath, made sure her expression communicated the absolute severity of the situation, and said, "I spoke to the new Lord Hyde almost a week ago. During our conversations he shared with me a prophecy." Cecilia was sure she spied recognition in Lyre's eyes at the mention of that, how odd that superstition would invoke the greatest reaction in him out of all she had said. "A great evil shall soon reawaken in this land. A monster we cannot survive if we do not stand together. I took him to mean that this monster was Artorius, and that if we were to destroy the keys—Artorius' sole means of return—we may conquer both threats at once. We will be united and the Ashen Lord will never be free again."

Silence took them, and Cecilia became conscious of how much the candle had already melted. Less than a quarter of its length remained. Lyre's eyes turned beyond her as he was consumed with thought. "Did this prophet have a name?"

"Not one that Hyde was willing to offer. I only know they met in Deserum."

Lyre's eyes locked in on hers. "Then this prophet may be one I know."

Cecilia's heart jumped. Of all the ideas she had constructed of Lyre, she had never expected him to be enraptured by mysticism. "How so?"

"I was also granted a prophecy, from one similarly born of the Gods' Land. He offered the same warning you have now given me. I believe we have common cause, Your Grace."

Cecilia felt a weight lift, it was working.

"I had business to conduct in Duster, but this is of far greater importance. I shall be in Avalass."

"You have my gratitude, Lord Lyre."

"Not yet. We cannot trust the other houses to do the right thing; you must take this into your own hands if we are to succeed."

And the weight returned. "What do you mean?"

"Destroy the cipher, make the keys of no use."

"I cannot." Cecilia braced herself for the lie she had prepared. "The cipher is beyond our understanding, I fear it cannot be destroyed." Truly, it was not an outright lie—Cecilia did not know whether it could be taken apart or not. But she did know that doing so would go against everything she was trying to accomplish. The Queen robbing her people of the chance to unite and choose of their own accord to stop Artorius' return would be taken solely as a display of tyranny. She needed the nobles to choose the path of unity themselves. Any other course could only be a last resort.

"A shame. Then we must ensure this event goes without any issue whatsoever. We must all be present, but do not allow the others to know the fear we do." Lyre's hand drifted toward his own key, tracing its metal teeth. "Our constitution for terror may be strong, but others will quickly crumble under the weight of what may yet come to pass. I suggest you concoct a secondary reason for this gathering. A banquet, a celebration, something worth their attention. Something that will distract them from the true weight of their decision, lest they turn it to their advantage."

Cecilia scolded herself inwardly that she had not thought to create a cover for the keys' destruction. They had all agreed to it, but without making the night more palatable, they may quickly raise questions once they were actually in attendance. "Yes, I shall see what can be done for it." The candle had almost entirely gone to melted wax. "I appreciate your understanding, Lyre. I am certain that we will emerge from this stronger than ever."

"Yes." His expression became serious once more. "Some of us shall."

As the candlelight gave way to darkness, Lyre vanished.

It was just as jarring as ever to emerge from the spell, and it took her a moment to find Corwyn and Chora in the room with her.

"Well?" Chora asked, the conversation had been heard by Cecilia alone.

"We have much to do." Indeed, they did. All parties would be on their way, but Cecilia thought an official invitation would do well to dull any potential confusion. "Let us speak with Lord Hyde, I believe that it is time he stepped out from the shadows."

Chapter Seventeen

The Same Page

Eric never considered himself one to be consumed by self-pity. Anger, sadness, and the rare hint of joy were feelings he knew well enough. But he tried his best never to direct those feelings inward. They were always for those around him, the ones who affected him and he affected in return. Perhaps that was not the healthiest way to go about life—he suspected it was not a very honest way either—but it had kept him relatively sane.

Whatever walls he had built up to shield himself—from himself—had crumbled the moment Greydeath removed the veil that had long obscured their relationship. Now, as Eric sat alongside the blind pseudo-prophetic child and his begrudged handler, he could only think of himself and what a fool he had been.

In his time as a bounty hunter, Eric had convinced himself he was pursuing a somewhat noble cause. The people whose lives he took were utter scum, surely deserving the fate that he forced upon them. The world was entirely bettered by the removal of such folk. But what had his actions actually yielded? What mark had his black hand left upon Duralaans? Sure, he had not known all he did had been in service to the underlord of Harbinger's Rest, but he had done his bidding all the same.

"Everyone's choices are dictated by something." The boy, whose name Eric had come to learn was Oedon, had been attempting to explain just how he knew where and when to find him. It had entailed a confusing string of metaphors but ultimately had been a nice distraction from their lengthy ride in the cart. "So-called choice is better described as reaction. From the moment we are born we are already conscripted to the will of a thousand others who came before us."

Eric had made the mistake of being curious, and the boy used it as an excuse to lecture him on the nature of causality and fate. He did not begrudge Oedon for being so enamoured by the concept, but it hit upsettingly close to home.

If the sum total of his life was decided by the scars others had left on him, then that left Eric in a terrible place. He was no more than Greydeath's weapon, something he could point and shoot at will, while keeping his own hands—*relatively*—clean. Eric did not want to believe that, but it forced into mind other memories, all that seemed to point him toward a similar conclusion. Raph had placed him on this path, impressed upon him the ability to heal his own wounds by healing others first, and for a time he thought it was working. But even at the pinnacle of his good deeds, Larina had torn him down with only a few words. Eric's mother had died, and he tried to become a hero. Eric's father and sister were murdered, thus he became Greydeath's pawn.

The most horrifying part was that it made some semblance of sense, and it terrified Eric that it almost made him feel better. If a person was entirely defined by the events forced upon them, then they could excuse all manner of cruelty, blame every insidious act on their upbringing, or a misdeed done to them. That was not too far from what Eric had done. He happily garbed himself in the scars, forged a new name to represent what he would become, and never once looked inward.

"Then what makes any of it worthwhile?" Eric interrupted Oedon's current monologue.

If the boy was offended, he did not show it. "A tree does not know that it was planted solely to be cut down. I explained myself to you because you asked, but you'll enjoy life more if you forget my words."

Eric frowned. "And what about you?" He had been only a few years older than Oedon when his own life had taken a dark turn. It upset him to know he was not alone.

"I am no tree." Oedon smiled. Something of humour behind the expression, as though he was referencing a joke Eric did not know the punchline to.

Eric's hand picked at the seams in his prosthetic. "Will Raph at least be alright, or is she still invisible to you?"

Oedon's crystalline eyes, somewhat obscured by his hair, seemed to bore through Eric, even as he presumed the boy could not actually see with them. "I can see her again."

"And?"

"Don't concern yourself with it. I've already said too much."

Never had Eric genuinely considered screaming at a child—that was no longer true. "Are all prophets this obtuse?"

Oedon shrugged, not a denial as far as Eric could tell.

"Quiet up now, fellas," Elias called back at them. "You won't be getting a repeat of Harbinger's, Blackhand."

"Greydeath had it coming."

Elias chortled, much to Eric's surprise. "That we can agree on, but there's a time and place for grand displays. This ain't one of them."

Eric allowed himself to focus on the town as it took up their surroundings. It was small, little more than a single wide street that looped around and back on itself, both sides of which were lined with buildings of all manner. It seemed the part they had entered into had a focus on the employed; a few small stores for general needs, a place for medicinal requirements, and what appeared to be a blacksmith's forge. The layout reminded Eric of Spirallos more than anything else, though that city had more layers to its circling districts.

He wondered if Duster possessed anything like Raph's store of antiques and oddities. Perhaps he could find a way to convince his captor to let him buy her a gift before they were through.

The years since Haevahn and Vécar had allowed Eric the time to mull over his feelings on all that had happened. He might have hoped to speak with her about it all at some point but was ashamed of the way he had allowed it all to break out of him in a single moment of passion. Raph was right, however; he did not know what person she had become over the course of that decade—she might not even enjoy odd trinkets anymore. Eric cursed himself for not asking, though there remained every chance she would not have answered if he had.

"What's going on here?" Elias muttered, suspicion icing his words.

Eric wasn't sure what concerned him. Nothing ahead or behind them stood out as odd, there were few people traversing the street, and many of the stores seemed closed for the day. Then Eric realised that was exactly what gave Elias reason for fear.

The sun remained high above them, it could not have been more than a few hours into the beginning of noon, yet the town was quiet as it would be if they were deep into the night. Even then Eric would have expected to catch a few folk wandering—likely in a drunken stupor, but still present.

Oedon's eyes remained affixed to Eric, but he spoke as though he could see the same troubling sight as them. "They knew we were coming."

"That's no reason to hide away like this," Eric said.

"That depends on what they were told."

Elias let a low rumble escape his mouth, a groan of utter annoyance. "Should've known Lyre wouldn't keep it simple; of course he has to make a fuss of everything."

Eric could only guess at what Lyre could achieve from imposing such a curfew on the townsfolk. If he wanted people off the street, it meant that he either aimed to keep them out of harm's way or hoped to keep something out of their sight. Either possibility did nothing to make Eric feel better about the situation.

Elias drove the cart toward the outer side of the street, came to a quick stop outside of what appeared to be an old tavern.

"Really?" Eric had not taken Elias as the type to drink on the job.

"You can wait out here if you want. Oedon can tell me if you try to run." He stepped down from the cart, took a moment to stretch his aging muscles.

Eric cast a glance behind them, the sight of an elderly woman watching through shuttered windows disturbed him. "I could do with a drink."

They entered the tavern, not at all surprised to find it as hauntingly quiet as the rest of the town. Oedon quickly directed Eric toward a table, one kept distant from any of the establishment's windows. Eric watched as Elias helped himself to the rack of colourful bottles behind the bar, taking a few glasses in one hand and the fullest bottle available in the other. He came to join them at the table, placing a glass before each of them—before quickly redirecting Oedon's toward himself.

All three glasses were filled with dark liquid, almost pitch black if not for what Eric thought to be a hint of blue within. The specks of colour seemed to appear and dissipate in short bursts, not a beverage Eric had ever held the privilege of enjoying. Elias threw back his first glass, then the second, finishing his display by taking in and letting out a rasp of air. He seemed to consider it for a moment more, then filled both glasses again.

Eric sipped at his own. "Didn't realise it was that kind of occasion."

"I saw nothing you didn't."

"Is it that bad?"

Elias finished his third glass, reacting less dramatically than the first time. "You don't clear out a town like that for no small reason. He's expecting trouble, I'll do the same."

"Aren't you just going to hand me over?"

"That was the plan, but men like Lyre don't often take to being given ultimatums."

"Then why risk giving him one?" Eric had tried to have Elias explain his reasoning along the journey but had been shut down each time. His greatest hope was that Elias' thirst had also loosened his lips.

"Because Lyre's asking for everything and giving me nothing." He downed his fourth drink, reached for another refill, pulled his hand back. "I took this job because it was simple; catch a troublesome youth kicking up too much muck, get paid, move on. Then suddenly it's complicated." He threw his hands up to articulate his exasperation. "And complicated is something I can deal with, I've done it before, and I'll do it again. But I need to know everything if there's any hope of it working out, and if I don't, then we get situations like this."

"If it's any consolation, it wasn't entirely *my* plan that got the better of you."

Elias cocked an eyebrow. "How so?"

"I got a letter, unsigned, no clue to who sent it. But it told me about Raph—my friend—and where she was. It even told me about you, told me your weaknesses and how to use them to my advantage."

Elias' eyes narrowed, not entirely convinced, but clearly disturbed. "And those weaknesses are?"

"It said you often get lost in the weeds of overthinking a thing. That you were the kind of person to get so focused on your own conclusion that you fail to see the bigger picture."

"Well I guess they weren't wrong. But in this job that's just what you got to do. I take what I have and use it as well as I can, there's no good to come from worrying about what I don't. The problem there is when those I'm trying to do a service keep things from me that would otherwise allow me to do better."

"You can't expect everyone to be entirely honest with you."

"In this job? Yes, I can. In fact, I have to, because I cannot let unknown factors cloud my judgement. Lyre keeping the detail that your friend was locked away in his cellar to himself meant that I couldn't figure out your motives. I still don't even know why he wants this girl, or where she could be going, because apparently the little prophet's powers are selective." He smiled sardonically at Oedon.

"I know where she's going." The boy chimed in quietly.

Elias' head snapped toward him. "Where?"

Oedon shook his head. "It matters little at this moment. If I told you, would it change your current course?"

Elias barked a laugh and sat back in his seat. He seemed on the verge of a breakdown, as though the fixtures that upheld his worldview were on the brink of crumbling to dust.

An idea came to Eric, a way to rebuild those fixtures. "I can tell you what our goal was."

Elias didn't even humour Eric with his gaze. "Why's that?"

"Because we might not be enemies at all. If you understood, if you saw the big picture then we might be able to stop this together."

That earned his eyes, dark and weary as they were. "Stop what?"

Eric had not even the chance to open his mouth before Oedon spoke up. "Lyre is not trying to resurrect Artorius."

Elias looked back and forth between the two of them, more vexed than surprised. "When did we start talking about folktales?"

"Raph was told that he was going to return, that Lyre was trying to find him and bring him back," Eric tried to explain, all while he was still knocked off kilter by what Oedon had said. If he did not believe the kid had some arcane form of prescience before, he was certainly coming around to it.

"Lyre is trying to find the Ashen Lord, yes. However, he does not want him to return."

"He tortured Raph for weeks!" Eric practically screamed.

"I did not say he was a good man."

"Woah there, let's slow down." Elias leaned forward, flattened his hands on the table. "Even if Lyre did want to bring this fella back, it's not like he could."

Neither Oedon nor Eric spoke.

"Right?" He pressed, a new edge to his tone. "Oedon?"

"No, *Lyre* will not succeed."

"Good, no problem then."

Eric grasped Oedon's shoulder and forced him to meet his eyes. "Don't think I didn't hear that. Why'd you specify Lyre?"

Oedon shrugged, eyes widened, like he was trying to play up his youthful ignorance. "Is he not the man we are discussing currently?"

Eric's jaw clenched, forcing back the rising chill in his heart.

"Oedon," Elias growled. "What do you see?"

The boy said nothing, and as such said everything he needed to. Raph was going to fail.

Eric shot to his feet, knocking his chair to the floor with the abrupt motion. He began to creep back. His breaths were coming too quick. Too short. Yet with each one he felt time slipping away.

"Sit down, we're not done," Elias spoke, not at all carrying any of the panic Eric felt himself.

"The world is about to end!" Eric could not be there. He had to find Raph. Had to fix this.

"And you're not gonna stop that."

Eric could only stare back at Elias; had to use all the remaining sanity he held not to scream and sprint out of that tavern.

"You're Eric Blackhand. You hunt murderers, and rapists, and whoever else you're paid to knock off. Our kind don't stop legendary villains of the apocalypse, we just survive."

"*We?*" The word was like poison on his tongue. "We are not the same, Elias. You . . . you just . . ." Eric searched for a point of difference that set them apart. Found none that did not make him feel like he was lying to himself. "And I . . . I'm . . ." No words came to him, and he fell back, luckily catching himself on the bar instead of collapsing to the hardwood floor.

Elias seemed almost apologetic; Eric only wanted to throw up for it. "No, we aren't the same. But this is above you. Let your friend handle it, and face the fact you're about to have enough on your own plate."

Eric was not surprised. Not disappointed either. He was not sure how he felt. "You're still handing me over?"

"I'm a professional, Eric. I won't be the one to betray this deal. They're paying me to hand you over, and that's what I'll do. They can expect trouble; doesn't mean I have to give it to them."

Eric pushed himself off the bar, finding his feet steadier as his mind worked. "And after that?"

"Job's done. I'll hunt down your friend—if they give me what I need to know, that is."

"And if they don't?"

Elias huffed. "Don't know. Find new work, I guess. Hope the world doesn't end before that."

"What if I paid you?" Eric was not sure where he was going with this new idea, had to only hope he would discover it as he spoke.

"For?"

"Your sword." Eric approached the table again, pressing his hands to the wood and leaning in. "You'd do it, right? As a professional?"

Elias stroked his beard, seemingly unconvinced. "I searched your bag; you don't have money."

"I left it all in Harbinger's Rest."

"I'm just supposed to trust that?" He clucked his tongue, like he was chiding a naïve child. "I'm not so old and my mind's not so gone that I'll be falling for that anytime soon."

"Oedon, will I pay him?" Neither of them turned to look at the prophet, but Elias smiled.

It was a shrill and disconcerting sound, but Oedon actually laughed. "Yes, he will."

Elias sat back, whistled. "Well then, what's the job?"

—

Elias Sorren hated so much of his time working to complete Lyre's demands. He was beginning to realise that may in part have been due to just how much waiting it had entailed. It was not until the sun was beginning to set that he finally spied a single carriage making its way through the streets of Duster.

Elias waved them over. It seemed odd that Lyre had not travelled with a larger escort. He was sure the carriage was packed with enough swords to put up a decent enough fight, but not enough for someone of his rank. Elias' hand fell to his pommel, they had planned out the series of events that would follow to a distinct point, he only needed to ensure nothing went wrong from there.

As the carriage came to a stop, there was a long moment of stillness. Elias could not see through the windows and could only guess at what reason Lyre had to delay. After Elias had been made to wait for frustratingly long enough, a banging came from within. The driver descended from his seat and made his way over to the door, addressing Elias in no way during the process. He drew open the door and stood back.

First came a lightly armoured man, metal covering his upper body and a few parts of his legs, but leaving various points open for mobility. It made a point of how skilled the man believed himself to be that he did not fear another blade's bite. He stood a short distance from Elias, swivelling his hairless head from side to side as he took in the locale. He coughed loudly and two more figures joined him, gruff-looking men without any piece of plate, but appearing far more impressive than those that Elias had originally been given as his own backup.

"They in there?" The leader took a step toward the tavern.

Elias took his own step to block the man. "It's Elias, and you are?"

"I know who you are."

And Elias thought he knew the armoured man as well. "Aron?" He was Lyre's captain, one of the guards who had been sent out from the throne room when Elias went to speak with the lord. Elias could not spot anybody else inside the carriage. "Where's Lyre?"

"Lord Lyre has been called to the capital so he may fulfill his lordly duties. I am handling the exchange." Aron seemed entirely disinterested in conversing with Elias. "Are they inside?"

Lyre being present was not integral to their plan, but it certainly made things more difficult without him. "Sure, got Blackhand safe and sound."

"And the girl?"

"No girl."

Aron's expression darkened. "Why not?"

"Blackhand was the target, girl was extra. I'll be happy to handle her next, but I'll need some questions answered first."

"I'm not here to answer to you."

"Then there's just no way I can find her. I'm not a god, just pretty good at figuring people out."

"Lord Lyre left you his prophet, even with him you failed?" Aron scoffed. "You can forget it, then. You're done."

Almost there. "All due respect, I'm supposed to deliver the guy straight to Lyre. If you'd tell me where he is, I'll finish the job myself."

"You're *done*," Aron repeated with a snarl, snapping his fingers and directing his men into the tavern.

Elias backed up, unsheathed his curved blade. "Not yet." He flinched none as the three took their own weapons in hand and Aron's eyes ignited with bloodlust. "You owe me something."

They stared each other down for a protracted few breaths, then Aron threw a small pouch Elias' way. "You have Lyre's thanks, Sorren."

Elias caught his pay, could feel it was even lighter than the original sum. He returned his sword to its sheath as the two entered the tavern, leaving Elias and Aron alone. "What does Lyre want from them?"

Aron did not respond.

"So much secrecy." Elias chuckled, forcing as much humour into his next words as possible. "He trying to kill a god or something?"

There was flicker of recognition, miniscule, but enough to tell Elias what he needed to know. He still found it hard to believe the Ash King of legend could be brought back after centuries spent being no more than a lesson of history. But Oedon had shown he could be trusted from time to time, and who was Elias to turn down good work and pay?

The doors swung open, and the men ushered Blackhand out. Oedon followed close behind but cut off to stand with Elias.

Oedon took a glance to make sure Lyre's men were distracted getting Blackhand bound and into the carriage, then said, "I told you he wouldn't be here."

"Yes, you're very clever."

"Plan B, then?" The boy kept on topic, but Elias could tell he was forcing himself not to smile at the compliment. He wondered if most simply took his abilities for granted. Given the trauma that had surrounded the way he'd gained them, Elias could see how that might hurt. If Lyre was so willing to just hand Oedon over to Elias, he clearly didn't respect him well enough as a person who had suffered greatly to be what he was.

"Yeah. Good luck." Elias removed the compass from his belt and took Oedon's hand, the way his grasp almost completely engulfed the boy's served as another reminder of just how young he was. It shouldn't matter what he could see or whether he could actually defend himself, no child deserved the life he led. Elias wanted to ask Oedon if he would be able to complete his job for Blackhand but knew better than to waste his breath on such things.

Oedon examined the compass as he joined Blackhand in the carriage. The captive was watching Elias, clearly not convinced yet that he would see through their agreement.

Elias came as close as he could before Aron stopped him. "Hey, Blackhand. I know why I couldn't figure you out."

A gag had been forced into his mouth, only his raised brows could tell Elias to continue.

"You're not just one guy." Of course, he meant that figuratively, for Elias had seen a disconnect between the man he had hunted and the man he had actually captured. "There's who you are: the killer bounty hunter with the black hand. Then there's who you want to be. I don't know him, but that's the man who broke into a lord's fortress to save a friend. All the same, I found the latter by following the former. That means they're both you, lad."

Aron gave him a dirty look. "When did you two get so close?"

"Know your enemy and all that." Elias shrugged and set off back toward the bar, let him wonder what they were planning, he wouldn't understand until it was too late.

Elias had a fifth and final drink as he listened to the carriage set off. He thought he did not like Blackhand, the arrogant hunter he had originally been tasked with bringing to justice reminded him too much of himself, and the world needed no more of that. But the man of hope he'd seen hints of, the one who thought he could stop the return of the land's greatest evil by himself, was what Elias wished he saw more of. His gut was telling him that he was being foolish. Blackhand chose what life he would live, and he would not stray from it.

That reminded Elias of his brother. The man ran away for a lie that called itself love and died for it. Elias had warned him, but Cleo just wouldn't listen, and for years he could not decide who to blame. Elias knew now that the fault was his. There was more he could have done. More than simply accept that Cleo was a good man in a cruel world. He could no longer protect that particular good man, but there were more good people that needed help, that could be kept on the right path.

Elias felt a strange sensation come over him, like an invisible thread had attached itself to his soul and was tugging him toward a particular destination. Oedon had activated the compass.

He collected Blackhand's supplies and exited the tavern. If Lyre would not come to them, they would go to him. Elias had no doubt that Aron would bring his captive straight to the lord rather than wait back at his fortress, and Oedon had done them the service of confirming the theory.

It was time to get back to work, he would not be blessed with a proper reprieve between jobs.

Elias decided that was for the best.

Chapter Eighteen

Sunset

Domina had arrived too late.

He passed through the boundary into Meergard and was instantly hit by the deathly quiet that emanated throughout, accompanied by the distinct scent of salt. It was like the city itself was holding its breath, unable to believe whatever had threatened them was truly gone, and only waiting for the next wave to strike.

Despite such dire sensations, the district he entered into appeared entirely undamaged. It was only further down the high coastline that Meergard had been built atop that he could see the ruins of homes, shipping vessels, and the docks they once took as port. Dark specks shifted among the wreckage, people doing what they could to piece their lives back together as soon as possible, rising above the threat of further destruction or perhaps simply ignoring the possibility.

Domina rode a horse he had hired from Haval through the streets, keeping an eye out for anyone who could point him toward Trethellyn's abode. He could only hope the lord had been spared the worst of whatever had transpired and that Domina's warning had given him the extra time he needed to stay out of danger's path.

It appeared as though something had come from the sea, thrashing whatever it could from the waters, but unable to make way onto the land. Domina had little experience with the creatures of the sea, and he shuddered to imagine just what could cause such disaster as that which he saw below.

He rode down one of the city's descending roads, leading his mount through and past each level of Meergard's streets. The scent of salt only grew as he neared the docks, coming to be accompanied by the pungent odour of smoke and blood.

"Hey, you!" A man's shout called Domina's attention to where he kneeled beside an elderly woman, a chunk of stone fallen on her leg. "Give us a hand!"

Domina dropped to his feet and was swiftly on the other side of the stone, hand gripping its underside as they lifted it high enough that another could drag her out.

"Alright. Thanks, fella." He offered Domina a pat on his left arm, stopping as he realised that was not something Domina possessed.

"What happened here?" Domina cast his eyes over the surroundings, wounded were sprawled about, alongside a few shapes covered in red-stained sheets.

The man gestured toward the docks, a point where the devastation appeared most focused. "Damn squid came out of nowhere, like nothing I've ever seen."

"A squid could do this?"

"You have no clue. Big as a ship, I tell you."

"Was it slain?"

He shook his head. "Nah, just slinked back to wherever it came from."

"I see." Then Domina suspected it was not at all finished. A sea beast was a step up from the fiery end the Hydes had met, but only added to his theory that spectacle was a part of the client's goals. They wanted for people to watch as their leaders were killed, unable to stave off even the most dramatic of ends. He also saw a suitable theme forming; fire to kill Hyde and water to prove the bane of Trethellyn. Uncovering just who would have such resources and contacts to set up such affairs would be difficult, Domina could understand why the client's chosen blood broker had come to fear them. "Do you have any idea where I might find Lord Trethellyn?"

"That old bastard?" The man was taken aback. "Doing whatever he can to forget about us and focus on his new favourite mage would be my guess."

Domina drew closer, urging the man to offer explanation.

"Some magic fella showed up while the squid was making a mess of us. Must have done quite the number on the thing because it was after that when it ran off."

That seemed exceedingly lucky. Though Domina was glad somebody had been there to protect the city when he failed to, it all seemed too simple. It was possible the attack was completely disconnected from the assassin he was hunting, which meant he could not stop his search now or the beast truly was a part of the conspiracy and likely would not give up so soon. Either way, Domina's work was not done. He needed to find Trethellyn.

Domina left the man to help others and strode through the ruined street, keeping an eye out for anyone that may have held some form of authority in the city. The sheer lack of any protectors among the injured populace was cause for concern. He did not know whether it would be worse if the reason was that many of the guard had been killed in the attack or that they simply did not take the aid of their people seriously. Domina had undoubtedly scared Trethellyn with his warning, he just hoped it didn't come at the cost of the citizenry's own safety.

"You the Black Rose?" a gruff voice asked from behind him.

Domina found a man coated in dust eyeing him. "I am."

"Lord Trethellyn told us to look out for you." He gestured to the ruins around them. "You're a touch late, but he still wants to speak with you. If you'll follow me?"

"Of course." Domina returned to his horse and followed who he took to be one of Trethellyn's swordsmen back up through the city.

They engaged in no conversation along the way, though his escort seemed to relax more as they moved further from the disaster zone. Soon enough they arrived before a large building of sand-coloured wood, about as wide as five of the regular houses Domina had seen throughout and two storeys in height. Besides its size, it was not a particularly elegant building, Trethellyn and his family must not have found it especially necessary to flaunt their wealth in excess. Domina did not care one way or another, what mattered more was how they used their wealth in relation to the people who relied on them, not the way they chose to present themselves at a glance.

Domina dismounted his horse and allowed the beast to be taken around to the nearby stables while his own escort led him inside the manor. Where Hyde's abode had been dark, moody, and drenched in the perpetuating state of drama, Trethellyn's home was the complete opposite. Brightly lit, the walls were lined with colourful banners Domina could only presume belonged to various seafarers the noble family had treated with. There was only one he recognised, an old family sigil that once belonged to the elven Forkh lineage. It invited unfortunate memories of his; Vécar Forkh was a dark shadow that hung over many points of Domina's life, but that was no more than his past. While it still hurt to think about those failures, he had to believe that as long as breath remained in his lungs he could forge something new for the days that awaited.

"Just this way, Black Rose." The swordsman sent him toward an open doorway to his right.

Domina could hear quiet chatter from that direction, surprisingly lively given the present circumstance. "Please, it's Domina."

"All the same, Lord Trethellyn awaits."

Domina entered the neighbouring room to find Trethellyn engaged in conversation with a man well and truly younger than him.

The door was shut quietly, but the motion was enough to call the lord's attention toward Domina's presence. "It is good to meet you in person, my lord. I am called Domina."

Shakily, Trethellyn came to stand. He was an aged man, frail form kept hidden by a bright blue tunic and large cloak of red fur. His mouth spread wide in a smile. "So you were real."

"I apologise for my means of communication; I would have taken a less dramatic approach if I had the choice."

"Well I remain glad for it. I was supposed to be greeting an ambassador at the docks just this morning, if not for your warning, I very well could have been among the casualties."

Domina allowed that to sink in. "Then your assassin knew your schedule?"

"I fear as much." He placed a hand on the younger man seated beside him. "Thankfully, Cortlan was passing through at the right moment. Our Mother and Father may not always treat us kindly, but their blessings come through when we need them most."

The man appeared somewhere in his third decade of life. His hair was a light red and his skin was tanned by years being kissed by the sun, but his attire appeared of the most interest to Domina. Cortlan wore a light grey tunic, decorated by shimmering specks of dark fabric that grew more prominent the closer they came to his shoulders. A golden cape was wrapped around his neck, adding to the overall appearance of dark opulence—this man was no ordinary mage, did not wear the telltale robes of any particular order, and seemed more akin to some pompous adventurer than a practitioner of the arcane arts.

"Fortunate as we were, I believe all is not yet done." Cortlan deftly passed a small glass orb between his fingers. "The kraken was not felled. I'm sure it will return once it has licked its wounds."

Trethellyn appeared far less concerned than he did when Domina had appeared before him in the night, confidence forged anew by his triumph over death. "I am sure it will pose no more of a threat a second time than it did the first, especially now that our Black Rose is here. I am correct that you are a warrior?"

"I am." Domina clutched Anamrath's hilt. He could see Cortlan force himself not to stare at the weapon. The mage must have been able to recognise its arcane strength, for he surely could not know the weapon itself. "Do you have any idea who could have set this creature upon you?"

Trethellyn opened his mouth to speak but was cut off by Cortlan. "I suspect one of the shipping vessels lured it toward port. Perhaps the crew did this wittingly. Perhaps not. But somebody must have left bait of a sort on the ship. Of course, this all means the ship in question would have been destroyed in the attack and we cannot discover which crew we should look further into."

"Apologies, but that sounds like a lot of supposition." Domina thought the theory was plausible but did not feel comfortable trusting it without solid truths to ground it. "My lord, do you have any reason to believe somebody may want you dead?"

"None at all. I may have my share of detractors, but to invite such lengths to bring about my demise, I cannot fathom the reason for it."

Domina did not take that as objective fact. It was possible the lord was simply ignorant to the true way his people thought of him. Domina would have to ensure he did his own research when he had the chance. "Then I suggest we focus on stopping the current threat. With this kraken eliminated, we might be able to draw out our foe, force them to do something foolish."

Domina waited for Trethellyn's take on the plan, but the lord's attention seemed completely snared by the sight of something that clung to Domina's belt.

"How did you get that?"

Domina found it was the key that he was interested in, the one he had accidentally removed from Chora's person. "A foe of mine lost it during combat. I mean to return it if given the chance."

Trethellyn glanced toward Cortlan, the mage appearing similarly taken by the key. "If I am not mistaken, that is no ordinary item."

The lord hummed in agreement. "You said you were present for Lord Hyde's demise, correct?"

"I was." Domina did not like the shift in the conversation's tone. "I'll need you to explain exactly what you're thinking."

Cortlan offered an answer, "That relic is one of eight very special keys. They were forged long ago, the only means of freeing the Ashen King Artorius after he was sealed away."

Domina coughed, finding it hard to believe the thing he had found in the dirt could be so important. Stranger still was the fact that the Artorian had it in her possession to begin with. "I don't suppose Hyde had one such key?"

"All of us do; the descendants of the lords who fought back during the Ashen Night," Trethellyn explained, he was trying his best to maintain a light tone, but he was clearly growing concerned.

Chora had been present at Hyde's fateful evening, Domina was sure of it. So for her to have such an important historical relic, she could only have taken it from the one who held it prior.

Cortlan had risen to his feet, the glass orb now gripped between his thumb and forefinger. "I take it you understand how this appears to us."

Of course he did, the same role in the death of Hyde that Domina now suspected Chora had played. "I did not warn you, Trethellyn, as part of any larger scheme. I was in Haval when I contacted you, and I have spent the days since journeying here. If I were to kill you, I would do it right now." He took his hilt in hand and threw it to the table with a loud clatter.

The mage appeared no less concerned, but Trethellyn eased back into his chair. "You say you took this key from someone?"

"Yes, a woman claiming to be of the Artorian Guard. Chora."

"I do not know the name, but if she was telling the truth then we have much reason for concern." His eyes went distant as his voice trailed off. "The Queen has invited me to Avalass, she asks that I bring my own key so it may be destroyed."

"That cannot be a coincidence." Cortlan's stance became less hostile, but he remained on his feet, body positioned so that he could spring into action at a moment's notice. "Though perhaps this is not a conversation we should be having."

"I cannot help it if that is the direction this trail leads."

Domina allowed them to discuss their fears without his interruption, he did not know enough about Duralaans' current monarch to add anything of value. Though he did not discount the fact that the monarch or simply somebody within the royal house would fit into the description of the client he was slowly piecing together. But Chora was just a part of the greater picture. She was not the assassin in Anderan and likely was not the one who summoned the kraken in Meergard either. But she had her part to play, had taken the key from Hyde's manor *herself*.

"Where do you keep your key?" Domina spoke up.

Trethellyn bristled at the question but quickly gave in to reason. "My family has never been particularly enamoured with the thing, I suppose it is somewhere within the loft."

"Then I believe that is our enemy's true target. When next the beast attacks, they will try to claim it during the chaos."

"Are you suggesting we do nothing but wait for it to strike?" Cortlan asked.

"Not if you have a better suggestion."

Trethellyn looked to the mage, eager for a solution. Cortlan snapped his fingers, and a key appeared midair, dropped to the table with a hefty *THUD*. "At the very least we use a decoy."

"What is that?" Trethellyn leaned forward to get a better look at the item. It appeared perfectly identical to Domina's own, but when Trethellyn tried to grasp it, he found that it only passed through his hand.

"It is but an illusion, you both saw its creation and thus know it to be false. That is why you cannot hold it. But our foe will not know so much, it will be a good lure while we have the real key removed.”

Domina reclaimed his hilt. “I've had no experience with krakens; do we have any estimate how long we have before it strikes again?”

“They are hardy creatures,” Trethellyn offered in answer. “If it means to finish us, it should return soon.

“Then I suggest you return to your safehouse.”

“I should first swap the real key for mine, but then I will accompany you, my lord. I will make sure nobody recognises you,” Cortlan suggested, helping Trethellyn back to his feet.

“Is there a limit to what you can do?” Domina asked.

Cortlan offered him a look of uncertainty. “There are limits, what do you have in mind?”

“Make it appear that I accompany you to the safehouse. That way our foe has no reason to believe somebody might be waiting for them.”

The three stood silent for a moment, as Domina allowed his new plan to solidify within his mind. It relied heavily on the assumption and hope that they had read their enemy correctly, otherwise Domina would be wasting time he could be utilising to face the attacking beast. But they did not have time to consider failure, let that come if it must, Domina would not let his fear of it hold him back. He clutched Anamrath in his hand and allowed the dark blade to ignite. Domina came to realise he had one aspect in common with his weapon—failure had starved him. It was time to feast.

—

It was a terribly cramped ride. On either side of Eric sat one of Lyre's men, with their leading man staring back from directly across the small carriage, and another armed guard to the plated man's right. Oedon sat to the leader's left, offering Eric no comfort as his crystalline eyes seemed to examine every inch of the interior that his captive self did not occupy.

Not one of the six attempted to speak along the way, truly there was no need for it, and Eric was not usually disturbed by extended periods of quiet. But he found himself currently growing impatient, anxious to know what fate had in store for him. Oedon's composure should have offered some comfort, if only the boy showing any hint of emotion was not a rarity of its own. Eric decided that was, in fact, a good sign—let his concern only mount in the event that the prophet suddenly found himself taken by surprise.

Eric tried to turn his thoughts toward the external; if Elias had not deceived them, he would currently be tracking their cart from a distance, though it would prove a while more before he could actually act. There was at least something soothing in believing there were greater forces acting in one's own benefit, even if those forces were little more than an aged mercenary with a satchel of Eric's finest devices in tow. It also helped to ease the feeling that had been gnawing at his subconscious since leaving Duster: that Eric was very much yielding to his enemy, giving into the cowardly whispering in his mind. But such thoughts were rooted in a path Eric no longer followed.

Now that he understood himself better, Eric would be the only one choosing the targets he hunted. No more bounties. No more gold. Just the delivery of what was owed.

"What's the smile for?" the lead guard grumbled, eyes narrowing as he stared Eric in the face.

Eric had not realised he was smiling—or that the man opposite could tell what his lips were doing behind the gag. He only shrugged in response, putting on the blasé performance he understood had become a staple characteristic of the idea that was Eric Blackhand. While his time with Raph had allowed for a momentary resurrection of the boy he had once been, that was not who these men had come to collect. Sometimes things were easier when you gave people precisely what they expected. Less painful too.

"You'll die tonight, Blackhand," the lead guard said, bolstered by the fact that Eric could not retort properly. "Smile if you want, it won't do you any good."

Eric began to lean forward, testing the limits of his escort with every inch he took, while his eyes remained locked to those of the plated man. A gesture from their commander's hand, and the men to either side of Eric tore him back against the wooden boarding behind him. The guards chuckled. Eric joined them. They had not realised his hand was now missing, its disconnection and fall to the floor gone unheard alongside the sound of Eric's head smacking the boards behind him.

With his bindings now useless, Eric seized the opportunity to take the blade from the laughing fellow to his right and bring the sharp end to kiss the throat of the guard's leader. Too stupid—or too arrogant—to consider the consequence, the two guards who still possessed weapons and did not have a blade at their throat brought their steel to bear, and suddenly the carriage seemed even more cramped.

"HOLD!" the armoured swordsman screamed.

Eric tried to speak, yet his voice came as little more than annoyed and muffled groans.

"Get that thing off him!" the leader demanded, and the disarmed man to his right carefully loosened the gag enough that Eric could spit it out. "You're a right fool, Blackhand. Or maybe just suicidal, is that it?"

Eric made a show of slowly examining each man and their weapon. His smile was gone, replaced with what he hoped would be interpreted as boredom. "I've survived worse."

"None of that arrogance will save you here, boy. You just died." A gurgled sputter of air and bodily fluid punctuated the end of his statement. A small dagger of some iridescent crystal had been thrust into his forehead, Oedon's hand gripping the hilt. The moment the boy released it, the weapon exploded into shards of the rock, puncturing the throats of the three remaining guards, and spraying blood throughout the interior. There were four bodies slumped within that carriage once the choked cries and gasps for air that would not come had dwindled.

"I wish you'd told me you were going to do that." Eric reattached his hand, taking care to fasten it properly.

Oedon cautiously extended a finger to make sure the armoured man's corpse did not fall his way. "What did you hope would be achieved with your little escape?"

"Had to make it look good, right? I'm sure there'd be a few questions if I actually came quietly." Everywhere he looked, there were lifeless eyes staring back at him, the fear of those final moments frozen in their gaze. "But this was a step further than I'd planned."

"There will be less for you and Sorren to kill later." Oedon spoke with the same casual disinterest Eric wore as a mask, and he tried to tell himself Oedon acted much the same, even as it felt more likely that this was no façade. "Kill now. Kill later. There is no difference."

Still, Eric could not shake the mewling within him that was horrified by the sight, even though he had enacted far worse in his own time. Something was awake in him that had not been there for some time, and he could not be sure whether it would do him good or ill.

Oedon snapped his fingers, summoning Eric's attention toward him again. The boy was smiling, a genuine appearance of comfort. "It had to be this way, Whitsin. You know this."

Eric wanted to argue, but who was he to debate with one who could see everything? He forced himself to remember the choice he had made.

No matter how much good Nath Whitsin achieved, it was all to fill a void within himself. A void that could never be filled. Eric Blackhand was simpler. He killed those he deemed deserving, and he did not fool himself into thinking that was for a noble cause. As nostalgic as it may have been to play the hero with his old friend once more, he would not progress without accepting the man he had been forged into. To fight that truth would be to fight himself, and there were true evils that needed to be dealt with first.

The carriage continued on, the sun nearly set completely. Lyre would likely be taking time to rest through the night, and that was when they would catch up to him.

It would not be a simple task, relying largely on taking Lyre by surprise. Though, with Oedon's information, they would be well prepared for whatever challenge their enemy posed. It would be enough because it had to be. This was the only way Eric was capable of aiding his friend—even from so far away.

Raph may have been set upon stopping threats as grandiose as Artorius' return, but Eric would have to settle on ensuring that Carlyle Lyre did not live to see another sunrise.

—

Domina immersed himself in the darkness of the unlit mansion, his cloak wrapped tight around his body. He did not consider himself a particularly stealth-inclined individual, but he knew how to disappear when he needed to.

Night had fallen hours prior. So far there had been no hint of the kraken's return—Domina supposed he should be somewhat gladdened by that fact, yet with every second that ticked by, he found himself questioning his own plan. He had to remind himself that this was not a spur of the moment decision like his attempt to protect Hyde. Cortlan was keeping Trethellyn safe, if somebody made an attempt on his life, the mage would be able to handle whatever they would try. It was a waiting game, but they were prepared. That would have to be enough.

It was better to not consider what it would mean if Chora, or whoever else was embroiled in this scheme, did not show their face. Domina could see the illusory key in the corner of the loft, sat atop a pile of crates. A great amount of their plan relied on the assumption that their enemy would know where to find the key, something that was not a certainty, but with everything else they had accomplished, it was likely safer to overestimate them than the opposite.

Domina kept his breathing quiet and slow, doing everything he could to focus solely on listening as he thought he had heard the sound of feet landing upon creaking planks come from below. The sound grew increasingly defined as it became clear they were approaching the ladder entrance to the loft. Domina tried to yield further to the shadows, only to find the slanted roof of the loft at his back. He took Anamrath into his hand, letting the black blade ignite. It would be practically invisible amid the rest of the darkness.

The intruder had reached the ladder, slowly pulling themselves up and into the space where Domina waited. He recognised them immediately; blue fabric cloaked their body, with a hood pulled low over their face. At the very least they were of the same occupation as Chora, though their overall figure matched her well enough that Domina suspected the similarities did not end there.

Domina watched as she quickly searched the room; it did not take her long to locate where the key sat. She took it in hand and wheeled toward her exit, stopping suddenly as she found Domina standing before her, the tip of his blade only inches from her throat.

"Is that you, Chora?" he asked, voice low with warning.

She raised her chin, revealing her masked face. "I hoped we would be reunited."

"So did I. Though I'm less inclined to return that key to you now that I know what it is." Domina recognised her voice, and the mask was identical to the one she had worn when they'd last met, although he distinctly recalled slicing it in two. "Get a new mask?"

"Of course." She responded quick, too quick to mask the uncertainty in her voice. "You still have Hyde's key, then?

He closed in on her, keeping his blade near to her throat. Thankfully, it seemed Anamrath was not particularly interested in her, it would prove problematic if the blade forced him to kill her before he had learned all he could. "What do you need them for?"

"I'm not at the leisure to offer you answers."

"Then this isn't your plan. Whose?"

A tiny shrug was all she offered as further conversation.

Domina stepped closer again, bringing the long side of his sword across her neck. "Don't throw your life away for this. I know the misery that is being consumed by this weapon, you don't want it." Even as he spoke them, Domina did not feel the threat in his words, and it was becoming an increasing oddity that Anamrath showed no interest in the prey set before it. The blade had never missed an opportunity to take life in the past, yet it felt in his hand like a weapon no different to any other.

"Was the kraken your work?" he asked, with only a glance out the window to see it had not yet returned as Trethellyn and the mage had anticipated.

Again, he received no proper response. Chora stood incredibly still, to a degree Domina found uncommonly unnerving.

"Take off the mask."

With it clear Chora would not break her silence, Domina reached out to take it from her himself, only to find his hand slip right through where it should have made contact with porcelain.

The shape twisted around his fingers like mist, fading in and out of existence as her entire body unfurled, taking a moment to decide what form it would take next.

The mask being repaired or replaced struck him as strange enough, but not implausible. It was Anamrath taking absolutely no interest in her soul that left him with only one conclusion. She did not have one. The Chora presented to him was no more than an apparition.

An illusion.

Domina leapt through the loft's sole window, landing on the lower level's rooftop and sprinting toward its edge. He should have known some mage appearing at just the right time to save the city was too good to be true.

"I do need that key, Domina," came a sharp voice from what remained of the window. The shape stepped forward and landed at the opposite end of the rooftop, unphased by the droplets of rain that tore through its wispy form, forcing it to constantly readjust itself as it struggled to take on Cortlan's own appearance.

Domina ignored him, looking out across the cityscape and realising he had never been told where he could find the safehouse Trethellyn would be taken to.

"You have come really quite close to the answers you seek, but I fear they do not belong to you. It was the broker's folly that brought you into this, you would be better off turning away now." The apparition of Cortlan took a few steps toward Domina, cautious—as if there were anything he could do to harm the phantom.

"You're the client, then." Domina held Anamrath before him, knowing just how little of a threat it posed in such a circumstance. "This is all your conspiracy?"

"Don't strain yourself thinking about it. I would be disturbed if one such as you could unravel it all. It is only out of blind luck that you have stumbled from one clue to another, and that is long run out. Give me the key."

"No. I've never needed to see the big picture, but I see you."

Cortlan raised his arms, a gesture that served only to point out the irony in Domina's statement. "If you do not give me what I ask for, this city will die."

To only add emphasis to his warning, a roar came from far below; down at the docks, the monster had finally returned. This was his play, why the kraken had not attacked when they had expected it would—because in truth Cortlan had his own scheme in mind. Domina would have cursed himself for failing to see through another plot if there was the time for it.

"Have you killed Trethellyn? This plot of yours doesn't work if we both make it out of this alive and knowing."

Cortlan smiled, pointed a playful finger Domina's way. "Now you're getting it."

"I can't give the key to you like this; are you sure you want to face me in person?"

"I know Anamrath well, Domina. I'll be quite fine." With that his form returned to smoke and the whisps trailed out through the stormy sky, drawn toward a clear destination, and beckoning to be followed.

Domina leapt forward, landing with a slide on the wet rooftop neighbouring Trethellyn's home. He maintained that momentum as he sprinted onward and threw himself across another gap between buildings, never losing sight as he followed the trail of Cortlan's illusive form.

There was that familiar hunger again, the black maw that was eager to consume from within to without. There was no time to think. No time to regret.

Chapter Nineteen
No Time to Lose

Eric was sure he should have felt his nerves heightened as the carriage that held him captive began to slow, yet it was something else which darkened his thoughts in that moment. A precipice was upon him, a moment defined by what had come, and a choice that would decide what would be. But that choice had already been made, unless Eric had misunderstood Oedon. "Do we have any choice in this?" he asked, confident that certainty in the matter would simplify things.

The boy released a heavy sigh, making no attempt to hide his vexation. Eric must not have been the first to be overtaken by such existential confusion. "Think to when you received that letter and decided you would save your friend, despite the inherent risks. I might have been able to predict that would happen, your past with her and the misery you experienced in her absence made it quite clear how you would react. Does my ability to predict your actions make them any less your own?" He paused for a few seconds, listening to what seemed like movement outside the cart, then returned his attention to Eric. "You choose."

Eric only half heard his final point, something Oedon had referenced all-too casually had caught his attention instead. "You knew I would save her." Of course he did, Oedon had made it clear there were very few events that he was genuinely blind to, yet Eric could not see the logic in that. Oedon was Lyre's, so why not do anything to hinder his rescue? "You wanted me to free Raph."

Oedon did not seem to be listening, instead continuing to listen to what happened beyond the cart. Eric did not have the boy's senses, could only look into the crystalline orbs that sat within those dark sockets and wonder at what they saw. There was something lively in those rocks, and Eric thought that if he only looked long enough he might discern its shape. He was so distracted that he did not notice Oedon swing a shockingly strong fist towards him, and turned his world black.

—

As soon as Nath Whitsin was assuredly unconscious, Oedon allowed himself a moment of relief. He did not dislike the man by any metric, only found his entire nature to be increasingly overwhelming. There was so much misery in his past, too much conflict in his present, and only the faintest glimmer of hope for his future.

Oedon did not often take the time to explain the way he viewed the world, precisely because he knew most could not stomach such revelation. Yet so many continued to insist upon stepping into the prophet's shoes for but a moment, stripping back the flesh of reality so they might bear witness to the sinew and muscle beneath. Time after time their stomachs proved too weak to bear it.

Let them see just how small they are, he thought. If they were so intent on dancing with the fires of fate, they could suffer the consequences when it kissed their flesh.

As the carriage door was opened, one such fool stood to greet him. Oedon had not anticipated his reunion with Lyre with much excitement, the man was about as delusional as one could be. Not because he was expressly heinous, but because he had managed to delude himself into thinking he portrayed this tale's hero. As if any single being could stand taller than another in the eyes of the immortal. Even among such people, Lyre was little more than an ant.

The lord was joined by at least ten of his guard, and they quickly moved to guard Lyre as the corpses within the carriage caught their attention.

Oedon stepped to the ground. "I warned them not to underestimate him."

Lyre waved off his overly eager guards before stepping forward to examine the damage himself. "Where's the girl?"

Oedon turned his gaze beyond, finding the pale green devola as she rode a brilliant white horse toward Duralaans' capital, taking little time to rest as she did. He returned his attention to Lyre after only a moment. "Out of our reach."

Lyre grimaced but seemed alleviated as his eyes located the second thorn in his side. "Blackhand will do for now. I trust you are aware of our heading."

"Yes, my lord. An invitation from the Queen herself, how prestigious." If Lyre had ever been antagonised by Oedon's thinly veiled disrespect, he had never spoken of it.

"What she plans, will it succeed?"

"No." Oedon did not bother turning to his visions to confirm what he suspected would be the result of Cecilia's gala. It was not that gazing toward the future was especially painful, though there was a discomforting strain that came from doing it too frequently or for too long a time. It felt much like forcing eyes he no longer possessed to focus on something that was not actually there; the flickering images of the time to come appeared as reflections within the prismatic angles of the crystalline orbs that filled his black-stained sockets. The more distant the future, the less clearly it was reflected, and the more strain it took to make out what he was seeing.

"Then I am glad to have you returned now." He snapped a look to one of his men, and they rushed forward to carry Whitsin out of the carriage. "We must discern a path we can take to avoid the

Queen's folly. I may need you to relieve my fellows of their own keys, if they do in fact bring them."

"I suggest you speak with Blackhand once he wakes. You will be surprised by how much he knows."

Lyre seemed surprised as he glanced toward where the captive was being hauled into a nearby tent. "You cannot tell me yourself?"

"Presently I am to commune with the Mother and Father." It was an excuse he had used to avoid Lyre's incessant demands often enough that the lord no longer questioned it, simply offering a curt nod before marching toward the same tent Whitsin had been placed within.

Oedon waited until his master was out of sight, then crossed through the campsite to find a place he could be alone. He made sure he was far enough from the campfire that it no longer made his hair stand on end. It had been long enough since his mother's death that the sound alone did not always force those buried memories to the surface, rather it was the sight and smell of the ash that came after which haunted him.

He thought there was irony in that. Of course the boy who was most disturbed by ash would be subjected to a land that would soon be smothered in the grey substance. But his task was too important to be forsaken out of personal distaste, and he had set up too many pieces to avoid being present for their fall.

Oedon let himself lie in a bed of grass, finding comfort in just how soft it was against his back. He was sure the sky before him presented a brilliant vista, though he could never be absolutely certain. His abilities allowed him to see every moment of history, in varying degrees of clarity, except the exact present he stood in. Oedon knew what that night sky looked like in the seconds to come and the moments that had been, but he would never truly see what it was that looked back at him in any given time. He knew there were worse fates, many lived truly blind and were perfectly happy in such a state. But that did not mean Oedon needed to be just as content.

He wondered why, despite his own innate suffering, he still insisted on comforting those who could not reckon with the nature of that which guided their actions. He did all he could to make them feel once again like their choices mattered, all while he did not share such beliefs.

Perhaps that was because, even if he stripped back the flesh of nature, everyone he shared it with could only see a sliver, the smallest scar of truth. Oedon saw the total mutilation, the complete structure of the misery that ensnared them.

Elias would arrive soon. Oedon had been so tempted to tell him what awaited him, but he knew it would change nothing. This was inescapable, no matter how much he wished otherwise.

—

Anamrath cut the wooden door to pieces as Domina charged through, allowing the hail of shattered wood to fall upon his back. He moved quickly, no time to waste on thought, relying solely on his blade's hunger to draw him toward the safehouse's inhabitants. He barely took notice of the mess of blood and flesh scattered throughout the premises. To have brought about so much violence, Cortlan must have been a creature of far more menace than Domina had allowed himself to presume.

The safehouse appeared as a typical home from outside, but within it contained only a few genuinely decorated rooms to trick any who passed by, while the rest was simply a maze of stone halls connecting those rooms to the bunker below.

Domina practically flew down the stairway, finding the metal door to the bunker already open, and only more reason for despair behind it. Cortlan sat back on a large leather chair, his fingers steepled together in consternation as he turned his attention away from the corpse splayed on the floor and to Domina's arrival.

The mage stood, spread his hands wide in apology. "I'm sorry, Domina. It is always so disappointing to be correct."

What a terrible plan, Domina thought as he rushed toward Cortlan, Anamrath eager to make up for the time it had gone without satisfying its hunger. What did Cortlan hope to achieve by slaying his hostage? Was he so powerful that he could defend himself without such cunning means? If so, Domina would have only this one opportunity to end their duel before it began, and he would not waste it.

Anamrath severed the matter of flesh without resistance, even as the shadow of Cortlan's face became that of another.

The world seemed to freeze for a moment, as Domina's eyes met the horrified expression of Lord Trethellyn, the light in him dimming as his soul was consumed whole. The movement of time returned all too quickly. Trethellyn began to contort with violent speed, the momentum of the slice spinning his torso as it flailed to the floor. His lower body buckled alongside it and came to lie a distance from its upper half.

It took Domina seconds too long to comprehend what had happened; the body that had supposedly been Trethellyn's had disappeared without a trace. Besides the bisected mass before him, Domina was the only thing in the room.

Though he could no longer be seen, Cortlan could be heard as his rapid footsteps echoed down the hall. "Guards! He's killed Lord Trethellyn!"

The cry was followed by heavy footfalls growing as they stampeded toward the bunker.

Domina's mind had gone blank, overtaken again by the numbing desire of his weapon. He gripped it tight in hand, choosing to focus on its chill rather than the revulsion growing within.

Domina spared himself the sight of his mistake, turned toward the steps, and slowly ambled back up to the hall. He found it packed with warm bodies, men and women armoured in heavy leathers and light steel, one blade for every two hands. Domina stood before them, did not—could not—hear their warnings as he continued forward.

—

Although he had spent a good deal of time around those with powerful arcane abilities, Eric still found himself surprised by what Oedon could do. Beyond even seeing into the future and summoning an exploding blade of crystal, knocking him out with a single precise strike was something many had tried and failed to do before the prophet. And as he came to wake once more, there was little lingering pain—what would surely be only a short respite.

Eric was strung up by his wrists, the ropes tied low enough that slipping his prosthetic off would not save him again, and his body ached enough to tell him it had been in that position for a while, though nothing about the tent's interior offered any sense of the time. A man was seated at the other end of the small space, a desk sat before him, though it was to Eric that his full attention was laid. His chest was bare, mahogany skin decorated by ornate markings, tattoos Eric was sure he had never seen prior, though there were trace symbols he could place as commonly used in magecraft.

"Eric Blackhand." He spoke carefully, savouring his own words. "You have been an issue."

Eric smiled but returned no vocal response. He had to draw this out as much as possible, give Elias all the time he needed to fulfill his part of the contract.

"I hope you realise by this moment just how foolish you have been. The end of Duralaans nears and you have only hastened it with your pitiful games."

Eric's silence was quickly broken as he said, "No games, Lyre. You hurt my friend. That will not stand."

"You've hurt many of my friends in return. Claustere. Orion. Aron. Stellos. Do you even know their names?" Lyre said the words without any true upset, as though he did not at all care that they were dead, only that he was able to use their demise as a barb.

"I suppose I do . . . *now*." Eric forced as much confidence into the remark as he could muster. Oedon had suggested Lyre was the kind of man who needed to be right, so as long as Eric fought back against his declarations, the lord would be compelled to keep him breathing—though Eric knew well enough that did not mean he would not suffer in the meanwhile.

Lyre approached, rubbing his thumb over his knuckles. The tattoos continued along his muscled arms, becoming more intricate as they reached his fingers. Then the ink flared to life, glowing a silver that illuminated his skin.

When the fist collided with his stomach, Eric felt a shuddering pain spread throughout his entire form. It was like every bone in his body shattered at once, before being reforged with some infernal energy that ignited his insides. He screamed, choking as blood quickly filled his throat—a smattering of which fell to the floor as dried black flakes.

He tried to breathe, the process quickly becoming a terrible cycle of perpetuated pain. The intake of air itself felt so much like swallowing glass that he could only bear small gasps, only for the sensation of suffocation to overwhelm him and force a deeper agonising breath.

Lyre stepped back to examine his work, appearing very much pleased by Eric's state. "I have a few questions you should answer."

Eric did not want to speak. Did not think he could at the time. If his mouth were to open again, he thought all that would exit would be mulched organs and blood.

"Where is Seraph?"

He could not answer. He did not know the answer. Still feared testing his ability to speak.

"Tell me." Lyre grasped Eric's face, forced him to meet his gaze, but Eric's eyelids did not want to remain open.

"No . . . idea . . ." Each word brought about a new agony, but Eric found himself overpowered by his unconscious desire to not give Lyre another reason to strike. "I . . . got caught—"

It was not enough. Even something as simple as the back of Lyre's hand across Eric's face made him feel like skin had been torn free. He thought his eyes would burst. Teeth should have shattered. It took everything to not bite through his tongue at the moment of impact.

The world around him flashed black for a moment—perhaps that had been enough to end his life, for as his vision slowly returned it was not the tent he saw.

There was a garden. A distant sea. Pitch black trees grew in a plain of pearlescent white grass. There may have been millions of the things, certainly more than he could ever count. A woman stood beneath one of them, turned toward him with a kind expression that gave way to panic as she seemed to recognise her new guest. She rushed toward him—only for the vision to bleed back to reality.

Stars littered his vision, accompanied by spots of darkness that seemed to shift every time he blinked. Lyre remained before him, an expression of total apathy upon his face.

Eric must have lost consciousness for a moment. The image of the strange place was quickly fading from his memory. He knew that woman, but even her image would not retain its shape in his mind.

"People like you disturb me." Lyre cracked his knuckles, smiling as the sound made Eric flinch. "There is some semblance of honour in your pursuits, and I can understand your fear. But your place is not in saving anyone, you have not the power to do so. That is for me alone. I will save Duralaans, that is my path. My destiny." He stepped closer again, the man's expression appeared so much like a predator savouring its hard-won victory. "I can only imagine yours. Your place in this world is a small one, but it was yours. I mourn anyone who sacrifices their place for another, only to find themselves lost without it. Though I will not mourn you, Eric Blackhand."

Lyre drew back his fist, making it clear he would not hold any more of his power at bay. If Eric had anything to offer that might save his life, he would not know another opportunity to present it.

"You'll fail!" he spat, feeling as though he had torn out his throat in doing so.

Lyre did not move, kept his fist ready to strike at will.

"Has he not told you?" Eric took Lyre's continued delay as reason to continue. "Artorius will be free. *That* is destiny, you won't be able to stop it."

Lyre seemed to consider Eric's words for only a moment before discarding them as drivel. "No. You have no idea what you speak of."

"But Oedon knows everything. You ask him." It was difficult to believe Lyre truly wanted to achieve the same goal as Raph and himself; Eric could only see the monster before him, only wonder if the pain he now felt was the same brutality Raph had endured. Yet there was no denying the vigour with which he proclaimed himself Duralaans' saviour-to-be. Perhaps that was Eric's leverage, what might buy himself and Elias the time they needed.

If Eric considered himself a selfish man who used heroics as his shield, this was his counterpart; the righteous lord, who wielded malice and pain as his tools of healing.

Lyre seemed further swayed by the mention of the fate-seeing boy. His eyes flickered toward the tent's entrance as he likely considered calling on him to settle the matter. That choice was stripped from him by what had begun outside those fabric coverings.

There was a faint hissing, followed by cries of frustration and the metallic ringing of blades being drawn. Then thin whisps of smoke began to snake their way into the tent, and Eric realised he had not needed to buy much more time after all. Lyre did not appear so pleased as Eric felt, and his fist had once again been sent toward him.

As the man who had called himself Eric Blackhand died, he briefly wondered which of them was the better person. Would it be their means or their ends that cemented their moral standing in the annals of history?

Those of immortal standing surely did not care what bloody work one had to perform in order to achieve a greater good.

Perhaps in some ways Lyre was right to proclaim himself the hero. Though it did not really matter.

They would both be ash soon enough.

—

For all of his aversions to Blackhand as a person, the gift that was his complete arsenal served as enough to make Elias reconsider his judgement.

He had thrown a small capsule into the campfire—once he was sure luring individual guards to a quiet death had reached its limit—and the campsite had suddenly been bathed in dark smoke. Of course, his vision would likewise be inhibited, but unlike his opponents, Elias had taken the time to mark everyone's positions before they were obscured.

Elias sprinted into the smoke, slipping his curved blade from its sheath and driving it into the closest man's neck. The sound of the body collapsing to the ground caught the attention of his fellows. Elias had to slip away before one of them stumbled into him, but not before leaving a small steel orb with the corpse. He watched as they struggled to locate where the noise had come from, and eventually one of them, a short bulky woman, called out as her foot caught something her eyes could not see.

"Stick together," she ordered. "Don't let them take us out one by one."

Bright orange flared to life as flame engulfed the guards who stood too close to their fallen ally, making their silhouettes momentarily visible amid the smoke. Elias counted four taken out by the explosion.

He took the roaring flame as opportunity to go loud, calculating where the nearest guard would be, based on the last Elias had seen them. Steel met flesh, but too briefly to leave a mortal wound. Elias' opponent rounded on him and was swinging his own blade in a flash. Elias was too slow to properly parry it but at least prevented it from making bloody contact. He deflected a second attack, then surprised his foe by drawing a new weapon that shot a burning hole through his chest.

The guard's mouth formed a shocked circle as he fell back, Elias figured he felt much the same. He had seen cinder powder weapons in use—and felt little respect for any who relied on them—but this was something else entirely.

The soft shifting of leather boots on dirt came from behind him, accompanied by the shy whisp of a thin weapon slicing through air. Elias thrust his sword towards the disturbance, catching his attacker with a wet *THUNK* as steel plunged through flesh and spilled blood. Though death was near, the guard had already been in the midst of his attack, and Elias had to pivot to avoid the worst of it, but grimaced as he felt the sword bite into his left arm.

He had been cut deep, but could not let himself waste any time on the wound. The guards had homed in on his position, and the smoke was beginning to clear. There were six, each with a blade of their own, and all assured of their victory.

He tested his arm. It was not his dominant, rather the one he used to hold Blackhand's firearm. Elias only hoped he would be able to raise it high enough to continue being useful. The rest of Blackhand's arsenal were within a pouch slung over his shoulder, and inside he found a second of the smoke capsules that he fastened to his shoulder, twisting the activation so it began releasing more smoke.

Elias' form was quickly cloaked by thick grey clouds, making him appear less of a man and more of a brimstone creature out of Diavollos.

While his enemies took a moment to further size him up, Elias sprung forward. He did all he could to draw his opponent's attention to his blade, before allowing it to swing purposefully wide to avoid a deflect and instead raised the firearm to light up the man's face. The act of lifting that arm brought incredible pain, but the man went down all the same, and Elias threw himself toward the swordswoman next.

She was fast, though her flurry of strikes were clearly not meant to hurt, merely exhaust him. Her attempts would not be a problem, if not for the other four simultaneously trying to take advantage of his distraction. Elias had to keep in motion, angling himself so none were able to surround him, though it was quickly becoming clear he had to do something to disrupt them. Chaos would be his only ally in a fight where he was completely outnumbered. He would need to time his own strike perfectly, but Elias knew that had been one of the many things age had taken from him. So when he kicked his leg out to catch the swordswoman in the stomach, it may have succeeded in catching her unaware, but the whirlwind that was her attack had no difficulty slicing across his shin, more than likely digging into bone during.

In the momentary reprieve that bought him, Elias threw himself toward the closest man, bringing them both down into the dirt. They tussled briefly before Elias managed to get a thick arm locked around the guard's throat.

With his newly acquired human shield, the rest of his combatants were hesitant to act. Despite the pain, Elias took the opportunity to raise his left arm and fire on them, even as he felt steel penetrate his waist. While keeping the man atop him made it difficult for the others to get at Elias, it also made it incredibly easy for his hostage to rapidly jab a dagger into his stomach. For every guard that went down, Elias was stabbed at least twice, and he could see more who had been awoken by the commotion were stumbling out of their tents.

These men and women had—to Elias' immense pleasure—not the time to properly armour themselves.

With the others dead, Elias pressed the firearm to his captive's skull and pulled the trigger, immediately regretting the decision as the sound ruptured his ears.

He threw the corpse off and stumbled back to his feet. Elias' hearing was shot, replaced by a piercing ringing and making balance near impossible to acquire. Eight more were studying him with confused anger, and now Elias noticed finally that Lyre himself was standing at the cusp of his own tent.

If Elias had more of those explosives, he might have been able to take a few of them down while they were grouped up, but Blackhand's designs held no recognisable label to tell him what each did.

He wondered if Oedon would make a move anytime soon, then decided that relying on the boy's aid would do him no favours. The best he could do was toss the last three capsules toward his encroaching enemies and hope they would serve him well. But he noticed that none of them were coming closer, content to only form a half-perimeter around him. They were waiting for Lyre to give them permission.

"You cannot tell me you grew so close to Blackhand that you'd throw your life away for him," Lyre said. He was trying to keep his tone calm, but there were inflections of irritation that Elias picked up.

Good. Let that keep him occupied. "That's just part of the job sometimes."

"Is that the mercenary way? An opponent makes such a fool of you that there's no choice but to yield them your life?"

"Don't take it so personally." Elias was not so glad for the break, it only allowed more time for the severity of his wounds to become clear. The slice to his leg and arm hurt, but could be dealt with, it was the savage punctures to his stomach that caused him the most concern; blood coated his thick tunic, and his combatants would be well aware of his weakened state. "We live and die by circumstance, that's all there is."

"Then let me offer you a new one. Blackhand is dead. Whatever it is he has put you up to is over. Drop your weapons and I shall allow you to walk away from this with at least some of your dignity."

Elias smiled. He was still amazed by how accurate Oedon's predictions were. "You asked me, not so long ago, to tell you what kind of person you were."

"Stalling will only waste your breath."

Elias hardly cared. "I only saw what you wanted me to. You think you're so complicated? A man burdened by purpose and the bloody means he uses to fulfill it." Elias laughed, felt disgusted by the taste of blood on his tongue. "That ain't you. No, you're simple as the rest of us."

"Really, is this how you wish to waste your final words?" Lyre had dropped any attempts to hide his frustration. "Who do you suppose I am, then?"

"A shadow that trusts only its own, and is therefore . . . irrelevant." As soon as the words had left his mouth, Elias raised his left hand and fired, sending a streak of fire through Lyre's side. It would not kill him, that was not part of the deal, but hopefully it would keep Lyre out of the fight.

As Lyre roared with rage, the perimeter closed in on Elias. He was no longer able to raise his arm high enough to take headshots, but burning a hole in a person's chest could be no less lethal. He took out two of the guards before the rest were close enough that he was forced to begin the melee again.

He brought his sword arm around in wide arcs, trying to force them back while he fetched another of Blackhand's capsules and threw it at their feet. There was no time to see what it would do, as one of his opponents saw the opportunity to strike. Elias was able to deflect that one, but it only allowed somebody to his right the chance to embed their sword in his so far unwounded side.

Elias pulled back, wrenching the embedded blade from its wielder's grasp. A new figure swung at him from the opposite direction—Elias thanked the Gods that it went wide, and parted the man's head from his shoulders with a single strong swing. He continued to back up, that finisher had taken too much out of him, and he could feel the blade still stuck in his side cutting at his organs in response to even the smallest of movements.

Elias noticed that the ground where he had thrown the capsule was now covered by a black liquid, only moments before it burst into flames, engulfing all who stood upon it.

Although his body dared to refuse, Elias managed to force it forward, making use of the chaos that was his only hope to see victory.

Elias was not fully conscious of what he did from that point onward. His body had been consumed by a blind fury, an ultimate burst of energy to see him through the searing pain that threatened to cripple him. Three of the swordsmen fell to the fire and another two were slain by Elias' metal during the immediate confusion.

Each kill came with a trade, and the pain that coursed through his flesh only grew. Something about it set his nerves on fire; he threw himself onward with the closest he could muster to a warrior's cry, drove his sword through a shocked guardsman, and emptied the remaining contents of Blackhand's arsenal.

There had been an explosive left after all—two of them, in fact. If Elias had not positioned himself behind the man he had just skewered, his life would have ended as they burst into a brilliant display of red and yellow heat.

He was thrown from his feet, crashing back to the ground with terrible force. Elias tumbled over once, twice, three times before he came to a stop and forced himself onto his back.

Elias found it odd how much it felt like he had just come from a swim in the ocean. His body was drenched in a liquid, but it was too warm to be water, and too thick to be anything else that was supposed to be outside his body.

Somebody was approaching him. Perhaps Cleo had been sent to bring him home? He had been away for so long, surely Mother and Father wondered where he was.

Instead it was a man that Elias did not know he recognised who loomed over him. He was injured, hand clutching at a wound on his side, face wrought with anger. Elias wondered what had happened to make him appear so grim, but the whisper of a memory told him this man deserved it. Still, amid the roaring fury, he could make out the flicker of terror in the man's eyes.

Elias felt a new life flow through him, and slowly, carefully he rose to his feet. The man, whose name he remembered was Carlyle

Lyre, stepped back, eyes wide with the totality of his incomprehension. It felt almost like he was floating, as his entire body had gone numb. Like he was being kept standing by a single thread that might give out at any moment.

Lyre appeared utterly dumbfounded.

Good, Elias thought. *That's how it feels.*

Chapter Twenty
The Clay Forest

Eric leaned back against the chair and threw his feet up over the wooden table before him. It had not quite been an hour, but the waiting was already getting on his nerves. He did not like these kinds of jobs; there was a simplicity removed in doing the work so personally, and something about the look in a person's eyes as they knew death was near disturbed him. Perhaps that was selfish of him. Perhaps his targets deserved the respect of looking their killer in the eyes as the life left them. It hardly mattered, the dead didn't care whether or not they were respected.

He felt a pang of guilt blossom within. Eric thought he should remember something, but the irony of his thoughts were lost as time ticked away.

The firearm in his hand seemed to grow heavier the longer he clutched it, but he refused to lower his best source of defence. The chances of Anton DeMarco posing a threat were slim, but not a risk worth taking, even if it meant making him marginally more uncomfortable.

About an hour went by before he heard any sort of shift downstairs. Anton was enjoying the night's dinner with his family, a fact that had made it easy enough for Eric to enter the upper office without being noticed, but also meant it would be quite the wait before he could confront the man. Of course, if Eric was really so desperate to see the job done, he could just walk downstairs and traumatise the man's children irrevocably. Eric had not even been conscious during his mother's death and that had put him on an already disastrous path, putting others through an even more horrid experience was not worth considering. Eric would wait.

He always found his heart racing the closer he came to ending a life, others had told him it was something that got easier. Like grief, a person was supposed to become numb to the guilt and pain after enough time, but that feeling had never left him, and grief continued to blacken his soul. Even more so with time. At least he was being paid for it now.

"I'll be there in a moment, just have to tidy up," came a cheerful voice from behind the door. It was time.

The door opened, a man entered, and Eric began to squeeze his weapon's trigger. Yet he did not fire.

It was not Anton DeMarco who had entered. This man was tall, heavily built, and sporting a thick red beard that shifted as he broke into a smile. "Son?"

Nath—for that was the person he was in this man's presence—could only stare back at his father.

"What are you doing in here?" He took a step forward, folding his muscled arms across his chest in such a way that Nath felt himself overwhelmed by heartrending nostalgia. "Your mother's fixed up quite the supper, I reckon you ought at least try it."

"Of course." Nath dropped his feet back to the floor and slowly rose, finding his legs shaking terribly. It was clear that whatever he had found himself amidst was not reality, but the vision of the dead almost moved him to tears.

"Come on then," Eric Whitsin said, holding the door open so Nath could catch up. He knew it was only a short walk to the dining room downstairs, but every step felt like wading through the deepest of waters, as though without utilising all the focus he had

Eric would collapse, and likely never have the strength to stand again.

Along the way it became clear this was not the place he remembered. Nath's recollection of the night he killed Anton had been taken and altered to be set within what seemed to be a cross between his childhood home and the farm he had spent the years since Haevahn living in with his father and sister.

Nath tried to remember how he had gotten there—recoiled as he felt pain shoot throughout his flesh.

"You alright there?" His father had stopped, noticing his son's pain and reaching out to offer any form of comfort.

It wasn't that Nath didn't want it, but he stepped back all the same. A part of him thought that if he felt his father place even a hand on him something horrible would happen. The illusion would die. Nath would close his eyes and see only remains when he opened them again. The place he called home would be reduced to smouldering cinders. Or perhaps—worst of all—it would actually feel real.

"What's the matter, lad?" Eric pulled his hand back, shoved it into a pocket instead.

Nath cast his eyes beyond and toward the staircase before them. "Are they down there?"

"Who?"

"Mother? Imma?"

"Of course they are." He seemed so honestly perplexed, sharing none of Nath's own disbelief. "What's the matter? Has something happened?"

"You died." The words came from his mouth before he could stop. "You all died."

Eric spread his arms and rotated on the spot. "I don't feel particularly dead, and what would that make you?"

There was pain again, this time resurrecting memory of those final moments. Lyre had killed him.

Did that make this new place the afterlife? It was possible, but raised the question of why it would take such a form. He should not be the only one who remembered his own death, yet Nath's father was apparently oblivious to his own demise.

"Son, whatever it is that has happened to you—to us—that's in the past now. Let's enjoy what we have."

That gave Nath all the answer he needed. "I'm not looking to serve a god. I don't care which one you are."

"Excuse me?"

"Is that you, Anni? I don't want your help."

This was a test. A lesson. Some means for a divine entity to understand Nath's mettle or twist it to their own ends, he was sure of it.

"Well?" he pressed, spurred on by his father's lack of response.

"I'm sorry." A whisper from behind rippled through the hall, seeming to shake the wooden architecture despite its soft timbre.

Nath turned toward it, found himself back in the white plain filled with black trees. Last time he had been standing at a distance. Now he found himself standing among the shadowy growths, surrounded in every direction by an infinite expanse of towering darkness.

They were all pitch black, but seemed to consist of two varieties. Some appeared soft, Eric imagined them to be malleable under enough force, there might have even been handprints on some he could make out. Others appeared solid, stonelike, some were cracked and bore chips. Eric stretched his metal hand toward one—decided it wouldn't be for the best to make contact.

"I don't want your apologies, Larina," Eric said, realising who it had been that had appeared to him among the trees. It was only natural that the Lord of Death's former lover would fall into the same disposition. It was not something he could fault her for; his family had been bandits before they finally settled down. The apple rarely did fall far. If at all.

Larina Yukkie stood a good distance from him, garbed in something like mourning attire, only it was coloured in ethereal white rather than the typical darker shades. It gave her an entirely ghostly appearance, especially with the veil shielding her face.

Eric took a step toward her but found he could not manage more than that. The memory of her words cutting him to shreds stung even after so many years. "I'm dead, then?"

"For the time being." Larina's dress billowed around her form despite the lack of any wind within the odd forest. Even the trees and grass remained perfectly still, as though she and him were the only entities of consequence. "Do you like this place? It is our garden, my husband and I's."

"Vécar?"

She bowed her head in affirmation.

"He's alive?"

"No. But this is what he started, when we thought he was amassing an army. He was also building a garden. A place to nurture those who have passed and prepare those who are soon to join them." She placed a hand on one of the solidified trees. "Do not mistake my meaning. What we did was indeed necessary, I know that now."

Eric tried not to dwell on the truth of that. The revelation of his work for Greydeath caused enough consequence to his mentality, further considering the morality in ending Vécar's undeath might have broken him entirely. "Well, I'm glad you've finally found peace."

"In fact, I have not. Not yet."

"Right. Need me to ease your conscience?" Eric tried to muster some humour into his tone, that was better than letting his circumstance weigh him down. "It doesn't matter anymore. It's like Father—or you—said: that's the past."

"I was in pain. It was not until later that I realised all my words did was pass that pain onto another."

"You don't have to explain it to me, Larina. You loved Vécar, I understand what you were going through. Pain makes fools of us all."

"And we let others suffer for it." It appeared to Eric as though she took only a single step forward, but in the next moment she was close enough to rest her hands on his face. "I am sorry, Nath. You *were* a hero, you still are."

Nath did break then, felt tears dampening his cheeks. He had told her there was no need to dredge up their past, could not bear to dissect that murky darkness any more than he already had. "Maybe I was, but that's changed. I've *been* changed. Everything that's happened has made me the man I am now; the only version of me that could survive this world. I know it's taken me too long to understand, but I accept it."

"Do you?" Her eyes bored into his soul. "Are you happy like this?"

Eric couldn't answer—not a physical incapability, but a simple unwillingness to address the corner he had backed into.

"If it is the world that shapes us, that moulds the man from the clay. Then what are *we* in that relationship?"

He could see where she was going, denied it with everything but his voice.

"Are we simply the sculpture that shall be? Unable to choose what form we deserve to take?"

"Something like that." He needed her to stop talking. But there was surely nothing he could do to oppose her in such a place.

Larina chuckled, a pleasantly soothing sound. "I see. Then why bother aiding Seraph?"

"She needed my help." His answer came quick, demanding no forethought.

"But you are no hero. That is your conceit, yes?"

"I thought I could be. That's the problem. That's what you told us. It's not about what we do, it's why we do it that matters."

"Then what is Seraph? What am I?"

"Raph *is* good. She helped people—people like me—even when it did nothing for her."

Larina's laugh rose to a shrill cackle.

"What?" Eric demanded. "Stop acting like you're so much better, like you know what I need. I've finally made peace with all of this, so please stop what it is you're trying to accomplish and let me die in peace."

"Oh, dear boy. I'm sorry, I just thought you knew her better."

Eric turned away, briefly considered putting distance between himself and the ghoul which haunted him, before recalling how quickly she had already shown herself able to traverse her domain. "You thought wrong. I'm nothing but a burden to her."

"Daft boy," she exclaimed. "I should not have to explain this. Those lessons, she may have shared with you, but they were never *for you*."

Eric was taken back to their first meeting; Raph's deal with him in return for the locket had asked that he aid those in the city who needed it. He had understood later that the point of that arrangement was to distract him from his grief and allow his need for vengeance to fade, but it never had. Instead he had simply been able to turn from defending the people of Spirallos to hunting the infamous Death Lord. The root of the issue had been eventually forgotten but never addressed or dealt with. It had lingered beneath the surface, a constant rot within his heart that he could always feel but thought was better to leave unvoiced.

In all that time, Eric had failed to consider that Raph might have been experiencing a similar pain, that she had also been using her spree of heroics to escape the shadow of melancholy that chased her.

"I can see that mind of yours working. If you are no hero, then neither is Raph. If she is a hero, then why aren't you?" He did not need to see her face to know she was smirking

"Oedon said—"

She did not let him finish that thought. "Oedon is no less confused than you are. His sight may be absolute, but his understanding is far from it."

She was right, Eric knew that she was. Even if he could not let himself accept it. "I've hurt so many people, Larina. This is the only way I can live with myself."

"I find your new obsession with the past quite dull. That is a thing that does not exist beyond memory, you do not need to let it shape you."

"If only that could be done so easily as it's said."

"Yes, that is why you have failed to come to this conclusion so far. I did not want to step in, but seeing as the path set upon you was largely pathed by myself, it felt only right."

Eric caressed his metal hand, finding it warmer than it had ever been since he'd lost the appendage. "What are we, then? If not the clay or the sculptor?"

Larina stood to his left and took his faux hand in hers—a sensation Eric was shocked to find that he could actually feel. "We are the kiln. That which decides what is to be the final shape we wish to hold." She chuckled again. "It's not a perfect metaphor, but I like it."

Eric realised that was what the trees were made of; the soft being the clay of those who continued to live and change. The solid, those who were otherwise incapable. He supposed his would appear like the latter.

"Why tell me all of this? Beyond whatever responsibility you feel for my state, why try to help me?" Eric asked.

"If you're going to have another shot at this, I can't have you repeating your mistakes."

Eric looked up at her, unable to believe the implication in her statement.

"I already told you that you're not dead yet; that boy really is something. Do keep an eye on him for me, would you?"

Pain shot through Eric's chest, but he wasn't ready—he didn't know that anything would actually change. "How am I supposed to be anything else after everything that's happened?"

She met his gaze and held it with a warmth he would not have expected from a creature of death. "Do you want to be something else?"

He knew that he did. Eric Blackhand might have been the only way he could survive the new life thrust upon him, but Nath Whitsin was the person he wanted to be. The person he sought to protect with the shield of a new man. "Should that matter?"

"Desire is often the soul's only way of telling us what it needs. You might survive like this, but you won't live for long."

He forced himself to take a deep breath, then came to a decision. "I could not save my mother, my father, not even my sister. But I want to save my home."

"Good."

Thus the life of Eric Blackhand and the death of Nath Whitsin simultaneously came to an end.

Chapter Twenty-One
One Last Breath

They were many.

And Domina was one.

If he had the space necessary to properly avoid the guards' attacks, success could have been more likely, the narrow corridor leading out of the safehouse's bunker offered nothing of the sort. Though even with more space, these were no common mercenaries; trained guards in service to a noble house would provide no small amount of threat.

Such facts were obvious to Domina from the moment he laid eyes on his opposition. Which left a simple and confounding question: why was he winning?

Anamrath became little more than a black smear as it severed flesh and brought lives to an end. It may have been his hand that the blade was in, but Domina was far away. A spectator only fit to bear witness to the onslaught. At least, that was such a way to view the situation that brought him comfort. More comfort than facing the fact of the matter; Domina was killing a lot of people.

A man, far taller than he, charged with blade held high. The steel was sharp, thick, a single strike would easily cleave apart flesh and bone. Domina did not falter. He took a single step forward and brought Anamrath up in such a way that it removed the man's sword arm—while also drawing a flesh-splitting line upon his face. That was followed by a simple twirl and Anamrath had bisected another of its prey. A furious leap and the blade punctured a third's chest.

As horrible as the violence appeared, it was not the worst part of the bloody dance—Domina figured he'd seen worse in the war he'd once waged on Azazel's behalf. No, he was no stranger to gory death. It was the consumption of the victims' souls that sent him spiralling into an almost catatonic despair. With every droplet of blood spilled by his black blade, he saw something of the former owner's life as their essence became one with Anamrath.

He decapitated an older woman.

She had just welcomed her first grandchild into the world.

Anamrath skewered a thin but challenging warrior.

He had run away from home to pursue a life of honour.

Another thought to strike Domina from behind; a well-timed dodge forced him to unwittingly hit an ally instead. Then Domina skewered the both of them.

One enjoyed troubling the poorer citizens of Meergard when he found himself inebriated enough. The other was struggling to work up enough coin to purchase the wedding bracer his beloved had been enamoured with months prior.

An armoured woman with thick arms attempted to grapple Domina, catching his wrist with one hand and clutching his throat with the other. He flicked the hilt at the closest wall and watched as it ricocheted throughout the hall, ending the lives of four more.

One had wanted to be a baker as a child.

For another there was no moment that he did not spend hoping his daughter would eventually be found.

She was supposed to retire from Trethellyn's service upon the day's end.

They had a dream that they still hoped to make a reality.

That dream died with them. All of them.

The hand on Domina's throat loosened and the woman fell, leaving him alone in the hall. He forced himself forward and found that he was genuinely stunned that his body still responded to his will, and wondered just how much of that massacre had been the work of his weapon and how much himself.

Anamrath was a biting chill in his palm; the blade refused to yield itself. Domina thought he could hear the souls within pleading for their freedom. He knew well enough the horror of being trapped within the thing, but there was nothing he could do for them.

He had to move on. Had to assess his situation. Trethellyn was dead—by his own hand, no less—but he had found the man behind Hyde's death. Cortlan, assuming he had offered his true name, had to be the man he was looking for. If not, he would at least be a meaningful step in the right direction. Domina pondered how the Artorian Chora fit into the puzzle, she could easily have been working alongside him, or just another victim of his manipulations.

"What are you doing?" asked a soft voice.

Domina wheeled in an instant and brought his blade's tip toward whoever had addressed him. A dark elf with grey-green skin stood just ahead of him. He wore a bloodied white tunic that disappeared beneath a leather corset and a tattered black cloak that hung off his shoulders. Domina did not recognise him at first. Those tired eyes, distant and predator-like, delayed Domina's realisation that what stood before him was no more than a reflection.

Anamrath wanted him to move, to turn away from the blatant illusion. But Domina was transfixed.

"I'm going to end this," he answered. "I have to avenge them. I must not fail."

The mirror said nothing more, instead it was Cortlan's voice which offered rebuttal. "You failed a long time ago."

Domina gripped Anamrath and slashed back at the illusionist with all of his fury. The blade froze, the void's edge refusing to connect with Cortlan's neck. He strained to force it onward, found it entirely unresponsive. Domina could not even pull the blade back, his entire arm had been overtaken by a tension that refused to let up.

Cortlan was smiling. "What's the matter? You had no issue killing everyone else."

"How are you doing this?"

"Oh, I'm not." He seemed to take a special amount of pleasure delivering that news.

Then something bizarre happened to the mage. Parts of his skin began to change colour and dry, becoming a light grey with the texture of chalk. Domina reminded himself that it was just an illusion; if he knew as much then it could do nothing to harm him. Yet the ashy corruption only continued to spread across Cortlan's face, consuming everything that made up his person.

Domina screamed, trying desperately to use whatever strength remained within him to tear his hand free from the hilt. It was no use.

He heard laughter but was unable to identify where it could have possibly come from. It was within his mind—not a new experience, but this sound did not belong to Morguein, or any other entity that should be within him.

A hand appeared. Somebody was wrapping their arm around Domina from behind, their fingers slowly trailing a path toward Anamrath's hilt. The appendage was grey, skin flaking off like the ash on Cortlan's face. When it finally reached its target, Domina braced himself for madness and horror, but was stunned to feel nothing at all.

Darkness was all that remained.

—

Logic, something that had once been Elias' comfort in times of struggle, now offered him only a daunting revelation: he was a dead man walking.

Everything hurt, and as much as he tried, he could not trace any of the pain to a particular injury, rather it felt as though his entire body was an open wound. Those technicalities should not have mattered to him, but it was all there was to keep him from letting his body collapse.

Elias ran a hand through his rough hair, shifted the ropey strands away from his face.

Carlyle Lyre had backed away from him, appearing taken aback by Elias' newfound vigour and trembling with rage. "Just die already, old man. This is not your fight."

Though his vision was blurred around the edges, Elias thought he could see a shape move behind Lyre. He refused to focus on it. Better that the lord kept his whole focus on the dying man before him.

Elias offered the ground a quick search, before making way toward where his blade had landed. His legs threatened to give out with each step. "So what's the plan, Lyre?"

Lyre only stared back at him, apparently perplexed by just how casually his former hire was acting, despite the situation. It was almost pitiable just how useless he was in the face of something he had not expected.

Elias tried to laugh, but the effort hurt too much for him to proceed. "Why keep it so close to your chest, even now?"

"Because it doesn't matter anymore."

"Oh, really?"

"You ruined it, Sorren." He spat the name like a curse. "I cannot save them, because of you."

"You weren't gonna save anyone. Let's be true to each other. For once." Elias had reached his blade. Inside himself, he was dreading the simple act of bending over to pick it up. But his time was running out, and any moment of delay would be a waste. So Elias lowered himself to the ground, took that familiar hilt in his hand, and rose again.

"They're all going to die, but I suppose you won't live to see that." Lyre's eyes were glazed over and the markings scrawled across his bare chest had begun to glow. His fists were pure light, as some terrible energy coursed through the ink.

Elias shifted the weight in his hand. The tip of the curved blade had been destroyed in the blast, but the sharpened length of the weapon remained mostly intact. Whatever power Lyre held, Elias had to hope he still bore the same weaknesses as any man. Prone to overconfidence, it would be easy to avoid his first strike and land a lethal hit, though Elias had to remind himself that he was not in his usual state. There was every likelihood his own body would give out before steel would make any connection to flesh.

Lyre shifted the fur cloak from his shoulders, standing before Elias less like a lord and more akin to a beast with nothing left to lose. "What you are about to experience, shall be nothing but a sliver of what the people of this land will know. Think on that as your mind abandons you."

Lyre leapt forward, so much faster than Elias had anticipated that he had no time for the logic he cherished. He swung his blade through the air before him, praying to The Fist that it would be enough to save him—perhaps the Old Gods no longer listened to their people, but Elias was an old man, and not one to abandon such habits.

The harsh song of metal reverberated from the weapon; it had saved Elias, and he allowed himself a moment of elation when he saw Lyre's fury grow.

Then their duel of blood and steel began truly. Elias immediately took the lead, swinging his curved weapon in wide arcs. Allowing Lyre to get close would be a lethal mistake, so the combat revolved largely around Elias not letting him have the chance to do so.

Perhaps Honouros had heard him, because Elias felt a newfound strength course through his body. His blood burned and urged him onward. It was pure instinct that guided him, faith that Elias knew the path that would see him through the heat of battle. Faith that he did not need to overthink every last detail of a situation to know the right way from the wrong turn.

Elias would die that day, so he would die a man who finally knew something he could offer all of his trust. Himself.

Lyre attempted to bat away Elias' weapon, with the shock of each strike passing from the blade and into his already aching arm. With each attack and deflect he grew wearier. This was not a fight Elias was going to win, and Lyre was only growing more eager for the kill with every second it was kept from him. But Elias did not have to win. Though he had not thought Oedon would need so long to do his part, everything that had happened was technically still a part of the plan they'd constructed. Elias only needed to keep going as long as he could.

With each trade of blows, streaks of blood scattered; if Lyre cared at all that he was being wounded, he didn't waste time showing it. The lord was pure frenzy and adrenaline, driven by his longing to gain something from the exchange, even if that was only the chance to kill a man who was already on his way to death's door.

Elias thought he saw more movement on the cusp of his vision, had to hope it was somebody on his side and not one of Lyre's who had recovered. When he was finally able to identify Blackhand between Lyre's flurry of blows, he was hardly alleviated.

The way he stood revealed that the man was wounded, and his eyes weren't watching the fight.

Lyre caught Elias while his attention was split, a fist striking him in the shoulder. The pain was immense, but his left arm was already useless to him, and the hit sent his body twisting. He used that motion to his advantage, swinging his steel toward Lyre.

He hit the ground, expecting Lyre to finish him off at any moment. But a fatal blow failed to come. Elias glanced up to find Lyre clutching at his own face, blood trickling out from under his palm. His counter had bought him precious seconds, they couldn't go to waste—then he found himself looking back at Eric anyway, now joined by Oedon.

The boy was pointing at something. Elias thought it was himself, at first, rather it was something a few feet ahead: Blackhand's firearm.

Lyre had recovered, terrible line of red left drawn across his furious visage.

Elias leapt for the firearm, and caught it just as Lyre was on him. All of the lord's strength was focused on Elias' throat. He was laughing, taken by mania as he tightened his grip on his prey's only source of air. Elias had made the mistake of taking the weapon in his left hand; he could not corral his muscles to defend himself. The only option left was to flick his wrist with the little strength that remained in him and hope it landed close enough to his allies.

And they were his allies. Not something Elias could say he'd had in a long time.

He tried to speak, to do anything he could to buy himself more time. Just a few more seconds. A few more moments. One last breath.

"This is what happens to people like you," Lyre hissed, his voice hoarse and laced with cruelty. "Enjoy it, Sorren. You earned this."

The night sky became so bright that Elias had to close his eyes, and the next moment, a sound like hell filled the air. When Elias looked upon the world again, he found Lyre was gone, having been sent flying by Blackhand's weapon. Elias could not be sure whether the man was still alive, and found that he hardly cared.

Elias had done his part, Eric and Oedon could handle the rest.

It was a shame his life had led to this ending. Though Elias thought he had made peace with his mortality decades prior—a person who chose to live the life of a hired sword was not one who cherished life nor feared death—he felt the whisper of disappointment all the same.

Here lay a man who had lived his life solely guided by his own eyes, and the moment he decided to follow another's instincts he had met death. There was a cruel beauty in that which Elias may have appreciated if he were a different person. But he was not. He was Elias Sorren, and he was not going to die because of another's choices. He knew the folly in facing a lord of Duralaans and his guardsmen alone, yet he did it anyway. And he would do it again.

He saw Blackhand focused on where Lyre lay, his firearm raised in warning. Elias knew he would not use it. This was not the man Elias had hunted. That man—if he ever existed at all— was a far cry from the youth before him. There was still hope for whoever he really was to choose a different path, no matter what Oedon thought of fate.

Elias smiled as he felt his body grow weaker, his breathing shallow. Oedon must have known this would be where Elias met his end, and the boy let it happen all the same. What a strange one he was.

"I'm sorry," and there was his voice, timed as though he could read thoughts as well.

Elias forced himself to turn his head away from Blackhand and toward where Oedon was sat on his knees. His hair was still such a mess.

"You're wrong," Elias tried to say, unsure whether or not he actually managed it. "If everything we do is only because of something else that's already happened, where do you fit in?" Elias did not expect a real answer but felt it was a worthy question to ask anyway.

"We all answer to something." Oedon tried and failed to brush a strand away from his face. "I only do what is necessary, no more."

"Then why do you keep trying to get that hair out of the way? Is that necessary?"

Oedon responded with a meek shrug.

"Sometimes you got to do what you want, not what you need."

"I fear that is not the world we find ourselves in."

"And why should you care what the world expects of you?"

If Oedon had any answer, Elias did not hear it. His hearing had finally failed him, and his vision was gone quickly afterwards.

Elias thought he had more that should have been said, but he found any idea of what those words were fleeting. His time was up, and not a moment too soon either.

Elias hated waiting.

—

"Do not pity me, boy," Lyre groaned. He had forced himself to his, knees despite how much pain it must have caused him. "Death will come for us all soon, at least put me out of my misery."

Nath considered it. Maybe it really wouldn't matter whether or not he pulled the trigger just one more time. But if he did have a chance to choose another life, that had to begin at some point. "Maybe that's true, but your life isn't mine to take." He had already promised Raph that justice would be hers. Nath never had found a true resolution to the pain that haunted him, he would not take that from her as well. He lowered his weapon. "Tell me where you were headed."

Lyre laughed. "It seems Oedon has betrayed me, he can tell you whatever you want to know. Though I might recommend against trusting that he gives you the whole truth."

"I'm giving you the chance to offer your own perspective. You can choose whether you waste it or not, I won't care if you do."

"Waste it?" Lyre took a moment to decide how much he wished to divulge. "It's all a waste. This was the last chance we had. There is no stopping it now."

"Stopping what? Artorius?"

"Our only hope was destroying these keys, shutting off the last route to his freedom."

Nath took a step forward "Then you should never have opposed us. Our goals have been the same, we could have been allies." Nath reached for the key, only for Lyre to pull back. "But it's not just the keys that you care about, is it? Not just stopping Artorius. It needs to be you."

"Of course it does. What hope do you have or the girl have? If I caught her as easily as I did, how could she have ever claimed the rest of them?" Lyre laughed. It was a forced and cruel sound that turned Nath's heart cold.

"Then I'll destroy it myself." He closed the distance and tore the key from its place, too quick for the wounded man to avoid.

"NO!" Lyre screamed with a rage Nath had not expected he could still possess and threw himself forward.

But he never reached Nath.

Seven glass dagger bit into Lyre's chest in rapid succession—though Nath saw the life had already left his eyes by the fourth. In those final moments Nath saw Lyre's eyes were filled not with anger, but with a terror like none he had ever known—and prayed he never would.

Lyre landed in the dirt, and did not move again.

"What did you do?" Nath saw Oedon standing over where Elias lay in the dirt, a few strands of his hair braided with rings Nath believed had belonged to the mercenary. "Is he?"

Oedon lowered his head. "Yes."

"I'm sorry."

"Don't be. We were not friends, barely knew each other."

"Even so, I asked this of him. It's on me."

Oedon caught the daggers as they flew back into his hand, conjoining to form the complete crystal blade. "We should not remain here. It is doubtful that nobody heard all of this."

"Where can we go?"

"Not we." Oedon turned his back on Nath and took a few small steps toward the night. "My part in this is over."

"Because you're free of Lyre?" Nath called, then began to understand the larger image. "Or because you've set us all up and now you just get to watch us fall down?"

Oedon stopped but did not turn.

"You had to know this would happen. Why not warn us? Why not tell Elias not to come, or at least use a better strategy?"

"That is not my place. I cannot turn others from the destined path."

"Then why are you here? Do you enjoy watching us suffer?"

"No." There was a tremble in the boy's voice.

Nath thought that he could help Oedon, if only he could get past the walls he kept up. "You could help so many people."

"That is not how this works."

"Why not?"

"You cannot understand."

"Is that another future you see? You tell me and I don't listen?"

"I do not know."

"Then see for yourself, right now. Tell me what you're supposed to do here, and we'll see how I respond together."

Silence engulfed them for a long few minutes. Nath's eyes glanced toward where Elias lay more than once. He appeared surprisingly peaceful in death, though that did not stop Nath from believing that there should have been another way.

He had just about given up any hope that Oedon would speak again when the boy finally turned to meet Nath's eyes. "Our world is governed by two celestial forces, rules of nature that dictate the flow of reality. These are cause and effect, the gods most know simply as the Mother and the Father. All action is simply reaction. A cascade of events that will continue until we return to the void. That is life. These gods found me months ago. I was near my own end, in despair over my mother's death, but they offered me purpose. I would ensure their laws were not broken, I would come to this place and see that the return of Artorius went as it was supposed to."

Nath shuddered. There was a part of him that had expected this all-seeing child must have played a part in the grander scheme he and Raph faced. But the rest of him was shocked to know he could allow such a thing to happen. "How?"

"There were already figures who moved to achieve this, but they would struggle without a counterbalance. It only took warning two of this threat, and the rest handled itself. It did not take long for word to reach both the Queen and your friend's Goddess of Growth. From there, all has proceeded as it must."

"That's hypocrisy, don't you see that?" Nath was stunned; it seemed so obvious to him. "If you had to act in order to make all of this happen, then how is it destined? You have interfered. You've changed things."

Oedon stood straighter, defensive over his purpose. "I do not stand outside of the Gods' will. My actions are just as reactionary as yours. I was always going to do this. Nothing has changed."

"How do you know if you've not tried?"

"Perhaps I do not want to." Oedon hesitated. "Perhaps it is easier this way."

Nath felt as though he had failed, something in Oedon was broken or missing entirely, and he did not believe he would be the one to find it. He turned their discussion in a new direction. "Lyre said he was taking his key somewhere to have it destroyed."

"The capital."

"Avalass?"

"The Queen is holding a gala to introduce the new Lord of House Hyde. It is a cover for the destruction of the Artorian keys."

"Then that's where I'm headed."

"Even if you know it will make no difference? Lyre is dead, they will react poorly to anyone else bearing his key. The return of the Ashen Lord is nigh."

"Even so." Nath put on his best smile. "You didn't have to save me."

"I know," Oedon whispered, suddenly shy in the face of his own actions.

"But you did it anyway." He made his way over to the calmest of the horses which still remained in the camp, found a nearby saddle and began to fasten it. "Fate? Choice? Maybe there's no difference." He considered mounting the beast, then looked back to where Elias still lay in the dirt. "Whether we bury him or not, he's gonna rot away and eventually return to the land. Same result, right? But I'm gonna bury him anyway. It doesn't matter why.

Maybe it's something my parents taught me, maybe something else. It doesn't matter. I'm still gonna do it."

He searched the camp until he found a suitable shovel, then began to dig a decent enough distance away that Elias' grave should not be connected to the other deaths. It was going to take a while to do, perhaps even more time than he had if he wanted to attend this gala. But it felt right. He did not know Elias well, maybe he deserved the fate he met, but he'd done something good for somebody he didn't have to help. That deserved a decent burial at the very least.

The sound of a second spade striking the ground startled Nath. Oedon stood opposite him, using a shovel that was made for men twice his age and size. Nath smiled and continued to dig.

It was almost sunrise by the time they had finally laid Elias to rest and filled in the hole. They had not spoken at any point during the ordeal, Oedon's decision said enough on its own. Nath reckoned that he was probably just as stubborn at that age, and he probably held less than half the power Oedon did.

Nath watched the sun peak over the horizon, hoping it symbolised more than just the start of another day.

Oedon had already climbed atop their new horse, and did not object when Nath joined him. Together, they set out for Avalass.

Chapter Twenty-Two
Intermission

It had been years since Cecilia had visited the old palace properly. Whenever she imagined it, the place still existed as the desecrated ruin from the history books, but in present it stood just as grandiose as its mountaintop counterpart. Positioned close to the mountain's base, the majority of its structure was shaped like a wide crescent moon, shielding the central palace from the rest of the city.

Cecilia had been wandering its halls for most of the day—certainly, it was large enough that she rarely revisited the same room—but there was reason for her exploration beyond becoming acquainted with her ancestral home. It allowed her mind to race. Not the messy, anxiety-bred racing of when she kept herself still, but the steady, measured mindset that allowed her to better unravel the tangled mess at her doorstep.

It was the day of Hyde's gala; the eight original houses would gather, celebrate their new compatriot's official arrival, and together end the greatest threat to ever darken Duralaans. It should have been a day for hope, Cecilia's first great work as queen, even if it would likely not be for another few generations before anyone knew what had been done. But that was better. Do a good deed, not for recognition or acclaim, but because it was good.

Despite such excuses for celebration, she remained on edge.

Cecilia had found herself in the old palace's throne room, gazing up at the glass ceiling. She could almost make out the magnificent towers far above that were her home. It seemed so small, so insignificant from her current perspective. Funny, how something so incredible could appear completely inconsequential from a distance. But appearances were often deceiving, and no matter how unconcerning Artorius' return might have seemed, she would not be fooled.

It was difficult to believe that this room was the same she had heard so many stories about. Artorius had once unknowingly slain his sister just a few short steps from where she stood, then sent the noble lords to join her. She knew there were endless theories which had attempted to explain that single event, apply reason to the seemingly unreasonable. Some claimed he was mad, others that the nobles were the ones to betray him first, none told the full tale Cecilia presumed existed between the cracks. Such things were far removed from her; it was better for Cecilia if she did not allow herself to dwell too heavily on the past. That was not a mindset her fellows shared.

Aester Hyde had asked for only one thing in return for using his commencement gala as the staging grounds for Cecilia's own plot, that being to set it within that old palace. The years he had spent removed from the land may very well have developed in him a yearning to present himself with a certain grandeur. It was nigh impossible that the other lords had not already made up their minds on him, but she could at least respect his wish to officially present himself on his own terms. That was no luxury Cecilia had the pleasure of knowing.

She turned her attention downward as a polite cough called for her attention. "Yes, Chora?"

"Lord Hyde has arrived."

She stretched her neck, already feeling exhausted. Cecilia had allowed herself to hope he were the kind to arrive late to his own occasion, but such luck would not grace her. "Does he expect to see me so soon?"

"I believe that was his intent."

"Then I suppose I should not keep him waiting." Cecilia turned toward her newly appointed personal guard. She stood at attention in shimmering black armour, hands folded neatly before her, but Chora's eyes were lost taking in the hall itself. "You're aware that your namesake was killed in this very room?"

Her eyes took another moment to drink in the ancient architecture before she offered Cecilia her attention proper. "We are taught the histories during training." She seemed to struggle with something internally, only delivered the thought at Cecilia's allowance. "To be true, it was Artoria II we were named after, I believe you are referring to Artorius' sister—she was killed within this place."

"Quite right. Even so, I'm surprised that you are so enamoured by it. Does it not bear ill for you?"

"Should a place forever be marred by the events that took place within its walls?"

"Perhaps not. Though it can be difficult to move on." She smiled, trying her best to instil in Chora the confidence she did not feel herself. "I'm glad to see you feeling better. Whoever is working against us, I did not want them to have ruined you."

"And you have my gratitude for it."

Cecilia placed her hand on the girl's shoulder. Chora was shorter than most knights, almost scrawny beneath her armour, but Cecilia recognised the grit within her eyes. Beneath the kind loyalty, there was something fierce that dwelled within this one. It did not threaten the Queen, she knew there was no reason to doubt Chora's commitment to her Artorian vows. Indeed, it was that commitment that shone through her—how lucky Cecilia was to have this one as an ally.

Loyalty could be a terrible thing when placed in the wrong hands. Whether or not that described Cecilia was what this gala would serve to decide.

Aester Hyde was to be found in the palace's main hall, where the lords, ladies, and whichever relatives elected to join them would mingle amongst themselves, undoubtedly, to share their developing opinions on their new compatriot. Space for dancing had been made out in the centre for those who felt the need, and it was there Hyde stood, rotating on the spot as though assessing the ongoing preparation.

"I must offer your people my utmost thanks." He smiled with approval. "Deserum was no stranger to a celebration, but there was an elegance that we lost towards the end of my time there."

"It is nothing less than the event calls for. This is a homecoming, after all."

Something dark crept into Hyde's eyes then. "And the beginning of a new age." Those eyes flickered pointedly toward Chora, and he waited for Cecilia to have her guard dismissed before continuing. "Quite the bold solution you've decided upon."

"But an effective one."

His expression turned sceptical. "So they are in agreement? I'm quite surprised, such ties to the past are difficult to sever. Especially in those whose power is inherited solely through those very ties."

"Some were reluctant," Cecilia admitted, "but none did not succumb to reason in due time."

Aester hummed a doubtful tune.

"You have an opinion to share?" Cecilia asked, losing the internal battle with herself to simply ignore it.

"I watched Deserum tear itself apart on the whim of men and women whose sole claim to their power was blood." He shook his head, dismissing his own memory. "These people should never have been allowed such an opportunity."

"You believe none of us should be where we stand today?"

"I believe everyone deserves a moment to prove themselves worthy."

So tempting it was to invoke the power he was referencing, to declare such conversation beneath her and be excused. Cecilia's father would have done so, but that was only in his final years, and Cecilia's term had only begun. "Is that not what I'm offering this very night?"

He smiled. "Tonight, will prove your own mettle, not theirs."

"Why not? They have agreed to do something for the good of Duralaans, should that not be applauded?"

"You said it yourself: they took convincing. They revealed their own colours when they asked for a reward in return for their *righteousness*." That last word was laced with derision. "If I may speak candidly?"

Cecilia struggled to believe he ever did anything but. "Of course."

Hyde began pacing back and forth, drawing out their already lengthy discussion. "You have gifted these lordlings too much agency. If they had rejected your proposal, what then?"

Cecilia would not admit that she had never considered that as a possibility, not because she thought them too altruistic to deny her request, but because she knew they would not reject the offer of a prize. "That was not an option."

"So you were ready to take the matter into your own hands if necessary?" Aester seemed intrigued by her wording.

"Not through the means you suspect," she shut him down. "I want you to understand the importance of this moment is two-fold. Yes, preventing the threat you have warned me of is a priority, but so is securing our bonds as a united body. You may believe that they cannot be trusted to achieve such a consequential feat—and you are not wholly wrong to do so—yet it is my duty as queen to place my people's will above my own. If they do not wish to save themselves, then there is little more I can do."

His lilted laugh echoed throughout the hall. "These are not mere people, Your Grace. They are brutes, pigs fattened by the decades spent supping at their gilded troughs. They will choose what they see as preserving their seats, even if that so ironically happens to bring about their demise in due course. They are small of mind, inward thinkers who cannot fathom something beyond themselves."

Cecilia felt a familiarity in his words. They were not exact, but the encompassing belief aligned with the teachings of those who followed Avandoras' primordial deities. They incentivised looking toward the grander scale of the world, seeing beyond individual moments, and instead focusing on the ultimate result. She reasoned that it had been his upbringing in Deserum that had instilled in Aester such views. They were difficult to reckon with her own more subjective worldview.

Duralaans had come a long way from its past as a land of conquerors. The land had once been created by the Gods to train a brutal populace of warriors who would one day challenge the rest of Avandoras. The intent was to force the rest of the world's people to grow stronger in return. Duralaans was a place of limits; few would have the luxury of possessing that which they needed to survive, and the only way to have such things was to take from those who had them.

Though such inclinations had been tempered over the centuries, issues still arose as a result of the mindset singularly ingrained in Duralaans' people. The monarchs had overcome this by viewing the land and its people as an extension of their own self. Though it had long been apparent that the lesser lords of the land did not share this view, and continued to crave that which would solely benefit themselves. That was why it was so important that Cecilia allow the decision to destroy the keys be their own. A single moment of definition that would tell her who exactly were the people she was bound to lead.

"I value your opinion, Lord Hyde." She paused to allow her words some weight and choose her next carefully. "Even so, you may not understand your fellows as well as you believe. It is true that they are prone to introversion, but stripping them of their agency, as you say, will do nothing but antagonise them."

Aester's expression hardened, that dark intrigue twisting into something colder, and suddenly Cecilia regretted having sent Chora away. "You place the lives of the many in the hands of these few?"

"They have agreed to the terms, Lord Hyde. Your concern is unwarranted." She projected finality in her tone. "Now, if you would excuse me, I must prepare myself for the night."

In a moment, Aester had returned to pleasantry, and Cecilia understood just how fake his entire persona truly was. "Very well, I look forward to seeing your work blossom."

He bowed, and Cecilia made a swift exit. There was no need to let Aester's fears weigh on her, yet that was precisely what they did.

Once Cecilia was certain she was far from the sight of others, she fell back against the wall of one of the palace's many corridors. Despite her proclamations of unity and collective decision, she felt much of the stress fell upon her alone. Her innards churned as the world seemed to spin and her body shivered with a sickening chill.

All she could think of was that damned painting in her room. The fire and destruction had consumed the land and left it scarred forevermore, the people forced to survive the sins of another. If she were to fail, if the lords did renege at the final moment, it would thus be her own mistakes that the people had to suffer for. That responsibility should not have belonged to her. Yet it did. And there was nothing she could do for it but stand tall. That was the decision she had made on the night of her coronation, the same she had made when Léonora had offered her a chance to leave it all behind.

Had Artorius felt similarly? Was his betrayal actually a result of his own desperation to maintain his land? Or had he succumbed to the same beliefs Lord Hyde possessed? If Artorius had decided that his own desires took greater precedent than the demands of his council, then Cecilia could not allow herself to make the same mistake.

Aester had only been warned of a great evil's return, not the exact series of events that allowed it to happen.

Cecilia forced herself to take a series of concentrated breaths and shut down the thoughts that threatened to overwhelm her. *May Diavollos take Aester Hyde and his prophecies.* They did her no good. The people of Deserum could keep such things, Duralaans was a place of present matter.

"Cecilia?" Cassidy's voice upset her attempts to find calm.

Cecilia pushed herself off the wall and took a stance more fitting of a queen. "Cassidy, when did you become so quiet of step?"

"Apologies, Cecilia."

"What do you need of me?"

"I thought it time you were dressed for the night. But if you are occupied I can—"

"That's alright. I was already on my way to find you."

And so, after a delightfully strenuous intermission, Cecilia stepped back into her role as Queen of Duralaans and led Cassidy to her dressing room.

Even if she did not feel deserving of her role, Cecilia might as well look the part.

—

Wrapped in angles of black and highlights of silver-grey, Cecilia looked herself in the eye. Cassidy stood behind her, wrapping a tight ribbon around her hair to keep it in place as it cascaded down her back. She wore no jewellery, nothing to distract from the royal memorabilia that sat on her shoulders. Her dress was elegant, though not excessively garish; the night belonged to Hyde, let him be the centre of the universe for once.

"It will be welcome to have this night over with, I have not enjoyed seeing the strain it has put on you," Cassidy said.

"Such is my duty. Don't concern yourself with it, I can manage."

"I am aware, Majesty. Do not forget that I was present for every change you made so that you might be ready for your inheritance."

Cecilia laughed at the prospect. "I did not change so much."

"Not *so much*, no. But there have been some things you've let go."

The Queen felt a smile take her lips. "Do enlighten me."

Cassidy seemed to take a moment to decide, as though there were truly too many for her to pick from. "You have not painted in quite some years."

Bizarrely, Cecilia found her eyes grow wet. Had it really been so long? "I suppose that is true. I simply haven't had the time."

Cassidy's expression turned serious. "That is my point, Cecilia. You have given up your own pleasures for duty."

"I am Queen. I share the kingdom's pleasures."

"But you are Cecilia Asche, also. You are more than a piece in a game that is only allowed to move as the rules dictate."

"Cassidy?" Cecilia laughed. "I have never known you to be so opinionated."

The handmaiden huffed, stroked her soft jaw with her hand. "I apologise. You are my friend, Cecilia. Perhaps much more, if I am not stepping too far in saying that."

"You are not." Cecilia turned to meet her eyes, then wrapped her arms around her friend of so many years. "I do not tell you enough just how valuable your confidence is to me."

Cassidy returned the embrace. "Do not worry, Your Grace. I am sure the night will go without issue."

"If you believe that to be so, then I truly do have nothing to fear." She pulled back, brushed Cassidy's short red hair out of her face. "When this is done, we shall find your brother. You have my word."

"Thank you." A flicker of doubt crossed Cassidy's face, though it was quickly replaced once more by a smile. "I'm sure that wherever he has found himself, Cortlan is fine."

Chapter Twenty-Three
A Simple Solution

So Domina had found himself a prisoner once more. 173 years he had walked upon the surface of Avandoras. 173 years he had gone without being taken captive and left at the mercy of an adversary. Now he had been imprisoned twice within the span of a week or so. It seemed he was losing his touch.

At least the transport Cortlan utilised was a simple cart, and not a carriage that might obfuscate Domina's view of their travel. Unfortunately, that did not make escape any more of a prospect worth consideration. A chain collar had been locked around his neck and attached to the cart itself; if Domina were to leap out, he would do nothing but hang himself.

Of course, Anamrath could slice through the chain without issue—assuming it actually decided to respond to him once again. Though it remained hooked to his belt, the somewhat sentient weapon had ignored his attempts to summon it to his hand and prove itself of any use. What a waste it had shown itself to be, and what a fool Domina was for expecting anything else.

Though its power was undeniable, Anamrath had always been a difficult thing to wield. That had not been such a problem during his Santoran days, in that land he had found no end to the enemies that needed to be dealt with, and he certainly proved to be more effective than before he was the weapon's master. Though he now found himself wondering just how much truth that thought actually held.

Domina had been especially young for an elf when he had left the village he'd grown up in and found what he considered purpose among the ranks of King Azazel's military force. He thought himself a failure for leading those in his charge to their death in battle against an impossibly powerful enemy. Those men and women had relied on him, and as he always seemed to do, he let them down. Later, Domina had failed to save his next master as meteors fell upon a festival they had visited together. But Domina recalled that he had already possessed Anamrath during that particular event. Even with the blade as his weapon of choice, Domina could not save those that relied on him. And of late, his luck had only worsened with it returned to his grip. So he wondered why it was that he still craved the support of something that had only ever hindered him.

By Domina's estimate they had been travelling northward for eight days, slowly approaching a distant mountain, and likely the city that dwelled in its shadow. Domina's best guess was that Cortlan planned to shift the ire of the lawmakers onto him—it was not that Domina deserved no retribution for his actions, but he would not allow himself to pay for his sins alone.

As night fell, Cortlan brought their journey to a halt. Resting in the light of a red fire, the mage deftly passed his glass orb between his fingers, examining the flickers of flame reflected on its surface.

Each night, Domina had considered escape. There was some hope that he might break the chain free from where it was attached to the cart, but he could only do so when he knew that Cortlan would not be monitoring him. He thought that would not be so difficult an endeavour, but it appeared as though the mage never slept, or rather, he maintained an illusion of himself sat up throughout the night.

Domina had deduced this trick on their first night and attempted to tear free the plank of wood his chain was latched to, only for a very real Cortlan to stop him with a projectile of magical red fire. It seemed his illusions were more complex than Cortlan had originally let on. The mage must have maintained some mental connection to his mirage which would alert him in the case Domina tried anything.

He watched the projection each night. The man appeared so distant, relaxed despite the atrocities he had committed only days prior. Domina thought it was all too easy, that he had stumbled upon the one he sought and practically been handed the answers to the questions that had stalked him all the way from Anderan.

Domina let the details work their way through his mind. Cortlan must have found an assassin through the blood broker and hired them to destroy Hyde's manor with the lord inside. Meanwhile, the Artorian Chora would use her position to be welcomed into the party, only to disappear after getting her hands on Hyde's ancient key. Cortlan must have also tried to set up a similar affair in Meergard, but had been forced to eliminate Callum once it became clear he was uncomfortable with the situation he'd found himself in. So Cortlan was forced to deal with Trethellyn himself. That fact gave Domina some room for hope; not everything had proceeded as this mage had intended. He was far from infallible. Domina could use that to his advantage.

This left only two questions he could not answer. In order to secure Domina's release and be allowed to attend Hyde's dinner, Chora must have truly been Artorian, so how could Cortlan have possibly brought her into his plot? He may not have known much about Duralaans and its history, but Domina was certain the Artorian Guard were not a group that could easily be made to break their sworn oath to serve only the land's monarch. It brought to life the daunting prospect that the Queen herself was the true director of these crimes. Though if that were the case, then Domina would have no hope of unmasking the truth. He could wield a sword better than most, but there were some battlefields even he would not tread upon.

Domina's second question revolved around motive. Cortlan's goal must have been to collect the relic keys of both Hyde and Trethellyn, but it was the ends that perplexed Domina. As far as he was aware, those keys served a single purpose, yet he could not determine Cortlan's reason for pursuing such devastation.

All of these factors offered Domina a simple solution: there was a piece of this puzzle that remained obscured from him, and he would not be done until it was unveiled.

With such clarity, sleep was finally able to take Domina. The strange visions of ash that had twisted his perception and allowed him to be captured had managed to infect his dreams as well. They were not visions he could make any sense of. Images came to him of a dark sky smothered in clouds of smoke and a land choked by ash fallen from the heavens. Each time he gazed upon the ruin, Domina felt as though something was trying desperately to tear out his heart and sever his soul from his flesh. He thought such horrors would force him to wake. Yet somehow, with every second he spent within the dream, he felt more inclined to stay; there was something like an itch in his mind, one he could scratch if only he remained a few seconds more.

He knew that was just the outcome that whatever had infected him desired, so there was no way he could allow himself to remain. It didn't matter how close he felt to answers—especially when he suspected they were to questions he hadn't even asked the question to yet.

It felt like he had to physically remind his body how to pry open its eyes, but Domina eventually returned to lucidity. He did not know how long he had been asleep for, but the sun was past rising, and Cortlan was ready to set off for what would be their final day of travel.

Dread grew in the depths of Domina's stomach as the mountain became less distant. He tried once more to call Anamrath into his hand, was met with the same ignorance as every time prior.

He cast his attention toward where the mage sat. Cortlan had offered Domina only a handful of words during their whole journey, that projected a level assurance he found concerning, and surely needed to crack.

"Vécar Forkh," Domina said, just loud enough that he knew Cortlan would hear. "Know that name?"

"I am aware of it," Cortlan responded, without turning away from the road ahead.

"I defeated him once. Drove this sword right through his heart, killed the unkillable. Wasn't easy. Almost took me with him, stripped Anamrath of its power just to do it. But I did it, didn't I?"

"Feeling boastful, are we?"

"Just trying to clear the air." He could only guess at what expression Cortlan held, but he hoped he was trying and failing to beat Domina to his point. "Tell me, if even the lord of death couldn't beat me, what makes you think anything you have planned will work?"

Cortlan turned to meet his eyes, and Domina was disheartened to see that he was smiling. "But it wasn't you who killed Vécar, was it?" He chuckled. "No, it was that lovely sword of yours that did the real work. I hardly see you being much trouble without it."

"I've only had that thing back for a few weeks, I did well enough for the ten years before that."

Another laugh, chillingly genuine. "You think Lady Frieda's power is so weak?"

Domina's mouth went dry, he had underestimated just how much this mage knew. It was only a minor stumble, he could win this bout yet. "How do you know that name?"

"Four years I spent in service to that pirate king, do you know what that taught me?" Cortlan shifted the conversation. "Choose who you follow wisely. It seems so simple in hindsight, yet we continue to pledge ourselves to those who cannot deserve such privilege. Léonora was driven by their desperation to know freedom—or anarchy, if you prefer—and that made them reckless, too reckless to be an apt leader."

"I don't care about your history."

"No? I thought we were clearing the air. You of all people must know something of inept masters. Did you not follow Azazel for a few decades?"

Domina tried to stand, but his binding chain seemed to have suddenly shrunk, and the wind was torn from his throat. He struggled to speak through his gasping for air. "How?"

"The shadows talk, and you've been carrying one for a long time."

He could almost laugh. Forty-six years he had carried Anamrath, between Azazel and his second encounter with Vécar, the blade had been his greatest companion. A part of Domina had to know that a cost would present itself eventually, even if the rest of him did not care so long as he was met with continued success. Though it may have seemed a worthwhile prospect at the time, accepting the sword again from that woodland witch had been a terrible mistake. Even if he could not—and still did not—know exactly what part Morguein played in Cortlan's schemes, he had been damned to do her dirty work for longer than he could have feared.

Domina took a deep breath, and said, "You are an apprentice of Frieda. She ordered you to take the keys of this land's lords and use them to free Artorius."

"No order was necessary. We understand each other, there is no man nor woman fit to rule while a King chosen by the Gods still lives."

"Then what does she need me for? Why have me collect so many souls?"

"You are not entitled to the answers you desire. I have given you some to alleviate your confusion, but that is enough."

"Very well." Domina was done with questions anyway. "She has used me as her tool without my knowledge for decades, what makes you think you're any different?"

Cortlan turned to match Domina's gaze once more. "While you refuse to accept your place, I welcome mine with open arms."

Domina considered, then decided against continuing their discussion. He had learned more than he'd dare hope for and found himself almost comforted by what he now knew. Cortlan undoubtedly thought he had emerged with the upper hand, but Domina knew better. Morguein's involvement simplified things, smoothed over the knots in the web entangling him and offering the faintest glimmer of light within the abyss.

Despite how long he had been tethered to the witch, he knew very little about her. That had to change. Domina would not let himself fall for Morguein's sins, and he certainly could not let the souls he had amassed for her be turned toward any more atrocity.

Anamrath may have been uninterested in heeding his need for aid, but he knew there was something it could not resist—something that had been taken from it and only Domina could return.

The hilt trembled in place, eager to take back what it was owed.

The words Domina needed to speak teased his tongue. There would be no turning back if he allowed them to come forth, the end would begin, and Domina would have little time to do what he must. He smiled, realising that was nothing knew, and said, "Take it."

The hilt moved on its own, unhooking from Domina's belt and flying through the air. He caught it, brought the void to life, and drove it through his own chest.

Never in his forty-six years with the weapon had he thought it a good idea to fall upon his own sword. Domina had now done so twice over the course of only a week or so.

Chapter Twenty-Four

Serpent's Tongue

And what was your name?" the woman asked, looking down on Raph with thin eyes.

"Seraph."

The apologetic frown the woman offered in return was in no way reflected by the rest of her face. "Sincerest apologies, it is not that I do not believe you, simply that there is a process I am required to follow. You were not penned an invitation, Miss Seraph, so I see no reason I can permit your entrance."

Raph huffed in exasperation. "The Lady Wintre will confirm my identity." She had been passed from official to official in the hours since she had arrived in Avalass. As it turned out, though Lady Wintre had asked Raph to complete this journey in her place, she had not deigned to inform the Queen and her aides of the change. A winged messenger had been sent to request verification, but that left Raph with very little to do in the meanwhile. The woman before her was called Cassidy, and seemed no more interested in conversation than Raph did herself.

"I'm sure she will." Cassidy folded her hands together and straightened her back. "In the meantime, might you enlighten me as to why it is you, and not the good Lady Wintre, who is attending tonight's gala?"

"That set of particulars might be a touch delicate."

The aide's polite façade was tested with every second that passed. "Would you prefer speak with somebody else?"

Raph fixed her eyes on Cassidy's, wondering just how far she could push her. "The Queen available?"

"Preparations for the night have seen that she is quite occupied."

"Fair enough." But it was worth a shot. "Given the nature of the task—so much at stake—I'm sure you understand why I can't be just telling anyone and everyone what I'm here for?"

"Naturally." The handmaiden passed her by and placed a hand on the door. "And you can see why it would be irresponsible for me to allow your attendance despite your refusal to elaborate?"

Raph bowed her head. "Yeah. I can understand that."

"So, I must bid you farewell, Seraph." She opened the door, allowing Raph to see the two guards on the other side.

For a moment, she considered letting this aide in on her task. That could surely make things easier for Raph—if Cassidy were inclined to believe her—but Lyre had taught her just how damaging the wrong noble could be, and she would not risk a similar encounter if there was still hope that she could avoid one.

She joined the guards on the other side of the doorway, deciding not to return Cassidy's faux smile as the door was closed behind her. Unlike the knights Raph had seen at the palace's entrance, these two wore no plate, only white uniforms decorated with silver, all the better to fit the night's dress code.

Impassive faces watched Raph, seeming to take the time to decide whether or not she would cause them any trouble. Raph forced them to make up their minds, passed them to follow her best guess of which way she'd come from.

There was no reason to check whether or not they had decided to follow her—there was no world where Raph could hope she might be allowed to wander out of the palace alone, especially with the likely chance she might find herself wandering long enough to bump into the monarch herself.

The journey to Avalass had thankfully gone without trouble. Stellarhoof was truly a gem of a mare—there was little chance Raph would return her to Wintre's stable anytime soon—and it had not been until they had safely reached the crown jewel of Duralaans that their progress had slowed.

Getting into the city was a simple enough task, but her following days had been spent using whatever leverage she possessed as a prestigious follower of the Floral Maw. Luckily, a few members of the city's upper echelon shared her faith and were glad to provide her means of getting into the royal house's closed circle. After being passed between a few more figures in the Queen's service, she had finally been granted a meeting with Cassidy—albeit a short one, given it had landed on the same day as the gala Raph was supposed to attend.

If only she had returned to Harbinger's Rest, Raph may have been able to collect something that could have helped verify her claims. She also might have had a chance to reunite with Nath—or Eric, as she recalled he had proclaimed himself to be. He would have been a fine ally, no matter what he called himself or how their last conversation had unfolded.

She understood Vyx's test. That entire hallucination was just her ridiculously dramatic means of determining whether Raph was more or less trusting—and trustworthy—than the Ash King who had stopped by generations earlier.

She had begged for help in what Raph expected were her final moments, and she still didn't know how to feel about that. It really would have been a better idea to ask Wintre for more aid, yet that had not occurred to Raph until after she was well past the city, and too far to turn back.

A part of her thought she hadn't given herself time to consider a better option on purpose, because when she had asked for help inside that lake, that same part of Raph was disappointed in herself.

"Get this for me?" She stood in place before one of the old palace's many entrances.

One of the guards pulled Raph back and began fumbling with a ring of keys as he took her place in front.

She cast a quick glance toward the guard that remained at her back. He was close, but there was enough room for her to strike him. It was far from Raph's best idea, though she was quickly running out of them, and that window would quickly be closed.

Take out his legs. Use the time that bought to handle the key man. Knock the light out of the first guard. Then—that was where she was struggling to form the rest of her plan. Stumbling around the palace until she was eventually caught and outnumbered didn't seem like a good idea on the surface, but Raph had conquered worse odds more times than she could count.

As the door was unlocked and forced open, a new thread appeared before her, one she decided to follow before better reasoning could subdue her.

Raph dropped to the floor, kicking out both legs in the process and sending the guard before her stumbling through the open door. She braced herself for a hard landing and twisted so she could sweep out the second man's legs. As he fell with a pained grunt, she tethered the door's handle to each of her fingers and pulled it shut. Raph could hardly stifle a laugh as she heard the guard on the other side impact the reinforced wood, failing to break through.

In the meanwhile, the second guard was back on his feet and reaching for his sheathed blade. Raph snapped her fingers, and two more vines wrapped around his neck and threw him toward a painful collision with her knee.

He groaned on all fours, reaching a cautious hand up to inspect what Raph suspected was now a broken nose.

"It'll heal. Where can I find the Queen?"

The man tried to stand again but was wise enough to stop as the vines tightened. "I don't know."

"Seems a tad negligent."

"She's been on the move all day," he rasped. "None of us know exactly where she is."

Raph strained to keep the door shut, the guard on the other side was trying fiercely to pull it his way, and—powerful as Anni's magic was—she knew it wouldn't hold forever. "If I asked you to help me find her, would you?"

"God's Grace, what do you think I am?" A fair, albeit vexing response.

"I only need to get this thing to her," Raph tried to impress the legitimacy of her ends. "You can escort me, if that makes you feel better."

"*You* attacked *us*," he snarled in return.

Raph could understand that had done nothing to gain any trust, but trust as a whole was a concept she was still working on.

She crouched down to his level and made the vines loosen their grip until the man's breathing eased. "That's fair enough. I'm used to handling these kinds of things alone, so I don't really know how to properly get somebody's help. That's not something I've ever had—or wanted to do. But maybe now I'm realising how ridiculous that is. Maybe it's one thing to be strong enough to go it alone when you have to, and another to reject help just because you can." She was rambling, and his incredulous expression made it clear she ought find her point. "Something really bad is coming and I'm looking to ask your queen for help. It would be best if you either aid me or get out of my way and let me do my job."

"Ask and you shall receive," came a voice to her left, belonging to a man she could only presume was a member of a noble family, based on his decorated white tunic and shimmering gold cape. "As it so happens, I was just on my way to speak with Her Majesty. I would not object to your company."

Raph glanced at the man with the bleeding nose before her and the trembling door behind; it was certainly a wonder that this man had no concerns about either.

Such confusion must have been plainly identifiable on her face as he next said, "Yes, you've made quite the display. Misunderstandings can be so very troubling."

Instinctually, Raph found him to be utterly untrustworthy. But she didn't have to trust him to follow him, and the potential of being provided her meeting with the Queen was well and truly worth the risk.

Raph rose to her feet and dissipated the vines, allowing the guard behind the door to burst back into the room. The noble man quickly calmed him, and both guards seemed willing to accept the man's dismissal, albeit with the same touch of confusion Raph felt herself. Once they were out of sight, the noble invited Raph to follow him.

"That went quite a bit better than I expected," she said.

"These things require a great level of care. Though I will not lie, I was tempted to see how your plan went."

"Less of a plan and more of a whim."

The sound that escaped his throat was deeply unnerving, something that was less than a laugh and more than a groan. "Does that often work in your favour?"

"More than it should." She tried to quell her discomfort but could not stop herself from slowing her pace enough that their distance grew.

"I've known many who have lived such a way, though most only for a short while. Better to think a few steps ahead, or at least entrust yourself to somebody who does."

Raph could feel her hairs stand on end. "I'm sorry, I didn't take your name." It was possible her unease was not entirely her own.

"Cortlan, and you are?"

"Seraph. Are you noble?"

"Not quite, but I have family who are friends of the crown."

"And that has its benefits?"

"Less than you might expect, but yes."

They reached a grand hall, incredible in its magnitude, yet Raph's eyes were caught solely by the woman alone in the centre.

She was beautiful, with softly rounded features framed by two strands of her gold-blonde hair, the rest tied behind her back. She wore a black dress, highlighted by streaks of silver and grey, a stunningly sombre attire for what was supposedly a celebration. But the Duralaansi were a people who applauded displays of strength, and Raph could not discount that that may even come in the form of a simple dress.

"Your Majesty, I hope we are not interrupting," Cortlan said. He did not bow, or kneel, or offer any such gesture that might pay respects to the hierarchy, only straightened himself so that even compared to this monarch he was imposing.

The Queen took her time in examining the both of them; her eyes lingered on Cortlan, before eventually falling to Raph. "Not at all. Though I'm afraid the gala is still a few hours away. If you would be willing to wait, I should gladly make time for the two of you then."

"I fear this cannot wait so long." Cortlan stepped forward, dramatically swishing his cape behind him and finally offering his bow. "I am called Cortlan, Your Grace, and although I have been gone a long while, finally, I am returned."

Raph had not realised his name was such an important factor, but the Queen seemed taken aback. She studied him for another moment before recognition fell upon her and she stepped toward the man, with eyes wide and shimmering as a silver plate.

"We all thought you lost; your sister will be so glad." The Queen's voice shook with emotion her station should have forbade, and Raph felt more like the intruder she was.

"She was the first I spoke to," he said. Then his expression turned grim. "I bring grave news."

The Queen looked over to Raph, clearly trying to discern what role she played in her friend's return.

Cortlan followed her gaze and too suddenly seemed to recall that he had not come alone. "Show her what you have brought, Seraph."

"How do you know I brought anything?" Raph allowed herself to drift away, not so far as to invoke notice, but enough to feel safer in the presence of those whose allegiance she was yet to guarantee.

"You told your escorts as much," Cortlan said, perfectly innocent in his explanation, until something darker eclipsed the light behind his eyes. "Unless you only lied so you might be permitted our Queen's presence."

There was little she could do to further argue against his request without earning the Queen's distrust. Of course, she had intended to present the woman with Wintre's artefact anyway, it was only Cortlan's all-too eager gaze which stained her resolve. Raph assured herself that she could handle whatever he might try and drew Wintre's key from her satchel and held it in an open palm toward the monarch.

"Wintre was sure that was lost, how did you find it?" Cecilia asked, eyes no less wide, though the emotion behind them was different now.

Raph shrugged, projecting confidence that was for her own benefit more than anyone else in the room. "Helen cast it into the Lake of Vyx. I just fished it out."

The Queen took a step toward her, folding her hands together to stop their twitching. "May I have it?"

"For what?"

"So that it may be destroyed. So that the Ashen King may never return, and this land can stand together in moving beyond such a great evil."

Raph felt more inclined to trust her than Cortlan. The Queen's reasoning was sound, and her own purpose fell closely in line with Raph's own. "And if I refuse?"

"Then I can only hope you will reconsider. If Wintre has trusted your judgement, so must I."

It would be easier to turn away. Raph knew next to nothing about the monarch before her; trusting her with something so important could prove disastrous. Yet Cecilia had placed her own faith in Raph, just as Vyx had done before her on the promise that when the time came she would be able to accept help from another.

Raph steeled her thoughts and tossed Wintre's key toward the Queen, who clutched it close to her chest as though she thought it would soon be stolen away.

Cortlan reached into a leather pouch tied to his belt and—to Raph's shock and the Queen's delight—procured two more identical keys. "I hope this softens the grim tide I bring."

Cecilia accepted the keys from him and held the three in her hand, seeming less glad and more disturbed by their reveal. "How did you come upon these?"

Cortlan's eyes went distant as he recalled something from his recent past. "I trust you are aware of the tragic deaths of late?"

The Queen confirmed that she was; Raph could only assume he was referring to Hyde's demise alongside his family, as she had come across no news that might rival it during her journey.

"During my travels, I encountered their killer, he had taken a key from both Hyde and Trethellyn before ending their lives."

That stunned Raph. Another lord dead so shortly after the first was more than a tragedy, it was the prelude to only further devastation. Raph had been right to follow this quest with such haste, and lucky that Cortlan had been pursuing a similar goal at the same time.

Cecilia clutched the three in her hand and asked the same question that stalked Raph's thoughts, "Where is this killer now?"

"That is the issue. I had him apprehended and intended to bring him to you so justice could be done." He cast a disappointed look toward the ground. "Alas, I underestimated him and he escaped. I fear now, with his treasures taken from him, he will do something extreme to make up for his failure."

Cecilia's eyes fell, and a wave of disappointment crossed her face. It was not until several moments passed that she continued the discussion. "And what exactly do you suppose that will be?" Her tone had shifted to something bizarrely calm, with even a hint of sardonic boredom lacing her words. Raph thought she must have missed something in the exchange, for the Queen seemed not to see any cause for concern in Cortlan's claims.

"I believe he will take the cipher of Artorius."

Cecilia seemed to at least consider the possibility this time. "And what do you suggest we do to stop him? Have the cipher moved?"

"Whatever you see as best, Your Grace."

An unspoken tension had developed between the two, as though they were both playing a game of strategy, while simultaneously trying their utmost to keep such a fact veiled from their opponent.

The Queen made her move. "Perhaps we should confirm that the cipher is where it should be."

And Cortlan countered. "That may be a risk to you. If you would permit it, I will happily do this alone."

"No need. I have a personal guard for such a necessity."

Raph saw Cortlan's face pale ever so slightly as a figure entered through the door opposite him. They were armoured in black, and steel echoed throughout the hall as she made her way to her queen's side.

Raph watched Cortlan's expression closely as the knight whispered to Cecilia, something about the guard's presence discomforted him. A chill ran along Raph's spine as he returned her gaze. Whatever charisma he had carried up until that point was gone, replaced by an empty void Raph could not penetrate.

—

So desperately Cecilia had wanted to take Cortlan's return as the good tiding it should have been. But a lie remained such, no matter how greatly one wished it were otherwise.

She racked her mind and tried to think of another explanation, but the pieces fit together in a way so disturbingly perfect that the picture they created could not be ignored. He had undoubtedly counted on Cecilia not looking so closely at Chora's extended absence from the palace, and now with the Artorian's arrival, he appeared on the verge of mania. She surely should have been glad to have foiled his plot, but the return of Cassidy's brother was something she had hoped would come to be for many years, for that moment to be corrupted by reality was like waking up from a dream she had enjoyed for longer than she could recall.

There was still the faintest glimmer of a chance that Cortlan was simply mistaken, that everything he had said was not part of some grand scheme to shift the blame away from himself. Rather he may have simply been swept up in the confusion, just as Cecilia had been. What came next would remove all room for doubt.

Cecilia looked from the pale green devola to the mage she had once trusted to monitor her closest friend, and said, "How fortuitous. Chora has just informed me that somebody was found sneaking through the vault below this very palace. Shall we see what we've caught?"

Cortlan smiled, nearly the perfect recreation of the real thing. "Of course."

The four marched through the halls of the old palace of Avalass. The devola stood at Cecilia's side, and Chora marched in step, with Cortlan shortly behind them. The relic keys remained in Cecilia's tight grasp; she wondered why it was that Cortlan had wanted her to have the three of them. If he was truly a major part of the scheme to return Artorius to Duralaans, why leave their only hope of accomplishing that goal with their enemy? Doubt began to creep into her heart.

Doubt . . . and the remnants of hope.

Could Chora have lied to her? It was possible, but Cecilia found the prospect unlikely to be true. The Artorian had only revealed her side of the story after her queen had placed considerable pressure on her. She had not gone out of her way to convince Cecilia of one thing or another like Cortlan had, and likely would not have said anything if not for Cecilia's queries. Chora also could not have had any direct hand in the events in Meergard. There was no doubt that she was a part of the picture, but the artist she was not.

Then there was this inexplicable devola, apparently a trusted friend of Lady Helen Wintre who managed to find the Lady's presumed lost key. She was grateful to have another ally in her fight, even if she could not be entirely certain of the devola's character.

"Thank you for trusting me." Cecilia had to bend considerably so she could whisper to Seraph.

"Well, I wasn't going to become an enemy of the crown just to protect some key."

"Yet it is not only 'some key.' I can see that you understand this as well as I."

The young woman's face scrunched with confusion. "Why not just take it, then? Why risk me turning you down?"

Cecilia considered, and quickly decided not to explain her thesis on what that would symbolise again, not everyone was so well versed on the politics of her kingdom. "If you would like, I can explain my reasoning another time."

"Sure," Seraph answered, clearly reluctant, but not without due courtesy.

Cecilia was far from sure what place this one had in the larger plot that seemed to be closing in from all sides, but she hoped Seraph would be an unlikely ally if anything. It seemed she was running out of those.

They arrived together at the entrance to the vault. It was a door, purposely like every other in the palace, but beyond lied a stairway that dug deep into the rock below. Without a glance to ensure her companions were following, Cecilia began the long descent.

As she drew closer to the base of the stairway, the sound of metal clashing reached her ears. Cecilia faltered for a moment. It might have been wiser to send Chora ahead of her, but she had to remain resolute in her belief. If she was not, then Cortlan would win; doubt could be the death of her here, and with so much at stake, that could not be allowed to happen.

At the bottom, she found a cruel sight. A shape fought back against the knights trying to apprehend it. A tall figure it was, cloaked in black and wielding a long blade that was the colour of the night itself. Her heart broke as it became clear just how little hope the guards had.

"Domina?" Seraph was beside her, eyes wide with shock and recognition.

"You know him?"

"Not for years, but we were allies."

Cortlan joined them, quickly placing himself in front, as if he would be able to protect them from the force of nature that was this warrior. "Put whatever past you had with him aside. This man is a killer." He turned back to Cecilia, plea in his eyes. "This man struck down Lord Trethellyn without sympathy. Whatever doubts you harbour in regard to my return can be settled in due course, but this man is our true foe."

Cecilia's eyes returned to the fighter. He bore the grey-green skin typical of the dark elves. "Is this him, Chora?"

"It is, Majesty."

"He spared you, did he not?"

"I would not still live otherwise."

It was possible this man had lost his way since Chora had faced him, but that did not discount the fact that the Artorian had testified he had played no role in making Hyde's death a reality. By that manner Cortlan was incorrect—or intentionally deceitful.

Seraph was shifting on the spot, unsure of whether it would do any good to join the fray. "Something's wrong, he shouldn't have that blade."

Cecilia allowed herself a moment to consider the weapon. The blade was a sharp plane of black matter, contrasting the pearlescent white hilt. It fit the description of a sword from legends long past, but that weapon had been lost, even the greatest of historians had failed to trace where it could be found.

She pushed past Cortlan and addressed the surviving guards. "Fall back!"

The remaining knights struggled to back away and maintain their defence, but once they had put a measure of distance between themselves and their enemy, he yielded his attack. Cecilia directed the men to stand behind her. She did not fear the elf before her, but it would be foolish not to have a counter in mind if things were to go wrong.

She stepped toward the man, her eyes finding the relic attached to his belt. "You should not have that."

The man remained perfectly still, offering no hint of reaction or inclination to respond.

"Domina?" Seraph had taken Cecilia's approach as encouragement to do the same. "Is that you?"

His dark eyes shifted to acknowledge her, portraying the faintest flicker of recognition. "Seraph, I didn't expect you to be here."

"I'd say the same." She halted her approach slightly ahead of Cecilia, holding out her hand to suggest neither of them progress any further. "Nath's here too, have you seen him?"

Domina returned to silence.

"Why do you want this thing, Domina?"

Recognition turned to menace, and the shadow held his sword aloft in warning. "Do not test me, Seraph. I have not struck you down yet because we were allies once. Do not let my mercy go to waste."

The small devola only laughed at such a threat. "Oh, has it been so long that you've forgotten? I was always stronger than you."

He leapt forward, blade prepared for a killing blow. Cecilia could hear her guards panic, trying desperately to reach her in time to save her life. In those precious moments before his steel could strike her down, Cecilia grasped Seraph's shoulder and threw her out of the way; she could not risk that the devola had failed to see through Cortlan's trick.

Domina's dark weapon reached her without doing harm; it simply passed through her body as though it were not there at all. Which of course, it was not.

"Your magecraft has improved, Cortlan." She turned to bask in his barely disguised contempt. "Though I must say, not enough."

"I don't understand." Seraph was still transfixed by the illusion.

"I believe you do—or at least were close to discerning the truth. Care to explain, Cortlan?"

Clearly he did not. The cadre of knights had seized Cortlan, now turning toward him the anger they held for the one who had slain their comrades. "How?" was all he could muster.

"I was not certain until I saw he possessed the cipher. When I spoke, I did not simply mean that he *should not* have it, rather he *could not* have it." Cecilia held out her hand and Chora was quickly at her side, removing an identical relic from an ornate leather bag and placing the true cipher in her queen's hand. "With such strange occurrences of late—all surrounding these very keys—I knew it would only be wise to keep the item they would unlock where it could not be accessed.

"Though I never would have anticipated you might have played a part in this insanity until you returned speaking of such things. For what, Cortlan? What could you possibly have hoped to achieve?"

The knights held him firm, forcing the mage to meet Cecilia's eyes. "You'll see soon enough, Lady Asche." Then he shifted his gaze toward Seraph. "Sorry about your friend, he was never supposed to be a part of any of this. If it offers any consolation, he died by his own hand."

In an instant, the devola's hand was raised, and strands of glowing thread shot forth from unreality to strangle the mage. "What did you do?"

Cecilia placed herself between them. "Stand down, Seraph."

"You're not my queen," she spat back, eyes bloodshot and furious.

"And I am not asking as one." She reached out a cautious hand and placed it on the devola's shoulder. "This is a problem of my kingdom; I must handle it myself. Please trust me to do so."

Cecilia stepped away, letting Seraph know that she would respect whichever decision she made. So, when Seraph lowered her arm and Cecilia heard Cortlan's breathing relax, she thought the loss of an old friend might have been worth it. Even this girl Cecilia did not know could be trusted to make the right choice given the opportunity.

She offered Cortlan her attention once more. "Did you ever consider what Cassidy might think of this?"

His smile disgusted her. "Of course I did."

Cecilia waved the guards off, and they hauled him away. Such a day it had been, and there was still so much to be done. But Cecilia had found hope once again.

While it would take some time to completely unravel the intricacies of what Cortlan had planned and how those schemes had come undone in the end, Cecilia could breathe easily knowing he could do no more harm. This was to be a night of celebration.

Seraph looked an emotional wreck. Cecilia could only guess at what she had expected to find in Avalass and how far that was from what she had actually encountered. "Lady Wintre sent you in her place, correct?"

Seraph nodded, her eyes not meeting Cecilia's.

"Then let's get you ready for a gala."

Cecilia fought back a laugh when she saw the girl's dumbfounded reaction and tried to let herself forget what had unfolded. Those were concerns for another day. This was to be a night of celebration.

Chapter Twenty-Five

Through Diamond Eyes

The nightmare was only just beginning.

His throat was raw from hours spent coughing, choking on the stench of ash, cinder, and burnt flesh. He screamed, and found his voice silent, leaving only another anguished whisper drowned out by the echoes of suffering within his mind. He wanted to claw off his skin, for that was the only way he could rid himself of the stain he knew must have coated him, though he could not see it for himself. It was for that reason alone, Oedon was glad to be blind.

He reached for the things that had been shoved into his scarred sockets. His hair had come loose and had to be brushed away.

But Oedon found no strands veiling his face. He had woven them together with Elias' own rings, leaving two braids framing both sides of his thin face.

Sometimes it became hard to discern the difference between that which lay before and beyond him. Ash awaited in both directions and in many ways there was no reason to care which one led to what destination. It was all a matter of perspective. While a man might waste his life dreading what the stains of yesterday would do to his tomorrow, a god would see no difference at all. Oedon had tried to adopt that perspective as his own, but he always failed to shake the mortality which still clung to his heart.

He watched Nath Whitsin, so focused on the road ahead despite the futility he must have seen in his actions. If Oedon so wanted he could witness just what awaited this man; every moment, struggle, love, and death that he would encounter in the days and years to come in his life.

Oedon might not have had absolute focus when gazing upon the furthest reaches of time, yet when compared to the sheer scope of eternity, even a hundred years appeared frighteningly close. A year was akin to an hour, a month to a minute, a day to a single second; there was no avoiding the wind of fate that breathed down his neck.

Oedon's thumb brushed against one of the golden rings that bound his hair, and he wondered why it was that despite those laws of reality he still felt a gnawing sensation within.

"Child, hear me," spoke a voice long before Oedon had ever set foot on the soil of Duralaans. It was as though the sky itself was addressing him. With the timbre of the wind itself, they were calm, yet carried the threat of thunder. "You are as a rock, forged into shape by the violent winds of time immortal."

Oedon attempted to speak in return, but whimpering sputters were all he could muster.

The sky flickered with golden light in tandem with its speech. "Are you to be whittled down into no more than the sand we tread upon, or will you let yourself be sculpted into the mountain that will remain steady through damnation?"

It had not been a question Oedon could answer quickly, and his mind was otherwise consumed by what he thought were more pressing issues. "My . . . mother?"

"Is gone. You may join her if you so wish, yet that is not the fate we had planned for you."

"Planned?"

"In a sense that you comprehend, yes."

"Why?"

"All is catalysed. The tides of life give to death and sees itself returned in time. But without proper cultivation, that relationship gives way to chaos."

Then Oedon had realised just what was addressing him, though it never identified itself. The embodiments of cause and effect, the deities who had spawned and chosen Avandoras as the canvas upon which they would create the world they envisioned. In Oedon, that had birthed awe, terror, and rage like none he had ever known.

"Is that all we are?"

"What's that?" Nath called back to him.

Oedon gasped, realising that he had been answering the past's voice in the present. "Nothing. Are we getting close?"

"Pretty close, yeah."

Oedon peered over Nath's shoulder to find that was an incredible understatement. They had arrived.

"My father was born here, always wanted to take us back one day, if he ever had the money to support it."

Though he already knew as much, Oedon fought back the reflex to say so. He could appreciate the man's willingness to set aside what he knew of Oedon's ability and treat him just as any other person. Since he had stepped out of the shadows and revealed just what he could do to a select few, many had chosen to either worship, ridicule, or use him as a tool. A part of him longed for a return to the normalcy of his past, but the choices he had made within that past were what made those hopes nothing more than a child's dream. These small moments were all he had left.

Presently, they found themselves at the back of a long line of travellers bidding for entrance into the capital city. Avalass' tall walls surrounded it on all sides—save for the ones where a mountain stood in place of any manmade barriers, leaving the grand gateways as the only chance of passing through.

"This may be more difficult than I'd thought," Nath said, running a hand through sweaty red hair.

"Don't worry, Whitsin. I can get us through."

"You'd be happy to do that?"

"Not happy." Oedon did not know how he felt about Nath's decision to march so confidently into folly. "But I am supposed to witness the devastation to come. I cannot do so from beyond a wall."

Nath twisted to look down at Oedon, seeming to study his expression with a smile. He turned back toward the gate ahead. "That's why you came along?"

"Lyre was supposed to bring me himself; you make an apt substitute."

"But Lyre is dead and was always going to die before he could get here. I got that right?"

"Essentially."

Nath shook his head. "I just can't believe it's so simple."

"In what way have I made anything out to be simple?" They had taken up this very conversation a number of times, countless even to Oedon, throughout their journey, and he could only plead with what divinity kept its eyes on him that this would be the last.

"We aren't slaves to a greater power. We get to choose what our past makes of us."

"Nath, I am glad for the revelation Lady Yukkie offered you and I truly do wish that I could share your beliefs, yet there are some truths of nature that I simply cannot ignore."

"I'm not suggesting you do. Just—I don't know—use what you do know to make things better. Isn't that the best any of us can do?"

"That is the most *you* can do. My limits are different."

The line began to move forward and Nath ushered their horse to keep up. "You're just too damn young."

Oedon smiled, but there was an ache in his heart. "Sorren said the same thing."

Slowly, they progressed toward the main gate. Oedon kept a keen eye on those around them, curious as to whether they were among others who planned to attend the Queen's gala. It seemed more likely that these were simpler folk, whether visiting on the short-term or returning after too long spent far from home, these people would surely regret choosing such a time to pass through that gate.

Oedon could easily warn them of what was coming. Though many would not believe him, some would be paranoid enough to take the message of the strange blind boy as gospel. With a few well-placed words, many lives could be saved.

Oedon thought he might have been about to open his mouth when Whitsin said, "Mind telling me what the plan is? For getting in, that is."

"It's simple." Oedon snapped out of his contemplation and re-moved an envelope from what had been Sorren's satchel. "Lyre was to be an honoured guest of Hyde's gala. I shall present his invite and declare myself his proxy."

"They'll believe that?"

"It will be enough to grant us audience. From there, Hyde will be able to verify my story."

Nath ran his metal hand over his eyes. "Then I have some bad news for you: Hyde's dead."

Oedon laughed. "No, I speak of the new Lord Hyde. Caster was killed, yes, but Aester Hyde is very much not."

"God's Grace, how do you know so many of these people?"

"You may be surprised by how many people of power are in-nately superstitious. While fate might scare some like you, others find it comforting."

"I'm sure they do," Nath said, then added a second thought. "And I'm not scared of fate."

The tension that remained in Whitsin's shoulders told Oedon that was not entirely true, though he felt that was another fact better left unaddressed. "I know."

They shared a few more words as the hours lapsed, nothing of any importance, only simple banter to fill the void. Nath was vying for more of Oedon's background, but he offered nothing that would greatly shift Whitsin's opinion of him. Some secrets were better left undisturbed, even as he felt that itch in the back of his mind again.

"The order of nature is threatened, Oedon Desera. We have never possessed the luxury of being truly removed from mortal affairs, yet we find ourselves hurtling toward doomsday all the same." The memory returned unbidden, as though it possessed a sentient desire to remind Oedon of his purpose.

He forced himself not to respond aloud, but the debate came all the same.

"You understand consequence better than most. We are farmers who sow seeds a millennia before their yield is necessary. The harvest awaits; shall you be as its reaper?"

That question he had answered with ease.

"Evening, fellas," called a man in light armour. "What brings you to Avalass?"

"We'll be attending Hyde's gala," Nath said, continuing when he saw doubt creep into the guard's eyes. "We're acting in Carlyle Lyre's stead."

"Right, might I see some confirmation?"

"Of course. Oedon?"

He tore his focus away from the fractals of his mind, took a moment to reacclimate himself with his present, and offered the guard Lyre's invite. There was a strange tingle when his fingers brushed the key also within the satchel, but that was for another time.

The guard took a moment to read the missive in full, pausing briefly a few times to glance up at the two of them. They surely did not fit the appearance of anyone who should be attending a royal gala, though Lyre himself had never been one to obey the typical trends of Duralaans' fashion.

"If you doubt us, may I suggest conferring with Lord Aester Hyde? He will verify our claims."

The guard responded with forced humour. "You think I have direct line to a lord?" He passed the invite back. "No. Besides, I'm sure he'll be well busy."

"So, we're clear?" Nath asked.

"To get through the gate? Sure. To get into the palace? That'll be your problem to solve."

He waved them through and turned focus to the next in line. Whitsin brought their mount through the expansive gate and into the opulence of Duralaans' capital. Oedon considered the gilded brutalism of Deserum's cities more to his liking, but the elegance of Avalass lit a new appreciation in him.

It screamed of strength, a collective need to declare a people's intent to rebuild in the wake of calamity. The streets were wide and inviting, lined on either side by homes built with the black stone so common to the land. They were tall structures, with their tiled red roofs rising at least three-storeys above them and casting half of the street in shadow.

Oedon directed Nath through the city. It was not technically the fastest route available, but it was the most efficient.

The sun dipped below the horizon, yet the streets grew no quieter. Rather, it seemed a new life was only just beginning with the presence of that night's moon. Three navigated the world, each with their own fables. That night it was the Moon of Dyseus which looked down on them, the pale rock that heralded festivity in many places—whatever form that took. There was no question why Hyde had chosen that particular night to hold his gala.

They made their way toward the base of Avalass' mountain, stopping a few times during to allow assorted denizens to pass by, before reaching the grand wall encompassing the old palace of Avalass' royalty.

Oedon dropped down from their horse and approached the knights on guard. Whitsin dismounted as well, but Oedon was glad to see he did not take the lead.

"My name is Oedon Desera, and this is my escort Nath Whitsin. We have been sent by Lord Carlyle Lyre to attend this gala as his proxy and fulfill any obligations he has to the crown," he said, offering Lyre's invitation once more.

Two of the five knights stepped forward. Most were armoured in pearlescent white, with only one in pitch black, denoting themselves as a member of the Artorian Guard. "Lord Lyre informed us of no such thing."

"It was a sudden necessity. The death of Lord Trethellyn caused him concern."

One of the knights who had held back shared a confused look with his allies, clearly they had not expected him to know of the Meergard lord's demise. Oedon hoped it would buy him some interest, if not trust outright.

The knight slipped the paper into a small satchel and walked back toward the other three without another word. Oedon met the eyes of the knight who'd remained, even hidden behind that slitted visor he could see them, and was glad to know a chill ran along that knight's spine as he pretended to glance back to check on his fellows.

"Aester Hyde is a friend of mine. If you don't mind, I would like to speak with him before the night begins proper."

The Artorian finally stepped forward, pointed directly at Whitsin. "And who'd you say this is?"

"Escort," Nath affirmed. "It's a dangerous road; there were two of us when we left Prometh."

Oedon felt his lips twitch at the reminder and silently had to chide himself for the display. He knew what response the guard would give before it was vocalised, yet he still felt a splinter of fear puncture his heart.

"He's clear," the Artorian said. "I'll see the both of you to Lord Hyde's quarters."

"Actually, I believe the lord would prefer our discussion kept private. May one of you lead my friend to the hall?" He knew Whitsin would not be especially fond of that idea, but there was no argument he could offer without putting stress on their cover story.

"Very well." They signalled one of their subordinates to lead.

Nath stepped forward, his expression sour. "Are you sure that's the best idea?"

"Quite sure, thank you." Oedon smiled, carrying enough of the arrogance his family had once possessed that he felt his skin grow cold. "I shall see you inside."

With no other option, Nath followed the knight waiting for him, and a moment later, Oedon was led through the palace grounds by the Artorian.

It was only a short walk through the gardens before they were inside the crescent-shaped building. Oedon found it odd how green everything was. So much life had been cultivated just to declare that it could be done. Although the royal family had long been relocated to their mountaintop palace, they still felt the need to display their survivability where it could be seen. The brilliant limestone premises may have stood out from the black and red city surrounding it, but these people were Duralaansi to the core.

The green vision before him was suddenly corroded by an unwanted addition, as Oedon felt ash coat his flesh once more. He tried to brush the flakes away, but they had disappeared as quickly as they had come about.

Chapter Twenty-Six
Matinée

As far as revelry's went, Lord Hyde's gala of debut could be considered far from dreary. Indeed, Cecilia actually thought she might enjoy the night's affairs. She had attended a number of similar events in the past. During his time as monarch, King Raine had made sure to host at least two gatherings per year, maintaining an insistence that communicating with his fellows in person was the simplest and most effective means of securing their allegiance. If that required indulging in the finest wines and music? All the better.

Cecilia recalled those gatherings had subsided with the deaths of her siblings and mother. Her father had claimed it was for fear of infecting those once enjoyable nights with his own misery. But within their shared mourning, Cecilia had glimpsed ulterior reasoning; the King did not believe his lordlings deserved such pleasures whilst he drowned solely in sorrow. While Cecilia could understand such feelings, and loved her father despite his flaws, she knew her duties to her people had to surpass emotion.

Her hand felt for the place Hyde's gemstone ought to be. *We'll just have to have a new stone cut.* She thought it could be so simple. That night everything could change.

Cecilia could make it change.

Cassidy stood with her, overlooking the lords from a raised area that offered some opportunity for private conversation. Cecilia had informed her of everything that had happened with Cortlan. Despite her own pains, Cecilia did not dare imagine that she knew just how Cassidy was feeling. The woman was as tall and beautiful as she ever was, and that only made the knowledge that her heart had to be a wreck of emotion ever more upsetting.

"You may be dismissed, Cassidy. Do not think you must wear a mask of stoicism for my sake."

Cassidy spoke without meeting her queen's eyes. "I have tried for so long to convince you to put yourself before duty—at least from time to time. You did not delay your responsibilities when your father passed. I will do no less."

"You suggest I speak hypocrisy?"

"Well, not in so many words." Now she awarded Cecilia her eyes—alongside a wry grin. "I can feel it within my soul; this night will be one to be remembered. I shan't miss it."

Sure that her friend would be well, Cecilia turned her attention back to the guests below. While a part of her thought she might question Cassidy for any hint of her brother's motives, she understood there was more to concern her presently.

The night would be split into two parts. First, Aester would have his time to ingratiate himself with his fellow lords and ladies. They would dance, and eat, and converse, and fall into as drunken a stupor as they could survive. Then the key bearing members of the retinue would be invited into a separate room so they may destroy the Artorian relics together and begin a better age with bonds forged anew.

For the time being, she would have to join the mass and simply enjoy the night. Cecilia could be glad that for once she was not the main attraction, yet there would still be many who desired the Queen's ear—more so because Hyde had decided to extend the invites to all lords of Duralaans, and not just those who possessed keys demanding destruction.

Many had brought along their children, eager to have them endear themselves to the new lord—likely even court the man, if it was appropriate.

Amongst her guests stood two figures who stood out like bruised flesh. One was a young man, with long red hair tied back, olive skin, and draped in a red cowl that covered much of his upper body. Cecilia's first impression had been that he was a mercenary, hired by one lord or another to guard them on their journey into the capital.

That seemed to be incorrect, as he did not linger around anyone in particular, instead drifting aimlessly through the room as he searched for a purpose to steady him. The only person he appeared familiar with was the second individual Cecilia did not know; a young boy in tattered black rags with braided blonde hair who had no obvious reason to be there.

Bizarrely, that one had entered with Aester Hyde himself, the two deep in conversation as though they were old friends. That was enough to confirm that they were not intruders, but when Amor's explanation for them eventually came, she was only given more reason for concern.

These two were acting on Lord Lyre's behalf, apparently having arrived with his invite and key in hand, alongside the explanation that Lyre had decided to stay away, out of fear of meeting the same fate as Hyde and Trethellyn. Cecilia could not guess how Lyre had already been alerted to Trethellyn's fate, but that was the least of her concerns. Lyre was one of the few who knew the true reason for her desire to destroy the keys, he had seemed sympathetic to the cause and more than willing to oblige, making his absence all the more frustrating.

Twice now, Lyre had neglected to attend her events. It seemed Cecilia would have to be the one to take the matter into her own hands and finally close the distance between them. As much as she abhorred stripping her fellows of their agency, there remained a point where a monarch could no longer accept disobedience.

Alas, that would be a matter for another day. As long as his proxies had indeed brought along Lyre's key, the man himself being present was technically unnecessary.

Cecilia took a deep breath as she approached the staircase connecting her level to the masses below. *Time for duty.*

—

"They simply ask for far too much." The woman, whom Nath had learned was called Daphne Raleigh, seemed inclined to continue her ramblings whether or not her audience was at all interested. "So Santora has grown especially cloudy? My home is under the constant siege of savages! And have they ever offered *me* aid? Have I ever stooped so low as to beg for it?"

Her thick brows raised as though the question was less rhetorical than Nath had anticipated. "No?"

"Of course not. You would hardly know they're of the same lineage as us with how often they have cowed before the slightest sign of adversity."

"What can you expect?" A new party had inserted himself into their discourse, a lanky man in sharp dress. "After allowing that devil Azazel to rule them for centuries, they finally cast him from the throne, only to invite his daughter to take over fifty years after the fact. They have proven themselves fools again and again, of course they cannot solve their own problems."

Nath wanted to interject. He had seen much of Santora's devastation himself. The land had been entirely bathed in shadow, making it a place of almost constant night. Though Nath had not returned since his journey took him to Haevahn, he could imagine conditions had not eased in the time since.

Ultimately, Nath could put none of those thoughts to words. This woman was the only guest who had deigned to speak with him, and it would not be wise to deny her—even if he would prefer to keep to himself. Solitude would only draw the wrong kind of attention. Nath could not afford anyone questioning his story too greatly and he did not possess Oedon's ability to know exactly what excuse would get him out of trouble.

"Consider for the moment that you are regarding Santora inadequately," said the man-of-the-hour as he joined their quickly growing group. Aester Hyde wore a golden tunic, inlaid with tiny red gemstones that matched the crimson strips of fabric that hung from his shoulders. He gestured toward the lanky man. "Perhaps, Harald, where you see folly, I see a capability to adapt."

That first man, who seemed to be Lord Harald, harrumphed with disregard. "Is that so? Please, enlighten me further; it is your night after all."

"The Nights of Vengeance, Gallius Ascendancy, and finally this rain of darkness. All took place within the land of Santora. Yet still the people remain, constantly evolving so they might survive catastrophe. To my eyes, that exhibits strength."

"I suppose I should not be surprised you would adopt such a view. Deserum is just as ruined, is it not? You know catastrophe as well as any." Harald sipped at the purple liquor in his chalice, seemingly confident he had won their bout.

Raleigh believed otherwise, rounding so she may stand closer to Hyde and oppose the withered lord. "Actually, Hyde is quite right. It is true that adversity forges us anew, such is the reason my people are some of this land's strongest."

With no interest to argue his stance further, Harald offered Hyde a weak nod before parting to engage with other attendees. Nath was slightly disappointed to see him go, if only because it meant there was more of a chance Hyde or Raleigh would instead try to converse further with him.

"This is my new friend," Raleigh began, intent to prove Nath's fears correct. "What was your name again, boy?"

"Nath."

"Nath!" She clapped her hands. "He is in the employ of our good fellow, Lyre—you'll be so incredibly fortunate if you ever get to meet him. It seems nobody can drag him out of that mountain anymore, not even the Queen."

Hyde flashed Nath a polite smile. "A pleasure, Nath. Oedon has told me something about you; you're quite the survivor as well." He turned back to address Lady Raleigh. "And indeed, I would like to meet with Lord Lyre. I have heard nothing but the best about what has become of Prometh. Truly, it is another example of what has become better for the suffering it once endured. May you remind me what reason the lord offered for his absence?"

"He was afraid, with two other lords dead, that the journey was not worth the risk," Nath explained, wary of the fact that Oedon had likely already divulged as much to Hyde. So whatever reason he had for asking Nath, it went beyond mere curiosity.

"Lyre afraid?" Raleigh chimed in. "I hardly believe it."

Hyde drained his cup, feigning disinterest. "You suspect ulterior reasoning?"

"Of course. As long as I've known that man, he has never been without plenty a scheme. Twice now, he has refused the Queen's summons. First, her very coronation, and now your introduction."

"It is as though he is beginning to shirk his duties to the crown. It is not uncommon for wise lords to grow tired of a monarch," Hyde mused. Though he treated the statement without much emphasis, Nath could see the point he was trying to make.

Raleigh shook her head, not yet convinced of Hyde's assertions. "Still, he sends his proxies." She acknowledged Nath's presence with a quick smile. "And I cannot say that his presence goes missed."

They shared a laugh that was laced with malign. Nath couldn't help but smile knowing that, even among his fellow nobles, Lyre was disliked.

Raleigh's eyes widened as she seemed to spy a woman across the hall. "You must excuse me for a moment, it seems I owe somebody a dance." She raised her cup toward Hyde before she parted, "I look forward to sharing a table with you, Hyde. It is a tragedy which took us to meet, I only hope it proves to be worth it."

Nath felt his shoulders relax as he watched her go and realised he had barely breathed the whole time. But Hyde remained at his side, and he could not let his guard down yet—unless, of course, he put himself on the offensive. "How'd your talk with Oedon go?"

"Well enough, it has been too long since we could commune in person."

"Harald said you're from Deserum, that where you two met?"

"It was." Hyde showed no refrain from the topic of their past. "The poor boy was in a horrible place, I like to think we gave him purpose, in return for his vision."

Nath thought that sounded all too similar to how Lyre had been using Oedon, no more than a tool to aid in a supposedly greater plan. "And what purpose would that be?"

"I did not think you dull, boy." Hyde pivoted his neck slowly until his dark eyes were on Nath alone. "Did my words truly fall on such deaf ears, or might we expense with the pretence?"

Nath considered leaving their discussion there, but that would take him no further. He had decided to face this threat head on, despite how slim his chances of succeeding were, so he could not back down when confronted himself. "You're the reason Oedon came here. He set Artorius' return in motion for you."

"That's better." He turned back to the party. "Though we did not set the ball rolling, merely ensured it did not miss its target."

"I'll stop you."

"You'll try."

"What do you really get from this? Don't pretend it's all for some noble pursuit of making this place stronger." There was a fire burning in his soul that was becoming harder to keep in check. "This is my home, Hyde. You don't get to come here and decide what's good for us. I don't care who you or any of these people are. I will save this place."

"Like you saved your mother?"

He felt the warm grip of his firearm within his hand. "I don't know what Oedon's told you about me, but I suggest you choose your words carefully."

"Or what? You'll kill me like you did Greydeath?" He masked his grin by sipping his drink. "You'd think a mercenary would be less susceptible to provocation. Even if I actually believed you would throw away your life over an insult, it would do you no good. My continued mortality has never had any bearing on what is to come. That remains entirely in the hands of another."

Nath followed his line of sight to where Oedon now stood before the Queen, bowing low in respects to her position. "He's just a kid. How can you excuse putting so much on him?"

"Well, that is quite simple. We make no excuses. This is his fate; he knows that better than any of us."

"And who's 'us' supposed to be?"

Hyde ignored the question. "The course has been set, Nath, we simply must follow it." He offered a polite nod, then made his way toward a broad man waving him over.

It was for the best, Nath had decided he needed to stop Oedon before he could say anything devastating to the Queen. He had no idea what exact words that might entail, but Nath was quickly realising he had barely scratched the surface in terms of figuring out where Oedon's ambitions lie.

Whatever he intended to say left him as he came face-to-face with the last person he'd expected to find, yet perhaps also the one being he wanted to see more than any other.

She was now dressed in a pale white dress, highlighted by linings of green. A far nicer article than he had managed to find her, and a better disguise within their current setting.

They stared at each other for what felt far longer than the few seconds they must have been. Raph broke the silence when she could apparently no longer contain her shock. "What the hell are you doing here, Nath?"

—

Raph immediately wished she had chosen her words better. "Sorry, that was rude." She looked him up and down, unconsciously checking him for injury—and coming away shocked that he had been allowed to attend in such a state of dress. "But it is weird that you're here."

"A man can't enjoy a royal gala every now and then?"

"Not this man." She let herself smile. "And not this gala."

"Well, if there's another gala about to be ground zero to an apocalypse, you let me know."

That brought their lively exchange to a halt. Raph had guessed that he would not be at this gala for any other reason, but the severity of his words was sobering. "Looks like we got a lot to catch up on."

Nath maintained his smile, even as pain lurked behind his eyes. "Yeah, if only there was some privacy."

"We don't need it." She held out her hand. "A dance?"

It took him a moment to find the words to respond. "I don't think I know how."

"Neither do I, but we used to be good at figuring things out together. Compared to all that, what's learning to dance?"

Gingerly, his hand took hers, and together they joined the few other nobles swaying to the music. Raph wrapped her arms around his neck as Nath gingerly placed his hands on her waist.

As long as they had known each other, neither had allowed themselves to pursue any sort of intimacy; the life they led dashed such hopes with the fear of the end they would inevitably see. There might have been moments Raph had let herself wonder what a different life could have meant for her, but that curiosity always lost out to greater responsibilities. This dance would be the closest she could ever get to the romantic life of normalcy.

It took a moment for them to find the right rhythm to their steps. The music was slow and melancholic. Settling into the careful motions of one another took time, but that also gave Raph the time she needed to organise her turbulent thoughts.

Nath spoke first. "I'm sorry."

She looked toward his eyes, only to find them unfocused and staring at the space just past her right ear. "About?"

"I wasn't right after I killed Greydeath. He got my mind all messed up, even if I didn't realise it. I said things I wish I hadn't. I lashed out, and you didn't deserve that."

Raph wanted to tell him that there was no need to apologise, that she would have reacted much the same if she were in his position. None of that would have helped him. Nath regretted his actions, denying that was not going to do either of them any good. It was time for honesty to prevail. "I haven't been great to you either."

He opened his mouth—no doubt to tell her the same thing she had thought to tell him—so she placed her palm over his lips to keep him quiet enough to listen.

"You can guess just how bad of a man Lyre was, how hard it was to be in his possession for so long. The only thing that kept me going was dreaming of the day I could be free. I spent every moment that I could actually control my thoughts planning my escape. There was never hope that somebody would come for me. The only person who could ever save me was myself."

She took a moment to recollect her thoughts but found them instinctually drifting back to the chill of Lyre's dungeon, so she pushed those memories back into the dark corner of her mind in which they belonged and pressed on. "You took that from me, and I felt like I was back to being that weak girl from Spirallos I've tried so hard to abandon all these years. A part of me hated you for that, and I know I wasn't strong enough to hide it. I wanted you to leave me again, so I could go back to just being myself and proving whatever it is I've been trying to prove.

"Feeling that way about you—of all people—just made it worse, because you matter a lot to me. You've mattered more than anyone else from the day you chose to stay and help a city you barely knew, even if that meant letting the people who killed your mother get away." She lowered her hand from his mouth when he finally met her eyes. "I just don't know how I'm supposed to help others if I can't even help myself."

It was a slight gesture, but she could feel Nath pull her closer. "You don't have to know how. You *have* helped a lot of people. We all did. We saved people who couldn't save themselves, because sometimes that's what we need. Sometimes we can know how to help everyone except ourselves."

She could hardly recognise the words coming out of his mouth. Raph thought she had come away from her time in Vyx's Lake a wiser person, but Nath seemed even more at peace than she had ever known him.

He must have noticed the confused way she looked at him because he was quick to explain further. "I spoke to Larina—*long story*—and she helped clear some things up for me."

"Larina's here?"

He shook his head sombrely. "I went to her."

There was only one thing that could mean, even if Raph feared to confirm it. "What happened after I left?"

He took a deep breath, steadying himself for his turn. "Elias found me and took me to Lyre. As it happens, he wasn't so bad a guy, and we made a deal to try and stop Lyre and all he had planned. That didn't go great, and I got pretty close to the end."

Raph wanted—needed, really—to know so much more, but all that mattered was where they were now. There would be time in the future to discuss the past. "So, Lyre?"

"Dead. I'm sorry. I know that should've been your justice to deliver, but Oedon acted before I could stop him."

That hurt, even if Raph knew it shouldn't. Knowing she could never stand witness as that vile creature met his ultimate fate felt too much like letting something go. Still she wanted to deliver upon her captor the penance she had dreamed of. But there was nothing to do for it now. "Oedon?"

"That blind kid we met in Prometh. He's been helping me somewhat." He nodded toward a place behind her, and Raph turned to see the same boy in conversation with the Queen.

"You've really had your share of adventure, Nath." She paused, recalling what he had said during their last meeting. He had clearly changed tune since then, but she needed to be sure of how he really felt. "Is it still okay for me to call you that?"

He beamed at her, eyes twinkling with a humour that she had not seen in years. "Of course it is. I want to be that person again. With your help, if you'll give it."

She returned the smile and felt her heart flutter, even as old memories returned to her. "Sera is what my Mother would call me in the letters she'd write. That name turned into one more thing that reminded me of the person I didn't want to be. She left me so I would be kept away from the life she had. So I'd be safe. But I didn't want her help, I didn't want the name she gave me, I just wanted her. If I couldn't have that much, then I'd do it all alone, because I had no choice. But now I do, and I choose to accept help. Maybe Sera is still a part of me. Maybe that's who am when I don't have to be strong."

Nath held her eyes for a few seconds more, then he leaned forward and whispered softly into her ear. "You're strong, no matter what name you use. That's just who you are. It doesn't die just because you pair it with another's. I think, if anything, that just makes you stronger."

They were so close now, their bodies pressed together as they swayed in tandem to music that only grew increasingly more sombre. "Strong enough to beat this?"

Nath's smile had died, but the light in his eyes had not. "I don't know. Oedon doesn't seem confident, but I'm still going to do everything I can."

"What does Oedon know?"

"A lot, actually. He thinks everything will come to a head tonight, but I just don't see how."

Raph considered it for a moment and came to the same conclusion. With Cortlan locked away somewhere within the palace, could his machinations continue? "A man arrived around the same time as I did. Tried to trick the Queen into granting him access to Artorius' cipher. She saw through his illusions and had him imprisoned, so he shouldn't be a threat anymore."

"Do we have any other leads?"

"You said Lyre's dead, so not really."

Nath's eyes left hers as he seemed taken by contemplation. "Hyde might be trouble as well, but I don't see us being able to do anything about him with so many people around. Can we talk to this man?"

Raph turned her chin upward with confidence. "I don't see why not."

Despite their decision, neither immediately pulled away from the dance. Raph felt slightly awkward about the fact she could be so comfortable on the brink of Duralaans' potential destruction, but she would not deny the comfort she found in the embrace.

"Are you ready to be a hero again?" It was her that whispered into his ear now.

"Don't let me be anything else."

Chapter Twenty-Seven
Behind the Curtain

Never had Cecilia been one to exaggerate. Such flowery extrapolations served only to muddle understanding. Thus, she had been taught at a young age to avoid them. So when she found herself believing the night to be an utmost success, Cecilia immediately began to seek out the flaws that could only be lurking beneath the surface.

The first came in the shape of young Davick Anderthread, the one whose marriage to Holly Harald Cecilia thought she had saved from being torn apart by their parents. This made it all the more disheartening to see that, though the gala had brought them under the same roof, the pair had not yet taken the time to speak with one another. She considered the possibility that their parents had discouraged further communication, and decided that in such a case she would take matters into her own hands.

It did not take long for Amor to have the two brought to speak with her. Both Davick, wrapped in his family's famous blue silk and Holly in her loose dress of maroon, seemed in high spirits as they greeted their queen.

Holly offered her lilted pleasantries. "Such a lovely night, Your Grace."

"Quite so, if only my father had the servants you do," Davick agreed.

"That is very kind, I shall offer our hires your best regard. But I did not request your presence for your acclaim alone." Cecilia could not help but notice how far apart they stood. The distance was not so great that it was awkward, but they certainly displayed nothing of the affection she hoped to witness in the apparent newlyweds. "When last they were in the capital, both of your parents discussed with me the terms of your marriage."

The two shared a glance, neither immediately volunteering to be the one to explain the situation. After a stern glance from Holly, Davick straightened and said, "You left the decision in our hands. I cannot thank you enough for that—"

"And we have made our decision," Holly cut in. "It is not the best outcome for either of our families if we were remain wed."

Cecilia felt her chest ache, though this time not from fear. It was fury that came alight within her soul, she had to be sure to quell it before she spoke next. "Quite the shame. What could have possibly brought you to such a conclusion?"

Holly frowned. "My father spoke to me after he had returned and impressed the importance of choosing a spouse carefully. Though I do care deeply for Davick," she offered him an affectionate glance, "I fear we allowed too much haste in furthering our relationship."

"Then take more time. Surely, this does not require your betrothal to be annulled outright." When they both delayed further comment, Cecilia was certain of the truth not being shared. Of course, neither Lord Harald nor Anderthread could keep from poisoning their children's minds, even if their monarch's orders were expressly to do the opposite. "I will see to your parents myself."

"That is not necessary, I assure you," Davick said. "We would not ask that you sever our bond this very moment, merely that you understand which choice we have made and see to its handling when you have the time spare."

As much as Cecilia wished to argue it, she could not make their choice for them. If they told her this was truly what they wanted, she had to accept their decision—misled as it may be. "Very well, expect it done by the third moon's rise."

She guided them back to the main floor of the party, watched them speak only a word or two more before splitting off again. Cecilia was not sure who she wished to greet next. None bore any semblance to a friend; the presence of such people as these was something to be endured rather than enjoyed. Her one true friend in attendance was speaking with Lyre's proxy, the crystal-eyed boy who had offered her Lyre's key and a concerning warning.

"Some keys are best left unused." Cecilia mouthed the words and wondered if they were his own or a message passed on from his master. She would have to ask Lyre herself whenever she finally had the pleasure.

It occurred to Cecilia that she now possessed five of the relics. Trethellyn's and Hyde's from Cortlan. Lyre's from the blind boy. Wintre's from the devola Seraph. And Asche's from her father. There was no need for fear anymore. If she so wished, those five could be destroyed, and Artorius would be sealed away forevermore. She could finally breathe without struggle.

Amor stood in wait at the hall's edge. Cecilia caught his eye, and he sprang into motion. Carefully, the attendant weaved through the guests and informed the three remaining key bearers that it was time to make for the private chamber which would house the main event.

Cecilia waited for them there. The room itself was simply a drawing room with a fire that roared in its hearth; she had been assured the flames would be enough to melt the metal, given enough time. Of course, Cecilia did not need the keys to be destroyed immediately, she reminded herself the symbol of the lords casting away the relics would be enough to assure her of their willingness to cooperate.

The five keys she had already collected weighed heavily in her hands. She gazed into the fire, finding herself reminded of the red blaze that had erupted from Promethus centuries ago. It had been that fire which united their people once, and though the flames that flickered before her possessed little of the might that volcano had, it would be burdened with the same task. Cecilia considered discarding her five at that moment, but it was then that Cassidy entered with the key bearing lords.

Redan Rosse, Daphne Raleigh, and Zephyr Mars were the three nobles who joined her. Each found their own seats throughout the room, making themselves comfortable as they awaited whatever would follow.

Cecilia spent a few more moments staring into that fire, letting the heat wash over and calm her mind. It was time to unite a people. It was time to be Queen.

"My friends, I thank you for joining me in this extraordinary moment. Though few will know what we have accomplished here tonight, its impact will be felt throughout the whole of this land. For tonight, we forge our home anew. Tonight, Duralaans returns to its glory of old. Tonight, Duralaans unites against a threat once bested, and to be bested once more." Cecilia turned to meet each of their eyes, punctuating her words. "Each of us were given an opportunity long ago. An opportunity, not to progress or grow ever stronger, but to wither away and yield to desperation. Yet we have endured. We have grown stronger without the Gods, without crawling back to the ashen kings we've rejected, and we are ready to cut off that path entirely."

Cecilia held her left hand high, showing off the two keys that sat between her fingers—the two she knew Cortlan had given her. Then she cast them to the fire.

What followed was silence—except for the crackling of the flame slowly consuming the ancient metal. None seemed particularly moved by her speech, though Raleigh did appear intrigued by something in Cecilia's words.

Rosse seemed just as unamused as ever, planting his chin atop his fist as he asked, "Where's the rest?"

Cecilia wasn't quite sure what he meant. Surely he understood the rest of the guests did not possess keys and therefore would do nothing but crowd the room with their presence.

"I agreed to destroy my own, if only everyone else did. So where are they?"

Mars laughed. "I hardly see how Hyde or Trethellyn are supposed to have joined us."

"And Carlyle? Helen?" He shook his thick head back and forth. "There are supposed to be nine of us, I count three."

"Four," Cecilia corrected him. "I retain the title of Asche so long as I have no kin to carry it for me."

"Four, then," Rosse agreed. "How am I supposed to treat this seriously if the most of us could not so much as deign to be present?"

"Both Lyre and Wintre had proxies sent forth to stand in their place." She held up the remaining three keys. "Nothing is lost in their absence."

Rosse sunk in his seat—not convinced, but at least momentarily willing to submit to her reasoning.

Mars was next to take issue. "I count two keys too many."

"How so?" Cecilia tried her utmost not to allow frustration into her voice.

"By my estimate, we each have a key of our own. You have one as Lady Asche, as well as Lyre and Wintre's. So, whose were the two you just threw to the fire?"

Raleigh looked at the eldest of their trio with a perplexed expression. "Would they not be the keys of Hyde and Trethellyn?"

Rosse's eyes lit up as he caught on. "And how did Her Grace come by those?"

All eyes turned to her and Cecilia realised the mistake she had made. As far as they knew, Hyde and Trethellyn's keys would have been with them at the time of their death. Her possessing Trethellyn's was not hard to explain, he had not been killed until after she had invited him to the capital, and it was reasonable that he also sent somebody to deliver his key. But Hyde had died before Cecilia had even been coronated, there was no reasoning she could see to explain how she had come by it—*nothing beyond the truth.*

If Cecilia were to trust them with destroying these items, she had to trust them with the truth. *Aester Hyde's jaded suggestions be damned.* "The events surrounding the deaths of both lords have been kept from you so far. This is because, until today, the truth had not been entirely discerned." She watched as the demeanours of all three shifted as they took in her explanation. "A man, who I will not presently identify, manipulated members of my own court and organised the assassination of Lord Hyde. Additionally, I believe he played a major part in Lord Trethellyn's death, though we have not had the time to further analyse this possibility. What we know for certain is that he came into possession of both men's relics."

"And how did you come to take them back from this unnamed individual?" Rosse asked.

"He gave them to me, in what I believe was a bid to portray himself as innocent and another as the culprit."

Mars seemed disturbed by that point. "His entire reasoning for collecting the keys was to give them to you? I fail to see the logic behind that."

"Neither do I." Cecilia needed to keep them on side. "But that is not our current concern. Our foe has been apprehended; you can all rest easy."

"I disagree." Rosse took to his feet, his tone combative. "If somebody would kill just to possess these trinkets, clearly we have underestimated their importance."

"That is entirely true, and the very reason they must be destroyed."

"And if we need them at a later time?"

"For what?" Cecilia's tone grew sharper than she should have allowed. "The only purpose they serve is to set Artorius free, and that is not an option we will discuss."

"Nor should we wish to." Mars stood as he spoke, holding out his hand as though to calm the rising tension. "Though perhaps we are realising that we rush toward a decision we don't entirely understand. Would it be better to wait for a time Lyre and Wintre are available? Discuss this properly with Trethellyn's heir present?"

"I assure you, that is not necessary."

Silence took them again, and Cecilia was left to wait with bated breath to see just how salvageable the situation was. She knew how obstinate these lords could be, but they were not so foolish as to risk the entirety of Duralaans for no real benefit in return.

Do you really believe that? she could not help but wonder. *What reason do these people have to give you what you want?*

Raleigh had remained silent the longest of the three lords, and those present seemed to all wait for what she had to say. Lady Raleigh leaned forward on her seat. "We do not know the reasoning behind these assassinations. Perhaps this man wants the keys for himself or perhaps he wants to scare us into destroying them. Either way, we lack proper vision of this scheme laid before us."

"Your point, Lady Raleigh?" Cecilia no longer cared that her impatience was clear. Let them know what she thought of their idiocy.

"It would be rash to act. I respect your reasoning, but we have kept these keys safe for generations. Why change things now?"

Her fellow lords nodded in agreement and returned to their seats. Cecilia turned back toward the fire, frightened by what she might do if she continued to stare back at them. Despite all of her hope, all of her trust that these men and women would make the right choice when given the chance, Hyde had been so terribly correct.

The irony almost made her laugh. They were finally united. Though in the place of a common threat, it was self-interest and a fear of change which bound them together.

It should not have mattered, not really. Cecilia had destroyed two of the keys. If she tossed the other three into the fire, then at least a fragment of her ambition would be achieved. Yet that was a hollow consolation. The lords would go on as they always had for as long as they could. The people would continue to be fragmented by lords who refused to play fair with one another, and the Duralaans that was once promised would be nought but a distant whisper.

Cecilia turned back toward them. She had not prepared a speech for this particular outcome, so her words would have to come straight from her bleeding soul. "Is this what we are now? So desperate to maintain any edge that we would clutch to worthless antiques?"

"Careful, girl," Rosse growled.

"I know you, Redan Rosse. I have known all of you since I was a child. I've seen you bicker at every table, drag your heels, and sulk like children at every slight that might bruise your ego." It was not a smart decision to test them like this, but she would not deny how good it felt to see their stupefied reactions. "We were gifted this land by the Gods themselves, made to survive a savage home that forced us take or be taken from. I understand how hard it is for us to change, but that time has been passed for *centuries*. We are not individuals. We are leaders. Think for just a moment, and ask yourselves what good will truly come from allowing this path to our own destruction to persist?"

No response came. She had to take that as a good sign. A sign that it was not too late. "Countless generations have come and gone. Yes, we have always put ourselves before others, and we have survived because of it. I will admit that way of life was likely what the Gods wanted for us, but they are gone, and this world is changing. We have to change with it."

Raleigh stood, her mouth twisted into a wide smile. "I could not agree more, Lady Asche." She paused, clearly hoping for a reaction that Cecilia was too tired to offer. "Your father was a man tradition demanded we tolerate, but you have actually earned my respect. Because you are entirely correct. It is time we changed, and I don't see why we need a monarch anymore."

Rosse returned to his feet, visage contorted in rage. "That is outrageous!"

"You defend her now?"

"I defend what we have built. We've not been without a monarch in two thousand years, what you propose would mean the end of Duralaans as we know it."

Mars shook his head. "I've had enough of this. Inform me once we know more about the situation, until then I shall be in Maross."

Cecilia watched him stride out of the room before she could formulate an argument that he remain. All the while, Raleigh and Rosse had descended into furious debate. It had been quite the shock to have Lord Rosse defending her, but that was hardly any prize. Cecilia thought that compared to their refusal to follow her plan, Raleigh suggesting an abolishment of the monarchy was inconsequential.

"Leave." Cecilia could barely hear her own voice over their discourse. "I demand you leave!"

They both shot her a harsh gaze, offended more than anything else to have their screaming interrupted. The door opened, somebody on the other side must have heard her order, and neither lord seemed too interested in remaining.

Cecilia was alone and unsure what she wanted to do most. Her mind wanted her to scream, her heart begged to cry, and her soul pushed her toward manic laughter. Instead, she simply stood by that fire, staring deep into it and wondering why neither of the keys had been reduced. Sure, not enough time had lapsed that they could have completely melted, but they appeared no different to the three she still held in her hand.

The wise choice to make would have been throwing those last few into the blaze and putting the threat of another Ashen Night to rest. But that night was already upon them. Was that not what she had decided on the night of her coronation? *Who will see us through it now?*

Cecilia pulled her dress up around her as she lowered herself to the floor. Perhaps Duralaans really did have no more use of a queen. Perhaps the only thing that could unite them now was that which had done it once before. *Fine.*

She reached her empty hand into the flame, felt the dancing orange and yellow lick her arm as it tasted flesh, and reclaimed that which had refused to burn.

Chapter Twenty-Eight
A Stage Reduced to Cinder

Raph wouldn't have been surprised if the dungeons below Carlyle Lyre's fortress had been designed by some duke out of Diavollos. It was cold, barely lit, and made purposefully to maximise discomfort between sessions of torture. Compared to that, the cell Cortlan had the pleasure of inhabiting might as well have been made up for whatever noble hoped to take an extended stay as the Queen's guest.

Cortlan had laid back on the bed set in his room's corner, propped up by a large pillow, and reading a leatherbound book. He paid no attention to Raph or Nath as they came to stand in front of the so-called cell. A large plane of clear energy sealed the prisoner inside, though they had been informed that as far as Cortlan could see, it was just another blank wall.

The armoured Artorian knight who had escorted them inside took stance behind them, having agreed only to let the pair question the prisoner under the condition they were kept under watch, a demand neither had any grounds to reject.

Raph stepped toward the energy field, then walked right through. She wondered just how shocked the knight must have been and was sure Nath would be quickly offering explanation.

One of the many benefits of being bound to her particular deity was Raph's ability to manipulate the currents of the Immortal Plane that intersected with the physical world. All mages could tap into the Immortal to varying degrees, allowing them to manipulate reality and create extraordinary displays of power. But instead of using those threads which bound the planes together to alter reality, Raph could shift the threads themselves. Though typically only to summon them as vines she could use to hinder her enemies, she could also get more creative when an excess of ties to the Immortal Plane were in play.

Cortlan finally looked up from his book. "Oh. Hello, Seraph. How goes the gala?"

"It's been pretty dull, so far. Any plans to liven things up?"

"From within my cell? I hardly see how."

"Then what was the point in coming here? The digs are nice and all, but there are easier ways to find a place to stay. And it looks like you were close enough with the Queen that she'd let you stay without the attempted theft."

Cortlan marked his page and laid the book on a side table, apparently having decided this conversation would be a long one. "You would like for me to explain my entire plan?"

"Not especially. I just got to know what's happening next." She snapped her fingers and vines of iridescent light began snaking their way around his neck.

"Intimidation, is it? And am I supposed to believe the guards on the other side of that wall will let you do such a thing?"

Raph shook her head. "Of course not, if they could see what I was doing they'd stop it immediately." She let her words hang, waiting for the telltale shift in his expression that would show he had taken her meaning.

He forced a chuckle, but the sound was hardly as confident as Cortlan must have intended it to be. "Of course they can see us, it's not exactly a complicated spell."

"No, which makes it very easily manipulated. A good enough witch could simply project a false display on the opposite side. Leaving those within complete—"

She was interrupted by a roaring explosion that knocked Raph from her feet. It was no more than a moment that Raph found herself disabled, but when she had risen again, she found Cortlan sprinting through the opening in the wall that had been magically sealed only moments prior.

Both the knight and Nath had disappeared, likely having rushed off to investigate the source of the blast. Raph sprinted back the way she had come, hoping Cortlan had not been given much of a head start.

Another explosion shook the palace walls as she climbed the stairway out of the dungeons. This time, the sound of devastation did not recede, instead growing into an ear-splitting roar that perpetually echoed throughout the halls.

Nobody alive remained within the palace—that would have been too difficult, not that Cortlan seemed to have noticed. The man stood just outside the palace's main entrance, the same terrace where Raph had faced Artorius within Vyx's accursed lake. His arms were held toward the sky as he basked in the vision of the erupting mountain of Avalass.

"How could you do this?" Raph fought to be heard above the cacophony.

"I didn't, that's the most disappointing part. He would never take one of us, no. He needed a true host, and nothing less." Cortlan turned to face her, his visage twisted with manic ecstasy. "They thought the cipher would lead to his tomb. No, the cipher was his tomb. Imagine the irony; the Ashen King reduced to ash himself. Left to wait centuries so the right host might release him. And here we are."

Something came alive in Raph's mind, like a dark room's shadows being chased away by newfound light. She remembered what she had made herself forget in the depths of Lyre's dungeons. Deep within the dormant beast that was Mount Promethus, she had found the rotted parchment that should have led to Artorius' tomb. But it had never been a map. Instead, it recorded the means of crafting a weapon, one that might contain a seemingly immortal entity and put an end to their reign of terror. A device which could contain just as easily as it could release.

It had to be destroyed. If those who sought power ever discovered its true purpose there would be no recourse. Possessing a key to finding Duralaans' most powerful being was one thing but taking that power for themselves was another. Now she realised there was just as much risk to be found in keeping that truth from them. Cecilia had no idea what danger she kept so close to her.

"Don't be scared," Cortlan crooned, "it's over now."

Raph raised her hand. "That's the scariest part; it's not." She snapped her fingers again and the world around them began to warp.

Cortlan's eyes went wide as he watched reality seemingly fold in on itself and colours begin to rapidly shift and invert—Raph even felt a wave of nausea, despite being fully aware of what was happening.

She closed her eyes for the duration of the transformation, only opening them when the sight of their true environment returned. Truly, Anni's gifts could be especially useful given the right circumstance. Raph had not been certain that folding the magic barrier around them to project a different environment would work, she also did not know that Cortlan would respond at all to the same vision of Avalass' fiery destruction that Vyx had shown her. That had undoubtedly used up all the luck she would receive for the next decade, but she was glad to see it had paid off.

Cortlan appeared especially stricken with confusion. He was on his hands and knees on the floor of his cell, looking almost as if he would throw up at any moment. "How dare you," he moaned. "Knowing will not change anything."

Raph took a single moment to be glad seeing Cortlan so distraught at having his own methods turned back on him, then she raced back out through the barrier to stand before Nath, who had seemingly only just finished explaining what Raph had attempted.

"Where's the Queen?"

—

Cecilia sat on the old palace's throne, wondering at just how many had placed themselves there before her, and how many of them had actually deserved to do so. They were all of the same ilk, all in place simply because a god had decided their lineage would be the best to govern the land forevermore. How utterly stupid that god had been.

She turned the ancient cipher over in her hand. All five of the keys required to open it had been placed within, but Cecilia had not dared to turn them and unlock the artefact properly. *Can't even do that right.*

The gala had ended some hours prior. Cecilia had not bothered to be present in bidding farewell. It felt more natural to bask in her misery than reprise her role.

For a moment, she had been so sure of her decision to unlock the cipher and locate Artorius' resting place, that would surely give the people something to stand against, but something had stopped her.

Some keys are best left unused.

Cecilia could not guess whether that boy or his master had truly suspected what she might do should her first plan fail, but the warning had stayed her hand as it echoed in her mind. And she was left alone with her thoughts and inaction.

The melancholy of Cecilia Asche was interrupted by the arrival of Chora, alongside two individuals she recognised. The girl was Seraph, the one who had been present during Cortlan's betrayal, and the other was escort to Lyre's proxy—Nath Whitsin, if she was recalling the name correctly.

"Now is not the best time," she called down as the trio hurried toward her.

"Quite the opposite, Queen," Seraph responded.

Cecilia met Chora's eyes, the Artorian's expression was grim enough to hold the Queen's attention. "Very well, what is the matter?"

Seraph took a moment to tear her eyes from the item in Cecilia's hand. "I thought you'd destroy those."

"I tried. It didn't take," was all the explanation Cecilia felt inclined to give.

"Then let's find another way," Whitsin joined the conversation. "Whatever you do, it cannot be opened."

Cecilia almost laughed. Of course it could be opened, he meant to say that it shouldn't be. And even that certainty had begun to wither.

Seraph tried to step forward, only to find Chora's firm grip holding her at bay. "It's not what we think it is. That thing will not lead you to Artorius' tomb, because it is his tomb. An urn to contain his remains until somebody decides to release him."

"You suggest our lore is incorrect? We have known what this relic is for generations," Cecilia said, though she felt no truth in the words.

"But do you know where it's from? Who crafted it?" Cecilia waved Chora off and allowed the devola's approach. "I found its designs and had them destroyed. But they were not signed, and none of my research could discern who—"

"Her name was Morguein Frieda," came a new voice echoing through the throne room. Cassidy stood in the entrance, fierce with a confidence Cecilia had rarely seen in her. The aide strode toward them, carrying in her hand something that could not be identified from such a distance. "My brother told me this long ago, after Frieda had saved him from certain doom in Léonora's service.

Cortlan was bound to serve her and her wish to see Artorius returned."

Cecilia stood from the throne and slowly descended from the dais to meet Cassidy. There was something about the woman's new demeanour, something Cecilia recognised but could not name. "You are certain he could be believed?"

"I am. He has never once lied to me."

Cecilia considered it for a moment, then caught something odd in what her aide had said. "It has been months since we lost track of Léonora. You kept this from me for so long?"

"I had to, Cecilia. It would have only been one more burden atop countless more."

Cecilia felt Cassidy's hand take hers and lift the cipher so that she held it out, as though presenting it to those before her.

"I know you have always been happy to bear that, but I could not continue to stand by as this duty of yours ruined you." She took a few steps away from Cecilia, tears shimmering in her eyes.

Cassidy was herself once more, and Cecilia realised what the momentary façade had been. Often, Cecilia would view herself as an actor and her duty as a role. It made dealing with the stresses she encountered somewhat easier, though the lines between character and performer had almost entirely blurred. She suspected those closest to her could see through the act and to the person beneath, people like Cassidy who had known her long before the role was hers to play. Now Cecilia stood on the opposite side of such an act, and though she knew Cassidy to be the same woman who had stood by her side since they were children, she hardly recognised what stood before her.

"You can hate me if you wish," Cassidy whispered. "But I will always love you."

A blade of pure black abyss burst forth from whatever it was Cassidy gripped in hand. In a single fluid motion, she swung the weapon high above her and brought it down through the artefact in Cecilia's hand. It shattered instantly, scattering shards of metal and grey powder everywhere, as though the relic had been waiting to erupt since its creation.

Amid the cloud of grey, Cecilia could make out bright threads of spectral energy forcing Cassidy to her knees. Whitsin had some kind of weapon in his hand, trained solely on Cassidy as he and Raph debated their next course of action. Chora was attempting to wave the dust cloud away so she might reach Cecilia within, but it was as though some unseen force was keeping her at bay; the grey had a mind of its own.

The cloud closed in on Cecilia, seizing her body and locking her limbs in place as it violated her mortal form. The Ashen Night that had waited upon the horizon since she first put paint to canvas had finally arrived. It was not what she had wanted, not how she hoped to do her people the justice they deserved. But fate had decided to twist the knife, and there was no leaving the stage now.

Cecilia took a deep breath and a bow.

It was Artorius who rose in her place.

Chapter Twenty-Nine
Duty and Death

Domina found himself adrift within a familiar void. Not simply the abyss that was his blade—though he was sure that engulfed him also—but the chilling embrace of his abject failure.

This feeling was not natural. Though it was passingly familiar, it went beyond the spells of doubt he had known time and again over his extended life. This was a tangible feeling. A weight that bound him whole. A poison that choked his lungs with malice. He had seen it in those he had slain. It had haunted his waking days as much as his dreams. It had followed him from one land to another.

And it had a name he knew.

Morguein Frieda. These were her snow-laden woods Domina now found himself within.

The last time Domina had been there, he had been offered a choice—one he knew had been answered too quickly now that he was benefitted by hindsight. He was certain the witch would not have brought him back without another in mind.

He trekked forward through the dense brambles. Not a single tree bore any sign of life, all were naught but violently twisted protrusions from the ground. In another time they might have struck fear in him. Perhaps it had been such fear that had encouraged him to yield to the witch's demands and take the blade up as his own the first time, though so long had passed since then that Domina could no longer be sure. In any case, if fear had played any part in his choice, he knew it was not Morguein who had spawned it. She had only preyed upon what already lurked within.

Time did not seem to affect him within Morguein's domain. Simultaneously, it felt like he had marched on for hours as it did mere moments. A falsehood that was only further perpetuated by the repetitive nature of the woods itself. With no distinctive elements to mark his progression, Domina almost wondered if he was just walking in place. Though there remained one sensation which made him suspect he was nearing something in particular.

An almost static feeling had dwelled within Domina since he had awoken. That gnawing buzz seemed to be just beneath his skin—if that were indeed something he at all possessed in this realm—and only grew stronger as he continued forward. It seemed to know something Domina did not, guiding his footsteps and ushering him toward that which awaited him.

It was not the same forceful control that Anamrath had imposed upon him. It was gentle, no more than the suggestion of a soothing hand tugging him toward a destination. Domina knew malice could take the form of kindness with ease, but somehow he felt that this was not one of those situations. This felt natural. Like the lullaby of sleep calling to a man in his final moments. And Domina supposed he was in his final moments.

He did not notice the cabin immediately. It was made of the same dark wood as the trees, and blended well among them, appearing to be woven from thousands of branches twisted together; it hardly made sense that it was standing at all. Domina supposed he was much like that cabin, something that continued to exist only of sheer grit and a blind eye to reality.

There were no windows to offer any idea of what awaited within. Domina could only trust that upon opening the door he would not immediately be slain. He had already made one incredible gambit that day, a gambit which had led him to the cabin which now sat before him, it would be a waste to turn away on the cusp of finding the answers he sought.

The moment his fingers found the door's surface, it began to peel away. The bramble and twigs that made up its form pulled back to unveil the cosy interior.

"I'm making tea." Morguein was standing over a cauldron, its bubbling loud enough to be heard from where he stood at the entrance. "If you'll wait a moment, I can fix you a serving."

The inside seemed larger than its exterior might have suggested. It had not expanded by any incredibly degree, but it was hard not to notice even small the transformation. There were windows now, as well.

Domina stepped further into her abode, fully aware that showing any form of hostility toward Morguein would do him no favours. Instead, he took a seat close enough that he could feel the cauldron's heat and watched her stir away. Whatever was within the boiling pot of iron, it was no supper—at least not one a mortal could effectively enjoy. No, within that pot was the very thing the energy inside of him was being summoned toward.

"Morguein, what is this?" he asked, instilling his tone with deathly gravitas. They had never been friends—nor even allies. Their relationship had been purely transactional so long as it had existed, and Domina suspected he would find it unlikely that she would be receptive to his questions. But there were few options left to him, and even the slightest hint of what she had planned could be turned toward salvation.

Morguein stopped her stirring, tapped the spoon a few times to cast off any lingering droplets of its contents. "My home or the plan?"

"What stake do you have in any of this? These keys? Cortlan?" Domina gave voice to his queries. "What do you have to gain?"

"Purpose, Domina. I would think you might understand that."

Of course he understood it. "But there's a line. Some things just aren't worth the cost."

"So you see why your life has been ever so marred by failure?" Morguein looked down at him, her expression far from cruel, yet offering no sympathy. "You lack the spine to be anything more than yourself, darling. Time to accept it."

Domina came to his feet. Despite standing at the same height as her, he still could not shake the feeling that Morguein was in fact far more imposing. This was her domain after all; he had to be aware of any trick she might pull. *Aware but not afraid.* "If it takes more killing just to think you matter, then that's worth less than dirt to me. A hundred years from now people won't remember your name. But they'll remember the ones who stopped you."

Morguein cackled, and it seemed as though the world joined her. "Oh, dear, I have persisted through far more than a measly hundred years. Yet still you know me. I am a piece of this puzzle. A brilliant fragment of the mosaic. You will amount to little more than a whisper in my memory, something only to awaken the faintest remnant of an irritation long in my past. You have joined everyone who has ever known you in death."

"Is that supposed to deter me?"

"From what? There is no role left for you to play. This"—she gestured to the structure around them—"is nothing more than consolation."

For a moment Domina took Morguein at her word. He had known his choice would not be one to survive. He had ventured into this void of his once already and only escaped with the aid of Enna's machine. But this was not that void, and it was more than a sanctum Domina's brain might have concocted to comfort him in his final moments. "When have you ever been so kind as to offer consolation? Why has my soul not joined the rest already?"

She smiled—a gesture to hide the fact Domina was close to unveiling something Morguein sought to keep secret, or so he hoped. "You know nothing of me. I can offer kindness to those I deem worthy. It was I who empowered dearest Artorius after he had fallen so far, I who offered a lost illusionist a path to call his own."

"And I wholly reject your kindness. So take my soul. Do with it what you will." Domina responded to her grin with his own. "If you can."

"Goading, really?"

Their attention was wholly taken by the cauldron as it began to shudder in place. The metal container seemed almost to expand as a sharp hiss emanated from within.

When Morguein returned her focus to Domina her confidence had only grown twice as fiendishly malevolent. "Too late for heroics, sweetling. Their Ashen Lord has returned." She took a few steps forward, and Domina could not help but retreat. Whatever ethereal sensation tugged him toward the bubbling pot was outmatched by Morguein's own control over their surroundings. The cabin shuddered as though a violent wind afflicted it, threatening to be torn apart at any moment. All the while, the cauldron's hissing grew into a shrieking chorus. "I want you to know their fates, Domina. Your allies of years long passed by; Seraph, Whitsin, both are irrevocably doomed. Their demise shall fall upon your head, old friend. Every life you have ended, every soul consumed in your lust for triumph has gone toward this."

Domina was thrown back against the cabin's door, its tiny twigs twisting into his flesh until they drew blood. It took all he could to not relinquish to his body's demand to cry out in pain.

"You wanted a purpose? You've always had one, Domina. You, child of Mina'lla, blade of Azazel, last of the Black Rose; you have been my means." Morguein spread her arms as though in welcome. "And this is the end."

With a flick of her wrists, the cabin exploded, and Domina was sent hurtling back into the dense woodlands. The sharp branches of the dead trees slapped against his flesh, leaving no inch of him that did not tingle with raw pain. He wondered just what trick Morguein had pulled to make agony a sensation that could still apply in whatever state Domina now found himself in. Though it surely was not, it felt so excruciatingly real.

As the spear-like ends of the branches sliced through grey-green skin, Domina was left with a new revelation, one that could at least instil in him some much-needed hope. If the pain could feel so real, everything else could as well.

Finally, Domina crashed down to the ground, the snow serving to cushion the landing enough to spare him further pain. Morguein's home was no longer visible to him—though he was not certain whether that was because he had been thrown so far away or because the cabin no longer existed. It hardly mattered; Morguein would not be far.

If the witch could sunder his soul, Domina knew she already would have done so. The simple fact that he still bore his mind as his own and had been thrown a far distance rather than immediately consumed by her void told Domina all he needed to know. Morguein was trying to keep Domina away from something, he posited that was the same thing his soul continued to call him toward.

Domina tried to stand and ready himself for the long sprint back the way from which he'd come, but the presence of a man standing over him made Domina falter. This man he knew. Though his hair was a bloodier shade of red, his face deathly pale, and clothes singed black; Domina recognised the dead Caster Hyde as well as he knew his own shadow.

—

Raph supposed there were very few people who knew the right way to react when met with doomsday incarnate. It was the type of threat that forced one to step back into the comfort of their basest instinct, hoping beyond reason that it would be enough to cushion the horror of what was inevitable. Raph's own instinct was to call on her otherworldly gifts and keep her foe immobile, an attempt that proved futile as the Queen's treacherous aide severed Anni's vines with a single slice of her blade—or Domina's blade, if Raph's memory proved correct.

How had she come across it?

Raph could recall having heard Cortlan tell the Queen that he had met with his sister—this Cassidy woman—before he had encountered Raph. She guessed that had provided Cortlan an opportune moment to leave Cassidy with the blade in the hopes she would use it to break him out at the right time. It also confirmed that this man had indeed met and bested Domina. A miserable thought, that would have to wait.

Neither Cassidy nor her brother seemed at all interested in hostility, instead they both watched the ashen cloud slowly wrap around Cecilia's silhouetted form. Cortlan's eyes alone told just how struck with awe he was as he saw the Queen clothed in history itself.

The ash began to solidify in select places, forming the stark-white armour of the Ashen King; with a cloak of black smoke and a winged crown to smother Cecilia's vision. The figure remained still for moments more, staring blindly toward those before it without any hint as to whether or not he truly took note of them.

Cortlan hurried forward, snatching Domina's sword from his sister and approaching the armoured shadow of the monarch. He slowed as he grew closer, dropping to one knee in utter reverence and raising the sword above his head as offering. "My lord. Recall thy name: Artorius. Recall thy nature and recall thy duty. You are at last returned to your rightful place. I beg of thee: recognise thy compatriots and offer unto us your strength."

Slowly, as though struggling to recall how to manipulate physical form, Artorius turned his gaze toward Cortlan and reached for his weapon's hilt. Raph could guess now why she had been so familiar with the weapon he wielded in Vyx's lake; Artorius had possessed that black blade before Domina, only at that point it had not been enhanced by the arcane magic that coated it in void.

As Artorius took the weapon in hand, he was met with a barrage of blazing red blasts that seemed to him as no more than a minor irritant. Nath strode forward with each shot, closing in on his target as Artorius appeared to size up his opponent.

The Artorian woman took the distraction for the opportunity it was and charged Artorius with a furious cry. Sword clenched in both hands, she swung hard, only to find her weapon posing no resistance to the black blade as it sliced cleanly through, and she was disarmed. But Artorius' choice to focus on the swordswoman had cost him, allowing Nath to get close enough to take the lord's throat in his black hand.

Artorius' voice came from Cecilia's mouth, his tone calm and measured as he said, "Is this pursuit truly worth the cost?"

Nath made no retort, instead only tearing a panel from his prosthetic and forcing a switch within to activate. Raph was not sure what it would do exactly but was thankful she made the quick decision to pull him back from Artorius with a few gilded tethers, as by the next second, his hand had exploded in a ball of red and black flame that sent them all hurtling into the hall's furthest reaches.

Though they had been far enough from the blast to avoid its lethal fire, Raph's body still felt its effects, and both Nath as well as the Artorian hadn't been able to refuse the allure of unconsciousness.

After making sure Nath had not been injured, Raph forced herself to her feet and toward the black cloud that had begun to dissipate. She tried to hope that Nath's attempt might have been enough—or at the very least might have done the demon some harm. Nonetheless, she felt no surprise when the smoke parted to reveal three unchanged figures. A shimmering veil of energy had shielded both siblings from the fire, but Artorius had persevered through his own mettle alone.

"Artorius," Raph said, projecting her voice with strength she hoped would hide her injury.

The Ashen Lord's face fell from his allies to her, and Raph was sure she could feel his eyes upon her, despite the mask blinding him. "Am I familiar to you?"

"We've spoken some, yeah."

"I cannot recall, though you do not seem to be a false one. Are we allies?"

Raph considered what opportunities a lie might grant her, though figured the chances of her effectively selling any of them were slim. "No, we're not."

"A pity, to be sure." Artorius' focus left Raph for his supporters. "You have done me good service, friends. Though the hour for which I require thee is not yet ended."

Cortlan straightened, newly invigorated by a victory that was hardly his. "I am yours to command, my lord. The Ashen Night shall begin anew."

A chilling moment passed before Artorius spoke again, the undead workings of his mind taking their time to reacclimate to existence. "You channel Lady Frieda's power through yourself."

"In service to you alone, be assured."

"It matters little to me. If only you fulfill your purpose, we shall see no quarrel between us." He began to address Cassidy alone, "And what of you?"

The Queen's aide showed conviction Raph might have admired had the circumstances been different, she did not cower or submit to the Ashen Lord before her, instead standing tall in the face of one of history's greatest villains. "I have fulfilled my pact. Will you complete yours?"

If Artorius was at all taken aback by her show of strength, he hid it well. "Your friend shall be released once I find an equally suited host, that is the terms to which you agreed?"

"It is no less than she deserves."

"Very well, it shall be done in time. However, in this moment my ascendance must take precedence. Then I shall see to delivering you what is owed."

Artorius marched forward with his supporters in tow, seemingly having forgotten Raph's presence until she placed herself between the trio and the exit. "You didn't think I was just going to let you walk out of here, did you?" She was far from certain through what means she would be able to stop his progress, but Raph was damned if she refused to try. "You told me why you chose this path; you've deluded yourself into thinking it's the only one you have left. Maybe that was true once. But this world has changed, and you don't have to let whatever role the Gods forced on you back then define who you are today."

Artorius' silence lasted longer than Raph could stomach. She was betting on the fact that the version of the man she had met in Vyx's lake bore some resemblance to the one before her now. *He must,* she thought. *Why else would Vyx use him?*

Cecilia's lips twisted into a smile as Artorius said, "I am *letting* nothing define me, child. Quite the opposite. Today, I define the future of Duralaans. Today, I do not simply follow the path, I pave it."

Raph only had a moment to glimpse Cortlan raise his hand, and only a moment more to have her eyes shut tight. *It's not real,* she tried to tell herself, such had been how the Queen had bested his illusions before her.

She repeated that simple litany over and over. Making sure she truly believed whatever Cortlan might throw at her was nothing more than a cruel trick. Yet the shudder of the floor beneath Raph's feet felt incredibly real. So too did the ear-splitting chorus of stone coming apart all around her.

When Raph could no longer help but open her eyes, she was met with the sight of the throne room's destruction, as the surrounding world shook violently. Thick cracks snaked through the once-pristine floor, growing larger as they neared where she stood with her wounded allies. The ceiling had shattered, and glass rained upon them. Raph could only watch as the floor gave way beneath her and she fell into the dark.

—

"I don't want to go," the child whimpered, refusing to release his mother from his grasp. "I can stay!"

"You cannot." His mother placed her hands firmly on the boy's shoulders and tore him free, looking pleadingly into his eyes. "I will not let them hurt you."

"I can keep hiding."

"They will find you."

"I'll fight."

"They will kill you."

That kept the boy quiet.

Cecilia watched this play out as though it were theatre.

The street was familiar to her; she stood somewhere in the midst of Avalass' mercantile sector, among a bustling crowd. It was difficult for her to keep track of the boy and his mother—given their clear attempts at maintaining a semblance of secrecy—she supposed they had chosen the time of day quite deliberately.

They snuck through the crowd, politely declining any merchants who offered them a special once in a lifetime deal, all the while searching. Or perhaps not exactly searching, Cecilia realised, the fear in the mother's eyes told that she was afraid somebody was searching for her.

Who are you? Cecilia wondered, and why was she a part of this?

It was difficult to recall, but she knew the broad strokes of what had happened. Cecilia failed to unite her council, failed to present herself as a queen worth any of their respect, and failed to prevent the return of the Ashen King Artorius. It could have been that Cecilia had found herself in the Infernal Plane of Diavollos for her sins, forced to be subject to whatever cruelty its reality of punishment deemed justice. Yet she did not recall death taking her, and this vision did not seem to her like punishment.

The woman noticed a hooded figure within the crowd and gradually adjusted the path she took so that it would bring her in contact with him. Just before the two met, he veered off to one side of the street and slipped behind a cart covered by a sheet of dark fabric. The mother followed him, an arm kept protectively over her son as she disappeared from sight.

Though none of them seemed to pay her any mind, Cecilia still struggled to make her way through the crowd. It was not until she reached the cart itself that she could finally hear the mysterious woman again.

"This is the boy?" That voice Cecilia did not recognise, meaning it had to be the hooded man. His tone was clipped and sharp, giving her the impression of a noble lord, or at least somebody frequently in their service. "He seems sickly."

"Food has been difficult to come by, and I have not dared allow any to know that I have two children to feed."

"There is another?"

"None of your concern. This is the one we've spoken of."

Cecilia felt her stomach twist. Whoever this man was, she clearly meant to hand her son over to them. Perhaps she thought he might offer a nicer life than she could. So why not do all she was able to send both of her children with this man? No possibility soothed the disgust boiling within.

The man seemed to weigh his options before speaking again. "Very well. Make your farewells quickly, I do not wish to delay." With that, the man turned his attention toward ensuring his horses were properly fastened to the cart.

The mother lowered herself to meet her son's eyeline. "Look at me, Artorius."

He refused. "I don't want to go."

"I'm afraid that choice is not yours."

Cecilia watched the Lord of the Ashen Night begin to cry before her very eyes, all the while certain he currently possessed her body in reality. Neither revelation gave her any solace. Instead, Cecilia only felt her pity for him mount—far from an issue for a leader to pity their enemy, but the fact that pity came from a place of familiarity was deeply concerning to her.

"Take it as a blessing. So many go their entire lives wanting for a purpose to call their own. You have been gifted perhaps the greatest purpose of all. Do not dare think yourself better." A flicker of something sterner corrupted her visage, but it was gone the next moment, and she removed something from the leather satchel she'd kept at her side: a thick necklace of glistening platinum. "Be grateful. Do not mar all that I have fought for."

Without another word, she laid the Platinum Chain around his neck, hoisted him off the ground, and placed him inside the cart. The boy did nothing to fight her, resigning himself entirely to his lot.

With a cry and the crack of a whip, the cart took off, and it began to weave its way through the dispersing crowd.

Cecilia's eyes were on Artorius' mother. She had read something of the woman in the histories, though her name had never been recorded. Cecilia had always thought that point odd given how long Artorius had held the throne—fully capable of divulging his own mother's name. Now Cecilia suspected he had withheld such information out of whatever residual spite he had retained for her choice to send him away.

Cecilia could feel that spite, though she could not tell whether it came from her own heart or his.

The sound of the cart grew distant, and Cecilia had to tear her attention from the mother to see the shape of the vehicle dwindling. A decision was made, even if she did not realise it, and Cecilia began to sprint toward the cart.

Thankfully, that cart was not moving with so much speed that catching up to it took much effort—only becoming easier as she cast off her heels and threw herself forward with every last hint of energy she had. That rage and terror which had only been building over the last few weeks seemed to finally prove useful, as it allowed her to leap up onto the cart and clamber inside.

Cecilia sat with Artorius in the shrouded cart of a man neither of them knew and joined the boy on the path fate had thrust upon him.

Chapter Thirty

The Next Best Thing

As consciousness was returned to Nath, it was the terror awake within his heart which greeted him first. His eyes were open, yet he could not see the ground before him, nor could he make out any hint as to what darkness he had found himself within.

Nath felt so immensely sore, and recalled his attempt to best Artorius by activating his prosthetic's explosive defence mechanism. Yet that offered no explanation as to where the light had gone.

"Hello?" he called into the void, hopeless that somebody might respond.

"Who's that?" Came a voice he could not identify but was sure he had heard recently. "Do you have a light?"

Nath hurriedly searched his pouches, and felt his racing heart calm ever so slightly as his fingers found an old alflight. Domina had left him with a few of the arcane twigs when they'd parted ways and Nath thanked whatever gods were keeping an eye on him that he still had some to spare.

With one hand missing, Nath was forced to scrape the bark off with his teeth until enough of the inner membrane had been exposed that golden light revealed their surroundings.

They were underground. Deep, if the length of the dark chasm above offered any insight. Tattered strands of golden thread lay strewn across the stone floor surrounding them. Nath realised that Raph must not have fallen as he had, instead maintaining enough lucidity to break their fall into the chasm.

Nath began to search for her, quelling the onset of panic only once his eyes found the spot on the floor she sat. The Artorian swordswoman was not much farther away, doing as much as she could to take in the surroundings, and seeming to find some familiarity possess her. Whether she knew the place or not did not matter to Nath in that moment. Raph knelt on the cold surface of the stone tunnel, hunched over with hands laid flat as though she were deep in prayer.

He placed a cautious hand on her back. "What's happening, Raph?"

"I'm fine. I just need to take a breath." Her hands balled into fists, and she shook her head.

Nath knew better than to believe her. He had seen the state of Lyre's dungeons. Dark, cold, claustrophobic, and not at all distant in appearance from their current location. Raph could hardly be blamed for being discomforted by returning to such a place, but he was sure she understood the greater precedence Artorius' return took. Raph deserved so much more after all she had already done, but the most Nath could offer in that moment was the embrace of a friend.

"What are we going do?" the Artorian asked, her tone soft as though she did not truly wish to interrupt.

Nath had no immediate answers for her. If Artorius had survived the infernal power of his prosthetic's blast, he was not sure there was much else he could do. But he had told Oedon he would not give up and had no inclination to turn back from that pursuit now. "We have to evacuate the city, help the people get free from whatever Artorius has planned."

"We have systems in place for that. The bell will go off at the first sign of trouble."

Raph sat up, resting an arm on Nath's shoulder as she came to her feet. "Good. Once the fire begins, they might not have much time."

"And what fire is this?"

"Artorius is going to make Avalass' mountain erupt. He will bathe the city in fire and rule among its ashes." Raph paused as though to decide whether she was certain her words were true. "We need to start the evacuation ourselves."

"Mount Avalass is no volcano, it cannot erupt."

"That mage's powers have grown beyond mere illusions. What the mountain is and isn't will not stop him."

"What about Artorius himself?" Nath asked. "We have to at least try and keep him occupied."

"You're sure you want to face him again so soon?" Raph asked.

Nath knew it was not because she doubted him, rather it was simply a realistic question to raise. He had been an asset in the fight against Vécar with his magic locket, but without it and Domina's aid as a buffer, there was the risk that he would be no more than a burden. But Nath had just seen Artorius' strength firsthand, nobody could face him alone. "Yeah, I'm ready."

She turned toward the swordswoman. "And . . . I apologise, I do not recall your name."

"Chora," she answered, her eyes falling to the ground as her hand felt at the empty sheath at her side. "I tried to fight him, and he destroyed my sword like it was nothing. I do not know what aid I could possibly offer against him."

If Raph was disappointed, she did not show it. "That's okay, Chora. What about his mage?"

"Cortlan?" Chora's face came alight with a wicked grin. "He forced me to be a part of this madness, made a fool of me and my oath, and brought harm upon the first person to see any true value in me. Yeah, I'll put him down."

"Good." Raph began to test her balance without Nath's help. "Now, how do we get out of here?"

"These are the palace's tunnels; they should be able to take us to practically any part of the city."

"Do we know where we'll find them?" Nath interjected.

Chora took a moment to think, then said, "I don't know about Artorius. But I'll bet Cortlan will be in the palace's observatory. Our greatest mages have always worked out of there, and I don't think Cortlan will turn up a chance to be among their number."

"Then we have a plan," Nath said, and was met with solemn silence for the next few moments. It seemed that none of them felt like being the one to take the first step toward what came next. "Artorius was beaten once before, but this won't be about beating him. I don't know that we can hope for such a thing. Instead, we can only save as many lives as possible. Slow him down, weaken him, distract his allies; this is as much as we can hope for. This city needs heroes; let's give it the next best thing."

Chora seemed no more convinced, but Raph smiled and echoed the moniker. "The next best thing."

Without another word, Chora strode forward into the dark. "We'll need steel."

And they found them. After a short while of walking, Chora led them into what seemed to be an armoury that had gone generations without use. Nath was confident enough with his firearm but decided to tuck a few daggers into his bandolier for good measure—seeing as it had been empty since Elias had used the last of his explosives against Lyre's men. Recalling the old mercenary's sacrifice only provided an additional reason to do all he could in Avalass. In many ways, everything Nath did henceforth was thanks to that begrudging ally; he would do all he could to make that final choice worthwhile.

Nath wondered what Oedon was doing with the chance Elias had bought them, and hoped he was not furthering the devastation to come. Nath could see the boy was beholden to his vision of prophecy, but he did not believe such malice came from within Oedon. Aester Hyde seemed to believe this horror was justified as long as it meant the people would be forced to grow stronger in response, and that ideology stunk of the same obsession with causality that possessed Oedon. Nath would have to find the boy when all was done. He could not let him leave with Hyde to repeat these mistakes elsewhere.

Chora equipped herself with an additional three blades, while Raph took a shortsword and bound the hilt to a length of her ethereal thread. With the trio satisfied with their new tools, they continued further through the darkness.

It took longer than Nath had hoped to fully traverse the tunnels. Their apparent age became increasingly concerning once the world around them began to rumble. Nath wondered just how long they would hold their shape and whether they'd even have the chance to reach the surface before the true destruction began.

"Do either of you feel that?" Chora called back; she was a few feet ahead of them despite not carrying any light source of her own. "It's getting hotter."

Nath had not been paying the temperature any attention, though now that he was, he could agree that it was noticeably warmer than when they had set off from the armoury. "Why would that be?"

Raph's feet ground against the stone, and Nath had to steady her before she fall. Her brow was furrowed with consideration, and Nath realised she had not nearly fallen due to any weakness, rather something terrible had crept into her mind. "Cortlan knows that I am aware of his plans with the mountain. What if they decided on a new course?" She laid her hand flat against the stone and stood still for several seconds. "The stone is charged, the immortal threads which run it through have been set aflame. Artorius means to ignite the city from below."

"And nobody will know it's coming until it's too late." Raph's plan had offered them insight into the plot of their enemy, but such windows are never one-sided. "One of us has to set off the evacuation ourselves."

"That seems the best way."

Nath knew there was nobody else for it. Anyone could set off a bell, but the women before him would be wasted on such a task. "I'll do it as quickly as I can."

"I'll try to leave something for you to take a shot at." Raph offered him a wink as they continued toward what appeared to be an ancient ladder, stretching far above them toward the surface.

It occurred to Nath how much harder climbing it would be with only one hand. *And Domina always made it look so effortless.* He decided to allow his allies to precede him, not wanting to slow them down, while also knowing a part of him did not want to be the first to see what state the city was in. He clambered slowly up each rung. It was shocking just how far below ground they had been, but soon enough he joined Raph and Chora through the trapdoor and into the city's streets.

Immediately, Nath found himself practically bowled over as a pedestrian rushed past. Nath could not blame him for wanting to escape the threat of death, yet when he cast his gaze toward the sky—actively dreading what he would see—he found nothing out of the usual.

"It hasn't started," he realised aloud.

"Not that we can see," Raph reminded him. "Let's get to work, yeah?"

Their eyes met. "Of course."

Raph held the same hesitation in her eyes that he felt. There was something between them, the lingering feeling that something important had gone forgotten and might never be recovered if it was not addressed at that very moment. But that was no more than a feeling. Anxiety having its way with his mind and forcing dread into his heart. Whatever words Nath thought needed to be shared, they could wait until Avalass had been saved. Those loose ends were something that they could share, if they were to be tied together now, that would only acknowledge the fear that this would be their last meeting.

Loose ends be damned, he thought, offering Raph a simple nod before turning toward where he'd spied the belltower standing tall above the rest of the cityscape, and taking off in that direction.

Shoving and weaving through the night's crowds, it was tempting to scream that the end was nigh. But there was little chance that would actually encourage anyone toward evacuation and might even cause delay to Nath's journey toward the belltower.

A dull rumbling of rock reverberated beneath Nath's feet. Whatever the plots of Artorius and Cortlan entailed drew near, yet the people around him were too focused on enjoying their libations to take any notice.

It became far easier for Nath to continue his race once he'd gotten off the streets and begun solely traversing the many narrow alleys between buildings, allowing him to slip around the hordes of nightgoers. He did not sprint, fearing that would mean attracting the populace's attention, but moved at a pace as close to it that could be mustered.

Finally, Nath reached the crimson tower that housed the city's alarm bell. It was a marvel of architecture, all vicious angles twisted toward the sky, as though offering a direct threat to the heavens themselves and those who would dwell within. At its highest level, Nath eyed the spot where the tower opened up but could not see the bell itself from so far below.

It took a well-placed shot from his firearm before Nath could get the entrance open and let himself inside. A single stairwell encircled the length of the tower's interior until the point it reached its second level far above.

Nath had to be careful during his ascent. The structure must have been built in the city's earliest days, and he considered it a genuine possibility that they had not done much to repair the stairway since that point. Each step was a battle of its own, as Nath's own caution went to war with his need to begin the evacuation as quickly as possible. He knew that if he fell to his death as a result of a mistaken step, the evacuation would begin too late anyway; survival had to come before haste.

A heavy iron trapdoor acted as the final obstacle before he could enter the belfry. It took almost all the strength Nath had to budge it, but his sheer will proved enough to throw it open eventually.

And there he found the bell—cut from the mechanism that would see it operatable and lying useless in the belfry's centre.

"I am sorry, Whitsin. Though I thought I had given you warning enough," came a voice from behind the bell.

Nath considered removing his weapon from its holster, though he knew he would not need it. "I was wondering where you'd gotten to."

"And I knew you would find me . . . eventually."

Nath expected to find Oedon as he circled the bell, instead found nothing. The boy was avoiding him. "You're not scared of me, are you?"

A lull, then Oedon said, "We are enemies, are we not?"

"Of course not." Nath continued his pacing around the bell in the vain hope the boy might decide to meet him. "Oedon, you're just a kid. That's not me discounting everything you're trying to do or what you've been through, but you're as much of a victim as the rest of us. I'm not letting anyone else get hurt today, and that includes you."

"Then you can rest assured, I am to escape this unharmed."

Nath gave up on his search, instead putting all his energy into his next words. "What are you actually here for? Because I don't buy any of that ensuring destiny bullshit. If this was meant to happen one way or another, then you wouldn't need to be here to set it up."

"I am bound to my fate, just as you are yours. Knowing what that entails does not equate to being able to avoid it."

Nath wanted to continue arguing his point, but he knew Oedon understood his own problems well enough. Nothing could be achieved by fighting a battle Nath was not equipped for.

The city streets were so far below, it was a difficult thing to rationalise that the blurred mass of shifting forms were indeed sentient beings, each with their own incomprehensible lives. It was that distance that always made Nath loathe how many lives he had taken. No matter what he saw or thought he knew, Nath could never condense a person's mortality into something that did or did not deserve to be snuffed out.

It would be nice if Nath could see the world as colourlessly as Elias Sorren had. He seemed to have viewed the world through a simple lens; there would be no good or bad, only those who offered him the coin to do a job and those who would be the job—both roles Nath had at one point taken up. But Nath did not have the leisure of possessing that particular point of view and he did not believe Elias had thrown his life away for coin. Maybe it was a naïve hope, but Nath thought somebody could not give so much without their heart being in it to some degree—no matter how small.

So where is Oedon's heart? Nath thought it was time to find out.

He thought the boy's tree metaphor was actually quite apt. To a single observer, they might seem like they were just mindless objects fulfilling their nature. But even trees made their own choices, twisting their growing branches so they might sap up as much sunlight as possible. It was time that Oedon decided whether or not the light was something he wished to see again, and Nath might have been the last person who could offer him that chance.

Nath gave himself no more time to consider the reckless decision he had made. That would only delay him, and he hardly felt comfortable wasting even a few seconds more. With as much speed as Nath could muster, he unholstered his firearm, pressed it to his temple, and pulled the trigger.

Chapter Thirty-One

The Art of Perpetuity

It was so incredibly bizarre to be among the few with knowledge of the impending doom that came for Avalass, all the while sprinting through the masses of those blissfully un-aware. Raph thought that should be what she wanted. The best possible scenario was that they dealt with this threat in such a way that the general citizenry would be none the wiser. Yet it unsettled her no less to think that these people could be reduced to ash in moments, with no chance to make peace with their fate before the end came. The sudden shift from raucous celebration to utter oblivion might be enough to kill all on its own.

"Are you sure you want to face him alone?" Chora called back from a few good strides ahead.

"I have a goddess at my beck and call," she answered, hoping she would be heard over the lively ongoings from within seemingly every home and tavern they passed by. "I'll be fine."

If Chora had any further misgivings regarding Raph's abilities, she allowed them no voice. That was for the best too. Anni's pow-ers could be incredible, but also frustratingly circumstantial. While Raph had never known any issue summoning her ethereal vines for assistance in binding a foe, she had to acknowledge the fact that it had been years since she had faced anyone on Artorius' level. There remained every possibility that her gifts would hold no bearing on this new enemy.

But she did not have to beat him. Her only goal was to buy Chora enough time to stop the machinations of the Ash Lord's mage or at least slow him down long enough to allow Nath the time to evacuate the city. None of them sought victory outright because they knew that was little more than a distant dream.

It would be a shame to die in Duralaans; Raph thought she still had so much to do elsewhere. It might have been nice to see her mother one last time. They had begun to speak again after the devastation in Spirallos, but their conversations had always been cold and focused solely on matters of the city and its people. Raph found herself—potentially for the first time ever—wishing for something other than the arduous path she had chosen, one where she might speak with her sole remaining family about matters that did not matter at all. Nath would have been shocked. Or delighted. Or confused. Raph realised she might never know.

Raph was not quite sure why the threat of death had awoken such an introspective part of her mind. It did not matter. They had returned to the Old Palace and the mountain of steps that led toward its entrance.

Artorius would be there. That had been the image Vyx chose to construct in her vision, a warning to prepare Raph for what was to come. "Artorius will be waiting for us. He'll know better than to think Cortlan's trick could have killed us all," Raph began to explain. "I'll do what I can to keep his attention on me, so take whatever opening you see and get to that mage."

Raph ascended a few of the steps, coming to pass the Artorian, and in doing so notice that she was trembling under her layers of black metal.

"They train you for this sort of thing, don't they?"

Chora made a show of checking her blade's edge, what was only the beginning of what must have been a series of pre-combat checks she had been taught to undergo. "They do. But I never thought it'd come real. Not like this." She raised a hand as though to check the fit of her helm, only to falter as she realised it was not there. "They gave me this job not all that long ago, and I've already failed all of the people who I'm never supposed to fail."

"Where are you going with this?"

"How do I know I won't fail here as well?"

Raph smiled. "Is an infant born knowing how to stand?" Then she forced herself to sprint as she began her ascent. Chora had a good enough heart to figure things out, she would make the right call when the time came. Raph did not need to guide her, only point her in the right direction. There was somebody else she had to deal with in the meanwhile.

Raph was immediately hit by a wave of heat once she had cleared the steps. It was unlike anything she had ever felt and came from no discernible source besides the pale shadow of a man that was before her.

"I had hoped that you would be the one to survive." Artorius stood in front of the grand entrance to the palace—his palace, lost centuries before, now returned to his claim. "You know more than you should. How is this so?"

Raph took a few steps toward him, found the heat grow exponentially with each one. It inflicted no pain, instead seeming to drain from Raph her very will to continue and fill that void left in its wake with utter exhaustion. "Ever had one of those dreams that made you feel like you were drowning?"

There came a laugh, a sound that was hollowed out and bore no true emotion. "Vyx persists to this day? I ought pay her a visit after so long, I never did thank her for gifting me that first gemstone."

"Did you think that made you special? Meant that you really were destined for all this?"

"I am destined for this," he spat. "Know that whatever that vixen allowed you to witness was naught but the faintest glimmer of my truth. Perhaps you spoke to a shadow of my past, a version of me long gone. That encounter will do you no good today."

Raph let her short blade fall from her hand, stopping it just short of touching the ground.

There remained a cautious distance between Raph and the Ashen Lord, though she was sure he could close it in an instant, it gave her the most security she would dare hope for.

"Do not be a fool, girl. My rule begins once more upon this day, you should not make yourself an enemy of my crown," he said, as though he truly did hold some inkling of genuine concern for Raph's wellbeing within his heart.

"You've killed a lot of decent people to come back. Can you justify that?"

"This land needs me. It will wither and rot in another's hands. It is my duty to do all I can to save these people, that is simply who I am. What right do you have to stop me?"

Raph cast her eyes back to the city behind her. The heat only grew with each passing second, and whether that came at the hands of Cortlan or Artorius, she was running out of time to stop it. But as the heat rose, so too did the fog that addled her mind, weighing down her desire to continue this fight.

Artorius held what had been Domina's sword tight in his clutches. The end of the void weapon had been embedded a foot or so into the ground and a strange aura seemed to come from it in waves. But the weapon itself had changed, no longer was its blade a pure slate of black, instead it had been set alight with flickers of pink flame that danced within the blade's form. That same fire had joined the cloud of ash that was Artorius' cape, embellishing his imposing form with the shape of his power.

It took no conscious effort for Raph to visualise the threads of immortal current that remained throughout the world. Those currents typically appeared to her as iridescent threads of light, yet those that surrounded Anamrath appeared sickly, a fiery crimson that dug into the ground like veins of corruption; here was the source of what they had found underground. Cortlan was not the one who was causing the rising temperature beneath the surface, it was Artorius.

With that thought came another. Raph's connection to Anni remained as strong as ever, but the Gods that had chosen Artorius were long gone. There existed no divine providence that strengthened his claim to destiny. His fate was a work left unfinished.

So too was Raph's. "I'll offer you only one chance to return the life of that woman to herself."

"Now you offer me the ultimatum?" The hollow cackle returned. "Good. My return would not be complete without proper opposition."

"So confident, but you probably felt the same way before they beat your ass last time, right?"

Artorius remained still for a moment more. Raph expected that he would combat her jab with one of his own, instead he seemed to have finally seen through her bid to buy time.

He roared and tore the burning void that was his weapon from the ground, running it along the flat surface before him and sending a hungry wave of fire to consume Raph. There was barely the time needed to escape its trajectory, but Raph managed it at the last moment, stepping out of its path and into that of Artorius' blade. He fell upon her from above, and instinct had Raph throw her own blade at him, catching the resurrected king in the shoulder and knocking him off course.

Raph wondered whether such wounds would be felt by Artorius' unwilling host, and if the cost of slaying Duralaans' Queen would be worth what it bought. Though Raph suspected if there had been a way to kill Artorius, his foes would have found it rather than relinquish to the plotting of this Morguein Frieda named by Cecilia's attendant.

The wound did nothing to slow Artorius; every attempt to maim and slaughter Raph came terrifyingly close to meeting the mark. She cursed herself for allowing him the upper hand so early in their bout, her opportunities had been relegated to nothing more than narrowly avoiding his own attacks.

Raph had to turn the tide against him. And if such attempts saw her killed, she would be no worse off than if she made no attempt at all. The issue would be finding the right moment and knowing what to do with it.

Artorius was a trained swordsman—a *well-trained* swordman—and his manner of carrying himself in battle made it clear why he had been such an object of reverence in his time. Every movement was made with precision and purpose; he acted without allowing the rush of the moment to guide him and almost seemed to predict how Raph would react to each strike and adjusted himself accordingly. If it were a fair fight, Raph knew she held no chance of beating him.

But it was not a fair fight.

Every slash of Anamrath was followed immediately by a trail of pink-hued flame, an afterimage of certain death that might have incinerated Raph if she did not stay focused. It was also birthed from some form of magic, and all works of magic could be traced back to the threads of the Immortal Plane. Raph could read those threads, even corrupted as they were by Artorius' augmented being, and she could predict his own moves as a consequence.

That was a feat more easily considered than it was executed. And Raph had already been avoiding his attacks; it was a way to turn the pressure back on him that she needed.

Raph avoided a few more sweeping arcs of Artorius' weapon, forcing herself not to smile as she noticed the slightest hint of confusion on the face that did not belong to him. That confusion made him reckless, not so much that Raph's odds saw incredible improvement, but enough so that she could better time her own motions.

With each strike she managed to avoid, Raph extended the distance between herself and her combatant. Finally, she was allowed a moment to truly consider what stood before her. That moment would have to be enough, as Artorius threw himself forward with a vicious thrust of his blade.

Given her foresight, Raph had an abundance of time to avoid what would otherwise be a fatal strike and throw out her own blade in return so that it might find itself in Artorius' shoulder.

It was the second instance of Raph managing a blow on Artorius. She was intent to not let herself waste that opportunity again.

A flick of the threads attached to its hilt was enough to tear the blade from where it tasted Artorius' shoulder and send it dancing through the air between them. Raph whipped it toward him again and again, not exactly with the goal of wounding the demon, more so that he might know something of the feeling that came from being kept under pressure.

That was the position Raph had known for the most part of the fight, and if she could find a means of escaping it, so could the aspiring king of ash and death.

As spectacular as the whirlwind of silver steel and gold thread appeared, it was little more than a move to aggravate Artorius—and not one that would keep him abated for long.

Then, from the corner of her eye, Raph spied a dark shape of shimmering metal pass by. Completely unseen by the warrior opposite Raph, who was entirely consumed with the act of defending his own ashen hide.

Raph allowed herself to smile.

It was her life's great purpose to defend those who could not do so for themselves. Still, it surprised her to find those willing to do the same in return. It seemed everyone had a part they were fit to play; Raph only wished that she had not been blind to that fact for so long.

The hilt was back in her hand, and to Raph's immense surprise, Artorius seemed to have become less enthused by their fight.

"I can only admit when I have been made a fool." He stretched Cecilia's arm, nursing wounds that did not belong to him. "You are blessed, not unlike myself. If it is so that the Gods have chosen you for this path, perhaps we should come to an—"

Raph leapt toward him, unleashing a scream that would surely render her throat sore in the days that might follow, and dug her blade into Artorius' chest.

She let her mouth widen into a smile—despite the searing heat radiating from his shape, despite the precarious position she held propped atop his upper body, and despite Artorius' own blade pressed through her stomach to burst from Raph's back.

Raph had never been happier to know so few could grasp the nature of the power Anni allowed her to manipulate. That power was the only thing keeping Artorius' flames from engulfing her entirely. Instead, she allowed her own blood to smother the fire and cut Artorius' otherworldly power off at the source.

He must have realised Raph's intent, and attempted to throw her off, only for her to wrap tight fingers around the blade's hilt and keep it where it was. Corrupted as they were, Raph could manipulate the threads empowering the weapon as well as anything else. Painful as that was, Raph could turn that power back on Artorius.

Perhaps it would be her undoing, but so long as the Ashen King's ire belonged solely to her, Raph intended to earn it.

She finally leapt back from him, flipping through the air, and landing a safe distance from Artorius—or at least enough distance that Raph could witness her work pay off.

Anamrath was now wrapped in shimmering gold thread, continuously layered atop itself like spider's webbing. Artorius attempted to tear it off, finding that the blade beneath had been returned to its former state as naught but pure black void.

Raph rested a hand on her new wound, taking the time to seal it enough that it would not immediately prove to be her doom. That hand came away coated in blood, charged with the remnants of the fire that had caused it, all Raph needed to do was run it along her own blade for it to come alive with golden fire of its own.

She smiled. "We're nothing without our toys."

Artorius approached Raph, slow as a predator sizing up its next victim. He seemed well and truly done with trading blows verbally.

A cut from that blade would still make her know pain like no other, but at least it could not so easily be used to sunder the city.

Raph had played her part to perfection. Now all that remained was to survive the encore.

Chapter Thirty-Two
Ghosts in a Snowfield

I must be entirely honest with you, sir." Lord Caster Hyde appeared much as he had in life, his thinning red scalp of hair and freckled face just as vibrant in colour as they had been under the candlelight of his own dining hall. "I expected your services to have done me more good."

"I'm sorry," was all Domina could muster; his throat felt suddenly dry. He considered rising from where he knelt in the snow but found that he did not have the strength. The wound Domina had inflicted upon himself may have finally been leaving a dire impact.

"I did not hire you to be sorry. I thought you would make good on your vow to protect my life."

"I did all that I could," Domina protested, hoping that whatever entity this was could not see through to his doubt. "I couldn't have known how deep this all went."

There was no emotion within the eyes that stared down at Domina, Hyde's face was little more than a slate that his visage sat atop. "Time and again you seem to do all you can, yet it is never enough. Everyone who puts their faith in you is betrayed by your foolishness. How many others are there just like me?"

Domina could not answer that—would not reward Morguein's trickery any longer. He forced himself to stand, taking a moment to steady the legs that shook beneath him. At full height, Domina towered over Hyde. "You would have died either way. My failure to prevent such a thing does not shift the blame to me." He brushed past the deceased lord, stopping only to offer the last piece of solace he could think up. "I will avenge you, Hyde. That much I can promise."

It was an incredible distance that Domina had been thrown from Morguein's cabin, it would take some time to trek the whole way back to it—if indeed Morguein permitted such a thing. The witch had more control over whichever plane Domina found himself in than any other, if she preferred that he wander the repetitive vision of her woods, she surely could make such a thing a reality.

Yet she had allowed Domina to live.

It had been mostly bluster that had led him to challenge her ability to fell him properly. Though perhaps Domina had touched at the truth without entirely intending to. Was it possible he had somehow found himself outside of her control? It was a gamble, and there was very little he could do for it in the meanwhile. Either Domina would confront his former patron with the benefits provided by this newfound turn of luck, or he would find Morguein Frieda's kindness utterly expended and be unwoven in an instant. It could not be considered a wise gambit, it was simply the one he had.

Domina attempted to pick up his pace, though his body proved infuriatingly unwilling. It was clear now that he was coming apart, his very being longed to become one with the mass of Anamrath and was pleading with his mind to allow it to do so. The only thing that continued to keep him together was that frail thread, tugging Domina even now toward Morguein's abode and the strange cauldron within.

He had to rely on that subtle pull just to remain as one piece—he put so much of his focus toward it that Domina did not hear the axe whistling through the air until it crashed into the snow a few steps ahead.

Domina knew that axe well enough to recognise it, a triple-pronged weapon that mimicked the tridents wielded by the devil lords of Diavollos. Truly, there were few who could not guess at its owner, after all there were few who could make use of an axe that was the length of two grown men.

The shadow of the Scapegoat King darkened the snow before Domina, stretching further and further as Azazel loomed over him. Domina did not turn; he could not stomach the face of his first master.

"Keep going, Domina. Why should you pay for your mistakes?" Azazel's voice was enough to still Domina's heart. It had not been so long since Morguein had last tested him with a vision of the devil, but this particular encounter felt far more chilling. There was more balanced in the space between success and failure, more at stake than one elf's freedom.

"This is not about me," Domina said, with more vitriol than he had expected from himself. He took a few breaths to calm his temper; Morguein's puppets could not be allowed to break his nerve.

"Of course it is." Azazel forced Domina to face him, then took the elf's throat in one hand and raised him from the ground. "It must always be about you. You had to lead my men. You had to slay Vécar. Now it is your blade that must slay the Lord of Ash?" In his empty hand he reclaimed his axe, brought the edge to Domina's cheek. "For what?"

Domina's attempts to fight back were short lived, a few measly kicks of his feet were nothing against Azazel's stone-like build. "Put me down."

A wry grin crossed the devil's face—a thing Domina had never witnessed while the man still lived—and he was pressed back to the ground with such force that Domina suspected he would have died a second time, if such a thing were possible. "I know how just your intent has always been, but is there not a time when you must confront the truth?"

"People are going to die." Domina wished he could have articulated a better argument, the words he sought simply refused to make themselves available when he needed them. "I cannot—will not do nothing."

Carefully, Azazel embedded his axe into the snow, Domina's neck fitted between two of the thick prongs. "The people of this land are not your responsibility, and those you have pledged your aid toward have only known misery. What drives your continued blunderings?"

Vision became a white haze, Azazel's colossal form a dark shadow that loomed over Domina in his addled state. He tried to focus, to turn what remained of his vision toward his destination. It was there. Far in the distance, he could sense a great wellspring of—was it energy? Life? It seemed so familiar, a fact that only made his difficulty to define it all the more troubling. But there was something else that caught Domina's attention. It was not so far away. Something that just barely stood out from the mass of white snow. A tiny pink flower.

"If you were who you pretend to be then you'd already know," Domina responded. Meanwhile, he tried to shift the blades away from his neck, yet they seemed as though they were one with the ground itself, completely incapable of movement. "It's not about us, Morguein."

Azazel's face bore no sign that anything lay behind his eyes which might understand the words Domina spoke. Something in that made Domina's heart sink; confirmation that this was no opportunity for him to speak once more with an old friend. Morguein's power only perverted that hope, turned it into a weapon to be wielded against him. Anger arose within—for once not to be directed inward, rather against those who would make him falter.

The assassin who bore such delight upon witnessing a man and his family reduced to cinder.

The illusionist who would turn allies against one another so that his cruel ambition may be fulfilled.

The witch who would not allow morality to sunder her—what was it she sought to gain from this madness? It did not matter.

These were people who would put their own ends far above those of countless others. They did not see beyond themselves, and in his worst moments, Domina feared he was hardly a contrast. Those fears no longer mattered. He did not seek to avenge Hyde only so he might prove himself, nor did he pursue this quest because he thought nobody else capable.

Domina fought these same battles—over and over again—because he could. Because no matter how countless his failures became, it only took a single victory to outshine the rest.

"You taught me to keep going. No matter what got in my way." The faintest light of recollection glimmered behind Azazel's dark eyes. "Even if you didn't mean to, you gave me a reason."

Azazel glowered. "A reason to suffer." They were Morguein's words and came unnaturally from the devil's tongue.

"Is that what this is?" Domina tried his most arrogant grin. "If you've been alive for centuries, how is it that you're still so weak?"

It was more than a flicker behind Azazel's eyes now; the flame of rage roared to life.

"You keep failing to leave your mark, so why are *you* still trying?"

The devil tore the axe from its place, raised it high above his head to cleave Domina apart—if only the dark elf did not evade the strike at the last moment.

Domina threw himself to the side and forced himself back to his feet, his body seemed all too eager to deny his will but seceded to the necessity of the situation. He moved as quickly as his legs would take him, refusing to offer the faux Azazel even one last glance.

Even as the forest grew dense around him once more, Azazel's furious roar found Domina's ears as though he were right behind him. Of course, Domina had anticipated the creature would not let up so easily. He could only hope that the constant sound of snapping branches meant the forest was proving a hinderance to the larger being.

"Still running?" Azazel's voice boomed, rebounding from the pillars of wood so that it seemed to come from every direction at once. "Who will it be next, Domina?" A loud *THWACK* punctuated the question, a sound that could only have been Azazel's colossal weapon tearing through whatever had the bad luck to get in his way.

Domina was not so tall that he could not duck and weave between the dark trees that stood before him, but he found himself having to do so with more frequency. The forest seemed to be growing inexplicably denser as he progressed, even as he was certain the path ahead had only moments prior appeared to leave enough room for him to pass through without issue. These were more of Morguein's manipulations. If Domina only continued—and found it within himself to move a little quicker—he would reach the end and hopefully leave Morguein's thrall within her own trap.

Domina struggled to make the pace he desired, that speed had to be traded for the ability to shift on his feet to weave between the growing number of trunks that sought to block his path.

Risking a glance back the way from which he'd come, Domina found Azazel had dropped behind considerably. He had not needed to outrun the devil after all—Morguein should have chosen a less cumbersome form to test Domina.

Domina's trials were not yet over. He had reached the forest's edge, only to find no space he could conceivably squeeze through. Domina was trapped, with even the path he had taken suddenly cut off. The hulking shape of his former master grew closer with every moment that slipped by, shattering his own obstacles into little more than black shards of bark.

It had been the hope of a fool. Whatever place this was, it belonged to Morguein Frieda alone. Domina could not escape it, not unless he did so according to her will.

Domina let his eyes drift shut. Morguein had asked him a question, one he had already answered to the best of his ability, but sometimes the situation required more than one's best. "You wanted to know why I keep doing this? The truth?" Domina was not such a complicated man, even if he often found himself facing complicated matters. "It's because I have nothing else."

Azazel showed no sign that he heard what Domina had said and continued his destructive march forward.

"When you live this long, you need something to focus on. Lest it all start to be far too much to bear. It's easy to serve, be that a man or something less mortal, either tends to be better than something grand like what you've put together. But I guess we've lost anyway, haven't we?"

A shadow passed between the trunks just ahead of him. "In what way have I lost?"

"You've been stuck in your own rotten mind for so long, you can't even hope to do something new. All these years wasted in service to a dead king who may very well be bested once more. We are, both of us, the sum of our lives, but our lives have only ever consisted of one thing. That is all we are. And that thing is loss so long as we continue."

Morguein responded with a surprisingly lilted cackle. "You dare speak as though we are one and the same? I have not been spending my years achieving nothing. I am a creature of patience. I bide my time so that when I decide to strike I do not waste my chance. You indulge in what you cannot do, throw yourself from one failure to another. You are alone. Do not drag me down just to comfort yourself."

"Of course, Morguein. We're similar, but not exactly the same. I know now why I need to do this. Not for me or so I can prove anything, but because this needs to be done."

"Incredible, I do believe this is the first time we have found ourselves in agreement."

There was no chance of getting through to her, Domina could not deny that, especially with Azazel moments away from being within striking distance. Given how easily his weapon could cleave through the surrounding nature, there was little hope of Domina's body maintaining its shape if it came into contact with its massive blades.

"If that's all there is, Morguein. I'd like to say one last thing, just to keep between us." Domina's words came softly, quiet enough that the witch would have to come nearer to the forest's edge. She crept toward a narrow gap between the trees, her dark eyes finding his with a look of utter disdain. Domina held his tongue, inching as close to his side of the bar-like trunks as he could come, while also keeping an eye on Azazel's progress.

The devil was so close now. It would only take two more swings, and he would have a clear shot at Domina.

THWACK.

One more.

For a woman of so-called patience, it appeared to be coming in short supply, as Morguein Frieda bared her teeth and said, "Spit it out, fool. Do not bother saving your breath now."

"When all is said and done," Domina began to say, waiting for Azazel to come a step closer.

THWACK.

And the last thing keeping them apart was undone in a wave of splinters. "Nobody will know that you were ever a part of this madness. They will blame Artorius, as they always have. Win or lose, nobody will care about all Morguein Frieda did. All the years you've lied in wait will amount to nothing. Everyone remembers the end, but the means? Not so much."

Azazel swung and Domina did his best to drop as far below the blade as the branches and trunks that surrounded him would allow. The axe met only a wall of wood, and cut straight through, knocking Morguein out of the way and leaving a wide enough gap for Domina to squeeze through.

Domina offered the woman no additional thought as he sprinted past the downcast witch, knowing that even a moment wasted might allow her to regain her bearing enough to conclusively stop him.

There was a hand upon his soul, guiding him toward the space where Morguein's wicked abode had once stood. Instead of a cabin of dark wood, a blinding column of white light burst forth from the ground. It pulsed with energy, rippling as though it wished to become more than the shape of which it had been confined. Here was the source of Morguein's power, the amalgam of souls Domina had all too easily gathered for her. He could not guess at how it was being used beyond the witch's domain, but there remained no doubt in Domina's mind as to whether such power could remain in her possession.

Domina did not delay, and gave himself entirely to the light. His body no longer felt as though it would fall apart, rather he felt more himself than he had in a long time, as light consumed each and every one of his senses. Of course this energy would be so familiar, he had drifted within it not so many days prior, though he was certain Anamrath's void had never been so bright.

All Domina could do was exist within it. Now that he had reached his goal, that sensation which drew him toward the void in the first place had dissipated, leaving Domina utterly alone with the souls of those he had slain. He could not make them out from the blinding white that the void had become. But he could feel their incorporeal hands attempting to grasp at him, whether that came from a hope that he may release them or a want for vengeance, Domina could not be sure.

Then came a shift and the appearance of a new shape within the white, a black figure of a more tangible appearance than the other souls that dwelled within the consuming weapon. Its appearance was followed by the roaring crack of a sound like thunder, something that reverberated through the essence of the void and into what remained of Domina's being. The thunder was joined by a flash of black energy, rendering the forms of those souls which still grasped at him briefly visible as the men and women they had been in life.

Domina knew this moment. He had seen it once before from another's perspective. Never before had Domina been given the opportunity to study the nature of Anamrath's void, but he did not find it unreasonable that time did not exist as a facet within its mass that held much sway. Every moment which took place within the blade happened concurrently; the moment Domina had utilised the souls within to create a weapon that could free him may have happened within his own past, but it was also taking place within the void's present.

Yet something was wrong. With each pulse of the Telanimus, the souls did not seem to heed his past self's call. Instead, they seemed to remain a part of the void, making real Morguein's will in Duralaans. Domina recalled the souls having willingly yielded to his request, allowing themselves to be forged into the white blade he had dubbed Anamchara. Yet he now saw it had not been the souls of those he'd slain at all. *Of course they would not aid their killer.*

The Telanimus' power burst forth from the past Domina's shape again. He could feel a whisper of that energy lingered still within his current form, and wondered how he might use it once again.

If the souls would not come to him of their own accord, Domina would have to bring them himself. He was one of them, after all, just another mortal damned by Anamrath's hungering edge. But unlike the rest, he had faced it and returned. No wonder they clung to him with such fervour, they believed Domina might escape once more and hoped they might join him.

There came another flash of black and Domina let it draw him closer to his former self. This had been what he had felt in the forest, the power of the Telanimus entangled within Anamrath's void had called out to the machine's remaining essence within his own being.

With each subsequent strike of the arcane iron, Domina brought himself forward. He felt heavier with every step taken within the surfaceless place, as the souls seemed to bear as much of the weight they would have in life. It did not matter. Domina had carried the heft of their deaths with him for as long as he could remember, he would not stop now.

Heat rose between them as the past and present forms of Domina neared one another, and the void itself seemed to protest. Spikes of white plane shot forth from every direction, running through Domina's not-flesh and pinning him to a place that did not exist.

None of it did.

And Domina was finished letting anything tell him to give up. In spite of the void's resistance, Domina pressed onward, letting his body unravel at the seams and shoot toward his past self, victims in tow.

A feeling like no other shot through Domina's form as his broken shape was reforged. There was no pain, only the feeling of complete and utter sensation igniting whatever passed as nerves for his spirit self.

Somehow the white void seemed to grow even more blinding as vision was stripped from Domina and he became more than he had ever before been. A being brought to a point, formed into a weapon that might repel the souls and that which fed upon it.

Anamchara, the blade forged from Domina's own spirit, was brought high, then struck down and through the essence of the void.

The white light peeled back, a wound that grew and festered until it encompassed the vast majority of the bright expanse. Beyond the veil was a violent sea of colour, where bright shards of glass shattered upon collision and birthed colours that had never before been witnessed. Islands drifted upon the sea, twisted shapes that seemed a parody of reality, unlikely to survive long as the ocean shredded them into nothing. Domina was no more than a spectator to this beautiful impossibility and could only feel so incredibly small compared to the madness that unfurled before him.

Domina's past self was gone, having returned to his body, and set on the road to Meergard. This was something he had not seen, something Domina could not fully realise. But he knew what it was not. Morguein had tethered the mortal soul to a single point, a well she could draw from whenever she so pleased her. This new sight had to be something beyond her control, at the very least, if not the proper returning place of the deceased spirit. Yet this vision could not be the Immortal Plane. It was too chaotic, too horrible, too wild to be held under any god's sway.

The only thing that seemed to survive the horrible expanse before him was a single vessel. It was red as blood, faceted as a diamond, and seemed to glide across the churning ocean as though it were ice, riding the ethereal breeze with sails of threaded cloud.

Domina could not be sure how long he stared at that ship, hoping it might come near enough that he could identify its crew, yet the longer he viewed the voyage, the more he felt as though something stared back.

It took great effort to tear his sight away. It would do him no aid. His past self had been able to return to his flesh after cutting through Anamrath's void, yet Domina now found himself without the pull of the Telanimus to lead him back to the Mortal Plane. He would need a new lead.

Domina reached out with his spirit—which remained all he had of himself at that moment—and let that remnant become one with the natural currents of power that swirled around him. Morguein's hold had been weakened, but she remained able to draw from her crucible of souls. That power manifested in the mortal realm, where a mage attempted to scour its ancient stones to ruin, and an undead spirit coiled around the flesh of the land's queen. Domina was within that current also, it would only take him to let go of his bearings if he wished to be swept away. But that would mean losing himself. Domina would become little more than energy to be wielded by Morguein's thralls, whose callous use of such power had led him down this road to begin with.

There was another option. Such a simple one that Domina feared it could not possibly succeed. But it was the option he had, and it was all he could do.

Domina threw himself into the rapids, swimming with the current of spirits rather than against them, and charting a course toward the destination he sought.

It felt like so long ago that Domina had failed Caster Hyde and unknowingly been swept up in the machinations of countless men and women who thought only to bring damnation. Amid such madness, Domina had maintained his vow, allowed it to steady his course as best he could, and protect him from the greater weight of what he faced. That vow was only reinforced by the small victory he had taken from Morguein.

It was simple.

Domina would avenge Lord Hyde. Domina would win.

—

Chora always seemed to find herself in the worst possible situations. It did not matter if she were the street rat who could not help but end every day marred by bruises and scrapes or the Artorian knight who had let herself be manipulated into taking part in what was surely the most devastating calamity to reach her home's shore in recent years. Chora should not have been a part of any of it. Yet the world cared little for what should be.

Queen Cecilia had never told her what madness it had been which made her promote Chora to such a dignified position. Chora vowed that she would see that answer given to her eventually. If *either* of them survived.

Chora also vowed to kill that devola should she fail to save their queen, but that only made her recall how terribly she herself had failed.

Such thoughts were enough to invigorate her anger enough that Chora could force herself to climb the last few steps leading into the palace's observatory.

The doors were wide open, inviting Chora into the circular room. A great glass dome served as roof, allowing any who stood within to view the totality of the great mountain which towered over their city. Chora might have wished to take in the spectacle for a few moments more, if she did not know her focus would be better kept on the man who sat cross-legged in the room's centre.

"I thought I had killed you," Cortlan murmured. His eyes were open, yet it was only their whites which Chora could see. "Or are you perhaps another? It is hard to tell with all the armour and masks. Or—my apologies, that's just your face."

Chora kept her sword close, unsure of what it might be that Cortlan would throw at her.

"Your strength is wasted on a ruler so inept that she did not realise her own aid sought to foil her. Artorius, on the other hand, earned his throne. There has never, and will never, be another like him. A leader who *deserves* our allegiance, can you even imagine it?"

Chora smiled, and was certain some mania had seized her, for she did not fear this man at all. "You mistake our history. Artorius did not earn the throne. It was his sister who led her people against the old kingdom, who fought so they might know a better day. All your king did was arrive at the right time, when the battle was already fought and won—"

"And he killed the poor woman; I am well aware." His eyes met hers, the first crack in his measured expression. "The Ashen King took what was promised to him."

Chora held her blade tight in hand. "And who cast him down from his stolen throne?"

Cortlan had lost interest in dialogue, that seemed fair given the circumstance. Chora's words served more to remind herself than anyone else. It had been Artoria II who had bested her father in single combat, named after the sister Artorius had slain, and first of the Artorian Guard.

Chora was no fool, she could not emulate the legendary warrior of centuries passed by. She could not face Artorius himself. But she could handle one mage.

As she closed the distance between them, Cortlan shot to his feet and raised his hand toward her. "You would have been better off had you stayed where your sins could not find you. Who will forgive you for slaying that poor broker? For allowing Lord Hyde's demise? All because you thought you were enacting your precious Cecilia's will."

A figure arose from the space between them, the tall and thin shape of an elven man with dark hair and grey-green skin.

"You should be punished, and I cannot think of anyone less fitting to be executor."

Cortlan had summoned a being she knew, somebody who she had already fought and been bested by once before.

Yet something was different about the dark elf. Not only did he no longer possess that black blade he had wielded against her, but his left arm had seemingly returned, or at least been replaced by something akin to one. The appendage glowed bright white and held in its hand a sword of similar luminescence. Strangest of all, this illusion bore a grin, a knowing expression, as though he and Chora shared a joke.

"Cortlan," Domina began to speak, "for conspiring towards the deaths of Lord Caster Hyde, his lady wife Marie, and son Henryk, as well as the murder Lord Leonis Trethellyn, and untold civilians of the city of Meergard: I sentence you to death."

Cortlan's eyes widened as his own creation turned on him, blade risen to strike. "That's not possible. You gave yourself to Morguein. You lost!"

"That's when I do my best work."

Cortlan summoned a shield of energy as Domina's blade came down. It did him no good. The sword sliced through both shield and flesh, leaving a deep gash in Cortlan's chest.

The air left the mage's throat in a harsh sputter, then he fell to his knees and remained in shock for a long moment.

The bright blade disappeared as Domina stepped away from his work. Chora saw now that, depending on how she took him in, Domina appeared somewhat translucent. She wondered how long he would remain once Cortlan was fully gone and no longer able to maintain his illusory form.

"Your mistress has failed you, mage," Domina said.

Cortlan seemed taken by a deep sadness. "No. Only I have failed." Whatever light remained within the mage left him with his final breath, and his head hit the observatory's floor.

Chora thought to say something, to ask what had brought the dark elf to this point, and what part he had played in everything that had happened. But Domina's attention snapped toward the distant mountain, seemingly having realised what was about to happen moments before it did.

Cortlan's final illusion disappeared, the veil of what appeared to be a peaceful night lifted to reveal a sky choked by dark clouds of smoke and illuminated by bright yellow fire.

"We were wrong." Chora had not meant to put the realisation to words, but the shock had drawn it out of her. Cortlan had already forced an eruption from the mountain; the true illusion had been making it appear as though nothing were wrong. And she had not yet heard the telltale tolling of an evacuation's commencement. "We need to evacuate the city."

"No." Domina had turned away from the horror at hand and bore his gaze into her. "We stop Artorius. It all means nothing if we leave him on the table."

"Okay, very well," Chora answered without letting herself dwell on what facing Artorius herself might mean. "Let's go."

Chora had begun to make her way back, only to stop once she realised Domina had not begun to follow her.

"I cannot join you, Chora. Not properly."

"Because you're just an illusion." She would have to do it. She would face Artorius herself. "I feared as much."

"I am more than an illusion, but less than I was." He seemed to consider a distant thought for a moment, before discarding it. "Where is my blade?"

"They gave it to Artorius, did you know it belonged to him?"

If he had an answer to her question, Domina did not give it. "Get it back and I can aid you."

His image grew less tangible, appearing as though he was incredibly far away, despite Chora knowing the opposite to be true.

"You're strong, Chora. Do this because you know it must be done, and you can see it through."

Then Domina was gone, as though he had been no more than a figment of Chora's stressed mental state. Of course this would be the way of things—Chora wondered what madness had made her believe the Artorian path was the one for her in the first place. But she had accepted it, and despite all that had come to pass in recent days, she had never regretted that decision.

Chora offered the dead mage a final glance, then descended the staircase alone. Perhaps not ready to face what awaited her, but more than willing.

Chapter Thirty-Three
A Veil Lifted

The plebeian ant is never one to question its own self, that which it does is simply because that is what it must do. Cattle consume the fields because it is their nature, they do not seek to rewrite their script, they simply follow it to the very letter. Not even the ever-loyal mutt would think to bite the hand that feeds it. Yet mankind, time and again, would rage against the facilities designed to support them.

Oedon found this utterly perplexing. Why would the Gods design a creature that would only rebel against them?

And why had they then decided to send him to quell their resistance?

Oedon thought he understood Elias a bit better, even with the man himself dead. He too served a master who frustrated him to no end, even more so, Oedon realised, since he had begun watching Nath Whitsin.

That foolish man. Oedon had known how this would end from the moment it began, yet he had never known how he would feel once it came to pass.

Even as Whitsin entered the belfry, Oedon thought things may go differently, hoped the man would not test him so thoroughly. Even as Nath drew his firearm, Oedon prayed that he would not have to witness the same violent end that had haunted his dreams nightly since he set foot in Duralaans.

And he did not.

A thin plane of crystal appeared in the space between Nath's skull and his weapon's barrel, shining a bright yellow as the flash lit it up, followed by a shrill ringing as the blast was kept from its target.

Oedon watched Nath's body still, forced himself not to see what would come next. The moments ticked by, each offering Oedon a new and terrifying revelation. He saw Nath's body fall to the ground, thought for a second that everything had gone as it was meant to, then realised that Nath was still breathing. Those breaths came fast, his lungs and heart seized by fear, but they came and went as they naturally did.

Oedon let himself drop to the belfry's floor from where he had hidden himself in the cramped rafters. He took a step forward, then another, and one more, each shorter than the last. Oedon thought it was possible the strain of witnessing the future had finally broken his mind, and it had constructed an entirely new vision to cope with what he knew was unavoidable.

Oedon opened his mouth to speak, thought that if only he said what he thought, it might be made real. But he hesitated, once more wondering whether he was even lucid.

He had tried already to change fate, had warned the Queen against unlocking Artorius' cipher, and betrayed his entire reason for coming to Duralaans in doing so. But the Ashen Lord had been freed all the same.

"I'm alive," Nath said, pulling Oedon back to the strange new vision he had uncovered.

"You are," he agreed. "*How* are you alive?"

"I reckon that's not so hard to figure out." Nath laughed as he returned his weapon to its holster. "You saved me, Oedon. Why do that if we're all doomed anyway?"

"I don't know." He felt a dark shadow behind him, chastising him for his actions.

"Of course you do. Everything matters. Every single choice we make, no matter how small or inconsequential, it has to mean something. If not to whatever divine influence you follow, then at least it can matter to us."

Oedon found Whitsin's words difficult to consider. He had followed a single path—not for an especially long while, but he had known there was no way to return to how things had been before, thus in many ways there had been nothing else to know. He could not believe that he had been wrong because that would mean that everything he had done . . . was for nothing.

The night sky darkened inexplicably, the smooth vision of deep night turned sickly grey, backlit by the bright essence of flame. Avalass' mountain had erupted, spewing forth fire and smoke, and trailing molten lava in a burning path down its side. It was already so close to the city.

Whitsin's attention had been captured by the sight, and it refused to let him go.

Oedon had known the revelation would arrive at any moment, though he had expected Nath to be dead before he could witness it. His poor horror-stricken face could barely comprehend the reality before him.

"We underestimated them," Nath groaned.

"I didn't," Oedon said. "I knew this would be how it happened. I *knew*." But he was less sure than ever before that he believed his own words. He certainly thought he knew how it all should have unfurled; the combined machinations of several minds were to bring about a wave of destruction that would leave Duralaans forever changed. Now, Oedon considered whether that had been the sole true course or if it had merely been the one he was allowed to see. "I had to know, Nath. I had to. Otherwise it all turned to bile, none of it worked. And if I did not know, if none of it was fixed, then I should have been able to save her.

"But I did not save her." Oedon was only beginning to realise he had been speaking aloud. Just another thing he should have known. "Why did I not save her?"

Oedon felt so numb that he hardly registered that Nath had wrapped his arms around him. "I was about your age when I lost my mother. I blamed myself for a long time, thinking I could have or should have done something more. But I was just a kid. It's not on you to be anything more than that. Just be who you are, Oedon. And if that's what fate wants you to be? Great. If not? Then fuck fate. We decide who we are."

Nath offered Oedon a light pat on the shoulder then made way toward the belfry's edge, offering the situation a more focused set of eyes. "If I'm looking at this right, that lava will hit the palace walls first, then probably spread around it before hitting any of the city streets. That means we still have time. Not enough to evacuate the whole city, but it's not as bad as it could be." He seemed to be speaking to himself for the most part, so Oedon was caught off guard when he turned back to address him. "You can see exactly where it'll hit us the worst, right?"

Oedon nodded, he was not entirely sure what words would come if he tried to speak again.

"Then we can use that. You can find the quickest route to that part of town and then we do everything it takes to help. They'll be panicking now, so we have to be precise."

Oedon thought he had misheard. "You want my help? I will only slow us down, Nath. My eyes see nothing but pain."

"Your eyes see every step we must avoid. I need that, kid." Nath held out his hand, the olive skin of his palm rough from years of work. They forced Oedon to consider the fact that this was not Nath's first brush with disaster, he had witnessed and survived so much, yet he still felt that he could do more.

Who was Oedon to debate such proof of self?

He did not take Nath's hand; there was no time for such point-less displays of camaraderie. Instead he took off down the steps leading out of the belfry and descending the tower itself, making sure to point out the few steps which were due to break the next time somebody put too much weight on them.

Oedon had defied something powerful in choosing to save Nath's life, it would be a shame for a short fall and a sudden stop to undo such work.

—

While the beginning of their confrontation had maintained some semblance of combative dignity, the duel between Artorius and the devola Raph had devolved into an animalistic, brutal back and forth. The woman's clothes were littered with blood-stained gashes, her short hair unkempt, and face a twisted picture of fury and focus. Artorius showed just as many signs of being worn down, large chunks of his armour being damaged to reveal the chalky texture beneath the smooth exterior.

Raph screamed as she leapt toward Artorius, planting her blade into his shoulder, and wrapping the attached strands around his neck. She landed on the ground behind her foe and pulled the cord tight. Artorius let out a choked gasp, then tore the blade from his shoulder, twisting so that he could cut down across Raph's back. She dropped with the strike, kicking out at Artorius' knee and staggering him long enough for her to reclaim ground and summon her blade back to her hand.

After less than a second of downtime, the two returned to their bloodletting.

Chora watched all of this from behind a large pillar which sat a few steps from the palace entrance. She awaited what would be her moment, a chance to take Artorius by surprise and part his weapon from his hand. Yet that moment had not presented itself, and while Raph's savage flurry of movement had kept her so far alive, Chora knew it could not be maintained, even with Artorius himself showing signs of weariness.

Chora had no choice; she would need to create her own opening.

She checked her new helmet, one she had collected during a quick visit to the palace's armoury, and made sure the visor covered enough of her face to properly sell the farce she was about to deliver. Without Raph's divine power for herself, Chora likely would not pose Artorius a threat for long, but there were other ways to fight.

"Hark, brother!" she called, stepping from behind the pillar to reveal herself. She had to force out a long and shaky breath to keep herself from losing control. That wave of heat she felt upon facing him directly was particularly difficult to bear; Chora wondered how long it would take to melt her armour and cook her body within.

To her tremendous relief, Artorius did not attack her immediately. He simply turned to face her and stared, that heat seemingly accentuated by his gaze.

"Have you no words for me?"

Artorius took a step forward, the heat following him. "Could it truly be you, Artoria?"

"Such is my duty. Neither of us should be here, yet you have been forced to return, and I to fell you once more."

"Should it come to that? Can we not at last be allies?"

"You have let ego and greed drive you for too long. Nothing less than death can redeem you now, in my heart and that of this land."

Chora could see Raph attempting to grasp the situation, then decide to use the distraction as an opportunity. Chora wanted to wave her off, or at least tell her to go for his sword, but Artorius' grip had tightened around his weapon, and Chora would not risk calling Artorius' attention back to her ally.

Her own weapon came to her hand, and she held it steady between herself and her foe.

Artorius gained another step. "Where is your spear, sister? Will you face me without your preferred weapon?"

"This form did not offer such choice." Chora took her own step forward, hoping to put enough pressure on Artorius that he would not be allowed to dissect her act.

"Very well. For what little it may be worth, I am glad to see you."

There came a surge of adrenaline, followed quickly by a loss in much of Chora's awareness, and the sharpening of her focus. The only thing that mattered was the man who stood before her. "I cannot say the same."

The moment was at hand, Chora only hoped it would not come as painfully as she expected. She would put up enough of a fight to guide the blade toward where it needed to be, then pry it from his grasp while Artorius believed he had won.

Then Raph made her strike, slashing at Artorius' calves and placing herself between Chora and the Ash King. Chora's distraction had allowed Raph the chance to reignite her flame, and she whipped her blade toward Artorius with more precision than Chora had ever witnessed in a warrior.

But Artorius had similarly regained his focus, and he strode forward with a dark intensity, letting each of her strikes hit their mark without so much as slowing.

Chora charged forward, her distance was not so great from the two, but it felt all too much given the circumstance.

Raph threw her blade at Artorius' heart, and he snatched it from the air. Chora could see him twist Cecilia's mouth into a wicked grin as he clutched the steel in hand, then pulled it hard enough that Raph came stumbling toward him.

Chora saw the next few moments within her mind's eye. Artorius raised his weapon. Raph failed to find her footing. The black blade thrust down to meet her heart.

It would not meet its mark.

Chora threw Raph to the side with no hint of care and caught Artorius' hands in hers. The black blade punched through her armour and penetrated the layers of her flesh. Her arms trembled with the difficulty of preventing it from digging any further.

It hurt less than Chora had expected.

Her feet wanted to give out, but Artorius held her in place. "I am sorry, Artoria. It is a shame that we must face this once more."

"Do not lie to me." Chora forced herself to continue breathing. "This is just what you do. You took the throne, you took that body, and you took that sword."

"This blade has served me longer than any other. It, like everything else in this land, belongs to me."

"Not anymore." Chora made his strength his enemy, pulling the blade toward her and letting it embed into her side.

Artorius could not have known what she was attempting, but he tried to stop it all the same, pulling the blade back toward himself with all the strength he had taken from Chora's queen.

With a wild scream, Raph stabbed her shortsword through Artorius' wrist. He knocked her back with a vicious backhand, but that had meant relinquishing his claim over his sword's hilt.

Chora staggered back, doing all she could to gain distance from him, before collapsing. Everything had gone numb. As though Chora had moved beyond her own fleeting form and now watched a scene from her life played out by an actor she did not know.

She watched Raph struggle to her feet, but it was clear the fight had finally left her. Artorius' strike must have addled her mind because her stance swayed and her eyes seemed unable to remain on Artorius for long.

The Ashen King himself took them in with nothing that could be described short of contempt. "I must admit, I will not soon forget how trying the two of you have been." He cast his eyes toward the burning sky. "Cortlan is dead?"

Chora tried to speak but her voice was overshadowed by a fit of coughing.

"Very well. I commend your efforts; it is nothing less than pitiable that you thought me your enemy."

A hand placed itself on Chora's shoulder, yet she did not possess the energy to confirm it was no more than her imagination. It offered her comfort and something of the strength which had been sapped from her by the wound. In truth, she found much of that strength begin to return, and her breaths came easily once more.

Artorius enjoyed a few moments of reprieve, then started toward Chora and his stolen weapon. "We are at an end." He took the hilt in hand and, with a surprising degree of care, removed the blade from Chora's flesh.

There was no pain whatsoever. Still Chora felt as though she were far from her own flesh.

Artorius raised his blade once more.

And froze.

Perhaps Artorius had realised Chora was not so wounded as she should have been, otherwise he had simply noticed his weapon's appearance had changed.

It retained the same shape and colour, but it no longer held the impenetrable darkness that it had. Instead, there was a new level of clarity to its blade, entirely unlike any sort of metal, and far more akin to a carefully sculpted shard of glass.

"What have you done?" Artorius asked, his voice for the first time small.

Chora tried to answer, but her mouth did not respond as it should have. Words came forth from her tongue, yet they were not hers. "So, you're Artorius?"

Her body rose, overtaken by the spirit of another for only a moment. Then she was called to herself once again. But Chora was not alone, something had escaped Artorius' weapon and found purchase within her soul, presenting itself as a bright light beneath the surface of her left arm and a shining sword in her hand.

He said he wanted to make this quick? Domina's voice echoed in her mind. *Works for me.*

Chapter Thirty-Four
For Anything and Everything

Nath followed Oedon's lead, struggling to replicate the same elegant manoeuvring through the hurried crowds that attempted to flee the city. Nath's heart bled for them. He wanted to do something to aid their escape, but he understood there was no alleviating the frenzy that had taken them.

They needed to reach the very edge of the city, where the lava would first touch sculpted stone. Thankfully, that being the one part of Avalass nobody wished to remain in, meant they faced far fewer fleeing citizens as they progressed.

A small part of Nath thought to take another path, and make way for the palace itself. But he would not leave Oedon to execute Nath's plan alone. It took no small amount of effort to keep himself from asking if the boy knew what had come of his allies. Of course, such news would be nothing more than distraction. He would see Sera again soon enough; it would just have to wait.

"Stop here. We have arrived." Oedon stood in the middle of the crescent-shaped street which outlined the palace wall. "The lava will enter the city at either end of this road and meet here. With time it will only grow, becoming a flood which will wash through the city whole. We can do nothing but slow it."

"Then what'll slow it the most?"

"Anything," Oedon said, his eyes searching the empty street. "Everything you can find. We are not going to pull hours or minutes from what we have, but perhaps a few seconds."

"Then that's exactly what we do." Nath made his way toward an abandoned cart. "Help me move this."

Eventually, they managed to form a barricade of upturned carts at the farthest end of the street. It had taken far too long, and they still had the other side to do. Nath had thought it may help to form multiple levels of the barricades, something that might slow the lava's progress further by staggering it. But the combined strength of a one-handed gunslinger and a child hardly made up the man-power necessary to achieve such a feat.

"Can you see a better way to do this?"

Oedon's gaze went distant, as it did when he was witnessing whatever shape his visions took. Then his attention snapped toward a distant alleyway. "Keep going, Whitsin. I will only be a moment."

Nath lost sight of Oedon beyond the alley, decided to heed his suggestion and search for the next cart to move. He hadn't realised just how much Oedon had been helping him until now that he had to shift the thing without him.

So great was the difficulty that he had barely moved the thing from where he'd found it when Oedon had returned with two armoured guardsmen in tow.

The first of the two placed a heavy hand on Oedon's shoulder, trying to keep him just a few more steps back from the looming threat of the volcano. "The whole city is under evacuation, you two cannot be here."

"Nobody's going anywhere at this rate, we need to slow it down," Nath explained.

The second of the two, a broad-shouldered woman was looking over their handiwork. "You're trying to barricade against a volcano with wooden wagons and carriages?"

Oedon brushed off the guard's hand. "We cannot save this city itself, but the people may have a chance."

"We don't have enough bodies." The guardswoman turned her attention down both ends of the street, as if weighing the odds of success herself.

"Four more and we can buy enough time for everyone to escape."

"How can you know that?"

Nath tried to push the cart once again, managing one step forward. "Help us or do not, but we need to do this now."

Oedon's eyes were closed, lucky enough to know how the guards would respond. Nath just had to wait and hear it for himself.

"I might be able to find a couple folk to help," the guardsman said. "Won't guarantee anything, but I'll see what I can do."

He took off without another word, and the woman helped them move the cart into position.

It was not until after they had set up a second barricade and half of a third that the guard returned alongside two of his fellow guardsmen and one woman who appeared to be no more than a citizen willing to help. It was not what Oedon had said they needed, but everyone had to make do with what they had. Nath was amazed enough that they had found anyone willing to stay behind during such a disaster; these poor people had no idea what had actually caused the seemingly impossible detonation of a non-volcanic mountain.

It was just as he had told Oedon: everyone simply had to do what they could. Breaking fate was simply a bonus.

—

It was a dance between two entities which represented polar opposites. A king in grey armour of ash with a blade of black glass and the knightess in plate the shade of shadow itself and a sword of pure light. Their furious ballet was both incredibly difficult to watch, as well as nearly impossible for Raph to tear her eyes from. The hunger behind each of Artorius' movements failed to do anything against Chora's grace as a warrior.

Even then, there was something else mixed into the combative equation. Just as the Queen's body had been made a puppet of another soul, something had merged with the knightess' being. Yet unlike Artorius, this other entity seemed to guide rather than control. It showed Chora what moves to make and trusted her to make them herself.

And Raph recognised those moves. She could remember a time when they had saved her life, and as impossible as it seemed, they had saved her again.

What a miracle you are, Domina.

The weapons of opposing definition clashed again and again, both combatants failing to land a blow on the other, but only Artorius' demeanour seemed to change as their fight progressed.

Raph wondered why Domina did not go for the kill. Perhaps Chora would not let him mortally wound her liege. So what was their goal if not to end the fight properly?

Artorius had lost the cloak of fire which had engulfed him, the heat that wafted from his being had diminished, and even his blade now seemed far more tangible than it had. Whatever Chora had hoped to accomplish in impaling herself with Anamrath had seemingly worked. The connection to the source of his power that Raph had dulled, Chora had cut off entirely.

Miraculously, as Artorius whirled his own sword above his head and brought it down against Chora, she seemed to counter it in precisely the same location each time. Even when Artorius left himself open to retribution, the Artorian seemed more focused on landing a blow against his weapon than its wielder.

Every time the two blades made contact, a distinctive crack reverberated between them, a sound which only grew with each connection.

Raph tried to follow their exchange, searching for some way she might aid them. But Artorius' blows had finally taken effect, and Raph was reeling in both body and soul. It took tremendous effort even to focus on the fight before her, let alone call upon her illuminating sight to do any good.

One moment it was Chora fighting the returned king of an age long gone, the next Raph thought it was Domina wielding his blade against the Death Lord Vécar. So long it had been, and so little had truly changed at all. They had told this story before, and they would doubtless tell it again. Though Raph hoped the next time would prove less trying.

Allowing divine inspiration to take hold, Raph summoned the iridescent tendrils of light and commanded them grasp Artorius around the leg. It was enough to restrain his next rapid strike, allowing for no more than a poorly timed defence.

Chora's weapon found its mark once again, and this time did more than simply crack the glass-like blade, instead cutting straight through. The blade shattered entirely with a sound that reached Raph's ears like a thousand anguished screams let loose in a single instant. She saw them as well, a whirlwind of violence spiralling upward and away from where they had been set forth from the blade, escaping into the immortal threads of existence, and repairing those Artorius' actions had damaged.

Chora held her blade at Artorius' throat. "Yield, Artorius. Return that body to whom it belongs." Chora's voice was clearly her own, but there was no mistaking the subtle intonations of Domina's whispering within her words.

"If only that were possible," Artorius mused, entirely unphased by his apparent loss. "You lack binding. I leave this woman behind and where am I to go? You would let me into your soul? Your mind?" He turned so he might address Raph. "Your heart? I fear not one of you possess the spine to make such a sacrifice."

"And it is not needed." That was Domina's voice, clear as day despite the inflections made by what were Chora's vocal cords. "I present to you, Artorius, the blade forged by and of the soul itself. Anamchara does not consume as yours did. It is a true blade. Anamchara severs."

Chora drew the blade down in an instant, drawing a thin line across Artorius' chest.

The Ashen King reared back and screamed, and for the first time since he had overtaken her body, the Queen joined him.

—

In total, they had managed to line up five barricades. A feat that would mean the survival of many of the city's occupants, allowing nearly enough time for every citizen to escape the disaster.

Nearly enough time.

Oedon watched the liquid fire cascade down the solid face of the mountain. He could feel the heat even at this distance—or perhaps he simply recognised a future where he too would be engulfed by Avalass' bane.

"Oedon!" Nath screamed. "Give us a hand with this one!"

Oedon did not have to turn away from the coming destruction to know Nath and one of their volunteers were attempting to move another cart. "Do not concern yourself with that one. You have done as much as you can."

To Oedon's surprise, Nath did not argue the point, he simply thanked the five who had joined them and suggested they return to the evacuation. "If we can't do anything else out here, then we should move into the palace."

Oedon kept his eyes on the magma. It was closing in on the city's outskirts. "Yes, that would be for the best."

Neither of them made a move. "What are you thinking?"

Oedon could feel the heat now, *really* feel it, beyond the sensations of potential futures to come. "I have a way that I might save everyone."

"I thought we didn't have time?"

"Not that way. But I can create one final barricade, and if my power holds, it shall be enough. Everyone will live."

Nath was smarter than he seemed at times. He must have detected the fatality in Oedon's tone, even if he did not intend for it to be there. "What about you?"

"What about me, Nath?"

Nath forced Oedon to face him. "When the barrier falls, Oedon. What happens then?"

Even without witnessing it himself, Oedon knew the lava flow had reached the city. Oedon could not waste his energy on convincing Nath that everything might still be alright. "You have done me more aid than I deserve. Let me help you now."

"I won't let you get yourself killed."

"I told you already that I am not to die today." A bubbling hiss came from the street's end, soon it would eat through the pathetic defence they had mounted. "Help your friends, Nath Whitsin. We will meet again when this is well and truly over."

"They need help?"

"More than I."

That managed to turn his mind, and Oedon let himself return his own focus to the approaching flame. Nath seemed unable to voice what new thoughts had come to mind, offered only: "Thank you." Before sprinting toward the open gateway to the palace grounds.

Of course, Oedon was no longer so certain that he would survive. He and his prophetic abilities had already been proven wrong once that same night, perhaps they were due to repeat their inaccuracy. Oedon decided he no longer cared. He would save the city and deal with whatever came next when it arrived.

A great wall of crystal appeared in the space ahead of him. Within its many fractals, Oedon witnessed infinite possibilities. He did not care for any of them. None were truly real until Oedon chose to make them so.

Perhaps, he was beginning to prefer it that way.

Chapter Thirty-Five

Reprisal

All members of the Duralaans nobility were aware of the Tale of the Ten Kings, yet to experience the legend firsthand was unlike even the greatest performances Cecilia had been privileged to witness. It was an epic written as a means of exploring the failings in the land's monarchy, it dissected the rot deep within the roots of those who held power and mapped the events which the original author believed had brought about a cycle of stagnation and ruin.

That tale had long been a favourite of Cecilia's, especially when portrayed live in theatre, but she acknowledged it must have been incredibly far removed from the truth of what had happened. Now came the chance for a new perspective.

Step by step, she followed Artorius through the phases of his life, residing within the shadow of the warlord-to-be at all times. Although, his earliest days bore no sign of the cruel lord of ash who he would become. Artorius was just a child, taken far away from his home, and given a purpose beyond his own will.

The province of Lord Constance Raleigh became the boy's home, Irisha and the family who held it had changed much by

Cecilia's time, but there was a certain glory in witnessing it through the eyes of another age.

Raleigh showed no great pleasure in taking the child as ward—and servant—but there was almost an amusement which he displayed during the time Artorius was a guest to his halls. He knew more than the boy did, had been informed of what the youth represented before ever laying eyes upon him—of course, he likely never would have accepted his presence had he not known what Artorius would someday bring.

That truth would only be placed upon Artorius' own shoulders when he was deemed ready.

Cecilia did not believe anyone could be truly ready for such a burden.

Those early days were so delightfully normal. Artorius completed his duties within the house of Lord Raleigh every day, then did what he could to entertain his childish need to have his attention consumed. Guindoline Raleigh, the heir to the house, became his frequent companion outside the guarded walls of the family abode. That friendship reminded Cecilia so much of the days she had been at leisure to spend with Léonora, exploring the reaches of Cendela's civilisation alongside them and her own family.

All gone now. Not even Cortlan's return inspired new hope that she might reunite with her lost friend. Anything he might be willing to share would not be worth trusting and could have been corrupted by whatever fellowship he held with the Ashen King alongside his sister.

Cassidy. That betrayal had stung, and Cecilia had not been granted the time to process and attempt to understand it. Her only hope was that through drifting among Artorius' own memories, she might decipher the larger meaning behind his machinations, and the reasoning that might motivate anyone to become his ally.

Artorius never wore the platinum necklace his mother had given him, instead it remained buried within an oak chest in the corner of his quarters. Cecilia found it seemed to frighten the child, something in him would shudder whenever his eyes touched it, and he would quickly find something to distract himself from its presence.

Thusly he continued for many of the years which followed, until one otherwise ordinary day an epiphany took him, and he resigned himself to his quarters for an entire week. Within this solitude he developed what would become his guiding beacon, a plan that he might execute over the course of his life, a means to strengthen Duralaans like never before, and unite the eight independent houses under one head.

What surprised Cecilia was that this head would not be his own . . . but Guindoline's. Such respect Artorius had for her that he would place the fate of the land in her hands. It was touching enough that Cecilia almost found herself believing that something had changed in the structure of this particular tale.

It would not last, and Guindoline would never know she had ever been held to such esteem, as Artorius would be taken by a sudden curiosity before that week's end. A curiosity which demanded he dig the Platinum Chain from its exile and place it upon his shoulders.

Cecilia witnessed the same vision Artorius had at that point. A man in shimmering robes of pearlescent white, his skin the sheen of gold, and eyes as cold and distant as any one of Avandoras' moons. This being was beyond anything a mortal should know, appeared both benign and furious in a single breath. Cecilia felt immense pain at the prospect that she might have displeased the entity, as though its will were intrinsically tethered to her own, as well as every other facet of mortal existence. She was so utterly overwhelmed in what truly could not have been more than a few seconds. She could not recall him offering any words or demands, but when the world shattered and Cecilia was allowed to return to herself, she knew his name.

Arokxa the Hand, God of Order.

He had shown them something of great importance, though Cecilia could not visualise what exactly she had seen following the moment, it was only the impression of meaning she was left with.

The old gold rusts, the night grows cold.

A change must be seen lest the world grow small.

A house taken by disunity cannot be.

Through crystallised faith, only you hold the key.

Chain them in platinum and wield harmony as your blade.

Let no discord persist and you shall be obeyed.

By the time Cecilia had fully regained her senses, much time had passed her by. The message she had been given had not been witnessed by her alone, and Artorius had allowed it to completely consume him.

Under the guise of seeking out a suitable match for Raleigh's heir, Artorius was allowed to travel the entirety of Duralaans and treat with the highest of the land's nobles. One by one, he allowed them to know of his plot, one that would assuredly benefit all who stood with him against the maligned King Grettir II. One by one, they all pledged their banners to his cause—after all, only the fool would not ally with the man the Gods had chosen to be king, and all who gazed upon the chain upon his shoulders knew this claim to be no lie.

In parting, each lord and lady left their guest with a gemstone that represented their claim in some small way, and Artorius carried that piece of their loyalty with him as he added to his circle. By the time Artorius returned to Irisha, Lord Raleigh had already deduced his true intent and permitted that he take Guindoline's hand in wedding and add their family to his allies.

Artorius returned to his birthplace with an army at his flank. Ready and willing they were to tear down the grand doors to the capital and storm Grettir's palace, but the way had already been paved.

During his time away, a young woman had rallied the city's people and led them in uprising against the King. Such was the first tragic twist of the tale; while Artorius had been sent away, his sister, Artoria, had remained to witness the cruelty of the King as he searched for the one who would usurp him. Grettir never even considered that it would be a girl from the gutters who would be his bane.

Cecilia followed Artorius as he ascended the steps toward Avalass' palace, armoured in glistening white and platinum. They crossed into the hall of the throne room, and everything changed.

Reality seemed to become hollow. The world went still, colour went to grey, and the two monarchs were left alone within their palace.

They were both awakened from that dream of a memory, and Cecilia finally came to terms with who it was that stood before her. "Artorius," she hissed, trading her noble intonations for something that carried more venom.

He turned to—for the first time since he had infected her body and she his mind—acknowledge her presence. "You do not belong here."

"Do you suppose I've enjoyed this journey through your recollections? Get out of my body, leave my kingdom in peace, and I shall leave you to your miserable memories."

"I cannot simply disappear, I have told your allies the same. My essence is immortal; I require a vessel."

"We'll recreate your cipher, then lose it somewhere nobody will ever find it."

"If only that were possible. No, the last copy of those designs were rendered to little more than—" his face twisted into an amused grin, "—ash. And the one who first created them will not do so again. We are bound now. There is no undoing my return as King."

Cecilia laughed. It was a hoarse and deliberate sound, but it lightened some of her pain. "You will never again rule over these people. I will draw a blade across my throat or bury myself in the darkest pit of Diavollos. I will go where no man nor woman shall follow, if it means protecting my people from you."

"Then you are not fit to be Queen!" he spat. "You are the only piece of this pathetic place that holds any worth. The people yield to your commands because they must, because you are their ruler. No monarch deserving of their crown would sacrifice themselves so that—what? A few miserable more of them will be content? You are better than them. You are so much *more*. They are nothing, so you must be everything!"

Cecilia responded with a screaming denial and leapt on Artorius, taking him to the floor. She struck him once upon the face as she said, "We are *no better*. We are men and women." She struck him twice more. "They did not choose us. What right do we have to lead them? How can we know what is best for people we will never meet?" She ignored the blossoming pain in her knuckles, reminded herself none of it was any more than the memory of pain. And memories could be forgotten. "I am Queen only so long as they want me, and I fight every single day to be worth that responsibility."

Artorius groaned. "Why should they choose you? There is no choice. Only the paths made for us."

Cecilia made him stop talking. "And where has that gotten you? Did you ever so much as try to stray from it? Did you never wonder if you could be more?"

"I am—"

She struck him again. "You are nothing; a coward who sought a throne because you thought it belonged to you. It is us who belong to it, who give all we are to this duty so nobody else must. We strip ourselves of freedom so that everyone else might know what we cannot." Suddenly, Cecilia's anger cooled, and she looked down at Artorius with clear eyes—his were gone, reduced to scarred hollows at some point during her rage. "But the choice to sacrifice my freedom was my own, and it was one you were never offered. A god made you a king, and we were surprised when you proved yourself inadequate?"

Cecilia expected him to combat that outlook. He did not.

"The greatest day of my life came when a friend offered me the chance to walk away from all of this. I was to inherit this kingdom simply for the fact that I was the sole living heir to my father, but my friend made it a choice when they gave me the chance to take another path."

Artorius appeared so weak to her now. Completely unlike the way she had painted him atop Mount Promethus. He was just a man resigned, given over to something his heart wanted no part of.

"You can remain a passenger, forever fighting for control over my mind, only so you may return to the path they chose for you. Or you can leave me, scatter yourself to the winds, and follow whatever destiny you choose. We will not follow you. You will be free."

Despite his protests, Cecilia felt that something had changed. They were not bound together as when he had first possessed her, something had severed that connection, and Cecilia was sure Artorius could abandon her of his own will.

Cecilia returned to her feet and helped Artorius do the same. They stood in silence. She did not want to push him any further. This had to be his decision alone.

Slowly, Artorius' hands rose to his collar, and he removed the Platinum Chain from where it had rested. He held it in hand, staring with a face bereft of eyes, yet seeing something Cecilia could not imagine.

Artorius did not meet her eyes as he spoke, and Cecilia thought that told of some newfound shame within his heart. "After everything I have done. Everyone I have killed. The fields I have burned. The damage that cannot be repaired. How can I turn away?"

"Our past might be written, but we choose what that makes of our future. We are not defined by damnation."

"Then what does define us?" His voice trembled. "What are we? What purpose do we possess?"

Cecilia shrugged. "I believe that is entirely up to us to decide."

For a moment, Artorius' fingers clutched the chain tighter. Then his grip loosened. And he let go entirely.

Chapter Thirty-Six
Rosebud

It was an odd thing to be passenger to another's being, like one was wading through thick waters and struggling to properly articulate their flesh so they would not sink. Domina was not sure why Artorius had willingly submitted himself to such a fate, but men did strange things when driven by emotion.

No more than a second had passed since he'd driven his blade across Artorius' chest—enough to separate his soul from the Queen's, but not so deep that she would be terribly wounded—and the warrior's grey armour had begun to degrade. The tiniest flakes of ash began to float away from their larger pieces, giving way to the guidance of the soft wind which had only just begun to permeate through the heat.

Domina could feel Chora's emotions surge within her, a mixture of calm for the knowledge that the fight was won and joy at the sight of her friend's safety.

"She's going to be alright," he said, making sure Raph was aware of what had happened below the surface. But when he turned to see her, it was not the defeated king her eyes clung to.

"And what about you, Domina?" Raph's voice was softened by worry. She approached him, her weight kept to her right leg.

"I have a feeling you know more about that than I do."

Raph's focus went beyond him, and he knew she was examining what remaining connection he had to the Mortal Plane. Domina could feel it dwindling, he had done what he needed to do, and now he did not possess the aptitude to maintain his presence where he did not belong. Raph looked at him again but could not find the words to deliver the news.

"It's good to see you're okay, Raph. I reckon you have as much to tell me as I do you."

She nodded along, forced a smile. "Yeah, it's been . . . a lot. But I guess we don't have time for that."

"Nah. Doesn't seem like it." Domina took a deep breath, enjoying the sensation for what might have been the last time. The fire had stopped rising from the mountaintop, and the magma which flowed down its face had begun to cool to black. "We did it, huh?"

"Just couldn't help ourselves."

A chuckle escaped the lips which weren't his own. "Somebody had to."

"We should've stuck together. We could have done so much better."

Domina wrapped Chora's arms around the devola, careful not to irritate her wounds further as he brought her close. "I've done enough of that kind of thinking for all of us, trust me. You saved a city, that's enough."

Domina smiled.

Zephyrus. Azazel. Esgar.

They had all given their everything to what they believed in. Finally, Domina felt like he had done the same.

Domina had done all he could . . . and that was more than enough.

—

Chora had watched and allowed Domina to have a moment with his friend, until she felt the last of his presence dissipate and leave her mind alone within her body. Still, she felt comforted by the devola's embrace, and would not let go before the short woman was ready. Better to allow Raph a few more moments before realising her friend was gone for good.

"Thank you, Chora."

She released Raph, patted at her own sides nervously to distract herself. "That's alright. You know that—"

"You're alone now, yes." Raph stretched out her arm, testing the pain in the tendons. "How are you?"

Chora felt her side, the spot Anamrath had impaled her left little more than a thin scar. "Better than I ought to be."

"Oh, thank the Gods," a familiar voice called out. Chora and Raph turned to find Nath sprint toward them and take Raph in his arms, the woman winced, but seemed more than glad to return the embrace. "I knew you'd be fine."

Raph's eyes suddenly went wide, as the reverie was interrupted by greater concerns. "The people, Nath, are they—"

"They'll be okay. We did it."

Chora left them to each other and made her way toward where Cecilia sat on the ground. Much of Artorius' armour had left her, and the Queen's face had been uncovered. Cecilia's mind had not yet returned to her, but Domina had assured her that no lasting damage would arise from the separation. Chora was not sure how he could know such a thing, but she chose to believe him.

Chora peeled off her helmet and sat beside her queen, immediately glad to be off her feet. A part of her mind demanded she dwell further on the night's events and the contributions she had made toward it. It would take some time to properly allocate the blame for such atrocity, and Chora was not sure that she did not deserve much of it. But she ignored that part of herself for the time being, instead turning toward the future.

A small part of her heart thought to abandon the Artorian life, that recent events had proven herself unfit for such a duty. But another—far calmer—part of herself believed that was also reason for her to continue, to learn, and to become what she needed to be.

Fiery light once again awoke at the mountain's peak, but it was only the first hints of daylight making its presence known.

Chora heard metal clatter against the cold surface, and found Cecilia's platinum necklace cast aside. It slid along the ground for a moment before finally stopping, and Chora looked up to find Cecilia's eyes fixed upon it.

"My lady?" she whispered, a part of her hesitating at the prospect that some of Artorius lingered.

Cecilia smiled, stretched her legs out before her, and smoothed over her black dress. It appeared just as it had before the ash had overtaken her, as though it had not been coated in the substance only moments prior. Only a thin diagonal line across her chest told of the strike Domina had guided Chora toward delivering. "I am alright, Chora. Thank you."

"Do you have orders?"

"I suppose that I should," she said, her voice soft and quiet. "Are there orders you wish me to deliver?"

"Not that I can think of, Your Grace."

"Then we can allow ourselves a moment to enjoy the new day, while you tell me what has come to be during my absence."

Chapter Thirty-Seven

The Ashen Queen

It should not have come to this, Cassidy," Cecilia said, stepping through the arcane barrier and into her former aide's cell. "I always considered you a trusted member of this household."

Cassidy's shoulders twitched, though she did not turn from where she sat in the room's corner, limbs pulled close to her chest. Cecilia was pained to see her deliberately avoid the comfort of her bed, and hoped the girl was not mistreating herself. She had made many mistakes and would need to pay for each in due time, but Cecilia did not want her to suffer. This had been the work of Artorius and the witch Morguein Frieda, turning good people toward their wicked ends was only one more of their many acts of evil. If they were to escape punishment, she did not think it fair that Cassidy should take their place.

The woman had been found waiting in the throne room to see what came of Artorius' work, and had not offered any opposition when Cecilia ordered Chora take her to the palace dungeons. There had even been the slightest glimmer of joy in Cassidy's eyes when Cecilia had entered, that had broken her heart more than the betrayal itself.

Cecilia crossed the room and sat on the cold floor beside her lifelong companion. "Perhaps I still do. But there must be a reason behind all of this, I ask only that you try and allow me to understand."

The red hair that curled around her head seemed darker than it ever had before. Cecilia wanted to brush it, to return it to the vision of care it had once been, but some things would never be as they were. Cecilia was willing to accept that, though not without first doing everything in her power to repair what she still could.

"I am truly sorry about Cortlan." She had been informed that the dark elf Domina, the sword for hire who had been a part of this mania from the start, had executed the mage out of retribution for Lord Caster Hyde. "I would not have wished for this outcome. He deserved a chance to explain himself. The years he did me service should have earned that much."

"I did not recognise him," Cassidy whispered. Her voice sounded awfully weak, as though her throat had been made raw from hours of sobbing. "He came to me, and I did not know him. Something took him while he was away, broke him so that she could put him back together however she liked."

"Be that as it is, I regret not being able to offer him the chance to return properly."

Cassidy's head shook slightly. "Not everyone can be redeemed."

"Perhaps not, but that is my decision to make."

Cassidy let her head fall against the stone wall. "I wanted to help you. That is all I have ever done." She turned ever so slightly toward where Cecilia sat behind her but could not bring herself to meet her eyes. "You deserve so much more than this life. You should be free to see the world as you like, as you once dreamed of doing. I know you think that was just a child's fantasy, but I think it was beautiful. Of course, you could not make it true. You had these burdens that you could not rightly abandon." The nails of her right hand dug into the soft flesh of her arm; Cecilia instinctively placed her own hand over it and forced Cassidy to ease her grip. "I thought, perhaps, if another were to take your place, you might finally have the chance to put yourself first. You deserve that, Cecilia."

The Queen caressed Cassidy's arm for a moment, then stood and embodied what she still retained of her monarch's hauteur. "You are my dearest friend. You know me better than any other, living or dead. You are correct that there are times when this duty weighs heavily upon me; the past few days have shown just how difficult my time as ruler will be. I value your concern, truly, I do. But I have chosen this way of life, and I continue to choose it so long as there remains life within me. You have no right to decide what is best for me."

"I'm sorry. I know how worthless my words are now, but you're right. You'll be the best of monarchs."

Cecilia offered Cassidy her hand. When she realised the woman still had no intention to forgive herself, she said, "Still, you are right that I have neglected my own interests for too long. I cannot make an entire people flourish if I cannot even maintain myself." Cecilia realised Cassidy's redemption would be a long road, but it was one she would walk with her.

At the wave of a hand, Chora entered with a large canvas, easel, and a number of painting supplies. Cecilia thanked her guard and bid her leave to do as she wished.

The Artorian had exhibited noticeable change in the short while since she had been appointed Cecilia's personal guard, the Second Ashen Night had forged in her a new confidence. Cecilia wondered if she had found a new mentor, somebody outside of the typical retinue, perhaps someone who better understood the nature of the ethereal white blade Chora now wielded. Whatever the reason, Cecilia was glad to see somebody emerge from the night better off, especially after the way the poor girl had been treated during the time leading up to it.

Chora bowed, turned toward the dungeon's exit, and hesitated. Cecilia wondered what Chora thought of Cassidy, what expression she bore under her repaired mask. It had been the aide who had forged Cecilia's writing. She would not blame the Artorian for holding a grudge, nor for hesitating to leave the traitor alone with her charge.

Cecilia waved her off and turned her focus toward the canvas. It truly had been some time since she had last touched one. "Would you mind offering a request?"

Cassidy had turned toward the blank sheet, her eyes red and tired. "Something less bleak than your old work would not go unwelcome."

"Yes." Cecilia dipped her brush into the lightest shade of blue she had on hand and began to paint. "I very much agree."

—

A blue sky, a clear sea, a green landscape, and a fleet of ships making port on the shore of Duralaans. The finished picture was mounted above the entrance to the observatory, a bright reminder of what had been, and perhaps would be once again.

While the mountain-turned-volcano had ceased its spewing of fire, it had continued to pump grey clouds into the air in the days and weeks following, soon obscuring the whole of Duralaans' sky. Momentary glimpses of sunlight had managed to penetrate the darkness, though that particular day had not been so blessed.

There was no telling how long it would last.

Cecilia had summoned the wisest people she knew to study the issue but could not shake the feeling that she already knew what the night would entail.

"They have arrived, Your Grace," Amor said as he slipped into the circular space.

Cecilia had been incredibly relieved to learn that he had survived Artorius' onslaught. The ghost had used her body to kill any who were unlucky enough to cross paths with him—thus Cecilia had been given one more reason to regret letting him go free. Amor had not joined the dead, instead managed to gather as many of the palace's attendants as he could, and escaped through the old tunnels beneath the surface.

There was much that would surely change in this age to come, so there came comfort in the pieces of familiarity that were still salvageable.

"You may bring them in, Amor. Thank you."

He excused himself, and Cecilia turned her back to the door, finding her eyes land on the mountain's peak high above. Her home was gone, decimated in the moment of eruption, alongside the many servants who had worked their days making her life easier. The memorial would not be held for a few days more, but it would be the chance many needed to celebrate the lives and mourn the loss of all who had been taken during such calamity.

Cecilia had confirmed that list included Hyde and Trethellyn, alongside Carlyle Lyre—whose death had left another scar upon her, but remained just as cloaked in mystique as the man himself.

She wanted to vow that this would be the end of such unnecessary loss, that she could simply dedicate herself toward something better and thus her will would be made real. But progress was slow and could not be achieved alone.

The door opened wide and the remaining nobles of Duralaans entered. Despite the losses, there were more who joined her in the observatory than were present at Aester Hyde's gala—of course, the man himself had also come up missing. Just another of many issues that would need resolving.

Redan Rosse, Zephyr Mars, Phemus Anderthread, Amber Strados, Ennard Harald, Daphne Raleigh, Jessick Stellari, and Helen Wintre each found a space of floor to call their own. Karla Trethellyn was also present, in place of her late husband, and Kiara Lyre stood for her father.

Cecilia rotated on the spot, taking in each lord and lady in turn. All wore the matching chain of platinum they had been gifted upon arrival. Some fashioned the item as a necklace, others a bracelet. Cecilia herself wore the thin metal atop her head, threaded into her hair to keep in place the new pendant that sat above her brow.

"Welcome, my friends. I am glad you decided to heed my call despite such dire times."

"It remains a pleasure, Your Grace, even amid such circumstances," said Lady Wintre, ever Cecilia's most ardent of allies.

Rosse crossed his arms in a show of displeasure, but nodded along to Wintre's sentiment. "It is due time we discussed a means to handle this."

"Quite true, Lord Rosse," Cecilia agreed. "We face a time none had hoped to see again, yet it is here and face it we must." She took a moment to adjust her shoulders, only to be delighted by the newfound weightlessness that came as result of doing away with the Platinum Chain. Surely the nobles had noticed its absence, she only wondered who would be the first to address it. "I had hoped to unite us in preventing its arrival, and the failure to do so was difficult to accept. However, I did learn something from that failure; one cannot force unity without losing its value. The most you can do is surround yourself with people you can trust and hope they are willing to rely on you when the need arises.

"Some of you raised an excellent point during our last encounter. Perhaps the time of the all-powerful ruler is over. I am not certain that such a person is what this land needs anymore, yet my life remains in service to the people of Duralaans. If you wish not to obey me any longer, I will accept that, but I will do everything that remains in my power to help my people. And I will hope that you shall each do the same for yours."

"No," Lady Raleigh said flatly, "this is not the time to relinquish control." Her strong voice boomed throughout the enclosed space. "I still believe there is merit to the concept, but now is a time for structure. Perhaps we have become too self-focused, I do not know. Nor do I care. It is within our best interest to be allies at this time, so allies we shall be."

"Agreed," Rosse spoke up, offering Raleigh respectful nod. "Lady Stellari, Sevran is the only land which has not yet seen ash cloud its skies. We must rely on you if our people are not to starve."

The woman brushed a knotted strand of hair out of her face. "Not a problem, Redan. Good to be needed from time to time." Next she turned her smile on Cecilia. "You'll be glad for our lot, Grace?"

"Always, my lady." Cecilia returned the smile.

"What of the land of poor Lord Hyde?" Strados asked, making no attempt to mask the motive behind such interest.

"For now, I have arranged capable hands to oversee Anderan." Cecilia raised her fingers to touch the pendant cresting her brow, the gemstone had been made of a piece from each stone which had once been a part of her Platinum Chain. "Though his successor will be found in due time, and I shall gift them the same artefact I have given each of you."

Cecilia thought that perhaps they did not need to ask what their newly acquired ornamentation was, something in their eyes told her they either already understood or at least recognised the meaning behind them. The Platinum Chain had been melted down and forged into smaller iterations of itself, then decorated with the shards from its gemstones. They sparkled in the darkness, bringing colours to the grey world they had entered which were impossible to ignore.

"I did not want to force you all toward this path," Cecilia said. "I knew it would mean so much more if I had been able to bring us together without the threat of doom. But damnation comes whether we like it or not. The only question is whether we are strong enough to survive it. I am glad that we stand together now. The choices that brought us toward this point have been made. Now it comes to us to decide what we make from it. Not for the benefit of any sole person in this room, but for everyone else."

Perhaps Cecilia should have been afraid, should have turned her back on the hardships she would surely face while the opportunity had been present. What awaited Cecilia and her fellow nobles were times unlike any that had been witnessed in generations, but they had been seen and survived once before. Not because of an ashen king, but because a people had found the strength to stand together within themselves.

They would face this threat again, and they would see its end.

They would do it together.

Chapter Thirty-Eight
Apocrypha

Oedon recalled the day a god had made his eyes their home and bestowed upon him the prescience which would guide so much of his life going forward.

His mother was dead, burned at a stake for the unholy work she had practiced on her son. He had been cast out also, left to starve among her ashes.

Never had he found somebody to blame for the suffering he had endured then.

There was his father, one of Deserum's most powerful men, who had treated Oedon as the runt of his litter. There was his mother, who had hoped to make Oedon indispensable through the crystalline art of summoning powerful spirits which had been an ancestral talent of her lineage. And there were *The* Mother and Father, the all-controlling deities who had created reality and everything Oedon knew.

They had treated his pain as no more than a stepping stone, a necessary point in his life which would shape the man he would one day be. They had offered him the chance to become their reaper, one who might ensure reality unfurled precisely as they wished.

He had answered them with ease.

Oedon had said *no.*

Yet those first of deities had laid their claws into him anyway, offering visions of times long gone and soon to come, and Oedon had learned there was no denying the will of the immortal.

But he had been wrong. He had strayed from the path and writ a new possibility. Or perhaps he had simply found something that had been kept from his sight. It no longer mattered. Now came the time for him to consider not what had been, but what could be.

Oedon stood on the foredeck of the vessel he had requisitioned for his purposes. Of course, the Artisans had planned for it to return him to their Gilded Sea upon the conclusion of his time in Duralaans, but Oedon had become enamoured with what other uses it could have.

Cendela intrigued him, another land which trod upon the edge of oblivion. It would also be another opportunity to avoid destiny, to stop doomsday before it could begin.

He felt somewhat poorly about leaving Avalass without bidding Whitsin farewell. He had been so instrumental in setting Oedon on his new path, it was unfair that Nath would not know for certain what had become of him. But he would have only insisted that Oedon stay, and he could not risk his heart outweighing his mind.

Oedon had left behind a single one of Elias' rings and hoped that would be enough for Nath to know he had not perished. Though he had gained much during his time in Duralaans, there were some things that must be left behind.

He felt the cold crystal of his eyes against a single finger. In truth, they had done more to blind him than return vision.

Oedon pressed the finger into the socket, intent to dig out the orb, until something appeared before him, and Oedon thought he should retain his sight for at least a few moments more.

A pair of feet were just ahead of him, stood atop the ship's railing, and so pale that they were difficult to see clearly in the day's light. "I don't think that's a good idea," came the shrill, teasing voice of a young girl. "You've got the right idea, kiddo. But that's not how you want to do this. You'll need those if I'm gonna help you."

Oedon looked up to find the ghostly image of a girl in a wispy white dress. She was pale as death itself, night-black hair extended below her waist, and thin as though she had gone long underfed before meeting a cruel end. Yet Oedon could not see that end. As far as he looked, he could not find her place in reality. "Who are you?"

She crouched down, placing her hand against her head as though displeased. She held a pair of scissors loosely in that hand, Oedon could not help but feel like they suited her. "It's been too long since my name mattered. I'm just a whisper now. The memory of an idea that the Gods found a touch displeasing."

"Displeasing, how?"

She twirled a strand of hair around a thin finger, eyes going distant as though recalling a pleasant memory. "It was a matter of obedience." Her eyes snapped back to him so suddenly he could not help but shudder. "You're not so different, but you're gonna get hurt if you give up your one advantage. There's another way. A better way. My way." She brought the scissors up and snapped them together with a soft *snip*.

"I do believe I'm quite done with following another's *ways*."

"And how do you know that isn't what Mama and Papa wanted? That they didn't put you through all this so that you would strike out on a path you only *thought* was your own."

Oedon met her eyes, found there was something undefinable about them. Something that felt disconnected, beyond all that was within reason. She appeared to be no older than he was, while simultaneously striking him as being unthinkably ancient.

"Don't you think it's time we stopped suffering for the benefit of others?"

"I do," Oedon answered, of course he did. That did not mean he could trust this girl.

"Then what are we waiting for?" She offered him a pale hand. "Let's save the world."

"Whatever you are, I will not be a blind follower to your orders."

"Of course not." She smiled. "How about partners?"

"Partners might work." He considered her for another moment, before taking her hand, surprised to find his fingers did not simply drift through her illusive form. "What might I call you?"

The girl seemed to think on it for a moment, as though deciding which title best fit her at that precise moment. "Moira."

"Very well, Moira. Shall we see just how much disobedience we can muster?"

That seemed to please her greatly, and for the first time since his eyes had been cut from their sockets, Oedon's sight was crystal clear.

Chapter Thirty-Nine
Sera

Raph felt better than she had in a long time.

Drifting within Anni's world of ethereal light and shifting colour, her aching body seemed to finally relax.

Only now did she realise just how tired she had been, just how much damage Lyre's work had done to her. The passage of time would be the only way to tell how ruinous that man had truly been to her wellbeing. But he was dead now, and though Raph would have liked to be the one to witness the light fade from his eyes, she knew that would not heal any scars.

Anni herself drifted through the open expanse, her form just as luminous, despite the dark times faced in reality. Raph wondered just how much pain her goddess was privy to on a daily basis, wondered how it did not break her to see so much that she could not change. Anni had not always been an entity of divine nature, her conscience was no less mortal than Raph's own. Perhaps, with ascendance also came a better understanding of nature, the value in letting some suffer so many more could flourish. It was a dark thought, and one Raph knew did not represent her friend accurately. But when one could do so much, it was hard not to wonder why they did not do more.

"*I cannot express just how much you have impressed me, Seraph.*" Anni turned her attention away from another aspect of nature so she could address her servant properly. "*You have exceeded my greatest of expectations, and that is saying quite a lot, given how much I ask of you.*"

"Thanks, Anni. I only wish I could have stopped Artorius' return entirely." Raph hugged herself, feeling suddenly cold.

"*I already ask for you to achieve the improbable, the impossible would be a step too far.*"

That, Raph did not understand. "You knew I couldn't stop him?"

"*I knew there were many pieces at work that you could not control. You are but one person—incredibly powerful, you may be, but there are some things not even you can prevent.*"

Raph had to accept that. As much as it irked her, she was trying to better manage herself. "I understand."

"*Good.*" Anni turned her eyes back to what lay beyond Raph's astral form. "*Now, I must ask that you make your return to Santora. The remnants of the Godless are making trouble again and Chancellor Adeline has requested somebody with experience handle them.*"

Raph's instinct was to accept the task without a second thought, so it took her a great amount of concentration to restrain that reaction. Even then she could not bring herself to say what she needed to.

Anni's eyes fell to her again, and she smiled. "*Oh, I see. My friend, I ask too much of you.*"

"It's not that," Raph said. She would have been glad to accept the task, but something inside her soul knew it would not be right. "I just . . . I've been fighting for so long that I'm not sure who I am beyond that. I truly love protecting people and life itself, but there's something I've been neglecting. I need to find what that is before I can keep doing this."

The space around the two women folded, and suddenly Anni was close enough to lay her hand on Raph's shoulder. *"I'm glad. We'll be able to find someone else, so don't worry, and enjoy your time away."*

"Thank you, Anni." Raph felt their connection slipping and prepared herself for the shock that always came upon returning to the Mortal Plane. But there was one last thing that came to mind. "Tell Mother that I'm thinking about her."

"She knows, Seraph. Of course she knows."

—

Nath thrust the gilded key into its socket, still amazed by how obviously valuable even they were within the palace. If he were any more a bastard he might consider pocketing the thing before his time in the place was over. Alas, the memory of his quarters' decadence would have to be enough.

He carried a basket of fruit and bread that he had picked up from the market, and struggled to carry it in one hand while pushing through his room's heavy door. Nath was still not used to the feeling of his new prosthetic and looked forward to the time it would feel a natural part of him again—and he might forget the memories it carried.

Sera sat cross-legged on the floor, as far from any other object as she could get. Nath assumed she was in communion with Anni and did his best to be quiet as he laid out his purchases on their dining table. The rooms in the palace's guest wing were far closer to a completely furnished house than a simple place to spend the night, and after so long on the road, neither he nor Sera had any reason to deny the offer.

Of course, they had been offered separate quarters by their hosts, but after the memorial, neither had wished to remain alone in such an expansive space.

Despite how many Nath, Oedon, and their volunteers had saved, there had been a number who had died in the immediate eruption of the mountain. And of course, there had been Domina.

Nath was glad to know his old ally had been aiding them without their knowledge, but also despaired that he would not have the chance to see him again. Sera had told Nath all Domina had said to her before passing, and the Artorian Chora had filled in what additional gaps had remained shrouded, but there came sorrow in knowing he would not hear the tales from the man himself.

Then there was Oedon. The boy had seemingly vanished entirely, swallowed whole by the cracks in reality, leaving behind nothing but a ring of gold he had used to braid his hair. Nath took it to mean the young prophet was alive, and could only respect his decision to leave without any passing words and hope that he found fulfillment wherever he took himself next. Nath knew Oedon had only just begun to understand what he could really do with his sight, the optimistic part within him believed that would only continue with time.

Nath had offered up that ring during the memorial, in respect to both Oedon Desera and Elias Sorren. He had originally thought to also pay his respects to Damian, the youth who had taken on the role of Eric Blackhand during their infiltration of Lyre's fortress, but had learned he had been spared the worst of the lord's wrath. Cecilia had then promised the kid would be freed and repaid for any harm done to him. It was a rare bright spark amid the dark, and Nath was glad for it.

"How were the markets?" Sera asked, returned from her communion and shakily coming to her feet.

Nath let her investigate his purchases. "Busy. I reckon a brush with death dulls the need to be frugal."

"I'd expect you to be smarter than that," she teased, selecting an apple to bite into, before offering it to him.

Nath declined and made for the bed, started to work off his shoes. "The monarchy's coin has to go somewhere."

"Oh, I agree. I just prefer that be *our* pockets." Sera joined him, leaning against Nath's arm while loudly chewing her snack. "You know they're feeding us, right?"

"I thought I'd try to cook something myself. It's been too long."

"What's the occasion?"

Nath took a deep breath, remembered the scent of fire and smoke. "It's time I put that particular fear to rest."

Sera lowered the apple and turned to silence, her breathing starting to come heavier.

"Are you alright?"

She remained silent, laid her apple down on the bedsheet.

"I know you don't always want to share everything you've been through. But you've done so much to help me, and I will be here if you need it."

"I do, Nath." She shuddered. "I need help, I'm just not used to asking for it. I'm not sure how to begin."

Nath put his arm around her, and she seemed to lean closer. "I think you just did."

Sera's breathing eased, coming back under her control. "I just need somebody else to hear me, to know what I do. There's so much that I've seen. And done. And survived. And lost. And it's just been building. But I can't do it anymore. I can't ignore it." Her voice quivered with every word. "It's like rot that's just been growing and growing, and killing me from the inside. I don't want to live like this anymore, but I can't die either. I need to keep going, even when I know that I can't." She choked, and it was clear she was fighting back the urge to cry.

"Just tell me everything, Sera. You've carried all of this, your entire life. I can carry it for at least one night, and however long you need me to after that."

There remained some hesitation in her. But she had opened the bottle and released the storm, there was no putting it back, and the lid would not be returned until everything had been allowed free.

So Sera told Nath what she could remember of her childhood, those dark days she had been alone in Spirallos. She told him of her first encounters with that city's malignant demon, how she had helped a band of heroes replace its darkness with Anni's light, and never quite stopped trying to push that darkness back. She recalled her first meeting with him and their adventures that followed, concluding with the defeat of Vécar Forkh. She explained what had become of her life following that battle, a never-ending pursuit of justice which gave her a righteous excuse to put every other person's problems before her own. Finally, she detailed her torture at the hands of Carlyle Lyre and his subordinates.

It took time. The sun had set and begun to rise again before she had finished. There were many times Sera fell to silence, lost in the dreadful web of her own memory, and Nath only waited until she was ready to continue. At some points they cried together. At others they laughed.

Despite the pain in her words, there was something of levity that came from the act of giving them voice. A power that Sera seemed to find as she took control of her own bleak narrative.

Sera gave Nath her truth. She said every word she needed to say in that moment.

And he listened.

Chapter Forty
The Artisan

It does not matter, does it?" Aester Hyde asked, his voice shaking with fear. "Artorius was released, the doomsday began, and the mosaic nears completion. We can turn toward Cendela without issue. The treason of one boy should not redefine the success that this is." Aester was searching for agreement from his fellow Artisans, but all eyes turned toward their leader.

Annat'thandir had not offered a word since the meeting had begun. He had been curious to know what immediate reaction each of his so-called Doomsday Artisans would have to the news from Duralaans. As he so often was in the face of such company, Annat'thandir was left dissatisfied—though far from surprised—to learn only Aester dared impose his own opinion. Annat'thandir supposed he had not chosen this particular arrangement of power-thirsting maniacs for their originality. Still, a surprise now and then would not go unwelcome.

Annat'thandir leaned forward, letting his pitch-black eyes drift from one Artisan to another, wondering what emotion each would derive as they stared into the abyss. "Hyde is quite right," he eventually responded, "Oedon's betrayal was always a possibility. It may not have been my preferred outcome, but the grand scheme remains undamaged."

"Cendela will proceed as promised?" That was Echidna, aspiring mother-to-be of the new age of dragons. So eager she was for the focus to belong to her once more.

"Naturally," Annat'thandir confirmed, convincingly enough that Echidna offered no further query. "Must we discuss anything more?"

The gathered Artisans seemed perfectly content as they were, and Annat'thandir fought off the displeasure that demanded to make itself known.

"Then this meeting is finished. I trust you shall all journey well."

Each rose from their seat and took a moment to bid their leader farewell, an almost convincing show of civility from Avandoras' most disturbed individuals.

When all was done, only Meliné remained, though Annat'thandir was sure few of his Artisans had known she was present at all. Perhaps a few years past, she would never have failed to catch somebody's eye, but she had since learned when to make herself known and when to become one with the darkness.

Annat'thandir took her hand as she approached his seat, and gazed up at the feminine mask which covered her face. He thought it unnecessary, but understood the thing made Meliné more comfortable, and he would never oppose something that made her glad.

"Shall I?" she asked, still finding it necessary to confirm Annat'thandir's will, despite assuredly understanding it better than any other possibly could.

"Deal with the good Lord Hyde? Yes," Annat'thandir said. "Though you must ensure there is no collateral this time. Only Aester has earned our ire today."

Meliné nodded. The motion sent her white hair falling across her face and Annat'thandir had to reject the desire to right it before she had left.

Perhaps it was petty, but Léonora had always spoken so highly of Cecilia, that Annat'thandir was sure she deserved some recompense for the way Aester had manipulated her. The devastation that had followed may have been entirely necessary, but small justices mattered no less than others.

Once Annat'thandir was sure he was completely alone, he made way toward the glass mosaic which had been fitted directly behind his own seat. It was a masterful approximation of the original piece which existed beyond mortal sight, depicting the five cataclysmic events which would damage the natural order of reality irreparably, but it was only Annat'thandir who could see the meaning which lay behind the art. That path would lead to an end that all but the farsighted would deem as truly sinister. Thankfully, his allies were anything and everything but.

Three of the five events depicted by the mosaic had already unfolded. The shrouding of Santora and subsequent removal of the old deities. The dissolution and redefinition of death in Haevahn. And finally, the ashen storm of Duralaans.

All that remained was the return of Cendela's dragon deities, and Annat'thandir's promise would be fulfilled. His sacrifice finally complete.

That fifth cataclysm would be brought about by that poor boy, the final crack that would spill forth the infinite waters of the Crucible. Annat'thandir had hoped to avoid that one, though he had never fooled himself into believing such a thing would actually be possible. He would simply have to ensure the world would be ready for it.

His thoughts drifted—as they often did—to Léonora, and everything they had tried to achieve. It was a shame they could not be convinced to do what was necessary, but Annat'thandir was sure they would understand once it was all over.

Soon, he thought. *I will rescue you from your gilded sea.*

For too long, Annat'thandir had enjoyed his own freedom. It was long due that he shared something of that with everyone else.

Annat'thandir smiled as he realised it was not the end at all that was sinister, only the journey.

The end would be liberating.

Acknowledgements

As arduous an experience this was, taking this story from being something that existed purely within my own mind and turning it into a product that others could consume was not the most difficult part of this journey. No, that remains to be how I will ever categorise the emotions I feel now that I have reached the final leg of this adventure's beginning.

I have always loved writing and have practiced the craft in a number of forms throughout the years, but to finally have something out there in a form that seems even mildly professional is another thing entirely.

So, to whoever is reading this, whether physically or not, whether this year or ten in the future, whether you enjoyed any of it or hated every moment, I must thank you for giving my work even a fraction of your time.

I also want to offer my gratitude to my incredible family for the support you have given me throughout the creation of this story and everything that has come before.

Thank you to everyone that has responded to the fact that this book exists with enthusiasm and interest, it kept me honest and ensured I would see it through.

And a special thanks to my friend, and assuredly biased beta reader, Gaspar. I may have had to take much of your praise with a grain of salt, but that does not mean I will not forever be grateful for your time.

About the Author

A. J. Anderson is the Australian author behind this book. They have spent much of their life studying and practicing within the creative industries, undertaking roles such as lead writer on short form narrative and live broadcast productions, director of a documentary production, and the vision editor on music video productions. Author may only be the latest in a number of titles, but it remains their favourite.